Longus

Longus

literally and completely translated from the Greek

Longus

Longus
literally and completely translated from the Greek

ISBN/EAN: 9783337188115

Printed in Europe, USA, Canada, Australia, Japan

Cover: Foto ©Andreas Hilbeck / pixelio.de

More available books at **www.hansebooks.com**

THE ATHENIAN SOCIETY'S PUBLICATIONS

IV

*LITERALLY AND COMPLETELY TRANSLATED
FROM THE GREEK, WITH INTRODUCTION
AND NOTES*

*ATHENS : PRIVATELY PRINTED FOR THE
ATHENIAN SOCIETY : MDCCCXCVI*

THE ATHENIAN SOCIETY has now completed the first year of its existence, and may reasonably congratulate itself upon its success.

The Council take the opportunity of expressing its regret at the loss of some of the original subscribers, owing to death or other unforeseen causes.

Although the number of applications for membership is in excess of the number of vacancies, the issues of the Society will remain, as before, strictly limited to 250 copies.

It is worth observing that three times the original subscription price

has had to be paid for copies of the Society's publications to enable some collectors to make up complete sets.

The volumes which it is proposed to issue during the ensuing year will be produced in the same style and on the same lines as those already issued, but it is thought advisable to avoid issuing more than one portion of an author or authors in the same volume, so that each may be complete in itself.

The present issue contains the Greek Romance of Daphnis and Chloe, which has probably been translated more frequently and into more European languages than any other Greek author of its kind. It has had an interesting history, and it is hoped that the somewhat lengthy letter of Paul Louis Courier will be considered to repay the

trouble of reading it. It is extremely vivacious, and is full of genuine French *esprit* of the best literary kind, and gives a full account of the great literary dispute which was carried on for nearly a year in reference to the famous ink-blot on the Florentine MS.

The style of the Greek narrative is very simple, and quite intelligible to any ordinary English reader ; there are no obscure allusions, and to have added notes where none were necessary would simply have increased the bulk of the book to an awkward size without any corresponding advantage.

The General Editor will in future attach considerable importance to the Bibliography of the works translated, in deference to the expressed wish of subscribers. It is hoped that the one

appended to the present volume will
be found fairly exhaustive and complete, and that the references to other
books and pamphlets bearing upon the
subject will be useful to those who may
desire to extend their knowledge of the
Greek romance writers, as a whole,
further than is possible within the
limits of the present Introduction.

During the ensuing year it is proposed to issue a further portion of the
inimitable LUCIAN; another of the
GREEK ROMANCES; some select plays
of ARISTOPHANES; and a portion of an
author of a more serious kind.

It is also proposed to found, on
the same lines and for the same object,
a Society, to be called THE ROMAN
SOCIETY, and members of the Athenian
Society know that the Latin authors

present a large field which has not been worked, and which will appeal strongly to the student. The names of JUVENAL, TERENCE, PLAUTUS, PETRONIUS ARBITER, and MARTIAL at once occur as authors who have rarely, if ever, been presented in a complete English dress. Full particulars will be announced in due course.

In conclusion, the Council of the Athenian Society begs to thank its members for their support, and hopes for a continuance of the same.

INTRODUCTION

Nothing is known of Longus, or of
the age in which he lived. Neither
Photius, nor Suidas, nor any of his
supposed contemporaries make any
mention of him. It has been conjectured, however, that he was a native
of Lesbos, and that he lived not later
than the fourth or fifth century. Others
are of opinion that he never existed at
all, since a Greek writer, it is argued,
could not have had a Latin name.
The title of Sophist, or professional
philosopher, is generally added to his
name.

Daphnis and Chloe is the earliest

example of a pastoral romance, or indeed of fictitious prose narrative of any kind. This style of composition appears to have travelled westward to the Ionian Greeks, to have been adopted from them by Greek and Latin writers, and transmitted to modern times. "It is not in Provence, nor yet in Spain, as many suppose, that we are to look for the fatherland of those amusing compositions called Romances. It is in distant and far different climes to our own, and in the remote antiquity of vanished ages: it is among the people of the East, the Arabs, the Egyptians, the Persians, and the Syrians, that the germ and origin of this species of fictitious narrative is to be found, for which the peculiar genius and poeti-

cal temperament of those nations particularly adapt them. For even their
ordinary discourse is interspersed
with figurative expressions: and their
maxims of theology and philosophy
are invariably couched under the guise
of allegory or fable. I need not here
stay to enlarge upon the universal
veneration paid throughout the East
to the fables of Bidpai and to Lokman,
the Aesop of the Greeks: and it is
well known that the story of Isfendiyar,
and of the daring deeds of the Persian
hero Rustan are to this day more
popular in those regions than the
tales of Roland and Amadis de Gaul
ever were with us. And so decidedly
is Asia the parent of these fictions,
that we shall find that nearly all those
who in early times distinguished them-

c

selves as writers of what are now called
"Romances" were of Oriental birth or
extraction. Clearchus, a pupil of Aristotle, and the first who attempted anything of the sort, was a native of Soli
in Cilicia: Iamblichus was a Syrian,
as were also Heliodorus and Lucian.
Achilles Tatius was an Alexandrian."[1]
The first real novels of which we
have any knowledge are the "Milesian Tales," short amatory narratives
chiefly written in prose. They were
characterised by extreme licentious-
ness. Although they have been lost,
some idea of them may be formed
from the stories of Parthenius of
Nicaea, the tutor of Virgil. Amongst
his Ἐρωτικὰ Παθήματα, or "tragical love-
stories" are several in which the cha-

---

[1] Huet, *de Origine Fabularum Romanensium.*

racters are all Milesian, and seem to have been taken from the Milesian Tales. The beautiful fable of Cupid and Psyche, in the Golden Ass of Apuleius, is admittedly borrowed from them, and, probably, the story of the Ephesian Matron in Petronius Arbiter. We also find " Sybaritic Tales " mentioned in Aristophanes.

Previous to the age of Alexander the Great, the European Greeks seem to have attempted few works of this kind ; but his conquests brought Greeks and Asiatics more closely together, and gave them access to the sources of fiction. Clearchus, one of Aristotle's pupils, wrote a history of fictitious love adventures, and seems to have been the first writer who distinguished himself in this manner.

Antonius Diogenes, who lived after the age of Alexander, wrote twenty-four books on " The Incredible Things beyond Thule," somewhat after the style of Sir John Mandeville's " Voyages in the Northern Seas," founded on the wandering adventures and amours of Dinias and Dercyllis. The idea of his work seems to have been taken from the Odyssey, and in fact many of the incidents seem to have been borrowed from it. An abridgment of the work is given by Photius, who praises it for its purity of style and the delightful variety of its adventures.

After this, there seems to have been a considerable interval of unproductiveness, as far as romances were concerned.

Lucius of Patrae, who lived during the reign of Marcus Aurelius, collected accounts of magical transformations: a considerable portion of his Metamorphoses was borrowed by Lucian, and incorporated in his Λούκιος ἢ ὄνος, "Lucius or the Ass," which in its turn furnished considerable material for the Golden Ass of Apuleius.

About this time Iamblichus (not the founder of the Syrian school of Neo-Platonic philosophy, who lived some hundred years later) wrote his "Babylonica," relating the love-adventures of Rhodanes and Sinonis. We only possess an abstract of it by Photius.

About the second half of the third century, Heliodorus,[1] a pagan sophist,

[1] At one time erroneously identified with Heliodorus, Bishop of Tricca, in Thessaly.

born at Emesa in Phoenicia, wrote
his Aethiopica, in ten books. It contains the strange story of Theagenes
the Thessalian, and Chariclea, the
daughter of the King of Aethiopia. It
served as a model for most of the later
Greek writers of romance, and may be
classed with Longus's Daphnis and
Chloe as one of the best specimens of
this kind of literature in Greek antiquity. It is remarkable for original
power, clear sketches of character,
beauty of drawing, and moral intention : the style is pure, simple, and
elegant.

We may next mention Achilles of
Alexandria (generally known as Achilles
Tatius), who wrote about 450 A.D. He
was the author of the story of Cleito-
phon of Tyre and Leucippe of Byzan-

tium, two lovers who pass through a
long series of adventures before they
meet. In point of style, Achilles is
said to excel Heliodorus, and all the
other writers of Greek romance. His
language has been especially commended for its conciseness, ease, and
simplicity.   Photius, the learned patri-
arch of Constantinople, says: " With
regard to diction and composition,
Tatius seems to me to excel. When
he employs figurative language, it is
clear and natural: his sentences are
concise and clear, and such as by their
sweetness greatly delight the ear."

We now come to Daphnis and Chloe,
the first specimen, as has been already
mentioned, of a *Pastoral* romance. A
brief outline of the story may be given.
Lamon, a goatherd, living near Mity-

lene, in the island of Lesbos, finds a
male infant, exposed and being suckled
by a goat, brings him up, and calls him
Daphnis.   Two years afterwards, his
neighbour, the shepherd Dryas, finds
a female infant being suckled by a ewe,
takes her home, and calls her Chloe.
The children, as they grow up, deve-
lop great beauty: when they are old
enough, one tends the goats, and the
other the sheep, and they fall in love
with each other.   Many incidents and
adventures are then introduced, which
have no actual connection with the
final *dénouement*.   At last, Dionysophanes, the proprietor of the estate
which Lamon cultivates, comes to
visit his property, with his wife
Cleariste and his only son Astylus.
Astylus asks his father to hand

Daphnis over to him as a slave,
that he may give him to his parasite
Gnathon, who has become enamoured
of him. Lamon, in order to prevent
this, then relates how he found
Daphnis, and produces the clothes
in which he was wrapped, and the
other tokens, or γνωρίσματα (means of
future recognition), which had been
exposed at the same time as the child.
Dionysophanes and Cleariste, by
means of these, recognise Daphnis
as their own son, whom they had
exposed from motives of economy, at
a time when they had three other
children. Gnathon, alarmed at hearing who Daphnis really is, in order
to recover his favour, rescues Chloe,
whom Lampis, a cowherd, had carried
off, while Daphnis was occupied with

his new parents. The lovers are greatly afraid lest they shall be separated; but Dryas, like Lamon, tells how he found Chloe, and exhibits the tokens left with her. Dionysophanes gives his consent to a marriage between the two; but first gives a feast, to which all the chief inhabitants of the city are invited, and displays Chloe's "tokens" to all the assembled guests: they are recognised by a certain Megacles, a rich man, who had exposed her in the days of his poverty, and is now greatly troubled because he has no heir. This naturally leads to everything being settled satisfactorily, and the marriage is celebrated on the following day.

The style in which Daphnis and Chloe is written, although it has been

censured on account of its frequent
reiteration, sophistical plays upon
words, and affected antithesis, is
considered as the purest specimen of
the later Greek language : the descriptions of rural scenery and rural
occupations are very pleasing. But
in some respects the romance is very
defective. It displays little variety,
except what arises from the vicissi-
tude of the seasons. The courtship
of Daphnis is in the last degree mono-
tonous, and the conversations between
the lovers extremely insipid. The my-
thological tales also are considered by
some to be totally uninteresting (although this opinion does not seem to
be altogether justified), and not very
happily introduced.

Although mainly on chronological

grounds, it does not seem probable
that Daphnis and Chloe was the
origin of the pastoral drama; it bears
a stronger, resemblance to the more
recent dramatic pastorals of Italy,
which frequently turn upon the ex-
posure of children, who, after being
brought up as shepherds by reputed
fathers, are discovered by their real
parents by means of tokens fastened
to them, or deposited by their side,
when they were abandoned. There
is also a considerable resemblance
between the story of Daphnis and
Chloe and that of the Gentle Shepherd, by Allan Ramsay. The work
formed the model of the *Sireine* of
Honoré d'Urfé, the *Diana* of Monte-
mayor, and the *Aminta* of Tasso.
Marmontel, in his *Annette* and *Lubin*,

has imitated the simplicity of the lovers of Longus, and the celebrated *Paul and Virginie* is an echo of the same story. But, of all modern writers, the author who has most closely followed this romance is Gessner, who, in his pastoral of *Daphnis*, exhibits the same poetical prose, rural descriptions, and the same innocence and simplicity on the part of the rustic characters.

The fragment of our author discovered by Courier in the library at Florence is here given in an Appendix. A brief account of the circumstances connected with it, which created a great stir in the learned world, may here be given. Courier, who had already visited Florence in 1808, paid a second visit there in the following year, and began to examine more

carefully the MS. which he had not previously had time to go through. He found it perfect, and copied about ten pages of Book I. which he knew were not found in any existing edition. Unhappily, just as at Strasburg, he emptied an inkpot, which he had mistaken for a sand-box, upon a splendid copy of Athenaeus, he smeared with ink one of the pages of the MS. and obliterated about twenty words. The librarian was furious, possibly also feeling aggrieved that he had been anticipated by Courier in the discovery of the fragment. Courier apologised for the mishap as follows: " The piece of paper, which was placed by mistake in the MS. to serve as a marker, was smeared with ink: I alone am to blame: I alone was guilty of this act

of carelessness." Nevertheless, guilty
intentions were attributed to him, and
a great disturbance arose. On the
10th of February, Courier wrote his
letter to M. Renouard[1] who was in
Florence at the time : " I will not
allow you to be hung for me, and I
am always ready to cry : *Me, me adsum
qui feci.* When you please, I will
declare that I alone made the fatal
blot, and that I had no accomplices."
On the 12th of March, he wrote to
Firmin Didot : " I think you will not
be sorry to know that there exists a
complete Longus, and my translation,
dry and slavish as it is, will give you
an idea of what is missing in the
printed copies. I am setting out for
Rome, where I shall be able to see

[1] See the end of the present volume.

other MSS. of Longus. By com-
paring them with the copy of the
one I have here, I shall perhaps
have a text which will not be unworthy to find a place amongst yours.
You might even do it still more
honour, if you felt inclined to enliven
with a few colours the rough draughts
of my sketches made to illustrate the
original." The edition was at last
printed. The first impression was
limited to 50 copies, which were
offered to the most famous Greek
scholars of France, Italy, and Germany. The authorities thought fit to
interfere: the Minister of the Interior
caused 27 copies of the translation to
be seized, and Courier was ordered
to leave Tuscany. The stir created
by the affair lasted for nearly a year.

DAPHNIS AND CHLOE

ΛΟΓΓΟΥ ΣΟΦΙΣΤΟΥ

ΠΟΙΜΕΝΙΚΩΝ,

ΤΩΝ ΚΑΤΑ ΔΑΦΝΙΝ ΚΑΙ ΧΛΟΗΝ,

ΠΡΟΟΙΜΙΟΝ.

Ἐν Λέσβῳ θηρῶν, ἐν ἄλσει Νυμφῶν, θέαμα εἶδον κάλλιστον ὧν εἶδον· εἰκόνα, γραφὴν, ἱστορίαν ἔρωτος. Καλὸν μὲν καὶ τὸ ἄλσος, πολύδενδρον, ἀνθηρὸν, κατάρρυτον· μία πηγὴ πάντα ἔτρεφε, καὶ τὰ ἄνθη καὶ τὰ δένδρα· ἀλλ' ἡ γραφὴ τερπνοτέρα, καὶ τέχνην ἔχουσα περιττὴν, καὶ τύχην ἐρωτικήν· ὥστε πολλοὶ τῶν ξένων κατὰ φήμην ᾔεσαν, τῶν μὲν Νυμφῶν ἱκέται, τῆς δὲ εἰκόνος θεαταί. Γυναῖκες ἐπ' αὐτῆς τίκτουσαι, καὶ ἄλλαι σπαργάνοις κοσμοῦσαι

THE PASTORALS

OF

LONGUS THE SOPHIST,

OR,

DAPHNIS AND CHLOE.

PREFACE.

WHILE hunting in a grove sacred to the Nymphs, in the island of Lesbos, I saw the most beautiful sight that I have ever seen : a picture representing a history of love. The grove itself was pleasant to the eye, covered with trees, full of flowers, and well-watered : a single spring fed both trees and flowers. But the picture itself was even more delightful : its subject was the fortunes of love, and the art displayed in it was marvellous : so that many, even strangers, who had heard it spoken of, visited the island, to pay their devotions to the Nymphs and examine the picture, on which were portrayed women in child-birth or wrapping children in swaddling-clothes, — poor babes exposed to the

παιδία ἐκκείμενα, ποίμνια τρέφοντα, ποιμένες ἀναιρούμενοι, νέοι συντιθέμενοι, λῃστῶν καταδρομὴ, πολεμίων ἐμβολή.

Πολλὰ ἄλλα, καὶ πάντα ἐρωτικὰ, ἰδόντα με καὶ θαυμάσαντα πόθος ἔσχεν ἀντιγράψαι τῇ γραφῇ. Καὶ ἀναζητησάμενος ἐξηγητὴν τῆς εἰκόνος, τέτταρας βίβλους ἐξεπονησάμην, ἀνάθημα μὲν Ἔρωτι, καὶ Νύμφαις, καὶ Πανὶ, κτῆμα δὲ τερπνὸν πᾶσιν ἀνθρώποις, ὃ καὶ νοσοῦντα ἰάσεται, καὶ λυπούμενον παραμυθήσεται, τὸν ἐρασθέντα ἀναμνήσει, τὸν οὐκ ἐρασθέντα προπαιδεύσει. Πάντως γὰρ οὐδεὶς Ἔρωτα ἔφυγεν, ἢ φεύξεται, μέχρις ἂν κάλλος ᾖ, καὶ ὀφθαλμοὶ βλέπωσιν· ἡμῖν δὲ ὁ θεὸς παράσχοι σωφρονοῦσι τὰ τῶν ἄλλων γράφειν.

mercy of Fortune,—beasts of the flock nurturing them, shepherds taking them up in token of adoption, young people binding one another by mutual vows, pirates over-running the seas, and enemies invading the land.

Many other subjects, all of an amatory nature, were depicted, which I gazed upon with such admiration that I was seized with a desire to describe them in writing. Accordingly, I diligently sought for some one to give me an explanation of the details : and, when I had thoroughly mastered them, I composed the four following books, as an offering to Love, the Nymphs, and Pan, and also as a work that will afford pleasure to many, in the hope that it may heal the sick, console the sorrowful, refresh the memory of him who once has loved, and instruct him who has never yet felt its flame. For no one has yet escaped, or ever will escape, the attack of Love, as long as beauty exists and eyes can see. May God grant that, unharmed ourselves, we may be able to describe the lot of others !

ΛΟΓΟΣ ΠΡΩΤΟΣ.

Πόλις ἐστὶ Λέσβου, Μιτυλήνη, μεγάλη καὶ καλή· διείληπται γὰρ εὐρίποις, ἐπεισρεούσης τῆς θαλάττης, καὶ κεκόσμηται γεφύραις ξεστοῦ καὶ λευκοῦ λίθου. Νομίσεις οὐ πόλιν ὁρᾶν ἀλλὰ νήσους. Ἀλλὰ ἐκ ταύτης τῆς πόλεως, τῆς Μιτυλήνης, ὅσον ἀπὸ σταδίων διακοσίων, ἀγρὸς ἦν ἀνδρὸς εὐδαίμονος, κτῆμα κάλλιστον· ὄρη θηροτρόφα, πεδία πυροφόρα, γήλοφοι κλημάτων, νομαὶ ποιμνίων· καὶ ἡ θάλαττα προσέκλυζεν ἠϊόνι ἐκτεταμένῃ ψάμμῳ μαλθακῇ.

Ἐν τῷδε τῷ ἀγρῷ νέμων αἰπόλος, Λάμων τοὔνομα, παιδίον εὗρεν ὑπὸ αἰγὸς τρεφόμενον. Δρυμὸς ἦν, καὶ λόχμη βάτων, καὶ κιττὸς ἐπιπλανώμενος, καὶ πόα μαλθακὴ, καθ' ἧς ἔκειτο τὸ παιδίον. Ἐνταῦθα ἡ αἲξ θέουσα συνεχὲς, ἀφανὴς ἐγίνετο πολλάκις, καὶ τὸν ἔριφον

BOOK I.

THERE is in Lesbos a flourishing and beautiful city, named Mitylene. It is intersected by numerous canals, formed by the waters of the sea, which flows in upon it, and adorned with several bridges of white polished stone: to look at it, you would say that it was not a single city, but a number of islands. About two hundred stades distant from the city, a wealthy man possessed a very fine estate: mountains abounding in game, fruitful cornfields, hillocks covered with vine - shoots, and ample pasturage for cattle; the sea washed a long stretch of soft sandy beach.

On this estate a goatherd, named Lamon, while feeding his flock, found a child being suckled by a goat. There was a thicket of shrubs and briars, over which the ivy straggled, and beneath, a couch of soft grass, whereon the infant lay. Hither the goat

ἀπολιποῦσα, τῷ βρέφει παρέμενε. Φυλάττει
τὰς διαδρομὰς ὁ Λάμων, οἰκτείρας ἀμελούμενον
τὸν ἔριφον· καὶ μεσημβρίας ἀκμαζούσης, κατ᾽
ἴχνος ἐλθὼν, ὁρᾷ τὴν μὲν αἶγα πεφυλαγμένως
περιβεβηκυῖαν, μὴ ταῖς χηλαῖς βλάπτοι πα-
τοῦσα, τὸ δὲ ὥσπερ ἐκ μητρῴας θηλῆς τὴν
ἐπιρροὴν ἕλκον τοῦ γάλακτος. Καὶ θαυμάσας,
ὥσπερ εἰκὸς ἦν, πρόσεισιν ἐγγὺς, καὶ εὑρίσκει
παιδίον ἄρρεν, μέγα καὶ καλὸν, καὶ τῆς κατὰ
τὴν ἔκθεσιν τύχης ἐν σπαργάνοις κρείττοσι.
Χλαμύδιόν τε γὰρ ἦν ἁλουργὲς, καὶ πόρπη
χρυσῆ, καὶ ξιφίδιον ἐλεφαντόκωπον.

Τὸ μὲν οὖν πρῶτον ἐβουλεύσατο, μόνα τὰ
γνωρίσματα βαστάσας, ἀμελῆσαι τοῦ βρέφους·
ἔπειτα αἰδεσθεὶς εἰ μηδὲ αἰγὸς φιλανθρωπίαν
μιμήσεται, νύκτα φυλάξας, κομίζει πάντα πρὸς
τὴν γυναῖκα Μυρτάλην καὶ τὰ γνωρίσματα,
καὶ τὸ παιδίον, καὶ τὴν αἶγα αὐτήν. Τῆς δὲ
ἐκπλαγείσης εἰ καὶ παιδία τίκτουσιν αἶγες,

often ran and wandered out of sight, and abandoning its own kid, remained by the side of the child.   Lamon, pitying the neglected kid, observed the direction in which the goat went : and, one day at noon, when the sun was at its height, he followed and saw it cautiously entering the thicket and walking round the child, so as not to tread on and hurt it, while the latter sucked vigorously at its teat as if it had been its mother's breast.   Astonished, as was natural, he approached closer, and found that it was a little boy, beautiful and well-grown, and wrapped in handsomer swaddling - clothes than suited a child thus exposed : it had on a little purple tunic fastened with a golden clasp, and by its side was a little dagger with an ivory hilt.

At first he was minded to take up the tokens, without troubling about the child : but afterwards, feeling ashamed at the idea of being outdone by the goat in humanity, he waited till night, and took everything to his wife Myrtale, — the tokens, the child, and the goat.   When

ὅδε πάντα αὐτῇ διηγεῖται, πῶς εὗρεν ἐκκείμενον, πῶς εὗρε τρεφόμενον, πῶς ᾐδέσθη
καταλιπεῖν ἀποθανούμενον. Δόξαν δὴ κἀκείνῃ,
τὰ μὲν συνεκτεθέντα κρύπτουσι, τὸ δὲ παιδίον
αὐτῶν ἐπονομάζουσι, τῇ δὲ αἰγὶ τὴν τροφὴν
ἐπιτρέπουσιν. Ὡς δ' ἂν καὶ τὸ ὄνομα τοῦ
παιδίου ποιμενικὸν δοκοίη, Δάφνιν αὐτὸν
ἔγνωσαν καλεῖν.

Ἤδη δὲ διετοῦς χρόνου διϊκνουμένου, ποιμὴν
ἐξ ἀγρῶν ὁμόρων νέμων, Δρύας τὸ ὄνομα, καὶ
αὐτὸς ὁμοίοις ἐπιτυγχάνει καὶ εὑρήμασι καὶ
θεάμασι. Νυμφῶν ἄντρον ἦν, πέτρα μεγάλη,
τὸ ἔνδοθεν κοίλη, ἔξωθεν περιφερής. Τὰ ἀγάλματα τῶν Νυμφῶν αὐτῶν λίθοις ἐπεποίητο·
πόδες ἀνυπόδητοι, χεῖρες εἰς ὤμους γυμναί,
κόμη μέχρι τῶν αὐχένων λελυμένη, ζῶμα περὶ
τὴν ἰξὺν, μειδίαμα περὶ τὴν ὀφρύν· τὸ πᾶν
σχῆμα χορεία ἦν ὀρχουμένων. Ἡ ὤα τοῦ
ἄντρου τῆς μεγάλης πέτρας ἦν τὸ μεσαίτατον.

she expressed her astonishment that goats should bring forth little children, he told her everything: how he had found the child lying exposed and being suckled by the goat, and how he had felt ashamed to leave it to die. His wife agreed with him, and they resolved to hide the tokens, to bring up thè child as their own, and to let the goat suckle him. Further, they decided to call him Daphnis, that the name might have a more pastoral sound.

When two years had passed, a shepherd belonging to the neighbourhood, named Dryas, while feeding his flocks, made a similar discovery and saw a similar sight. In his district there was a cave sacred to the Nymphs: a large rock hollowed out within, and circular without. Inside were statues of the Nymphs, carved in stone, with feet unshod, arms bared up to the shoulders, hair falling down over the neck, a girdle round the waist, and a smile on the face: to judge from their attitude, you would have said they were dancing. The dome of the grotto was the centre

Ἐκ δὲ τῆς πηγῆς ὕδωρ ἀναβλύζον, ῥεῖθρον ἐποίει χεόμενον, ὥστε καὶ λειμὼν πάνυ γλαφυρὸς ἐκτέτατο πρὸ τοῦ ἄντρου, πολλῆς καὶ μαλακῆς πόας ὑπὸ τῆς νοτίδος τρεφομένης. Ἀνέκειντο δὲ καὶ γαυλοί, καὶ αὐλοὶ πλάγιοι, καὶ σύριγγες, καὶ κάλαμοι, πρεσβυτέρων ποιμένων ἀναθήματα.

Εἰς τοῦτο τὸ νυμφαῖον οἷς ἀρτιτόκος συχνὰ φοιτῶσα, δόξαν πολλάκις ἀπωλείας παρεῖχε. Κολάσαι δὲ βουλόμενος αὐτήν, καὶ εἰς τὴν προτέραν εὐνομίαν καταστῆσαι, δεσμὸν ῥάβδου χλωρᾶς λυγίσας ὅμοιον βρόχῳ, τῇ πέτρᾳ προσῆλθεν, ὡς ἐκεῖ συλληψόμενος αὐτήν. Ἐπιστὰς δὲ, οὐδὲν εἶδεν ὧν ἤλπισεν· ἀλλὰ τὴν μὲν διδοῦσαν πάνυ ἀνθρωπίνως τὴν θηλὴν εἰς ἄφθονον τοῦ γάλακτος ὁλκήν, τὸ δὲ παιδίον ἀκλαγγὶ λάβρως εἰς ἀμφοτέρας τὰς θηλὰς μεταφέρον τὸ στόμα καθαρὸν καὶ φαιδρόν, οἷα τῆς ὄϊος τῇ γλώττῃ τὸ πρόσωπον ἀπολιχμωμένης μετὰ τὸν κόρον τῆς τροφῆς. Θῆλυ

of this mighty rock. Water, gushing from a fountain, formed a running stream; a beautiful meadow extended in front of cave, the soft and abundant herbage of which was nourished by the moisture of the stream. Within were to be seen hanging up milk-pails, flutes, pipes, and reeds, the offerings of the older shepherds.

A sheep, which had recently lambed, went so often to this grotto, that more than once she was thought to be lost. Dryas, wishing to punish her and make her stay with the flock to feed, as before, twisted a bough of pliant osier into a collar in the form of a running noose, and went up to the rock, in order to snare her. But, when he drew near, he beheld quite a different sight from what he had expected: he saw the sheep giving her teat, just like a human being, for a copious draught of milk, to a child, which, without a cry, eagerly shifted its clean and pretty mouth from one teat to the other, while the sheep licked its face, after it had had enough. It was a female child, and by its side also

ἦν τοῦτο τὸ παιδίον, καὶ παρέκειτο καὶ τούτῳ
σπάργανα, γνωρίσματα, μίτρα διάχρυσος, ὑποδήματα ἐπίχρυσα, καὶ περισκελίδες χρυσαῖ.

Θεῖον δή τι νομίσας τὸ εὕρημα, καὶ διδασ-
κόμενος παρὰ τῆς ὄϊος ἐλεεῖν τε τὸ παιδίον καὶ
φιλεῖν, ἀναιρεῖται μὲν τὸ βρέφος ἐπ' ἀγκῶνος,
ἀποτίθεται δὲ τὰ γνωρίσματα κατὰ τῆς πήρας,
εὔχεται δὲ ταῖς Νύμφαις ἐπὶ τύχῃ χρηστῇ
θρέψαι τὴν ἱκέτιν αὐτῶν. Καὶ, ἐπεὶ καιρὸς
ἦν ἀπελαύνειν τὴν ποίμνην, ἐλθὼν εἰς τὴν
ἔπαυλιν, τῇ γυναικὶ διηγεῖται τὰ ὀφθέντα,
δείκνυσι τὰ εὑρεθέντα, παρακελεύεται θυγάτριον νομίζειν, λανθάνουσαν ὡς ἴδιον τρέφειν.
Ἡ μὲν δὴ Νάπη (τοῦτο γὰρ ἐκαλεῖτο) μήτηρ
εὐθὺς ἦν, καὶ ἐφίλει τὸ παιδίον, ὥστε ὑπὸ τῆς
ὄϊος παρευδοκιμηθῆναι δεδοικυῖα, καὶ τίθεται
καὶ αὐτὴ ποιμενικὸν ὄνομα πρὸς πίστιν αὐτῷ,
Χλόην.

Ταῦτα τὰ παιδία ταχὺ μάλα ηὔξησε, καὶ
κάλλος αὐτοῖς ἐφαίνετο κρεῖττον ἀγροικίας.
Ἤδη οὖν ὁ μὲν πέντε καὶ δέκα ἐτῶν ἀπὸ
γενεᾶς· ἡ δὲ τοσούτων, δυοῖν ἀποδεόντοιν.

lay swaddling-clothes and tokens, a cap
interwoven with gold, gilded shoes, and
gold-embroidered anklets.

Thinking that what he had found was sent
from Heaven, and being moved to pity by
the example of the sheep, he took the child
up in his arms, put the tokens in his wallet,
and prayed to the Nymphs that he might
be permitted to bring up their suppliant
happily. Then, when it was time to drive
back his flock, he returned home, told his
wife what he had seen, showed her what he
had found, and bade her adopt and bring
up the child as her own, without telling
anyone what had happened. Nape—that
was his wife's name—immediately took up
the child and caressed her, as if afraid of
being outdone in kindliness by the sheep :
and, that it might be more readily believed
that the child was her own, she gave it the
pastoral name of Chloe.

The two children soon grew up, more
beautiful than ordinary rustics. When
the boy was fifteen years of age, and
the girl thirteen, Lamon and Dryas both
dreamed the following dream the same

Καὶ ὁ Δρύας καὶ ὁ Λάμων ἐπὶ μιᾶς νυκτὸς ὁρῶσιν ὄναρ τοιόνδε τί· εἶναι τὰς Νύμφας ἐδόκουν ἐκείνας, τὰς ἐν τῷ ἄντρῳ, ἐν ᾧ ἡ πηγὴ, ἐν ᾧ τὸ παιδίον εὗρεν ὁ Δρύας, Δάφνιν καὶ τὴν Χλόην παραδιδόναι παιδίῳ μάλα σοβαρῷ καὶ καλῷ, πτερὰ ἐκ τῶν ὤμων ἔχοντι, βέλη σμικρὰ ἅμα τοξαρίῳ φέροντι· τὸ δὲ ἐφαψά- μενον ἀμφοτέρων ἑνὶ βέλει, κελεῦσαι λοιπὸν ποιμαίνειν, τὸν μὲν, τὸ αἰπόλιον, τὴν δὲ, τὸ ποίμνιον.

Τοῦτο τὸ ὄναρ ἰδόντες, ἤχθοντο μὲν οἱ ποι- μένες εἰ ἔσοιντο καὶ οὗτοι αἰπόλοι, τύχην ἐκ σπαργάνων ἐπαγγελλόμενοι κρείττονα, δι' ἣν αὐτοὺς καὶ τροφαῖς ἁβροτέραις ἔτρεφον, καὶ γράμματα ἐπαίδευον, καὶ πάντα ὅσα καλὰ ἦν ἐπ' ἀγροικίᾳ. Ἐδόκει δὲ πείθεσθαι θεοῖς περὶ τῶν σωθέντων προνοίᾳ θεῶν. Καὶ κοινώ- σαντες ἀλλήλοις τὸ ὄναρ, καὶ θύσαντες τῷ τὰ πτερὰ ἔχοντι παιδίῳ παρὰ ταῖς Νύμφαις, (τὸ γὰρ ὄνομα λέγειν οὐκ εἶχον) ὡς ποιμένας ἐκπέμπουσιν αὐτοὺς ἅμα ταῖς ἀγέλαις, ἐκδιδά-

night. They dreamed that the Nymphs of the grotto with the fountain, in which Dryas had found the little girl, delivered Daphnis and Chloe into the hands of a saucy and beautiful boy, who had wings on his shoulders and carried a little bow and arrows: and that this boy touched them both with the same arrow, and bade them tend, the one goats, the other sheep.

When they saw this vision, they grieved to think that Daphnis and Chloe were destined to tend sheep and goats, since their swaddling-clothes seemed to give promise of better fortune: for which reason they had brought them up more delicately than shepherds' children, had taught them to read, and given them all the instruction possible in a country place. They resolved, however, to obey the gods in regard to those who had been saved by their providence. Having communicated their dreams to each other, and offered sacrifice, in the cave of the Nymphs, to the winged boy (whose name they did not know), they sent the maiden and the lad into the fields, having instructed them in all that they

ξαντες ἕκαστα· πῶς δεῖ νέμειν πρὸ μεσημβρίας,
πῶς δεῖ νέμειν κοπάσαντος τοῦ καύματος, πότε
ἄγειν ἐπὶ ποτὸν, πότε ἀπάγειν ἐπὶ κοῖτον· ἐπὶ
τίσι καλαύροπι χρηστέον, ἐπὶ τίσι μόνῃ φωνῇ.
Οἱ δὲ, μάλα χαίροντες, ὡς ἀρχὴν μεγάλην
παρελάμβανον, καὶ ἐφίλουν τὰς αἶγας καὶ τὰ
πρόβατα μᾶλλον ἢ ποιμέσιν ἔθος· ἡ μὲν, ἐς
ποίμνιον ἄγουσα τῆς σωτηρίας τὴν αἰτίαν·
ὁ δὲ, μεμνημένος ὡς ἐκκείμενον αὐτὸν αἲξ
ἀνέθρεψεν.

Ἧρος ἦν ἀρχὴ, καὶ πάντα ἤκμαζεν ἄνθη, τὰ
ἐν δρυμοῖς, τὰ ἐν λειμῶσι, καὶ ὅσα ὄρεια.
Βόμβος ἦν ἤδη μελιττῶν, ἦχος ὀρνίθων μουσι-
κῶν, σκιρτήματα ποιμνίων ἀρτιγεννήτων· ἄρνες
ἐσκίρτων ἐν τοῖς ὄρεσιν, ἐβόμβουν ἐν τοῖς
λειμῶσιν αἱ μέλitται, τὰς λόχμας κατῇδον
ὄρνιθες. Τοσαύτης δὴ πάντα κατεχούσης
εὐωρίας, οἱ ἁπαλοὶ καὶ νέοι μιμηταὶ τῶν
ἀκουομένων ἐγίνοντο καὶ βλεπομένων. Ἀκούοντες μὲν τῶν ὀρνίθων ᾀδόντων, ᾖδον· βλέ-

had to do: how they ought to feed their
flocks before midday, and when the heat
had abated: when they should drive them
to drink, and when drive them back to the
fold: when they should use the shepherd's
crook, and when the voice alone. They
undertook this duty as joyfully as if they
had been intrusted with some important
office, and were fonder of their goats and
sheep than shepherds usually are: for
Chloe felt that she owed her life to a
ewe, while Daphnis remembered that,
when exposed, he had been nurtured by
a goat.

It was the beginning of spring, and all
the flowers were blooming—in the woods
and meadows, and on the mountains.
The humming of bees, and the twittering
of tuneful birds was already heard, and the
new born young were skipping through the
fields: [the lambs were gamboling on the
mountains, the bees were buzzing through
the meadows, the birds were singing in
the bushes.] Under the influence of this
beautiful season, Daphnis and Chloe, themselves tender and youthful, imitated what

ποντες δὲ σκιρτῶντας τοὺς ἄρνας, ἥλλοντο
κοῦφα· καὶ τὰς μελίττας δὲ μιμούμενοι, τὰ
ἄνθη συνέλεγον.   Καὶ τὰ μὲν εἰς τοὺς κόλπους
ἔβαλλον· τὰ δὲ, στεφανίσκους πλέκοντες, ταῖς
Νύμφαις ἔφερον.

Ἔπραττον δὲ κοινῇ πάντα, πλησίον ἀλλήλων
νέμοντες.   Καὶ πολλάκις μὲν ὁ Δάφνις τῶν
προβάτων τὰ ἀποπλανώμενα συνέστελλε·
πολλάκις δὲ ἡ Χλόη τὰς θρασυτέρας τῶν
αἰγῶν ἀπὸ τῶν κρημνῶν κατήλαυνεν.   Ἤδη
δέ τις καὶ τὰς ἀγέλας ἀμφοτέρας ἐφρούρησε,
θατέρου προσλιπαρήσαντος ἀθύρματι. Ἀθύρ-
ματα δὲ ἦν αὐτοῖς ποιμενικὰ καὶ παιδικά. Ἡ
μὲν ἀνθερίκους ἀνελομένη ποθὲν ἐξ ἕλους
ἀκριδοθήραν ἀνέπλεκε, καὶ περὶ τοῦτο πονου-
μένη, τῶν ποιμνίων ἠμέλησεν· ὁ δὲ, καλάμους
ἐκτεμὼν λεπτοὺς, καὶ τρήσας τὰς τῶν γονάτων
διαφυὰς, ἀλλήλας τε κηρῷ μαλθακῷ συναρτήσας,
μέχρι νυκτὸς συρίζειν ἐμελέτησε. Καί ποτε δὲ
ἐκοινώνουν γάλακτος καὶ οἴνου, καὶ τροφὰς, ἃς

they saw and heard. When they heard
the birds sing, they sang: when they
saw the lambs gambol, they nimbly
skipped in rivalry: and, like the bees,
they gathered flowers, some of which they
placed in their bosoms, while they wove
garlands of others, which they offered to
the Nymphs.

They did everything in common, and
tended their flocks side by side. Daphnis
frequently gathered together Chloe's wandering sheep: while she often drove back
his too venturesome goats from the pre-
cipices. Sometimes one of them tended
the two flocks alone, while the other
was intent upon some amusement. Their
amusements were those of children or shepherds. Chloe would pluck some stalks
of asphodel from the marsh, to weave a
locust-trap, without any thought for her
flock: while Daphnis, having cut some
slender reeds, and perforated the intervals
between joints, joined them with soft
wax, and practised himself in playing
upon them until nightfall. Sometimes
they shared the food they had taken with

οἴκοθεν ἔφερον, εἰς κοινὸν ἔφερον. Θᾶττον ἄν τις εἶδε τὰ ποίμνια καὶ τὰς ἀγέλας ἀπ' ἀλλήλων μεμερισμένας, ἢ Χλόην καὶ Δάφνιν.

Τοιαῦτα δὲ αὐτῶν παιζόντων, τοιάνδε σπουδὴν Ἔρως ἀνέπλασε. Λύκαινα τρέφουσα σκύμνους νέους, ἐκ τῶν πλησίον ἀγρῶν, ἐξ ἄλλων ποιμνίων πολλάκις ἥρπαζε, πολλῆς τροφῆς ἐς ἀνατροφὴν τῶν σκύμνων δεομένη. Συνελθόντες οὖν οἱ κωμῆται νύκτωρ, σιῤῥοὺς ὀρύττουσι τὸ εὖρος, ὀργυιᾶς, τὸ βάθος, τεσσάρων. Τὸ μὲν δὴ χῶμα τὸ πολὺ σπείρουσι, κομίσαντες μακράν· ξύλα δὲ ξηρὰ μακρὰ τείναντες ὑπὲρ τοῦ χάσματος, τὸ περιττὸν τοῦ χώματος κατέπασαν, τῆς πρότερον γῆς εἰκόνα· ὥστε κἂν λαγὼς ἐπιδράμῃ, κατακλᾷ τὰ ξύλα κάρφων ἀσθενέστερα ὄντα, καὶ τότε παρέχει μαθεῖν ὅτι γῆ οὐκ ἦν, ἀλλὰ μεμίμητο γῆν. Τοιαῦτα πολλὰ ὀρύγματα, κἂν τοῖς ὄρεσι, κἂν τοῖς

them from home, their milk, or wine. In short, it would have been easier to find sheep and goats feeding apart, than Daphnis separated from Chloe. ⸳

While they were thus engaged in their youthful sports, Love contrived the following trouble for them. There was a wolf in the district, which, having recently brought forth young, frequently carried off lambs from the neighbouring fields to feed them. The villagers accordingly assembled together by night, and dug some trenches, one fathom in depth and four in breadth : the greater part of the earth which they dug out they removed to a distance from the trenches : then, placing over the hole long pieces of dry wood, they covered them with the remainder of the earth, so that it looked level ground just as it had been before : this they did so cunningly that, if even a hare had run across, it would have broken the pieces of wood, which were more brittle than bits of straw; and then it would have been seen that it was not solid earth

πεδίοις, ὀρύξαντες, τὴν μὲν λύκαιναν οὐκ
εὐτύχησαν λαβεῖν (αἰσθάνεται γὰρ καὶ γῆς
σεσοφισμένης) πολλὰς δὲ αἶγας καὶ ποίμνια
διέφθειραν, καὶ Δάφνιν παρ' ὀλίγον, ὧδε.

Τράγοι παροξυνθέντες, εἰς μάχην συνέπεσον.
Τῷ οὖν ἑτέρῳ τὸ ἕτερον κέρας, βιαιοτέρας γενομένης συμβολῆς, θραύεται· καὶ ἀλγήσας, φρι-
μαξάμενος ἐς φυγὴν ἐτράπετο. Ὁ δὲ νικῶν
κατ' ἴχνος ἑπόμενος, ἄπαυστον ἐποίει τὴν
φυγήν. Ἀλγεῖ Δάφνις περὶ τῷ κέρατι, καὶ,
τῇ θρασύτητι ἀχθεσθεὶς, ξύλον καὶ τὴν καλαύροπα λαβὼν, ἐδίωκε τὸν διώκοντα. Οἷα δὲ τοῦ
μὲν ὑπεκφεύγοντος, τοῦ δὲ ὀργῇ διώκοντος, οὐκ
ἀκριβὴς τῶν ἐν ποσὶν ἡ πρόσοψις ἦν· ἀλλὰ
κατὰ χάσματος ἄμφω πίπτουσιν· ὁ τράγος
πρότερος, ὁ Δάφνις δεύτερος. Τοῦτο καὶ ἔσωσε
Δάφνιν χρήσασθαι τῆς καταφορᾶς ὀχήματι τῷ
τράγῳ. Ὁ μὲν δὴ τὸν ἀνιμησόμενον, εἴ τις
ἄρα γένοιτο, δακρύων ἀνέμενεν· ἡ δὲ Χλόη

at all, but an imitation. Although they
dug several similar trenches on the
mountains and plains, they could not
succeed in catching the wolf, which perceived the snare, but were the cause of
the loss of a number of sheep and goats,
and Daphnis also nearly lost his life, in
the following manner.

Two goats, in a fit of jealousy, charged
each other so violently that the horn of one
was broken, and, mad with pain, he took to
flight bellowing, closely and hotly pursued by
his victorious adversary. Daphnis, grieved
at the sight of the mutilated horn, and
annoyed at the insolence of the victor,
seized his club and crook, and started in
pursuit of the pursuer. But, while the goat
was trying to make his escape, and Daphnis
was in angry pursuit, they could not see
clearly what was in front of them, and both
fell into one of these pits—the goat first,
and Daphnis after him. This saved Daphnis from injury, since he was able to hold
on to the goat to break his fall. In this
situation he waited in tears to see if anyone would come to pull him up again.

θεασαμένη τὸ συμβὰν, δρόμῳ παραγίνεται εἰς τὸν σιῤῥόν· καὶ μαθοῦσα ὅτι ζῇ, καλεῖ βουκόλον ἐκ τῶν ἀγρῶν τῶν πλησίον πρὸς ἐπικουρίαν. Ὁ δὲ ἐλθών, σχοῖνον ἐζήτει μακρὰν, ἧς ἐχόμενος, ἀνιμώμενος ἐκβήσεται. Καὶ σχοῖνος μὲν οὐκ ἦν· ἡ δὲ Χλόη λυσαμένη ταινίαν, δίδωσι καθεῖναι τῷ βουκόλῳ. Καὶ οὕτως οἱ μὲν ἐπὶ τοῦ χείλους ἑστῶτες εἷλκον· ὁ δὲ ἀνέβη ταῖς τῆς ταινίας ὁλκαῖς ταῖς χερσὶν ἀκολουθῶν.

Ἀνιμήσαντες δὲ καὶ τὸν ἄθλιον τράγον συντεθραυσμένον ἄμφω τὰ κέρατα, (τοσοῦτον ἄρα ἡ δίκη μετῆλθε τοῦ νικηθέντος τράγου) τοῦτον μὲν δὴ τυθησόμενον χαρίζονται σῶστρα τῷ βουκόλῳ· καὶ ἔμελλον ψεύδεσθαι πρὸς τοὺς οἴκοι λύκων ἐπιδρομὴν, εἴ τις αὐτὸν ἐπόθησεν. Αὐτοὶ δὲ ἐπανελθόντες, ἐπεσκοποῦντο τὴν ποίμνην καὶ τὸ αἰπόλιον· καὶ ἐπεὶ κατέμαθον ἐν κόσμῳ νομῆς καὶ τὰς αἶγας καὶ τὰ πρόβατα, καθίσαντες ἐπὶ στελέχους δρυὸς, ἐσκόπουν μὴ τι μέρος τοῦ σώματος ὁ Δάφνις ἤμαξε κατα-

Chloe, having seen what had happened,
ran up, and, finding that he was still alive,
called one of the herdsmen from the neighbouring fields to her assistance. The
herdsman came up, and looked for a
long rope with which to haul him out,
but found none. Then Chloe unloosed
the band which fastened her hair, and
gave it to the herdsman to let down.
Then they stood on the edge of the pit
and pulled : and Daphnis, holding on to
the band as it was being hauled up, at
last succeeded in reaching the summit.

Then they drew up the wretched goat,
whose horns were both broken—so fully
was his vanquished adversary avenged—
and made a present of him to the herdsman, in return for his assistance, having
agreed to tell those at home that he
had been carried off by a wolf, if anyone
missed him. Returning to their flocks,
and finding them all feeding peacefully
and in good order, they sat down on
the trunk of an oak, to see whether
Daphnis had been wounded in any part of
his body by his fall. But they found no

πεσών. Τέτρωτο μὲν οὖν οὐδὲν, οὐδε ἤμακτο
οὐδεν· χώματος δὲ καὶ πηλοῦ πέπαστο καὶ
τὰς κόμας, καὶ τὸ ἄλλο σῶμα. Ἐδόκει δὲ
λούσασθαι, πρὶν αἴσθησιν γενέσθαι τοῦ συμ-
βάντος Λάμωνι καὶ Μυρτάλῃ. Καὶ ἐλθὼν ἅμα
τῇ Χλόῃ πρὸς τὸ ἄντρον τῶν Νυμφῶν, ἐν ᾧ
ἡ πηγὴ, τῇ μὲν ἔδωκε καὶ τὸν χιτῶνα, καὶ
τὴν πήραν   .   .   .   .

.   .   .   .

ἐγένετο, τοιαῦτα πρὸς αὐτὸν ἀπελήρει· "Τί
ποτέ με Χλόης ἐργάζεται φίλημα; Χείλη
μὲν ῥόδων ἀπαλώτερα, καὶ στόμα κηρίων γλυ-
κύτερον· τὸ δὲ φίλημα κέντρου μελίττης πι-
κρότερον. Πολλάκις ἐφίλησα ἐρίφους· πολλάκις ἐφίλησα σκύλακας ἀρτιγεννήτους, καὶ τὸν
μόσχον, ὃν ὁ Δόρκων ἐχαρίσατο· ἀλλὰ τοῦτο
φίλημα καινόν. Ἐκπηδᾷ μου τὸ πνεῦμα,
ἐξάλλεται ἡ καρδία, τήκεται ἡ ψυχὴ, καὶ
ὅμως πάλιν φιλῆσαι θέλω. Ὦ νίκης κακῆς. Ὦ
νόσου καινῆς, ἧς οὐδὲ εἰπεῖν οἶδα τὸ ὄνομα.
Ἆρα φαρμάκων ἐγεύσατο Χλόη μέλλουσά με
φιλεῖν; Πῶς οὖν οὐκ ἀπέθανεν; Οἷον ᾄδουσιν

trace of any injury or blood: only his hair and the rest of his person were covered with earth and mud. Daphnis therefore resolved to wash himself, before Lamon and Myrtale found out what had happened. He went with Chloe to the grotto of the Nymphs, where the foun-tain was, and gave her his tunic and wallet . . . .

. . . .

Meanwhile, Daphnis raved to himself as follows: "What has Chloe's kiss done to me? Her lips are tenderer than roses, her mouth is sweeter than a honeycomb, but her kiss is sharper than the sting of a bee. I have often kissed my kids: I have often kissed newly-born puppies, and the little calf which Dorcon gave me: but this kiss is something new. My pulse beats high: my heart leaps: my soul melts: and yet I wish to kiss again. O bitter victory! O strange disease, the name of which I cannot even tell! Can Chloe have tasted poison before she kissed me? why then did she not die? How sweetly sing the nightingales; but

αἱ ἀηδόνες, ἡ δὲ ἐμὴ σύριγξ σιωπᾷ ; Οἷον
σκιρτῶσιν οἱ ἔριφοι, κἀγὼ κάθημαι ; Οἷον
ἀκμάζει τὰ ἄνθη, κἀγὼ στεφάνους οὐ πλέκω.
Ἀλλὰ τὰ μὲν ἴα καὶ ὁ ὑάκινθος ἀνθεῖ, Δάφνις
δὲ μαραίνεται. Ἀρά μου καὶ Δόρκων εὐμορ-
φότερος ὀφθήσεται ; "

Τοιαῦτα ὁ βέλτιστος Δάφνις ἔπασχε καὶ
ἔλεγεν, οἷα πρῶτον γενόμενος τοῦ ἔρωτος
καὶ ἔργων καὶ λόγων. Ὁ δὲ Δόρκων, ὁ
βουκόλος, ὁ τῆς Χλόης ἐραστής, φυλάξας
τὸν Δρύαντα φυτὸν κατορύττοντα πλησίον
κλήματος, πρόσεισιν αὐτῷ μετὰ τυρῶν καὶ
συρίγγων τινῶν [γαμικῶν]. Καὶ τοὺς μὲν
τυροὺς δῶρον εἶναι δίδωσι, πάλαι φίλος ὢν
ἡνίκα αὐτὸς ἔνεμεν· ἐντεῦθεν δὲ ἀρξάμενος
ἀνέβαλε λόγον περὶ τοῦ τῆς Χλόης γάμου.
Καὶ, εἰ λαμβάνοι γυναῖκα, δῶρα πολλὰ καὶ
μεγάλα, ὡς βουκόλος, ἐπηγγέλλετο· ζεῦγος
βοῶν ἀροτήρων, σμήνη τέτταρα μελιττῶν,
φυτὰ μηλεῶν πεντήκοντα, δέρμα ταύρου τε-
μεῖν ὑποδήματα, μόσχον, ἀνὰ πᾶν ἔτος, μηκέτι
γάλακτος δεόμενον· ὥστε μικροῦ δεῖν ὁ Δρύας

my pipe is silent! How wantonly leap
the kids, but I sit still! How sweetly
bloom the flowers, but I weave no garlands! The violets and hyacinths bloom,
but Daphnis fades. Shall even Dorcon
appear more beautiful than Daphnis?"

Such were the passionate outbursts of
the worthy Daphnis, who then for the
first time felt the influence of love.
But Dorcon, the herdsman, the lover of
Chloe, seizing the opportunity when Dryas
was planting a tree near a vine-shoot,
went up to him with some cheeses
and pipes. He gave him the cheeses,
since he had been an old friend of his,
at the time when he himself pastured
his flock. Then he began to speak of
marriage with Chloe, and promised him
a number of valuable presents, if he
should gain her hand: a yoke of oxen for
ploughing, four swarms of bees, fifty
young apple trees, an ox-hide for making
shoes, and, every year, a calf that had
been weaned. Allured by the prospects
of such presents, Dryas was on the point
of giving his consent. But afterwards,

θελχθεὶς τοῖς δώροις, ἐπένευσε τὸν γάμον. Ἐννοήσας δὲ ὡς κρείττονος ἡ παρθένος ἀξία νυμφίου, καὶ δείσας μὴ φωραθείς ποτε, κακοῖς ἀνηκέστοις περιπέσοι, τόν τε γάμον ἀνένευσε, καὶ συγγνώμην ἔχειν ᾐτήσατο, καὶ τὰ ὀνομασθέντα δῶρα παρῃτήσατο.

Δευτέρας δὴ διαμαρτὼν ὁ Δόρκων ἐλπίδος, καὶ μάτην τυροὺς ἀγαθοὺς ἀπολέσας, ἔγνω διὰ χειρῶν ἐπιθέσθαι τῇ Χλόῃ μόνῃ γενομένῃ. Καὶ παραφυλάξας ὅτι παρ' ἡμέραν ἐπὶ τὸν ποτὸν ἄγουσι τὰς ἀγέλας, ποτὲ μὲν ὁ Δάφνις, ποτὲ δὲ ἡ παῖς, ἐπιτεχνᾶται τέχνην ποιμένι πρέπουσαν. Λύκου μεγάλου δέρμα λαβών, ὃν ταῦρός ποτε πρὸ τῶν βοῶν μαχόμενος τοῖς κέρασι διέφθειρε, περιέτεινε τῷ σώματι, ποδῆρες κατανωτισάμενος· ὡς τούς τ' ἐμπροσθίους πόδας ἐφηπλῶσθαι ταῖς χερσί, καὶ τοῖς κατόπιν τοῖς σκέλεσιν ἄχρι πτέρνης, καὶ τοῦ στόματος τὸ χάσμα σκέπειν τὴν κεφαλὴν, ὥσπερ ἀνδρὸς ὁπλίτου κράνος. Ἐκθηριώσας δὲ αὐτὸν ὡς ἔνι μάλιστα, παραγίνεται πρὸς τὴν

thinking that the maiden deserved to
make a better marriage, and being afraid
that, if he were found out, he might be
punished and even put to death, ´he refused his consent, at the same time
asking Dorcon not to be offended.

Dorcon, thus for the second time
cheated of his hopes, and having lost his
fat cheeses for nothing, determined to
lay violent hands on Chloe when he
found her alone. Having observed that
Daphnis and Chloe took it in turns to
drive their flocks to drink, he contrived a
scheme worthy of a shepherd. He took
the skin of a large wolf, which one of
his oxen, fighting in defence of the kine,
had killed with his horns, and flung it
over his shoulders, whence it hung down
to his feet, so that the forefeet covered
his hands, and the hinder his legs down
to his heels, while the head with its
gaping mouth enclosed his head like a
soldier's helmet. Having thus transformed himself into a wild beast as best
he could, he proceeded to the spring
where the goats and sheep used to drink

πηγὴν, ἧς ἔπινον αἱ αἶγες καὶ τὰ πρόβατα
μετὰ τὴν νομήν. Ἐν κοίλῃ δὲ πάνυ γῇ ἦν ἡ
πηγὴ, καὶ περὶ αὐτὴν πᾶς ὁ τόπος ἀκάνθαις,
καὶ βάτοις, καὶ ἀρκεύθῳ ταπεινῇ, καὶ σκολύμοις
ἠγρίωτο· ῥᾳδίως ἂν ἐκεῖ καὶ λύκος ἀληθινὸς
ἔλαθε λόχῳ. Ἐνταῦθα κρύψας ἑαυτὸν, ἐπετήρει τοῦ ποτοῦ τὴν ὥραν ὁ Δόρκων, καὶ
πολλὴν εἶχεν ἐλπίδα, τῷ σχήματι φοβήσας,
λαβεῖν ταῖς χερσὶ τὴν Χλόην·

Χρόνος ὀλίγος διαγίνεται, καὶ Χλόη κατήλαυνε τὰς ἀγέλας εἰς τὴν πηγὴν, καταλιποῦσα
τὴν Δάφνιν φυλλάδα χλωρὰν κόπτοντα, τοῖς
ἐρίφοις τροφὴν μετὰ τὴν νομήν. Καὶ οἱ κύνες,
οἱ τῶν προβάτων ἐπιφύλακες καὶ τῶν αἰγῶν,
ἑπόμενοι, οἷα δὴ κυνῶν ἐν ῥινηλασίαις περιεργία,
κινούμενον τὸν Δόρκωνα πρὸς τὴν ἐπίθεσιν τῆς
κόρης φωράσαντες, πικρὸν μάλα ὑλακτήσαντες,
ὥρμησαν ὡς ἐπὶ λύκον· καὶ περισχόντες πρὶν
ὅλως ἀναστῆναι δι᾽ ἔκπληξιν, ἔδακνον κατὰ
κράτος. Τέως μὲν οὖν τὸν ἔλεγχον αἰδούμενος,
καὶ ὑπὸ τοῦ δέρματος ἐπισκέποντος φρουρού-

after they came from pasture. This fountain was in a hollow valley, and the
whole spot around was full of wild
brambles and thorns, low-growing juniper
bushes and thistles, so that even a real
wolf could easily have concealed himself
there. Here Dorcon hid himself, waiting
for the time when the animals came to
drink, hoping to frighten Chloe under the
guise of a wolf, and so easily lay hands
upon her.

After he had waited a little while, Chloe
came driving the flocks to the spring,
having left Daphnis cutting fresh foliage
for the kids to eat after pasture. The
dogs who assisted them to guard the
sheep and goats followed her: and, with
the natural curiosity of keen-scented animals, they tracked and discovered Dorcon
preparing to attack the maiden. With a
loud bark, they rushed upon him as if he
had been a wolf, surrounded him, before he
was able in his astonishment to rise upon
his feet, and bit at him furiously. At first,
afraid of being recognised, and being for
some time protected by the skin which

μενος, ἔκειτο σιωπῶν ἐν τῇ λόχμῃ· ἐπεὶ δὲ ἥ τε
Χλόη πρὸς τὴν πρώτην θέαν διαταραχθεῖσα,
τὸν Δάφνιν ἐκάλει βοηθὸν, οἵ τε κύνες περι-
σπῶντες τὸ δέρμα, τοῦ σώματος ἥπτοντο
αὐτοῦ, μέγα οἰμώξας, ἱκέτευε βοηθεῖν τὴν
κόρην καὶ τὸν Δάφνιν ἤδη παρόντα. Τοὺς μὲν
κύνας δὴ ἀνακλήσει συνήθει ταχέως ἡμέρωσαν,
τὸν δὲ Δόρκωνα, κατά τε μηρῶν καὶ ὤμων δεδηγ-
μένον, ἀγαγόντες ἐπὶ τὴν πηγὴν, ἀπένιψαν τὰ
δήγματα, ἵνα ἦσαν τῶν ὀδόντων αἱ ἐμβολαὶ,
καὶ διαμασσησάμενοι φλοιὸν χλωρὸν πτελέας,
ἐπέπασαν· ὑπό τε ἀπειρίας ἐρωτικῶν τολμη-
μάτων ποιμενικὴν παιδιὰν νομίζοντες τὴν ἐπι-
βολὴν τοῦ δέρματος, οὐδὲν ὀργισθέντες, ἀλλὰ
καὶ παραμυθησάμενοι, καὶ μέχρι τινὸς χειρα-
γωγήσαντες, ἀπέπεμψαν.

Καὶ ὁ μὲν κινδύνου παρὰ τοσοῦτον ἐλθὼν,
καὶ σωθεὶς ἐκ κυνὸς, φασὶν, οὐ λύκου στόματος,
ἐθεράπευε τὸ σῶμα· ὁ δὲ Δάφνις καὶ ἡ Χλόη

covered him, he lay in the thicket without uttering a word: but when Chloe, terrified at the first sight of the supposed animal, shouted for Daphnis to help her, and the dogs, having torn off the skin, began to fix their teeth in his body, he cried out loudly and implored Chloe and Daphnis (who had just come up) to assist him.

They quickly calmed the dogs with their familiar shout; then taking Dorcon, who had been bitten in the legs and shoulders, to the fountain, they washed his wounds, where the dogs' teeth had entered the flesh, and chewed the green bark of an elm-tree and spread it over them. In their ignorance of the audacity prompted by love, they thought that Dorcon had merely put on the wolf's skin for a joke: wherefore they felt no anger against him, but tried to console him, and, having helped him along a little distance, sent him on his way.

Dorcon, having been in such deadly peril, after he had made good his escape from the mouth of a dog (not, as the proverb goes, of a wolf), devoted his at-

κάματον πολὺν ἔσχον μέχρι νυκτὸς τὰς αἶγας
καὶ τὰς οἶς συλλέγοντες. Ὑπὸ γὰρ τοῦ
δέρματος πτοηθεῖσαι, καὶ ὑπὸ τῶν κυνῶν
ὑλακτησάντων ταραχθεῖσαι, αἱ μὲν εἰς πέτρας
ἀνέδραμον, αἱ δὲ μέχρι τῆς θαλάττης αὐτῆς
κατέδραμον. Καίτοι γε ἐπεπαίδευντο καὶ φωνῇ
πείθεσθαι, καὶ σύριγγι θέλγεσθαι, καὶ χειρὸς
παταγῇ συλλέγεσθαι· ἀλλὰ τότε πάντων
αὐταῖς ὁ φόβος λήθην ἐνέβαλε. Καὶ μόλις,
ὥσπερ λαγὼς ἐκ τῶν ἰχνῶν εὑρίσκοντες, εἰς τὰς
ἐπαύλεις ἤγαγον. Ἐκείνης μόνης τῆς νυκτὸς
ἐκοιμήθησαν βαθὺν ὕπνον, καὶ τῆς ἐρωτικῆς
λύπης φάρμακον τὸν κάματον ἔσχον. Αὖθις
δὲ ἡμέρας ἐπελθούσης, πάλιν ἔπασχον παρα-
πλήσια. Ἔχαιρον ἰδόντες, ἐλυποῦντο ἀπαλ-
λαγέντες, ἤλγουν, ἤθελόν τι, ἠγνόουν ὅ, τι
θέλουσι. Τοῦτο μόνον ᾔδεσαν, ὅτι τὸν μὲν,
φίλημα, τὴν δὲ, λουτρὸν ἀπώλεσεν. Ἐξέκᾳε
δὲ αὐτοὺς καὶ ἡ ὥρα τοῦ ἔτους.

tention to his wounds. Daphnis and
Chloe, however, found considerable difficulty in getting together their goats and
sheep, which, alarmed by the sight of the
wolf's skin, and thrown into confusion by
the barking of the dogs, had fled to the
tops of the mountains or down to the sea-
shore. Although they had been trained to
obey their masters' voice and to be soothed
by the sound of the pipe, and to gather
together when they merely clapped their
hands, fear had caused them to forget
everything; and they could only get them
back to the fold with difficulty, after track-
ing them like hares. During that night
alone they slept soundly, and weariness
was a remedy for their amorous uneasi-
ness: but, as soon as day came again,
they felt the same passion as before. They
were glad when they saw each other, and
sorrowful when they parted : they suffered,
they wanted something, but they did not
know what they wanted. They only knew,
the one that he had been undone by a kiss,
the other that she had been destroyed by
a bath. In addition to this, the season

Ἦρος οὖν ἤδη τέλη, καὶ θέρους ἀρχὴ, καὶ πάντα ἐν ἀκμῇ· δένδρα ἐν καρποῖς, πεδία ἐν ληΐοις. Ἡδεῖα μὲν τεττίγων ἠχή· γλυκεῖα καὶ ἡ τῆς ὀπώρας ὀδμή· τερπνὴ δὲ ποιμνίων βληχή. Εἴκασεν ἄν τις καὶ τοὺς ποταμοὺς ᾄδειν, ἠρέμα ῥέοντας· καὶ τοὺς ἀνέμους συρίττειν, ταῖς πίτυσιν ἐμπνέοντας· καὶ τὰ μῆλα ἐρῶντα πίπτειν χαμαί· καὶ τὸν ἥλιον, φιλόκαλον ὄντα, πάντας ἀποδύειν. Ὁ μὲν οὖν Δάφνις θαλπόμενος τούτοις ἅπασιν, εἰς τοὺς ποταμοὺς ἐνέβαινε· καὶ ποτὲ μὲν ἐλούετο, ποτὲ δὲ καὶ τῶν ἰχθύων τοὺς ἐνδινεύοντας ἐθήρα· πολλάκις δὲ καὶ ἔπινεν, ὡς τὸ ἔνδοθεν καῦμα σβέσων. Ἡ δὲ Χλόη, μετὰ τὸ ἀμέλξαι τὰς ὄϊς καὶ τῶν αἰγῶν τὰς πολλὰς, ἐπὶ πολὺν μὲν χρόνον εἶχε πηγνῦσα τὸ γάλα· δειναὶ γὰρ αἱ μυῖαι λυπῆσαι καὶ δακεῖν, εἰ διώκοιντο. Τὸ δὲ ἐντεῦθεν, ἀπολουσαμένη τὸ πρόσωπον, πίτυος ἐστεφανοῦτο κλάδοις, καὶ τῇ νεβρίδι ἐζώννυτο, καὶ τὸν γαυλὸν ἀναπλή-

of the year still further inflamed their passion.

It was the end of spring and the commencement of summer: all Nature was in full vigour: the trees were full of fruit, the fields of corn. The chirp of the grasshopper was sweet to hear, the fruit sweet to smell, and the bleating of the sheep pleasant to the ear. The gently flowing rivers seemed to be singing a song: the winds, blowing softly through the pine-branches, sounded like the notes of the pipe: even the apples seemed to fall to the ground smitten with love, stripped off by the sun that was enamoured of their beauty. Daphnis, heated by all these surroundings, plunged into the river, sometimes to bathe, at other times to snare the fish that sported in the eddies of the stream: and he often drank, as if he could thereby quench the fire that consumed him. Chloe, after having milked her sheep and most of Daphnis's goats, was for a long time busied in curdling the milk: for the flies annoyed her terribly and stung her, when she endeavoured to drive them away.

σασα οἴνου καὶ γάλακτος, κοινὸν μετὰ τοῦ
Δάφνιδος ποτὸν εἶχε.

Τῆς δὲ μεσημβρίας ἐπελθούσης, ἐγίνετο ἤδη
τῶν ὀφθαλμῶν ἅλωσις αὐτοῖς. Ἡ μὲν γὰρ
γυμνὸν ὁρῶσα Δάφνιν, ἐπ᾽ ἀνθοῦν ἐνέπιπτε τὸ
κάλλος, καὶ ἐτήκετο, μηδὲν αὐτοῦ μέρος μέμ-
ψασθαι δυναμένη· ὁ δὲ, ἰδὼν ἐν νεβρίδι καὶ
στεφάνῳ πίτυος ὀρέγουσαν τὸν γαυλὸν, μίαν
ᾤετο τῶν ἐν τῷ ἄντρῳ Νυμφῶν ὁρᾶν. Ὁ μὲν
οὖν τὴν πίτυν ἀπὸ τῆς κεφαλῆς ἁρπάζων,
αὐτὸς ἐστεφανοῦτο, πρότερον φιλήσας τὸν
στέφανον· ἡ δὲ, τὴν ἐσθῆτα αὐτοῦ λουομένου
καὶ γυμνωθέντος ἐνεδύετο, πρότερον καὶ αὐτὴ
φιλήσασα. Ἤδη ποτὲ καὶ μήλοις ἀλλήλους
ἔβαλον, καὶ τὰς κεφαλὰς ἀλλήλων ἐκόσμησαν,
διακρίναντες τὰς κόμας. Καὶ ἡ μὲν εἴκασεν
αὐτοῦ τὴν κόμην, ὅτι μέλαινα, μύρτοις· ὁ δὲ,
μήλῳ τὸ πρόσωπον αὐτῆς, ὅτι λευκὸν καὶ
ἐνερευθὲς ἦν. Ἐδίδασκεν αὐτὴν καὶ συρίττειν·
καὶ ἀρξαμένης ἐμπνεῖν, ἁρπάζων τὴν σύριγγα,

After this, she washed her face, and
crowned with branches of pine, and girt
with the skin of a fawn, filled a pail with
wine and milk to share with Daphnis.

When noon came on, they were more
enamoured than ever. For Chloe, having
seen Daphnis quite naked, was struck by
the bloom of his beauty, and her heart
melted with love, for his whole person was
too perfect for criticism : while Daphnis,
seeing Chloe with her fawn skin and garland of pine, holding out the milkpail for
him to drink, thought that he was gazing
upon one of the Nymphs of the grotto. He
snatched the garland from her head, kissed
it, and placed it on his own : and Chloe
took his clothes when he had stripped to
bathe, kissed them, and in like manner
put them on. Sometimes they pelted each
other with apples, and parted and decked
each other's hair. Chloe declared that
Daphnis's hair, being dark, was like myrtle
berries : while Daphnis compared Chloe's
face to an apple, because it was fair and
ruddy. He also taught her to play on the
pipe : and, when she began to blow, he

τοῖς χείλεσιν αὐτὸς τοὺς καλάμους ἐπέλειχεν·
καὶ ἐδόκει μὲν ἁμαρτάνουσαν διδάσκειν, εὐπρεπῶς δὲ διὰ τῆς σύριγγος τὴν Χλόην ἐφίλει.

Συρίττοντος δὲ κατὰ τὸ μεσημβρινὸν, καὶ
τῶν ποιμνίων σκιαζομένων, ἔλαθεν ἡ Χλόη
καταννστάξασα. Φωράσας τοῦτο ὁ Δάφνις,
καὶ καταθέμενος τὴν σύριγγα, πᾶσαν αὐτὴν
ἔβλεπεν ἀπλήστως, οἷα μηδὲν αἰδούμενος, καὶ
ἅμα καὶ αὐτῇ ἠρέμα ὑπεφθέγγετο· " Οἷοι
καθένδουσιν ὀφθαλμοί· οἷον δὲ ἀποπνεῖ τὸ
στόμα. Οὐδὲ τὰ μῆλα τοιοῦτον, οὐδὲ αἱ
λόχμαι. Ἀλλὰ φιλεῖν μὲν δέδοικα· δάκνει
τὸ φίλημα τὴν καρδίαν, καὶ, ὥσπερ τὸ νέον
μέλι, μαίνεσθαι ποιεῖ· ὀκνῶ δὲ μὴ καὶ φιλήσας
αὐτὴν ἀφυπνίσω. Ὦ λάλων τεττίγων. Οὐκ
ἐάσουσιν αὐτὴν καθεύδειν μέγα ἠχοῦντες.
Ἀλλὰ καὶ οἱ τράγοι τοῖς κέρασι παίουσι
μαχομενοι· ὦ λύκων ἀλωπέκων δειλοτέρων, οἳ
τούτους οὐχ ἥρπασαν."

Ἐν τούτοις ὄντος αὐτοῦ λόγοις, τέττιξ

snatched it away, and ran over the reeds
with his lips : and, while he thus pretended to show her where she was wrong,
he speciously kissed the pipe in the places
where her mouth had been.

While he was piping in the noonday
heat, and the flocks were resting in the
shade, Chloe unwittingly fell asleep. When
Daphnis perceived this, he put down his
pipe, and gazed at her all over with greedy
eyes, without any feeling of shame, and
at the same time gently whispered to himself : "How lovely are her eyes in sleep !
how sweet the perfume from her mouth,
sweeter than that of apples or the haw-
thorn ! Yet I dare not kiss it : her kiss
pricks me to the heart, and maddens me
like fresh honey. Besides, if I kiss her, I
am afraid of waking her. O chattering
grasshoppers ! you will prevent her from
sleeping, if you chirp so loudly ! And on
the other side, the he-goats are butting
each other with their horns : O wolves,
more cowardly than foxes, why do you
not carry them off ?"

While he was thus talking to himself,

φεύγων χελιδόνα θηράσαι θέλουσαν, κατέπεσεν
εἰς τὸν κόλπον Χλόης· καὶ ἡ χελιδὼν ἐπομένη,
τὸν μὲν οὐκ ἠδυνήθη λαβεῖν, ταῖς δὲ πτέρυξιν
ἐγγὺς διὰ τὴν δίωξιν γενομένη, τῶν παρειῶν
αὐτῆς ἥψατο. Ἡ δὲ οὐκ εἰδυῖα τὸ πραχθὲν,
μέγα βοήσασα, τῶν ὕπνων ἐξέθορεν. Ἰδοῦσα
δὲ καὶ τὴν χελιδόνα ἔτι πλησίον πετομένην,
καὶ τὸν Δάφνιν ἐπὶ τῷ δέει γελῶντα, τοῦ
φόβου μὲν ἐπαύσατο, τοὺς δὲ ὀφθαλμοὺς
ἀπέματτεν ἔτι καθεύδειν θέλοντας. Καὶ ὁ
τέττιξ ἐκ τῶν κόλπων ἐπήχησεν ὅμοιον ἱκέτῃ
χάριν ὁμολογοῦντι τῆς σωτηρίας. Πάλιν οὖν
ἡ Χλόη μέγα ἀνεβόησεν, ὁ δὲ Δάφνις ἐγέλα-
σεν. Καὶ προφάσεως λαβόμενος, καθῆκεν αὐτῆς εἰς τὰ στέρνα τὰς χεῖρας, καὶ ἐξάγει τὸν
βέλτιστον τέττιγα, μηδὲ ἐν τῇ δεξιᾷ σιω-
πῶντα. Ἡ δὲ ἥδετο ἰδοῦσα, καὶ ἐφίλησε
λαβοῦσα, καὶ αὖθις ἐνέβαλλε τῷ κόλπῳ
λαλοῦντα.

Ἔτερψεν αὐτοὺς τότε φάττα βουκολικὸν
ἐκ τῆς ὕλης φθεγξαμένη. Τῆς Χλόης ζητούσης
μαθεῖν ὅ, τι λέγει, διδάσκει αὐτὴν ὁ Δάφνις,

a grasshopper, pursued by a swallow, fell
into Chloe's bosom: the swallow followed,
but could not catch it: but, being unable
to check its flight, touched Chloe's cheek
with its wing. Not knowing what was the
matter, she cried out loudly, and woke
up with a start: but, when she saw the
swallow flying close to her, and Daphnis
laughing at her alarm, she was reassured,
and rubbed her still drowsy eyes. The
grasshopper, as if in gratitude for its
safety, chirped its thanks from her bosom.
Then Chloe cried out again, and Daphnis
laughed: and, seizing the opportunity,
thrust his hand into her breast, and
pulled out the grateful insect, which continued its song, even while held a prisoner
in his hand. Chloe was delighted, and
having kissed the insect, took it and put
it, still chirping, into her bosom.

Another time, they were listening with
delight to the cooing of a wood-pigeon.
When Chloe asked what was the meaning
of its song, Daphnis told her the popular
story: " Once upon a time, dear maiden,
there was a maiden, beautiful and bloom-

μυθολογῶν τὰ θρυλλούμενα. "Ἦν παρθένος, παρθένε, ὡς σὺ οὕτω καλὴ, καὶ ἔνεμε βοῦς πολλὰς, οὕτως ἐν ἡλικίᾳ. Ἦν ἄρα καὶ ᾠδικὴ, καὶ ἐτέρποντο αἱ βόες αὐτῆς τῇ μουσικῇ, καὶ ἔνεμεν οὔτε καλαύροπος πληγῇ, οὔτε κέντρου προσβολῇ· ἀλλὰ καθίσασα ὑπὸ πίτυν, καὶ στεφανωσαμένη πίτυϊ, ᾖδε Πᾶνα καὶ τὴν Πίτυν. Καὶ αἱ βόες τῇ φωνῇ παρέμενον. Παῖς οὐ μακρὰν νέμων βοῦς, καὶ αὐτὸς καλὸς, ᾠδικὸς ὡς ἡ παρθένος, φιλονεικήσας πρὸς τὴν μελῳδίαν, μείζονα ὡς ἀνὴρ, ἡδεῖαν ὡς παῖς, φωνὴν ἀντεπεδείξατο. Καὶ τῶν βοῶν ὀκτὼ τὰς ἀρίστας ἐς τὴν ἰδίαν ἀγέλην θέλξας, ἀπεβουκόλησεν. Ἄχθεται ἡ παρθένος τῇ βλάβῃ τῆς ἀγέλης, τῇ ἥττῃ τῆς ᾠδῆς· καὶ εὔχεται τοῖς θεοῖς ὄρνις γενέσθαι, πρὶν οἴκαδε ἀφικέσθαι. Πείθονται οἱ θεοὶ, καὶ ποιοῦσι τήνδε τὴν ὄρνιν, ὄρειον ὡς παρθένον, μουσικὴν ὡς ἐκείνην. Καὶ ἔτι νῦν ᾄδουσα μηνύει τὴν συμφορὰν, ὅτι βοῦς ζητεῖ πεπλανημένας."

ing as yourself. She tended cattle and
sang beautifully: her cows were so en-
chanted by the music of her voice, that
she never needed to strike them with her
crook or to touch them with her goad:
but, seated beneath a pine-tree, her head
crowned with a garland, she sang of Pan
and Pinus, and the cows stood near, en-
chanted by her song. There was a young
man who tended his flocks hard by, beautiful and a good singer himself, as she was,
who entered into a rivalry of song with
her: his voice was more powerful, since he
was a man, and yet gentle, since he was
but a youth. He sang so sweetly that he
charmed eight of her best cows and en-
ticed them over to his own herd, and drove
them away. The maiden, grieved at the
loss of her cattle, and at having been vanquished in singing, begged the Gods to
transform her into a bird before she returned home. The Gods listened to her
prayer, and transformed her into a moun-
tain bird, which loves to sing as she did.
Even now it tells in plaintive tones of her
misadventure, and how that she is still
seeking the cows that strayed away."

Τοιάσδε τέρψεις αὐτοῖς τὸ θέρος παρεῖχε.
Μετοπώρου δὲ ἀκμάζοντος, καὶ τοῦ βότρυος
ἤδη περκάζοντος, Τύριοι λῃσταὶ Καρικὴν
ἔχοντες ἡμιολίαν, ὡς ἴσως μὴ δοκοῖεν βάρ-
βαροι, προσέσχον τοῖς ἀγροῖς, καὶ ἐκβάντες
σὺν μαχαίραις καὶ ἡμιθωρακίοις, κατέσυρον
πάντα τὰ εἰς χεῖρας ἐλθόντα, οἶνον ἀνθοσμίαν,
πυρὸν ἄφθονον, μέλι ἐν κηρίοις· ἤλασάν τινας
καὶ βοῦς ἐκ τῆς Δόρκωνος ἀγέλης. Λαμβάνουσι
καὶ τὸν Δάφνιν περὶ τὴν θάλατταν ἀλύοντα·
ἡ γὰρ Χλόη βραδύτερον, ὡς κόρη, τὰ πρόβατα
ἐξῆγε τοῦ Δρύαντος, φόβῳ τῶν ἀγερώχων
ποιμένων. Ἰδόντες δὲ μειράκιον μέγα καὶ
καλὸν, κρεῖττον τῆς ἐξ ἀγρῶν ἁρπαγῆς, μηκέτι
μηδὲν, μηδὲ εἰς τὰς αἶγας, μηδὲ εἰς τοὺς ἄλλους
ἀγροὺς, περιεργασάμενοι, κατῆγον αὐτὸν εἰς
τὴν ναῦν κλάοντα καὶ ἠπορημένον, καὶ μέγα
Χλόην καλοῦντα. Καὶ οἱ μὲν, τὸ πεῖσμα
ἄρτι ἀπολύσαντες, καὶ τὰς κώπας ταῖς χερσὶν
ἐμβαλόντες, ἀπέπλεον εἰς τὸ πέλαγος· Χλόη
δὲ κατήλαυνε τὸ ποίμνιον, σύριγγα καινὴν τῷ

Such were the enjoyments which the
summer afforded them. But, in mid-
autumn, when the grapes grew ripe, some
Tyrian pirates, having embarked on a
light Carian vessel, that they might not
be suspected of being barbarians, landed
on the coast: and, armed with swords and
corslets, carried off everything that came
into their hands, fragrant wine, a great
quantity of wheat, and honey in the honeycomb, besides some cows belonging to Dorcon. They also seized Daphnis as he was
wandering on the shore: for Chloe, being a
simple girl, for fear of the insolence of the
shepherds, did not drive out the flocks of
Dryas so early. When the robbers beheld
the tall and handsome youth, a more valuable booty than any they could find in the
fields, they paid no heed to the goats or
the other fields, but carried him off to
their ship, weeping and in great distress
what to do, and calling the while for
Chloe in a loud voice. No sooner had
they loosed the cable, and begun to ply
their oars, and put out to sea, than Chloe
drove down her flock, bringing with her a

Δάφνιδι δῶρον κομίζουσα. Ἰδοῦσα δὲ τὰς αἶγας τεταραγμένας, καὶ ἀκούσασα τοῦ Δάφνιδος ἀεὶ μεῖζον αὐτὴν βοῶντος, προβάτων μὲν ἀμελεῖ, καὶ τὴν σύριγγα ῥίπτει, δρόμῳ δὲ πρὸς τὸν Δόρκωνα παραγίνεται, δεησομένη βοηθεῖν.

Ὁ δὲ ἔκειτο πληγαῖς νεανικαῖς συγκεκομμένος ὑπὸ τῶν λῃστῶν, καὶ ὀλίγον ἐμπνέων, αἵματος πολλοῦ φερομένου. Ἰδὼν δὲ καὶ τὴν Χλόην, καὶ ὀλίγον ἐκ τοῦ πρότερον ἔρωτος ἐμπύρευμα λαβών· " Ἐγὼ μὲν, εἶπε, Χλόη, τεθνήξομαι μετ' ὀλίγον· οἱ γάρ με ἀσεβεῖς λῃσταὶ πρὸ τῶν βοῶν μαχόμενον κατέκοψαν ὡς βοῦν. Σὺ δὲ σοὶ καὶ Δάφνιν σῶσον, κἀμοὶ τιμώρησον, κἀκείνους ἀπόλεσον. Ἐπαίδευσα τὰς βοῦς ἤχῳ σύριγγος ἀκολουθεῖν, καὶ διώκειν τὸ μέλος αὐτῆς, κἂν νέμωνταί ποι μακράν. Ἴθι δὴ, λαβοῦσα τὴν σύριγγα ταύτην, ἔμπνευσον αὐτῇ μέλος ἐκεῖνο, ὃ Δάφνιν ἐγώ ποτε ἐδιδαξάμην, σὲ δὲ Δάφνις· τὸ δὲ ἐντεῦθεν τῇ σύριγγι μελήσει, καὶ τῶν βοῶν τῶν ἐκεῖ. Χαρίζομαι δέ σοι καὶ τὴν σύριγγα αὐτὴν, ᾗ

new pipe as a present to Daphnis. But, seeing the goats scattered hither and thither, and hearing Daphnis calling to her ever louder and louder, thinking no more about her sheep, she flung away the pipe, and ran to Dorcon, to implore his aid.

She found him lying prostrate on the ground, hacked by the swords of the robbers, and almost dead from loss of blood. But, when he saw Chloe, revived by the smouldering fire of his former passion, he said : " Chloe, dear, I am at the point of death : when I tried to defend my cattle, the accursed brigands hewed me to pieces like an ox. But do you save Daphnis for yourself: avenge me, and destroy them. I have taught my cows to follow the sound of the pipe, and to come when they hear it, however far off they may be feeding. Come, take this pipe, and play the same strain upon it which I once taught Daphnis, and he in turn taught you. Leave the rest to my pipe and my cows that are on yonder ship. I also make you a present of the pipe, with which

πολλοὺς ἐρίζων καὶ βουκόλους ἐνίκησα καὶ
αἰπόλους. Σὺ δὲ ἀντὶ τούτων καὶ ζῶντα ἔτι
φίλησον, καὶ ἀποθανόντα κλαῦσον· κἂν ἴδῃς
ἄλλον νέμοντα τὰς βοῦς, ἐμοῦ μνημόνευσον."
Δόρκων μὲν τοσαῦτα εἰπὼν, καὶ φίλημα φιλήσας ὕστατον, ἀφῆκεν ἅμα καὶ τῷ φιλήματι
καὶ τῇ φωνῇ τὴν ψυχήν. Ἡ δὲ Χλόη λαβοῦσα
τὴν σύριγγα, καὶ ἐνθεῖσα τοῖς χείλεσιν, ἐσύριξε
μέγιστον ὡς ἐδύνατο· καὶ αἱ βόες ἀκούουσι, καὶ
τὸ μέλος γνωρίζουσι, καὶ ὁρμῇ μιᾷ μυκησά-
μεναι πηδῶσιν εἰς τὴν θάλατταν. Βιαίου δὲ
πηδήματος εἰς ἕνα τοῖχον τῆς νεὼς γενομένου,
καὶ ἐκ τῆς ἐμπτώσεως τῶν βοῶν κοίλης τῆς
θαλάττης διαστάσης, στρέφεται μὲν ἡ ναῦς, καὶ
τοῦ κλύδωνος συνιόντος, ἀπόλλυται. Οἱ δὲ
ἐκπίπτουσιν, οὐχ ὁμοίαν ἔχοντες ἐλπίδα σω-
τηρίας· Οἱ μὲν γὰρ λῃσταὶ τὰς μαχαίρας
παρήρτηντο, καὶ τὰ ἡμιθωράκια λεπιδωτὰ ἐνε-
δέδυντο, καὶ κνημίδας εἰς μέσην κνήμην ὑπεδέ-
δεντο· ὁ δὲ Δάφνις, ἀνυπόδητος, ὡς ἐν πεδίῳ
νέμων, καὶ ἡμίγυμνος, ὡς ἔτι τῆς ὥρας οὔσης
καυματώδους. Ἐκείνους μὲν οὖν ἐπ' ὀλίγον

I have gained the victory over many
herdsmen and shepherds. Kiss me once
in return, and lament for me when I am
dead : and, when you see another tending
my cattle, then think of me."

When Dorcon had thus spoken, and had
kissed her for the last time, he breathed his
last as he spoke and kissed her. Chloe
took the pipe, put it to her lips, and blew
with all her might. And the cows heard
it, and, recognising the strain, began to
low, and all with a bound sprang into the
sea. As they had leaped from the same side
of the vessel, and caused the sea to part,
it upset and sank under the waves that
closed over it. Those on board were
flung into the sea, but with unequal prospect of safety. For the pirates were
encumbered with swords, and clad in scaly
coats of mail, and greaves reaching half-
way down the leg. But Daphnis, who
had been tending his flocks, was unshod,
and only half-clothed, owing to the burning heat. The pirates had only swum
a little way, when the weight of their
armour dragged them down into the

νηξαμένους τὰ ὅπλα κατήνεγκεν εἰς βυθόν· ὁ δὲ
Δάφνις τὴν μὲν ἐσθῆτα ῥᾳδίως ἀπεδύετο, περὶ
δὲ τὴν νῆξιν ἔκαμνεν, οἷα πρότερον νηχόμενος
ἐν ποταμοῖς μόνοις. Ὕστερον δὲ, παρὰ τῆς
ἀνάγκης τὸ πρακτέον διδαχθεὶς, εἰς μέσας ὥρμησε τὰς βοῦς· καὶ δύο βοῶν κεράτων ταῖς δύο
χερσὶ λαβόμενος, ἐκομίζετο μέσος ἀλύπως καὶ
ἀπόνως, ὥσπερ ἐλαύνων ἅμαξαν. Νήχεται δὲ
ἄρα βοῦς ὅσον οὐδὲ ἄνθρωπος· μόνον λείπεται
τῶν ἐνύδρων ὀρνίθων, καὶ αὐτῶν ἰχθύων. Οὐδ᾽
ἂν ἀπόλοιτο βοῦς νηχόμενος, εἰ μὴ τῶν χηλῶν
οἱ ὄνυχες περιπέσοιεν διάβροχοι γενόμενοι.
Μαρτυροῦσι τῷ λόγῳ μέχρι νῦν πολλοὶ τόποι
τῆς θαλάττης, βοὸς πόροι λεγόμενοι.

Ἐκσώζεται μὲν δὴ τοῦτον τὸν τρόπον ὁ
Δάφνις, δύο κινδύνους παρ᾽ ἐλπίδα πᾶσαν δια-
φυγών, λῃστηρίου καὶ ναυαγίου. Ἐξελθὼν δὲ,
καὶ τὴν Χλόην ἐπὶ τῆς γῆς γελῶσαν ἅμα καὶ
δακρύουσαν εὑρών, ἐμπίπτει τε αὐτῆς τοῖς κόλποις, καὶ ἐπυνθάνετο, τί βουλομένη συρίσειεν.
Ἡ δὲ αὐτῷ διηγεῖται πάντα· τὸν δρόμον τὸν

depths: Daphnis easily threw off the
clothes he had on, yet it cost him some
effort to swim, since he had hitherto only
swum in rivers: but soon, under the impulse of necessity, he reached the cows by
an effort, and, while with each hand he
grasped one by the horns, he was carried
along between them without difficulty or
danger, as if he had been driving a cart:
for an ox swims far better than any man:
it is only inferior to the water-fowl and
fishes. An ox would never sink, were it
not that the horn falls off their hoofs when
it gets wet through. The truth of what I
say is borne out by many places on the
coast which are still found bearing the
name of "Ox fords."

Thus Daphnis, against all expectation,
was saved from the double danger of the
robbers and shipwreck. When he came
to land, and found Chloe weeping and
smiling through her tears, he threw himself into her arms, and asked her what she
had meant by playing on the pipe. And
she told him everything, how she had run
to Dorcon for help, how his cows had

ἐπὶ τὸν Δόρκωνα, τὸ παίδευμα τῶν βοῶν, πῶς
κελευσθείη συρίσαι, καὶ ὅτι τέθνηκε Δόρκων·
μόνον, αἰδεσθεῖσα, τὸ φίλημα οὐκ εἶπεν. Ἔδοξε
δὴ τιμῆσαι τὸν εὐεργέτην· καὶ ἐλθόντες μετὰ
τῶν προσηκόντων, Δόρκωνα θάπτουσι τὸν
ἄθλιον. Γῆν μὲν οὖν πολλὴν ἐπέθεσαν, φυτὰ
δὲ ἥμερα πολλὰ ἐφύτευσαν, καὶ ἐξήρτησαν
αὐτῷ τῶν ἔργων ἀπαρχάς· ἀλλὰ καὶ γάλα
κατέσπεισαν, καὶ βότρυας κατέθλιψαν, καὶ
σύριγγας πολλὰς κατέκλασαν. Ἠκούσθη καὶ
τῶν βοῶν ἐλεεινὰ μυκήματα, καὶ δρόμοι τινὲς
ὤφθησαν ἅμα τοῖς μυκήμασιν ἄτακτοι· καὶ,
ὡς ἐν ποιμέσιν εἰκάζετο καὶ αἰπόλοις, ταῦτα
θρῆνος ἦν τῶν βοῶν ἐπὶ βουκόλῳ τετελευ-
τηκότι.

Μετὰ δὲ τὸν τοῦ Δόρκωνος τάφον, λούει τὸν
Δάφνιν ἡ Χλόη πρὸς τὰς Νύμφας ἀγαγοῦσα,
εἰς τὸ ἄντρον εἰσαγαγοῦσα. Καὶ αὐτὴ, τότε
πρῶτον Δάφνιδος ὁρῶντος, ἐλούσατο τὸ σῶμα
λευκὸν καὶ καθαρὸν ὑπὸ κάλλους, καὶ οὐδὲ
λουτρῶν ἐς κάλλος δεόμενον· καὶ ἄνθη τε

been trained to obey the sound of the
pipe, what strain she had been bidden to
play, and how Dorcon had died : only,
from a feeling of modesty, she said nothing about the kiss she had given him.
Then both resolved to honour the memory
of their benefactor, and went with his re-
latives to bury the unhappy Dorcon. They
heaped earth over him in abundance, and
planted a number of cultivated trees round
about, and hung up as an offering to the
deceased the first fruits of their labours :
they poured libations of milk over his
grave, crushed grapes, and broke several
shepherds' pipes. His cows lowed piteously,
wandering hither and thither the while :
and to the herdsmen and shepherds it
seemed that they were mourning for the
death of their master.

After the burial of Dorcon, Chloe led
Daphnis to the grotto of the Nymphs,
where she washed him, and then she herself, for the first time in Daphnis's presence, also washed her own fair and
beautiful person, which needed no bath
to set off its beauty: then, plucking the

συλλέξαντες, ὅσα ἄνθη τῆς ὥρας ἐκείνης, ἐστε-
φάνωσαν τὰ ἀγάλματα, καὶ τὴν τοῦ Δόρκωνος
σύριγγα τῆς πέτρας ἐξήρτησαν ἀνάθημα. Καὶ
μετὰ τοῦτο ἐλθόντες, ἐπεσκόπουν τὰς αἶγας
καὶ τὰ πρόβατα. Τὰ δὲ πάντα κατέκειτο
μήτε νεμόμενα, μήτε βληχώμενα, ἀλλ', οἶμαι,
τὸν Δάφνιν καὶ τὴν Χλόην ἀφανεῖς ὄντας πο-
θοῦντα. Ἐπειδὴ γοῦν ὀφθέντες καὶ ἐβόησαν
τὸ σύνηθες, καὶ ἐσύρισαν, τὰ μὲν ἀναστάντα
ἐνέμετο, αἱ δὲ αἶγες ἐσκίρτων φριμασσόμεναι,
καθάπερ ἡδόμεναι σωτηρίᾳ συνήθους αἰπόλου.
Οὐ μὴν ὁ Δάφνις χαίρειν ἔπειθε τὴν ψυχήν·
ἰδὼν τὴν Χλόην γυμνήν, καὶ τὸ πρότερον
λανθάνον κάλλος ἐκκεκαλυμμένον, ἤλγει τὴν
καρδίαν, ὡς ἐσθιομένην ὑπὸ φαρμάκων. Καὶ
αὐτὸ τὸ πνεῦμα ποτὲ μὲν λάβρον ἐξέπνει,
καθάπερ τινὸς διώκοντος αὐτόν, ποτὲ δὲ ἐπέ-
λειπε, καθάπερ ἐκδαπανηθὲν ἐν ταῖς προτέραις
ἐπιδρομαῖς. Ἐδόκει τὸ λουτρὸν εἶναι τῆς
θαλάττης φοβερώτερον. Ἐνόμιζε τὴν ψυχὴν
ἔτι παρὰ τοῖς λῃσταῖς μένειν, οἷα νέος ἄγροικος
καὶ ἔτι ἀγνοῶν τὸ Ἔρωτος λῃστήριον.

flowers that were in season, they crowned
the statues of the Nymphs, and hung up
Dorcon's pipe against the rock as an
offering. After this, they went to look
after their sheep and goats, which were
all lying on the ground, neither feeding
nor bleating, but, I believe, pining for the
absent Daphnis and Chloe. But, as soon
as they came in sight, and began to shout
and pipe as usual, they jumped up and
began to feed : the goats skipped wantonly, as if delighted at the safe return
of their master. Daphnis however could
not bring himself to feel happy : for, since
he had seen Chloe naked, in all her beauty
formerly hidden and then revealed, he felt
a pain in his heart, as if it was consumed
by poison. His breath now came rapidly,
as if someone was pursuing him : and now
failed him, as if exhausted in previous
attacks. Chloe's bath seemed to him
more terrible than the sea. He thought
that his soul was still amongst the pirates,
since he was merely a young rustic and as
yet knew nothing of the thievish tricks of
Love.

ΛΟΓΟΣ ΔΕΥΤΕΡΟΣ.

Ἤδη δὲ τῆς ὀπώρας ἀκμαζούσης, καὶ ἐπείγοντος τοῦ τρυγητοῦ, πᾶς ἦν κατὰ τοὺς ἀγροὺς ἐν ἔργῳ. Ὁ μὲν ληνοὺς ἐπεσκεύαζεν· ὁ δὲ πίθους ἐξεκάθαιρεν· ὁ δὲ ἀρρίχους ἐπελύγιζεν· ἔμελέ τινι δρεπάνης μικρᾶς ἐς βότρυος τομὴν· καὶ ἑτέρῳ λίθου θλῖψαι τὰ ἔνοινα τῶν βοτρύων δυναμένου· καὶ ἄλλῳ λύγου ξηρᾶς πληγαῖς κατεξασμένης, ὡς ἂν ὑπὸ φωτὶ νύκτωρ τὸ γλεῦκος φέροιτο. Ἀμελήσαντες οὖν καὶ ὁ Δάφνις καὶ ἡ Χλόη τῶν προβάτων καὶ τῶν αἰγῶν, χειρὸς ὠφέλειαν ἀλλήλοις μετεδίδοσαν. Ὁ μὲν ἐβάσταζεν ἐν ἀρρίχοις βότρυς, καὶ ἐπάτει ταῖς ληνοῖς ἐμβάλλων, καὶ εἰς τοὺς πίθους ἔφερε τὸν οἶνον· ἡ δὲ τροφὴν παρεσκεύαζε τοῖς τρυγῶσι, καὶ ἐνέχει ποτὸν αὐτοῖς πρεσβύτερον οἶνον, καὶ τῶν ἀμπέλων τὰς ταπεινοτέρας ἀπετρύγα. Πᾶσα γὰρ κατὰ τὴν

BOOK II

It was now the middle of autumn, and the vintage was close at hand; everyone was in the fields, busily intent upon his work. Some were repairing the wine-presses, others cleaning out the jars: some were weaving baskets of osier, and others sharpening short sickles for cutting the grapes: some were preparing stones to crush those full of wine, others preparing dry twigs which had been well beaten, to be used as torches to light the drawing off of the new wine by night. Daphnis and Chloe, having abandoned the care of their flocks, assisted each other in these tasks. Daphnis carried bunches of grapes in baskets, threw them into the press and trod them, and drew off the juice into jars: while Chloe prepared food for the vintagers, and poured some of the older wine for them to drink, while at the same time she picked some of the lowest bunches from the trees. For

Λέσβον ἦν ἄμπελος ταπεινή, οὐ μετέωρος,
οὐδὲ ἀναδενδράς, ἀλλὰ κάτω τὰ κλήματα ἀπο-
τείνουσα, καὶ ὥσπερ κιττὸς νεμομένη· καὶ παῖς
ἂν ἐφίκοιτο βότρυος, ἄρτι τὰς χεῖρας ἐκ σπαργάνων λελυμένος.

Οἷον οὖν εἰκὸς ἐν ἑορτῇ Διονύσου καὶ οἴνου
γενέσει, αἱ μὲν γυναῖκες ἐκ τῶν πλησίον ἀγρῶν
εἰς ἐπικουρίαν κεκλημέναι, τῷ Δάφνιδι τοὺς
ὀφθαλμοὺς ἐπέβαλλον, καὶ ἐπῄνουν ὡς ὅμοιον
τῷ Διονύσῳ τὸ κάλλος. Καί τις τῶν θρασυ-
τέρων καὶ ἐφίλησε, καὶ τὸν Δάφνιν παρώξυνε,
τὴν δὲ Χλόην ἐλύπησεν. Οἱ δὲ ἐν ταῖς ληνοῖς
ποικίλας φωνὰς ἔρριπτον ἐπὶ τὴν Χλόην, καί,
ὥσπερ ἐπί τινα Βάκχην Σάτυροι, μανικώτερον
ἐπήδων, καὶ ηὔχοντο γενέσθαι ποίμνια, καὶ ὑπ'
ἐκείνης νέμεσθαι· ὥστε αὖ πάλιν ἡ μὲν ἤδετο,
Δάφνις δὲ ἐλυπεῖτο. Ηὔχοντο δὲ δὴ ταχέως
παύσασθαι τὸν τρυγητὸν καὶ λαβέσθαι τῶν
συνήθων χωρίων, καί, ἀντὶ τῆς ἀμούσου βοῆς,
ἀκούειν σύριγγος, ἢ τῶν ποιμνίων αὐτῶν βλη-
χωμένων. Καὶ ἐπεὶ διαγενομένων ὀλίγων ἡμε-

all the vines in Lesbos grow low, and
are not trained to trees : their branches
hang down to the ground, spreading like
ivy, so that even a child that is, so to
speak, only just out of its swaddling
clothes, could reach them.

As is customary at the festival of Bacchus, on the birthday of the wine, women
had been summoned from the neighbouring fields to assist; and they cast
amorous eyes on Daphnis, and extolled
him as vying with Bacchus in beauty.
One of them, bolder than the rest, kissed
him, which excited Daphnis, but annoyed
Chloe.   On the other hand, the men who
were treading the wine-presses, made all
kinds of advances to Chloe, and leaped
furiously, like Satyrs who had seen some
Bacchante, declaring that they wished they
were sheep, to be tended by her : this,
again, pleased Chloe, while Daphnis felt
annoyed.   Each wished that the vintage
was over, and that they could return to
the familiar fields, and, instead of uncouth
shouts, hear the sound of the pipe and the
bleating of their flocks.

ρῶν, αἱ μὲν ἄμπελοι τετρύγηντο, πίθοι δὲ τὸ
γλεῦκος εἶχον, ἔδει δὲ οὐκέτι οὐδὲν πολυχειρίας,
κατήλαυνον τὰς ἀγέλας εἰς τὸ πεδίον· καὶ, μάλα
χαίροντες, τὰς Νύμφας προσεκύνουν, βότρυς
αὐταῖς κομίζοντες ἐπὶ κλημάτων, ἀπαρχὰς τοῦ
τρυγητοῦ. Οὐδὲ τὸν πρότερον χρόνον ἀμελῶς
ποτε παρῆλθον, ἀλλ' ἀεί τε ἀρχόμενοι νομῆς
προσήδρευον, καὶ ἐκ νομῆς ἀνιόντες, προσε-
κύνουν· καὶ πάντως τι ἀπέφερον, ἢ ἄνθος, ἢ
ὀπώραν, ἢ φυλλάδα χλωρὰν, ἢ γάλακτος
σπονδήν. Καὶ τούτου μὲν ὕστερον ἀμοιβὰς
ἐκομίσαντο παρὰ τῶν θεῶν. Τότε δὲ κύνες,
φασὶν, ἐκ δεσμῶν λυθέντες ἐσκίρτων, ἐσύριτ-
τον, ᾖδον τοῖς τράγοις καὶ τοῖς προβάτοις
συνεπάλαιον.

Τερπομένοις δὲ αὐτοῖς ἐφίσταται πρεσβύτης, σισύραν ἐνδεδυμένος, καρβατίνας ὑπο-
δεδεμένος, πήραν ἐξηρτημένος, καὶ τὴν πήραν
παλαιάν. Οὗτος πλησίον καθίσας αὐτῶν, ὧδε
εἶπε· "Φιλητᾶς, ὦ παῖδες, ὁ πρεσβύτης ἐγώ·

In a few days the grapes were gathered
in, the casks were full of new wine, and
there was no need of so many hands : then
they again began to drive their flocks down
to the plain, and joyfully paid homage
to the Nymphs, offering them grapes still
hanging on the branches, the first fruits
of the vintage. Even before that they had
never neglected them as they passed by,
but when they drove their flocks to pasture,
as well as on their return, they reverently
saluted them ; never omitting to bring them
a flower, some fruit, some green foliage, or
a libation of milk. And they afterwards
reaped the reward of this piety from the
Gods. Then they gamboled like dogs
loosed from their bonds, piped, sang to
the goats, and wrestled sportively with
the sheep.

While they were thus amusing themselves, an old man appeared before them,
clad in a goatskin, with shoes of undressed
leather on his feet, and carrying a wallet, a
very old one, round his neck. Seating himself close by them, he addressed them as
follows : " My children, I am old Philetas :

ὃς πολλὰ μὲν ταῖσδε ταῖς Νύμφαις ᾖσα,
πολλὰ δὲ τῷ Πανὶ ἐκείνῳ ἐσύρισα, βοῶν δὲ
πολλῆς ἀγέλης ἡγησάμην μόνῃ μουσικῇ.
Ἥκω δὲ ὑμῖν, ὅσα εἶδον, μηνύσων, ὅσα ἤκουσα,
ἀπαγγελῶν. Κῆπός ἐστί μοι τῶν ἐμῶν χειρῶν·
ὃν, ἐξ οὗ νέμειν διὰ γῆρας ἐπαυσάμην, ἐξεπονησάμην, ὅσα ὧραι φέρουσι, πάντα ἔχων ἐν αὐτῷ
καθ' ὥραν ἑκάστην. Ἧρος, ῥόδα, κρίνα, καὶ
ὑάκινθος, καὶ ἴα ἀμφότερα· θέρους, μήκωνες,
καὶ ἀχράδες, καὶ μῆλα πάντα· νῦν, ἄμπελοι,
καὶ συκαῖ, καὶ ῥοιαί, καὶ μύρτα χλωρά. Εἰς
τοῦτον τὸν κῆπον ὀρνίθων ἀγέλαι συνέρχονται
τὸ ἑωθινόν, τῶν μὲν, ἐς τροφὴν, τῶν δὲ, ἐς
ᾠδήν· συνηρεφὴς γὰρ, καὶ κατάσκιος, καὶ πηγαῖς
τρισὶ κατάρρυτος· ἂν περιέλῃ τις τὴν αἱμασιὰν,
ἄλσος ὁρᾶν οἰήσεται.

"Εἰσελθόντι δέ μοι τήμερον ἀμφὶ μέσην
ἡμέραν, ὑπὸ ταῖς ῥοιαῖς καὶ ταῖς μυρρίναις
βλέπεται παῖς, μύρτα καὶ ῥοιὰς ἔχων, λευκὸς·

I have sung many songs to these Nymphs,
I have often played the pipe to Pan yonder,
and guided a whole herd of oxen by my
voice alone.   I am come to tell you what
I have seen, and to declare to you what I
have heard.

"I have a garden, which I have planted
and cultivated myself, ever since I became
too old to tend my flocks.   You will always
find there everything that grows, in its
proper season : in spring, roses, lilies, hyacinths, single and double violets : in summer, poppies, wild pears, and all kinds of
apples : and, in the present autumn season,
grapes, figs, pomegranates, and green
myrtles.   Every morning flocks of birds
assemble in the garden, some to seek
food, others to sing : for it is thickly
shaded by trees, and watered by three
fountains : if you were to remove the
wall that surrounds it, you would think
it was a native forest.

"When I went into it yesterday about
mid-day, I saw a lad under the myrtles
and pomegranate trees, with some of their
produce in his hands : he was white as

ὥσπερ γάλα, καὶ ξανθὸς ὡς πῦρ, στιλπνὸς ὡς
ἄρτι λελουμένος. Γυμνὸς ἦν, μόνος ἦν· ἔπαιζεν
ὡς ἴδιον κῆπον τρυγῶν. Ἐγὼ μὲν οὖν ὥρμησα
ἐπ' αὐτὸν ὡς συλληψόμενος, δείσας μὴ ὑπ'
ἀγερωχίας τὰς μυρρίνας καὶ τὰς ῥοιὰς κατα-
κλάσῃ· ὁ δέ με κούφως καὶ ῥᾳδίως ὑπέφευγε,
ποτὲ μὲν ταῖς ῥοδωνιαῖς ὑποτρέχων, ποτὲ δὲ
ταῖς μήκωσιν ὑποκρυπτόμενος, ὥσπερ πέρδικος
νεοττός. Καίτοι πολλάκις μὲν πράγματα
ἔσχον ἐρίφους γαλαθηνοὺς διώκων· πολλάκις δὲ
ἔκαμον μεταθέων μόσχους ἀρτιγεννήτους· ἀλλὰ
τοῦτο ποικίλον τι χρῆμα ἦν καὶ ἀθήρατον.
Καμὼν οὖν, ὡς γέρων, καὶ ἐπερεισάμενος τῇ
βακτηρίᾳ, καὶ ἅμα φυλάττων μὴ φύγῃ, ἐπυν-
θανόμην τίνος ἐστὶ τῶν γειτόνων, καὶ τί
βουλόμενος ἀλλότριον κῆπον τρυγᾷ. Ὁ δὲ
ἀπεκρίνατο μὲν οὐδέν· στὰς δὲ πλησίον, ἐγέλα
πάνυ ἁπαλὸν, καὶ ἔβαλλέ με τοῖς μύρτοις, καὶ,
οὐκ οἶδ' ὅπως, ἔθελγε μηκέτι θυμοῦσθαι. Ἐδε-
όμην οὖν εἰς χεῖρας ἐλθεῖν, μηδέν φοβούμενον
ἔτι, καὶ ὤμνυον κατὰ τῶν μύρτων ἀφήσειν, ἐπι-

milk and ruddy as fire, and his body
shone as if he had just been bathing.
He was naked and alone, and he was
amusing himself with plucking the fruit
as if the garden had belonged to him.
I rushed at him to seize him, being afraid
that, in his wantonness, he might break
my trees : but he nimbly and easily
escaped my hand, now running under the
rose-bushes, now hiding himself under the
poppies, like a young partridge. I have
often had trouble in chasing young kids,
and tired myself with running after newly-
born calves : but this was a wily crea-
ture, and could not be caught. Being an
old man, and obliged to support myself
with a stick, I soon became tired : and,
being afraid that he might escape, I asked
him to which of my neighbours he belonged, and what he meant by plucking the fruit in a stranger's garden. He
made no answer, but, coming close to
me, laughed quietly, flung some myrtle-
berries at me, and, somehow or other,
appeased my anger. I asked him to come
to me without fear, and I swore by my

δοὺς μήλων καὶ ῥοιῶν, παρέξειν τε ἀεὶ τρυγᾶν
τὰ φυτὰ καὶ δρέπειν τὰ ἄνθη, τυχὼν παρὰ
αὐτοῦ φιλήματος ἑνός.

"᾿Ενταῦθα, πάνυ καπυρὸν γελάσας, ἀφίησι
φωνὴν, οἵαν οὔτε χελιδὼν, οὔτε ἀηδὼν, οὔτε
κύκνος, ὅμοιος ἐμοὶ γέρων γενόμενος. ᾿Εμοὶ
μὲν, ὦ Φιλητᾶ, φιλῆσαί σε πόνος οὐδείς· (βούλομαι γὰρ φιλεῖσθαι μᾶλλον, ἢ σὺ γενέσθαι
νέος·) ὅρα δὲ εἴ σοι καθ᾽ ἡλικίαν τὸ δῶρον.
Οὐδὲν γάρ σε ὠφελήσει τὸ γῆρας πρὸς τὸ μὴ
διώκειν ἐμὲ μετὰ τὸ ἓν φίλημα. Δυσθήρατος
ἐγὼ καὶ ἱέρακι, καὶ ἀετῷ καὶ εἴ τις ἄλλος
τούτων ὠκύτερος ὄρνις. Οὗτοι παῖς ἐγὼ, καὶ
εἰ δοκῶ παῖς, ἀλλὰ τοῦ Κρόνου πρεσβύτερος,
καὶ αὐτοῦ τοῦ παντὸς χρόνου. Καί σε οἶδα
νέμοντα πρωθήβην ἐν ἐκείνῳ τῷ ἕλει τὸ πλατὺ
βουκόλιον, καὶ παρήμην σοι συρίττοντι πρὸς
ταῖς φηγοῖς ἐκείναις, ἡνίκα ἤρας ᾿Αμαρυλλίδος·
ἀλλά με οὐχ ἑώρας, καίτοι πλησίον μάλα τῇ
κόρῃ παρεστῶτα. Σοὶ μὲν οὖν ἐκείνην ἔδωκα·

myrtles, and, in addition, by my apples
and pomegranates, that I would let him
pluck the fruits of my trees and cull my
flowers whenever he pleased, if he would
only give me one kiss.

"Then, laughing loudly, he began to
speak in a voice sweeter than that of
a swallow, or nightingale, or swan as
old in years as myself: ' It would be easy
for me to kiss you, Philetas: for my wish
to be kissed is stronger than your desire
to become young again: but look to
it whether the gift is suitable to your
age.   For, when you have once kissed
me, your years will not exempt you from
a desire to pursue me: but neither the
hawk, nor eagle, nor other bird that is
swift on the wing can catch me.   I am not
a child, even though I seem to be: I am
older than Kronos, more ancient than all
time.   I knew you in the bloom of your
first youth, when you tended your numerous flock in yonder marsh, and I was by
your side when you played upon your pipe
under the beech-trees, when you were in
love with Amaryllis, but you did not see

καὶ ἤδη σοι παῖδες ἀγαθοὶ βουκόλοι καὶ
γεωργοί. Νῦν δὲ Δάφνιν ποιμαίνω καὶ Χλόην·
καὶ ἡνίκα ἂν αὐτοὺς εἰς ἓν συνάγω τὸ ἑωθινὸν,
εἰς τὸν σὸν ἔρχομαι κῆπον, καὶ τέρπομαι τοῖς
ἄνθεσι καὶ τοῖς φυτοῖς, κἂν ταῖς πηγαῖς ταύταις
λούομαι. Διὰ τοῦτο καλὰ καὶ τὰ ἄνθη καὶ τὰ
φυτὰ, τοῖς ἐμοῖς λουτροῖς ἀρδόμενα. Ὅρα δέ
μή τί σοι τῶν φυτῶν κατακέκλασται, μή τις
ὀπώρα τετρύγηται, μή τις ἄνθους ῥίζα πεπάτηται, μή τις πηγὴ τετάρακται. Καὶ χαῖρε
μόνος ἀνθρώπων ἐν γήρᾳ θεασάμενος τοῦτο
τὸ παιδίον.

"Ταῦτα εἰπὼν, ἀνήλατο, καθάπερ ἀηδόνος
νεοττὸς, ἐπὶ τὰς μυρρίνας, καὶ κλάδον ἀμείβων
ἐκ κλάδιου, διὰ τῶν φύλλων ἀνεῖρπεν εἰς ἄκρον.
Εἶδον αὐτοῦ καὶ πτέρυγας ἐκ τῶν ὤμων, καὶ
τοξάρια μεταξὺ πτερύγων καὶ τῶν ὤμων, καὶ
οὐκέτι εἶδον οὔτε ταῦτα, οὔτε αὐτόν. Εἰ δὲ
μὴ μάτην ταύτας τὰς πολιὰς ἔφυσα, μηδὲ
γηράσας ματαιοτέρας τὰς φρένας ἐκτησάμην,
Ἔρωτι, ὦ παῖδες, κατέσπεισθε, καὶ Ἔρωτι
ὑμῶν μέλει."

me; and yet I was very close to her. I gave her to you, and the fruit of your union has been stalwart sons, good herdsmen and labourers. But now Daphnis and Chloe are my care: and when I have brought them together in the morning, I come into your garden, to enjoy the sight of the plants and flowers, and to bathe in this spring. This is why all the produce of your garden is fair to see, since it is watered by my bath. Look whether any branch is broken, whether any fruit is plucked, whether any flower is trodden upon, or your springs disturbed. Think yourself happy that you are the only man who has seen this child in your old age.'

"With these words, he sprang up, like a young nightingale, upon the myrtles, and, mounting from branch to branch, at length reached the top. Then I saw that he had wings on his shoulders, and a bow and arrows between the wings and his shoulders, and after that I saw him no more. But, unless my grey hairs count for nothing, unless I have grown more foolish with age, you are consecrated to Love, my children, and Love watches over you."

Πάνυ ἐτέρφθησαν ὥσπερ μῦθον, οὐ λόγον,
ἀκούοντες, καὶ ἐπυνθάνοντο τί ἐστί ποτε ὁ
Ἔρως, πότερα παῖς, ἢ ὄρνις, καὶ τί δύναται;
Πάλιν οὖν ὁ Φιλητᾶς ἔφη· "Θεὸς ἐστὶν, ὦ
παῖδες, ὁ Ἔρως, νέος καὶ καλὸς, καὶ πετό-
μενος. Διὰ τοῦτο καὶ νεότητι χαίρει, κάλλος
διώκει, καὶ τὰς ψυχὰς ἀναπτεροῖ. Δύναται
δὲ τοσοῦτον, ὅσον οὐδὲ ὁ Ζεύς. Κρατεῖ μὲν
στοιχείων, κρατεῖ δὲ ἄστρων· κρατεῖ δὲ τῶν
ὁμοίων θεῶν· οὐδὲ ὑμεῖς τοσοῦτον τῶν αἰγῶν
καὶ τῶν προβάτων. Τὰ ἄνθη πάντα Ἔρωτος
ἔργα· τὰ φυτὰ ταῦτα τούτου ποιήματα. Διὰ
τοῦτον καὶ ποταμοὶ ῥέουσι, καὶ ἄνεμοι πνέουσι.
Ἔγνων δὲ ἐγὼ καὶ ταῦρον ἐρασθέντα, καὶ ὡς
οἴστρῳ πληγεὶς ἐμυκᾶτο· καὶ τράγον φιλή-
σαντα αἶγα, καὶ ἠκολούθει πανταχοῦ. Αὐτὸς
μὲν γὰρ ἤμην νέος, καὶ ἠράσθην Ἀμαρυλλίδος·
καὶ οὔτε τροφῆς ἐμεμνήμην, οὔτε ποτὸν προσ-
εφερόμην, οὔτε ὕπνον ᾑρούμην. Ἤλγουν τὴν
ψυχὴν, τὴν καρδίαν ἐπαλλόμην, τὸ σῶμα
ἐψυχόμην· ἐβόων ὡς παιόμενος, ἐσιώπων ὡς
νεκρούμενος, εἰς ποταμοὺς ἐνέβαινον ὡς καό-

Daphnis and Chloe were as delighted as
if they had heard some fable, and not a true
story, and asked what Love was; whether
it was a bird or a child, and what it could
do. Philetas replied: "My children, Love
is a winged God, young and beautiful.
Wherefore he takes delight in youth, pur-
sues beauty, and furnishes the soul with
wings: his power is greater than that of
Zeus. He has power over the elements
and over the stars: and has greater control over the other Gods that are his equals
than you have over your sheep and goats.
The flowers are all the work of Love; the
plants are his creation. He makes the
rivers to run, and the winds to blow. I
have seen a bull smitten with love, and
it bellowed as if stung by the gadfly: I
have seen a he-goat kissing its mate, and
following it everywhere. I myself have
been young, and was in love with Amaryllis: then I thought neither of eating nor
drinking, and I took no rest. My soul was
troubled, my heart beat, my body was
chilled: I shouted as if I were being
beaten, I was as silent as a dead man, I

μενος· ἐκάλουν τὸν Πᾶνα βοηθὸν, ὡς καὶ
αὐτὸν τῆς Πίτυος ἐρασθέντα· ἐπήνουν τὴν
Ἠχὼ, τὸ Ἀμαρυλλίδος ὄνομα μετ᾽ ἐμὲ
καλοῦσαν· κατέκλων τὰς σύριγγας, ὅτι μοι
τὰς μὲν βοῦς ἔθελγον, Ἀμαρυλλίδα δὲ οὐκ
ἦγον. Ἔρωτος γὰρ οὐδὲν φάρμακον, οὐ πινό-
μενον, οὐκ ἐσθιόμενον, οὐκ ἐν ᾠδαῖς λαλούμενον,
ὅτι μὴ φίλημα, καὶ περιβολὴ, καὶ συγκατακλιθῆναι γυμνοῖς σώμασι."

Φιλητᾶς μέντοι ταῦτα παιδεύσας αὐτοὺς,
ἀπαλλάττεται, τυρούς τινας παρ᾽ αὐτῶν καὶ
ἔριφον ἤδη κεράστην λαβών. Οἱ δὲ μόνοι κατα-
λειφθέντες, καὶ τότε πρῶτον ἀκούσαντες τὸ
Ἔρωτος ὄνομα, τάς τε ψυχὰς συνεστάλησαν
ὑπὸ λύπης, καὶ ἐπανελθόντες νύκτωρ εἰς τὰς
ἐπαύλεις, παρέβαλλον οἷς ἤκουσαν τὰ αὐτῶν.
"Ἀλγοῦσιν οἱ ἐρῶντες· καὶ ἡμεῖς. Ἀμελοῦσιν
ἴσως· καὶ ἡμεῖς ἠμελήκαμεν. Καθεύδειν οὐ
δύνανται· τοῦτο μὲν καὶ νῦν πάσχομεν ἡμεῖς.
Κάεσθαι δοκοῦσι· καὶ παρ᾽ ἡμῖν τὸ πῦρ.
Ἐπιθυμοῦσιν ἀλλήλους ὁρᾶν· διὰ τοῦτο θᾶτ-

plunged into the rivers as if I were consumed by fire : I called upon Pan, himself
enamoured of Pitys, to help me : I thanked
Echo, who repeated the name of Amaryllis
after me : I broke my pipes, which, though
they charmed my kine, could not bring
Amaryllis to me. For there is no remedy
for Love, that can be eaten or drunk, or
uttered in song, save kissing and embracing, and lying naked side by side."

Philetas, having thus instructed them,
departed, taking away with him a present
of some cheeses and a horned goat. When
they were left alone, having then for the
first time heard the name of Love, they
were greatly distressed, and, on their return
to their home at night, compared their
feelings with what they had heard from
the old man : " Lovers suffer : so do we.
They neglect their work : we have done
the same. They cannot sleep : it is the
same with us. They seem on fire : we are
consumed by fire. They are eager to see
each other : it is for this that we wish the
day to dawn more quickly. This must be
Love, and we are in love with each other

τον εὐχόμεθα γενέσθαι τὴν ἡμέραν. Σχεδὸν
τοῦτό ἐστιν ὁ ἔρως, καὶ ἐρῶμεν ἀλλήλων
οὐκ εἰδότες. Εἰ τοῦτο μή ἐστιν ὁ ἔρως,
ἐγὼ δὲ ὁ ἐρώμενος, τί οὖν ταῦτα ἀλγοῦμεν;
Τί δὲ ἀλλήλους ζητοῦμεν; Ἀληθῆ πάντα
εἶπεν ὁ Φιλητᾶς. Τὸ ἐκ τοῦ κήπου παιδίον
ὤφθη καὶ τοῖς πατράσιν ἡμῶν ὄναρ ἐκεῖνο, καὶ
νέμειν ἡμᾶς τὰς ἀγέλας ἐκέλευσε. Πῶς ἄν τις
αὐτὸ λάβοι; Μικρόν ἐστι, καὶ φεύξεται. Καὶ
πῶς ἄν τις αὐτὸ φύγοι; Πτερὰ ἔχει, καὶ κατα-
λήψεται. Ἐπὶ τὰς Νύμφας δεῖ βοηθοὺς κατα-
φυγεῖν; Ἀλλ᾽ οὐδὲ Φιλητᾶν ὁ Πὰν ὠφέλησεν
Ἀμαρυλλίδος ἐρῶντα. Ὅσα εἶπεν ἄρα φάρ-
μακα, ταῦτα ζητητέα· φίλημα, καὶ περιπλοκή,
καὶ κεῖσθαι γυμνοὺς χαμαί. Κρύος μὲν, ἀλλὰ
καρτερήσομεν δεύτερον μετὰ Φιλητᾶν."

Τοῦτο αὐτοῖς γίνεται νυκτερινὸν παιδευτή-
ριον· καὶ ἀγαγόντες τῆς ἐπιούσης ἡμέρας τὰς
ἀγέλας εἰς νομὴν, ἐφίλησαν μὲν ἀλλήλους
ἰδόντες, ὃ μήπω πρότερον ἐποίησαν καὶ περιέβαλλον τὰς χεῖρας ἐπαλλάξαντες. Τὸ δὲ
τρίτον ὤκνουν φάρμακον, ἀποδυθέντες κατα-

without knowing it. If this be not love,
and I am not beloved, why are we so distressed ? why do we so eagerly seek each
other ? All that Philetas has told us is
true. It was that boy in the garden who
once appeared to our parents in a dream,
and bade us tend the flocks. How can we
catch him ? he is small and will escape.
And how can we escape him ? he has wings
and will overtake us. We must appeal to
the Nymphs for help. But Pan could not
help Philetas, when he was in love with
Amaryllis. Let us, therefore, try the re-
medies of which he told us : let us kiss and
embrace each other, and lie naked on the
ground. It is cold : but we will endure it,
after the example of Philetas."

This was their nightly lesson. At daybreak they drove out their flocks, kissed
each other as soon as they met, which they
had never done before, and embraced : but
they were afraid to try the third remedy,
to undress and lie down together : for it
would have been too bold an act for a
young shepherdess, even for a goatherd.
Then again they passed sleepless nights,

κλιθῆναι· θρασύτερον γὰρ οὐ μόνον παρθένων,
ἀλλὰ καὶ νέων αἰπόλων. Πάλιν οὖν ἀγρυπνία
ἔχουσα καὶ ἔννοιαν τῶν γεγενημένων, καὶ κατά-
μεμψιν τῶν παραλελειμμένων. "Καὶ ἐφιλή-
σαμεν, καὶ οὐδὲν ὄφελος· περιεβάλομεν, καὶ
οὐδὲν πλέον ἔσχομεν. Τὸ οὖν κατακλιθῆναι
μόνον φάρμακον ἔρωτος. Πειρατέον καὶ τούτου·
πάντως ἐν αὐτῷ τι κρεῖττον ἔσται φιλήματος"

Ἐπὶ τούτοις τοῖς λογισμοῖς, οἷον εἰκὸς, καὶ
ὀνείρατα ἑώρων ἐρωτικά, τὰ φιλήματα, τὰς
περιβολάς· καὶ ὅσα δὲ μεθ' ἡμέραν οὐκ ἔπραξαν,
ταῦτα ὄναρ ἔπραξαν· γυμνοὶ μετ' ἀλλήλων
ἔκειντο. Ἐνθεώτεροι δὲ κατὰ τὴν ἐπιοῦσαν
ἡμέραν ἀνέστησαν, καὶ ῥοίζῳ τὰς ἀγέλας κατήλαυνον, ἐπειγόμενοι πρὸς τὰ φιλήματα· καὶ
ἰδόντες ἀλλήλους, ἅμα μειδιάματι κατέδραμον.
Τὰ μὲν οὖν φιλήματα ἐγένετο, καὶ ἡ περιβολὴ
τῶν χειρῶν ἠκολούθησε· τὸ δὲ τρίτον φάρμακον
ἐβράδυνε, μήτε τοῦ Δάφνιδος τολμῶντος εἰπεῖν,
μήτε τῆς Χλόης βουλομένης κατάρχεσθαι, ἔστε
τύχῃ καὶ τοῦτο ἔπραξαν.

Καθέζοντο ἐπὶ στελέχους δρυὸς, πλησίον

thinking of what they had done, and regretting what they had left undone. "We
have kissed each other," they complained,
"but it has profited nothing. We have
embraced, but nothing has come of it.
The only remaining remedy is to lie
down together: let us try it: surely there
must be something in it more efficacious
than in a kiss."

With such thoughts as these their
dreams were naturally of love and kisses
and embraces: what they had not done in
the day, they did in a dream: they lay
naked together. The next morning, they
got up more inflamed with love than ever,
and drove their flocks to pasture, whistling
loudly, and hurried to embrace each other:
and, when they saw each other from a
distance, they ran up with a smile, kissed,
and embraced: but the third remedy was
slow to come: for Daphnis did not venture to speak of it, and Chloe was
unwilling to lead the way, until chance
brought them to it.

They were sitting side by side on the
trunk of an oak: and, having tasted the

ἀλλήλων· καὶ γευσάμενοι τῆς ἐν φιλήματι
τέρψεως, ἀπλήστως ἐνεφοροῦντο τῆς ἡδονῆς.
Ἦσαν δὲ καὶ χειρῶν περιβολαὶ, θλῖψιν τοῖς
στόμασι παρέχουσαι. Κατὰ τὴν τῶν χειρῶν
περιβολὴν βιαιότερον δὴ τοῦ Δάφνιδος ἐπισπα-
σαμένου, κλίνεταί πως ἐπὶ πλευρὰν ἡ Χλόη,
κἀκεῖνος δὲ συγκατακλίνεται τῷ φιλήματι
ἀκολουθῶν· καὶ γνωρίσαντες τῶν ὀνείρων τὴν
εἰκόνα, κατέκειντο πολὺν χρόνον ὥσπερ συν-
δεδεμένοι. Εἰδότες δὲ τῶν ἐντεῦθεν οὐδὲν, καὶ
νομίσαντες τοῦτο εἶναι πέρας ἀπολαύσεως
ἐρωτικῆς, μάτην τὸ πλεῖστον τῆς ἡμέρας
δαπανήσαντες, διελύθησαν, καὶ τὰς ἀγέλας
ἀπήλαυνον, τὴν νύκτα μισοῦντες. Ἴσως δ' ἂν
τι τῶν ἀληθῶν ἔπραξαν, εἰ μὴ θόρυβος τοιόσδε
πᾶσαν τὴν ἀγροικίαν ἐκείνην κατέλαβε.

Νέοι Μηθυμναῖοι πλούσιοι, διαθέσθαι τὸν
τρυγητὸν ἐν ξενικῇ τέρψει θελήσαντες, ναῦν
μικρὰν καθελκύσαντες, καὶ οἰκέτας προσκώπους
καθίσαντες, τοὺς Μιτυληναίων ἀγροὺς περιέ-
πλεον, ὅσοι θαλάττης πλησίον. Εὐλίμενός
τε γὰρ ἡ παραλία, καὶ οἰκήσεσιν ἠσκημένη

delights of kissing, they could not have enough: in their close embrace their lips met closely. While Daphnis pulled Chloe somewhat roughly towards him, she somehow fell on her side, and Daphnis, following up his kiss, fell also on his side: then, recognising the likeness of the dream, they lay for a long time as if they had been bound together. But, not knowing what to do next, and thinking that this was the consummation of love, they spent the greater part of the day in these idle embraces; then, cursing the night when it came on, they separated, and drove their flocks home. Perhaps they would have found out the truth, had not a sudden disturbance occupied the attention of the whole district.

Some wealthy young Methymnaeans, wishing to amuse themselves away from home during the vintage, launched a small vessel, manned with their servants as oarsmen, and coasted along the shore of Mitylene, which affords good harbourage, and is adorned with splendid houses, baths, parks, and groves, some natural,

πολυτελῶς. Καὶ λουτρὰ συνεχῆ, παράδεισοί
τε καὶ ἄλση· τὰ μὲν φύσεως ἔργα, τὰ δὲ
ἀνθρώπων τέχνης· πάντα ἐνοικῆσαι καλά.
Καταπλέοντες δὲ καὶ ἐνορμιζόμενοι, κακὸν
μὲν ἐποίουν οὐδὲν, τέρψεις δὲ ποικίλας ἐτέρ-
ποντο· ποτὲ μὲν ἀγκίστροις καλάμων ἀπηρ-
τημένοις ἐκ λίνου λεπτοῦ, πετραίους ἰχθῦς
ἁλιεύοντες ἐκ πέτρας ἁλιτενοῦς· ποτὲ δὲ κυσὶ
καὶ δικτύοις λαγωοὺς, φεύγοντας τὸν ἐν ταῖς
ἀμπέλοις θόρυβον, λαμβάνοντες. Ἤδη δὲ
καὶ ὀρνίθων ἄγρας ἐμέλησεν αὐτοῖς, καὶ ἔλαβον
βρόχοις χῆνας ἀγρίους, καὶ νήττας, καὶ ὠτίδας·
ὥστε καὶ ἡ τέρψις αὐτοῖς καὶ τραπέζης ὠφέλειαν παρεῖχεν. Εἰ δέ τινος προσέδει, παρὰ
τῶν ἐν τοῖς ἀγροῖς ἐλάμβανον, περιττοτέρους
τῆς ἀξίας ὀβολοὺς καταβάλλοντες. Ἔδει δὲ
μόνον ἄρτου καὶ οἴνου καὶ στέγης· οὐ γὰρ
ἀσφαλὲς ἐδόκει, μετοπωρινῆς ὥρας ἑστώσης,
ἐνθαλαττεύειν· ὥστε καὶ τὴν ναῦν ἀνεῖλκον
ἐπὶ τὴν γῆν, νύκτα χειμέριον δεδοικότες.

Τῶν δὲ δή τις ἀγροίκων, ἐς ἀνολκὴν λίθου θλί-
βοντος τὰ πατηθέντα βοτρύδια χρῄζων σχοίνου,

others artificial, but all pleasant to dwell
in. Coasting along and putting in to land
from time to time, they did no damage, but
amused themselves in various ways. They
fastened hooks to the end of a fine line
attached to the end of a reed, and caught
fish from a rock that jutted out into the
sea : or, with dogs and nets, captured the
hares which were scared by the noise of the
labourers in the vineyard; or again, they
set snares for ducks, wild geese, and bus-
tards, which, besides affording them sport,
provided them with an addition to their
repast. If they wanted anything else, they
bought it from the villagers, at a higher
price than it was worth. They only needed
bread, wine, and lodging, for, as it was
late in the autumn, they did not think it
was safe to pass the night on the water :
they accordingly drew up the ship on land,
being afraid of a storm by night.

It chanced that a peasant, being in need
of a rope to lift up the stone that was
used for crushing the grapes after they had
been trodden (his own being broken), went
secretly down to the sea-shore, and, finding

τῆς πρότερον ῥαγείσης, κρύφα ἐπὶ τὴν θάλατταν ἐλθών, ἀφρουρήτῳ τῇ νηῒ προσελθών, τὸ
πεῖσμα ἐκλύσας, οἴκαδε κομίσας, ἐς ὅ, τι ἔχρη-
ξεν, ἐχρήσατο. Ἕωθεν οὖν οἱ Μηθυμναῖοι νεα-
νίσκοι ζήτησιν ἐποιοῦντο τοῦ πείσματος, καὶ
(ὡμολόγει γὰρ οὐδεὶς τὴν κλοπὴν) ὀλίγα
μεμψάμενοι τοὺς ξενοδόκους, παρέπλεον· καὶ
στάδια τριάκοντα παρελάσαντες, προσορμί-
ζονται τοῖς ἀγροῖς ἐν οἷς ᾤκουν ἡ Χλόη καὶ ὁ
Δάφνις· ἐδόκει γὰρ αὐτοῖς καλὸν εἶναι τὸ
πεδίον ἐς θήραν λαγωῶν. Σχοῖνον μὲν οὖν
οὐκ εἶχον ὥστε ἐκδῆσασθαι πεῖσμα· λύγον δὲ
χλωρὰν μακρὰν στρέψαντες ὡς σχοῖνον, ταύτῃ
τὴν ναῦν ἐκ τῆς πρύμνης ἄκρας εἰς τὴν γῆν
ἔδησαν. Ἔπειτα τοὺς κύνας ἀφέντες ῥινηλατεῖν
ἐν ταῖς εὐκαίροις φαινομέναις τῶν ὁδῶν, ἐλινο-
στάτουν. Οἱ μὲν δὴ κύνες ἅμα ὑλακῇ διαθέοντες,
ἐφόβησαν τὰς αἶγας· αἱ δὲ, τὰ ὀρεινὰ κατα-
λιποῦσαι, μᾶλλόν τι πρὸς τὴν θάλατταν ὥρμησαν. Ἔχουσαι δὲ οὐδὲν ἐν ψάμμῳ τρώξιμον,
ἐλθοῦσαι πρὸς τὴν ναῦν αἱ θρασύτεραι αὐτῶν, τὴν

the ship unguarded, unfastened the cable, took it home, and used it for what he wanted. In the morning, the young Methymnaeans looked everywhere for the rope, and, as no one admitted the theft, after abusing their hosts, they put out to sea again. Having sailed on about thirty stades, they put in at that part of the coast where was the estate on which Daphnis and Chloe dwelt: since it seemed to them to be a good country for coursing. But, as they had no rope with which to moor their vessel, they twisted some long green osiers into a cable, and with them fastened it to land: then, having let loose their dogs to scent the game in the most likely spots, they spread their nets. The dogs, running in all directions and barking, frightened the goats, which left the hills and fled hastily in the direction of the sea. There, finding nothing to eat in the sand on the shore, some of them, bolder than the rest, went up to the boat, and gnawed off the osiers with which it was fastened.

It so happened that the sea was rather rough, as there was a breeze blowing from

λύγον τὴν χλωρὰν, ᾗ δέδετο ἡ ναῦς, ἀπέφαγον.

Ἦν δέ τι καὶ κλυδώνιον ἐν τῇ θαλάττῃ, κινηθέντος ἀπὸ τῶν ὀρῶν πνεύματος· ταχὺ δὴ μάλα λυθεῖσαν αὐτὴν ὑπήνεγκεν ἡ παλίρροια τοῦ κύματος, καὶ ἐς τὸ πέλαγος μετέωρον ἔφερεν. Αἰσθήσεως δὲ τοῖς Μηθυμναίοις γενομένης, οἱ μὲν ἐπὶ θάλατταν ἔθεον, οἱ δὲ τοὺς κύνας συνέλεγον· ἐβόων δὲ πάντες, ὡς πάντας τοὺς ἐκ τῶν πλησίον ἀγρῶν ἀκούσαντας συνελθεῖν. Ἀλλ' ἦν οὐδὲν ὄφελος· τοῦ γὰρ πνεύματος ἀκμάζοντος, ἀσχέτῳ τάχει κατὰ ροῦν ἡ ναῦς ἐφέρετο. Οἱ δ' οὖν οὐκ ὀλίγων κτημάτων Μηθυμναῖοι στερόμενοι, ἐξήτουν τὸν νέμοντα τὰς αἶγας· καὶ εὑρόντες τὸν Δάφνιν, ἔπαιον, ἀπέδυον. Εἷς δέ τις καὶ κυνόδεσμον ἀράμενος, περιῆγε τὰς χεῖρας, ὡς δήσων. Ὁ δὲ ἐβόα τε παιόμενος, καὶ ἱκέτευε τοὺς ἀγροίκους, καὶ πρώτους τε τὸν Λάμωνα καὶ τὸν Δρύαντα βοηθοὺς ἐπεκαλεῖτο. Οἱ δὲ ἀντείχοντο σκιρροὶ γέροντες, καὶ χεῖρας ἐκ γεωργικῶν ἔργων ἰσχυρὰς ἔχοντες· καὶ ἠξίουν δικαιολογήσασθαι περὶ τῶν γεγενημένων.

the mountains: and, as soon as the boat was unfastened, the tide carried it away into the open sea. When the young Methymnaeans saw what had occurred, some of them ran down to the shore, and others called their dogs together: and all raised such a shout that all the labourers hurried up from the neighbouring fields. But it was all in vain: for, as the breeze freshened, it bore away the vessel down the current with irresistible force.

Then the Methymnaeans, having thus sustained a considerable loss, looked for the keeper of the goats, and, having found Daphnis, flogged him and stripped him of his clothes. One of them, taking up a dog-leash, twisted Daphnis's hands behind his back, intending to bind him. He shouted loudly as he was being beaten, and implored the countrymen to help him, above all Lamon and Dryas. They, being vigorous old men, whose hands were hardened by their labours in the fields, assisted him stoutly, and demanded that a fair inquiry should be held into what had taken place.

Ταῦτα δὲ καὶ τῶν ἄλλων ἀξιούντων, δικαστὴν καθίζουσι Φιλητᾶν τὸν βουκόλον· πρεσβύτατός τε γάρ ἦν τῶν παρόντων, καὶ κλέος εἶχεν ἐν τοῖς κωμήταις δικαιοσύνης περιττῆς. Πρῶτοι δὲ κατηγόρουν οἱ Μηθυμναῖοι σαφῆ καὶ σύντομα, βουκόλον ἔχοντες δικαστήν· " Ἤλθομεν εἰς τούτους τοὺς ἀγροὺς, θηρᾶσαι θέλοντες. Τὴν μὲν οὖν ναῦν λύγῳ χλωρᾷ δήσαντες, ἐπὶ τῆς ἀκτῆς κατελίπομεν· αὐτοὶ δὲ διὰ τῶν κυνῶν ζήτησιν ἐποιούμεθα θηρίων. Ἐν τούτῳ πρὸς τὴν θάλατταν αἱ αἶγες τούτου κατελθοῦσαι, τήν τε λύγον κατεσθίουσι καὶ τὴν ναῦν ἀπολύουσιν. Εἶδες αὐτὴν ἐν τῇ θαλάττῃ φερομένην, πόσων οἴει μεστὴν ἀγαθῶν; Οἷα μὲν ἐσθὴς ἀπόλωλεν, οἷος δὲ κόσμος κυνῶν, ὅσον δὲ ἀργύριον· Τοὺς ἀγροὺς ἄν τις τούτους, ἐκεῖνα ἔχων, ὠνήσαιτο. Ἀνθ' ὧν ἀξιοῦμεν ἄγειν τοῦτον, πονηρὸν ὄντα αἰπόλον, ὃς ἐπὶ τῆς θαλάττης νέμει τὰς αἶγας ὡς ναύτης."

Τοιαῦτα οἱ Μηθυμναῖοι κατηγόρησαν. Ὁ δὲ Δάφνις διέκειτο μὲν κακῶς ὑπὸ τῶν πληγῶν,

As the others who had come up pressed
the same demand, the herdsman Philetas
was chosen as umpire: for he was the
oldest of those present, and he had the
reputation amongst his fellow villagers of
being perfectly impartial. First the young
Methymnaeans briefly and clearly made
their complaint :

" We came to these fields to hunt. We
had fastened our boat to the shore with a
green osier-withe, and left it there: after
which, we set out with our dogs to look for
game. Meanwhile, this man's goats went
down to the shore, ate the osiers, and set
loose the boat. You yourself saw it being
carried away out to sea : what do you think
was the value of the property with which
it was loaded ? of the clothes and dog-
trappings, besides money, enough to pur-
chase this estate ? Wherefore, by way of
recompense, we claim that we have a right
to carry away this rascally goatherd, who
pastures his flock on the sea-shore, as if he
were a sailor."

Such was the charge brought by the
Methymnaeans. Daphnis, although suf-

Χλόην δὲ ὁρῶν παροῦσαν, πάντων κατεφρόνει, καὶ ὧδε εἶπεν· "᾿Εγὼ νέμω τὰς αἶγας καλῶς. Οὐδέποτε ᾐτιάσατο κωμήτης οὐδὲ εἷς, ὡς ἢ κῆπον αἲξ ἐμὴ κατεβοσκήσατο, ἢ ἄμπελον βλαστάνουσαν κατέκλασεν. Οὗτοι δέ εἰσι κυ- νηγέται πονηροὶ, καὶ κύνας ἔχουσι κακῶς πεπαιδευμένους, οἵτινες τρέχοντες πολλά, καὶ ὑλακτοῦντες σκληρὰ, κατεδίωξαν αὐτὰς ἐκ τῶν ὁρῶν καὶ τῶν πεδίων ἐπὶ τὴν θάλατταν ὥσπερ λύκοι. ᾿Αλλὰ ἀπέφαγον τὴν λύγον· οὐ γὰρ εἶχον ἐν ψάμμῳ πόαν, ἢ κόμαρον, ἢ θύμον. ᾿Αλλὰ ἀπώλετο ἡ ναῦς ὑπὸ τοῦ πνεύματος καὶ τῆς θαλάττης· ταῦτα χειμῶνος, οὐκ αἰγῶν, ἔστιν ἔργα. ᾿Αλλὰ ἐσθὴς ἐνέκειτο καὶ ἄργυρος· καὶ τίς πιστεύσει νοῦν ἔχων, ὅτι τοσαῦτα φέρουσα ναῦς, πεῖσμα εἶχε λύγον;"

Τούτοις ἐπεδάκρυσεν ὁ Δάφνις, καὶ εἰς οἶκτον ὑπηγάγετο τοὺς ἀγροίκους πολύν· ὥστε ὁ Φιλητᾶς, ὁ δικαστὴς, ὤμνυε Πᾶνα καὶ Νύμφας, μηδὲν ἀδικεῖν Δάφνιν, ἀλλὰ μηδὲ τὰς αἶγας· τὴν δὲ θάλατταν καὶ τὸν ἄνεμον, ὧν ἄλλους

fering terribly from the blows which he
had received, seeing Chloe amongst those
present, made light of the pain, and spoke
as follows:

" I tend my goats properly. No one in
the village has ever complained of a goat of
mine browsing in his garden or breaking
down his sprouting vines. It is the fault of
these sportsmen, who have dogs so badly
broken, that they keep running about and
barking so loudly, that, like so many wolves,
they have driven my goats from the hills
and plains to the sea-shore. But they
have eaten the osiers: could they find
any grass, or wild arbutus, or thyme to
eat on the sand? Again, their boat has
been destroyed by the winds and waves:
the storm, not my goats, is to blame for
this. Again, there was a large store of
clothes and money on board: who would
be so foolish as to believe that a boat,
carrying so valuable a freight, would have
been fastened with nothing but a rope
made of osier-withes?"

Having thus spoken, Daphnis began to
weep, and moved the villagers to great

εἶναι δικαστάς. Οὐκ ἔπειθε ταῦτα Φιλητᾶς
Μηθυμναίοις λέγων· ἀλλ' ὑπ' ὀργῆς ὁρμή-
σαντες, ἦγον τὸν Δάφνιν πάλιν, καὶ συνδεῖν
ἤθελον. Ἐνταῦθα οἱ κωμῆται ταραχθέντες,
ἐπιπηδῶσιν αὐτοῖς ὡσεὶ ψᾶρες, ἢ κολοιοί· καὶ
ταχὺ μὲν ἀφαιροῦνται τὸν Δάφνιν ἤδη καὶ
αὐτὸν μαχόμενον· ταχὺ δὲ ξύλοις παίοντες,
ἐκείνους εἰς φυγὴν ἔτρεψαν. Ἀπέστησαν δὲ
οὐ πρότερον, ἔστε τῶν ὅρων αὐτοὺς ἐξήλασαν
ἐς ἄλλους ἀγρούς.

Διωκόντων δὲ τοὺς Μηθυμναίους ἐκείνων, ἡ
Χλόη κατὰ πολλὴν ἡσυχίαν ἄγει πρὸς τὰς
Νύμφας τὸν Δάφνιν, καὶ ἀπονίπτει τε τὸ
πρόσωπον ἡμαγμένον ἐκ τῶν ῥινῶν ῥαγεισῶν
ὑπὸ πληγῆς τινος, καὶ τῆς πήρας προκομίσασα
ξυμήτου μέρος καὶ τυροῦ τμῆμά τι, δίδωσι
φαγεῖν, τό τε μάλιστα ἀνακτησόμενον αὐτὸν,
φίλημα ἐφίλησε μελιτῶδες ἁπαλοῖς τοῖς
χείλεσι.

compassion : so that Philetas, who had to pronounce the verdict, swore by Pan and the Nymphs, that neither Daphnis nor his goats were in the wrong, but the sea and the wind, which were under the jurisdiction of others. However, Philetas could not convince the Methymnaeans, who, in the impulse of their rage, again seized Daphnis, and would have bound him, had not the villagers, roused at this, rushed upon them like a flock of starlings or jackdaws, and speedily rescued Daphnis, who also was stoutly defending himself. Then, with vigorous blows of their clubs, they routed the Methymnaeans, and did not cease from pursuing them, until they had driven them out of their territory.

While they were thus engaged in the pursuit of the Methymneans, Chloe quietly led Daphnis to the grotto of the Nymphs, where she washed his face which was smeared with the blood from his nostrils : then, taking a slice of bread and some cheese from her wallet, she gave him to eat, and — what comforted him most of all — she imprinted upon his mouth a

Τότε μὲν δὴ παρὰ τοσοῦτον Δάφνις ἦλθε κακοῦ· τὸ δὲ πρᾶγμα οὐ ταύτῃ πέπαυτο· ἀλλ' ἐλθόντες οἱ Μηθυμναῖοι μόλις εἰς τὴν ἑαυτῶν, ὁδοιπόροι μὲν ἀντὶ ναυτῶν, τραυματίαι δὲ ἀντὶ τρυφώντων, ἐκκλησίαν τε συνήγαγον τῶν πολιτῶν, καὶ ἱκετηρίας θέντες, ἱκέτευον τιμωρίας ἀξιωθῆναι· τῶν μὲν ἀληθῶν λέγοντες οὐδὲ ἕν, μὴ καὶ προσκαταγέλαστοι γένοιντο, τοιαῦτα καὶ τοσαῦτα παθόντες ὑπὸ ποιμένων· κατηγοροῦντες δὲ Μιτυληναίων, ὡς τὴν ναῦν ἀφελομένων, καὶ τὰ χρήματα ἁρπασάντων πολέμου νόμῳ. Οἱ δὲ πιστεύοντες διὰ τὰ τραύματα, καὶ νεανίσκοις τῶν πρώτων οἰκιῶν παρ' αὐτοῖς τιμωρῆσαι δίκαιον νομίζοντες, Μιτυληναίοις μὲν πόλεμον ἀκήρυκτον ἐψηφίσαντο, τὸν δὲ στρατηγὸν ἐκέλευσαν, δέκα ναῦς καθελκύσαντα, κακουργεῖν αὐτῶν τὴν παραλίαν· πλησίον γὰρ χειμῶνος ὄντος, οὐκ ἦν ἀσφαλὲς μείζονα στόλον πιστεύειν τῇ θαλάττῃ.

Ὁ δὲ εὐθὺς τῆς ἐπιούσης ἀναγόμενος αὐτερέταις στρατιώταις, ἐπέπλει τοῖς παραθαλατ-

kiss sweeter than honey with her tender
lips.

Thus Daphnis had a narrow escape, but
the matter did not rest there : for the
Methymnaeans, having reached their home
with great difficulty on foot, whereas they
had come in a ship, full of wounds instead
of in the enjoyment of luxury, called
an assembly of their fellow-citizens, and,
holding out olive branches in sign of
supplication, besought them to deign to
avenge them : they did not, however, utter
a word of truth, for fear that they might
be laughed at, for having allowed themselves to be so maltreated by a few shepherds : but they accused the Mitylenaeans
of having plundered them and seized their
vessel and its contents, as if they had been
at open war.

The Methymnaeans believed what they
said when they saw their wounds, and,
thinking it their duty to avenge their
wrongs, since the young men belonged to
the highest families in the place, they
immediately decided to make war without
the usual formalities, and ordered their

τίοις τῶν Μιτυληναίων ἀγροῖς. Καὶ πολλὰ
μὲν ἥρπαξε ποίμνια, πολὺν δὲ σῖτον καὶ οἶνον,
ἄρτι πεπαυμένου τοῦ τρυγητοῦ, καὶ ἀνθρώπους δὲ οὐκ ὀλίγους, ὅσοι τούτων ἐργάται.
Ἐπέπλευσε καὶ τοῖς τῆς Χλόης ἀγροῖς, καὶ
τοῦ Δάφνιδος· καὶ ἀπόβασιν ὀξεῖαν θέμενος,
λείαν ἤλαυνε τὰ ἐν ποσίν. Ὁ μὲν Δάφνις οὐκ
ἔνεμε τὰς αἶγας, ἀλλὰ ἐς τὴν ὕλην ἀνελθών,
φυλλάδα χλωρὰν ἔκοπτεν, ὡς ἔχοι τὴν τοῦ
χειμῶνος παρέχειν τοῖς ἐρίφοις τροφήν· ὥστε
ἄνωθεν θεασάμενος τὴν καταδρομὴν, ἐνέκρυψεν
ἑαυτὸν στελέχει κοίλῳ ξηρᾶς ὀξύης. Ἡ δὲ
Χλόη παρῆν ταῖς ἀγέλαις· καὶ διωκομένη κατα-
φεύγει πρὸς τὰς Νύμφας ἱκέτις, καὶ ἐδεῖτο
φείσασθαι καὶ ὧν ἔνεμε, καὶ αὐτῆς, διὰ τὰς
θεάς. Ἀλλ' ἦν οὐδὲν ὄφελος· οἱ γὰρ Μηθυμναῖοι πολλὰ τῶν ἀγαλμάτων κατακερτο-
μήσαντες, καὶ τὰς ἀγέλας ἤλασαν, κἀκείνην
ἤγαγον, ὥσπερ αἶγα, ἢ πρόβατον, παίοντες
λύγοις.

chief captain to put to sea with ten galleys and ravage their coast: for, as the winter was close at hand, it was not safe to intrust a larger fleet to the mercy of the waves.

On the following day, the captain put out to sea, using his soldiers as oarsmen, and directed his course towards the coastland of Mitylene. He carried off a large number of cattle, and a quantity of corn and wine, since the vintage was only just over, and also took prisoner a considerable number of those who were working in the fields. He at last landed on the estate where Daphnis and Chloe were tending their flocks, and carried off everything that he could find. At the time Daphnis was not with his flock: for he had gone up to the wood to cut some green branches to serve as fodder for the kids during the winter. Seeing the inroad from a distance, he hid himself in the hollow trunk of a dry beech-tree. Chloe, who was with her flocks, being pursued, fled to the grotto of the Nymphs as a suppliant, and besought her pursuers to spare

Ἔχοντες δὲ ἤδη τὰς ναῦς παντοδαπῆς ἁρπαγῆς μεστὰς, οὐκέτ' ἐγίγνωσκον περαιτέρω
πλεῖν, ἀλλὰ τὸν οἴκαδε πλοῦν ἐποιοῦντο, καὶ
τὸν χειμῶνα καὶ τοὺς πολεμίους δεδιότες. Οἱ
μὲν οὖν ἀπέπλεον εἰρεσίᾳ ταλαιπωροῦντες,
ἄνεμος γὰρ οὐκ ἦν· ὁ δὲ Δάφνις, ἡσυχίας γενομένης, ἐλθὼν εἰς τὸ πεδίον ἔνθα ἔνεμον, καὶ
μήτε τὰς αἶγας ἰδὼν, μήτε τὰ πρόβατα
καταλαβὼν, μήτε Χλόην εὑρὼν, ἀλλὰ ἐρημίαν
πολλὴν, καὶ τὴν σύριγγα ἐρριμμένην, ᾗ συνή-
θως ἐτέρπετο ἡ Χλόη, μέγα βοῶν καὶ ἐλεεινὸν
κωκύων, ποτὲ μὲν πρὸς τὴν φηγὸν ἔτρεχεν
ἔνθα ἐκαθέζοντο· ποτὲ δὲ ἐπὶ τὴν θάλατταν,
ὡς ὀψόμενος αὐτήν· ποτὲ δὲ ἐπὶ τὰς Νύμφας,
ἐφ' ἃς ἑλκομένη κατέφυγεν. Ἐνταῦθα καὶ
ἔρριψεν ἑαυτὸν χαμαὶ, καὶ ταῖς Νύμφαις, ὡς
προδούσαις, κατεμέμφετο.

herself and her flocks, out of respect for
the goddesses. But it was all in vain :
the Methymnaeans insulted the statues
and drove off the flocks, and Chloe with
them, as if she had been a sheep or a
goat, whipping her with switches.

Their ships being now loaded with all
kinds of booty, they made up their minds
to sail no further, but directed their course
homewards, being afraid of the wintry
season and hostile attacks. Accordingly
they rowed away as hard as they could,
but made slow progress, as there was no
wind. Daphnis, when all was quiet, went
down to the plain where their flocks had
been in the habit of feeding, and finding
neither goats nor sheep nor Chloe, but
everywhere desolation, and Chloe's pipe,
with which she used to amuse herself,
lying on the ground, he cried aloud and
lamented piteously, now running to the
beech under which they used to sit, and
now to the seashore, to look for her, and
then to the grotto of the Nymphs, where
she had taken refuge when she was being
carried off. There he flung himself on the

" 'Αφ' ὑμῶν ἡρπάσθη Χλόη, καὶ τοῦτο ἰδεῖν ὑμεῖς ὑπεμείνατε—ἢ τοὺς στεφάνους ὑμῖν πλέκουσα, ἢ σπένδουσα τοῦ πρώτου γάλακτος, ἧς καὶ ἡ σύριγξ ἥδε ἀνάθημα; Αἶγα μὲν οὐδὲ μίαν μοι λύκος ἥρπασε, πολέμιοι δὲ τὴν ἀγέλην καὶ τὴν συννέμουσαν. Καὶ τὰς μὲν αἶγας ἀποδεροῦσι, καὶ τὰ πρόβατα καταθύσουσι, Χλόη δὲ πόλιν λοιπὸν οἰκήσει. Ποίοις ποσὶν ἄπειμι παρὰ τὸν πατέρα καὶ τὴν μητέρα, ἄνευ τῶν αἰγῶν, ἄνευ Χλόης, λειπεργάτης ἐσόμενος; Ἔχω γὰρ νέμειν ἔτι οὐδέν. Ἐνταῦθα περιμενῶ κείμενος ἢ θάνατον, ἢ πόλεμον δεύτερον. Ἆρα καὶ σὺ Χλόη τοιαῦτα πάσχεις; Ἆρα μέμνησαι τοῦ πεδίου τοῦδε, καὶ τῶν Νυμφῶν τῶνδε, κἀμοῦ; Ἢ παραμυθοῦνταί σε τὰ πρόβατα καὶ αἱ αἶγες αἰχμάλωτοι μετὰ σοῦ γενόμεναι;"

Ταῦτα λέγοντα αὐτόν, ἐκ τῶν δακρύων καὶ τῆς λύπης, ὕπνος βαθὺς καταλαμβάνει· καὶ αὐτῷ αἱ τρεῖς ἐφίστανται Νύμφαι, μεγάλαι

ground and reproached the Nymphs with having abandoned her:

"Chloe has been carried off from you, O Nymphs, and you have had the heart to see and endure it—she who used to weave for you chaplets of flowers and offer you libations of fresh milk, whose pipe hangs suspended yonder as an offering to you. No wolf has ever carried off a single goat of mine, but an enemy has carried off the flock and she who tended it with me. They will flay the goats and sacrifice the sheep, and Chloe will have to dwell in some distant city. How shall I dare to return to my father and mother without my goats and without Chloe, as if I had proved false to my charge? For I have no longer anything to tend.

"Here I will lie and await death, or some other attack. Are you suffering like myself, Chloe? do you still remember these fields, these Nymphs, and me? or do you find some consolation in the sheep and goats that are your fellow-prisoners?"

While he was thus lamenting, a deep sleep overcame him in the midst of his

γυναῖκες καὶ καλαὶ, ἡμίγυμνοι καὶ ἀνυπόδητοι, τὰς κόμας λελυμέναι, καὶ τοῖς ἀγάλμασιν ὅμοιαι. Καὶ τὸ μὲν πρῶτον ἐῴκεσαν ἐλεοῦσαι τὸν Δάφνιν· ἔπειτα ἡ πρεσβυτάτη λέγει ἐπιρρωννύουσα· "μηδὲν ἡμᾶς μέμφου, Δάφνι· Χλόης γὰρ ἡμῖν μᾶλλον ἤ σοι μέλει. Ἡμεῖς τοι καὶ παιδίον οὖσαν αὐτὴν ἠλεήσαμεν, καὶ ἐν τῷδε τῷ ἄντρῳ κειμένην αὐτὴν ἀνεθρέψαμεν. Ἐκείνη πεδίοις κοινὸν οὐδὲν καὶ τοῖς προβατίοις τοῦ Λάμωνος. Καὶ νῦν δὲ ἡμῖν πεφρόντισται τὸ κατ' ἐκείνην, ὡς μήτε εἰς τὴν Μήθυμναν κομισθεῖσα δουλεύοι, μήτε μέρος γένοιτο λείας πολεμικῆς. Καὶ τὸν Πᾶνα ἐκεῖνον, τὸν ὑπὸ τῇ πίτυϊ ἱδρυμένον, ὃν ὑμεῖς οὐδέποτε οὐδὲ ἄνθεσιν ἐτιμήσατε, τοῦτον ἐδεήθημεν ἐπίκουρον γενέσθαι Χλόης· συνήθης γὰρ στρατοπέδοις μᾶλλον ἡμῶν, καὶ πολλοὺς ἤδη πολέμους ἐπολέμησε τὴν ἀγροικίαν καταλιπών· καὶ ἄπεισι τοῖς Μηθυμναίοις οὐκ ἀγαθὸς πολέμιος. Κάμνε δὲ μηδὲν, ἀλλὰ ἀναστὰς ὄφθητι

grief and tears. The Nymphs appeared to
him, three tall and beautiful women, half-
naked, without sandals, with their hair float-
ing down their backs, just like their statues.
At first they seemed to feel compassion for
Daphnis: then the eldest addressed him in
the following words of comfort :

" Do not reproach us, Daphnis : Chloe
is more our care than yours. We took
pity on her when she was but a child,
and adopted her when she was exposed
in this cave and brought her up. She
has no more to do with the sheep and
fields than you have to do with the goats of
Lamon. Besides, we have already thought
of her future: she shall neither be carried off as a slave to Methymna, nor
become part of the enemy's spoil. We
have begged the God Pan, whose statue
is under yonder pine, to whom you have
never offered so much as a chaplet of
flowers in token of respect, to go to the
assistance of Chloe : for he is more used
to the ways of camps than we are, and
he has often left the country to take
part in battle. He will set out, and the

Λάμωνι καὶ Μυρτάλῃ, οἳ καὶ αὐτοὶ κεῖνται
χαμαί, νομίζοντες καὶ σε μέρος γεγονέναι τῆς
ἁρπαγῆς· Χλόη γάρ σοι τῆς ἐπιούσης ἀφίξεται
μετὰ τῶν αἰγῶν, μετὰ τῶν προβάτων· καὶ νεμή-
σετε κοινῇ, καὶ συρίσετε κοινῇ· τὰ δὲ ἄλλα
μελήσει περὶ ὑμῶν Ἔρωτι."

Τοιαῦτα ἰδὼν καὶ ἀκούσας Δάφνις, ἀναπηδήσας τῶν ὕπνων, καὶ ὑφ᾽ ἡδονῆς καὶ λύπης
μεστὸς δακρύων, τὰ ἀγάλματα τῶν Νυμφῶν
προσεκύνει, καὶ ἐπηγγέλλετο, σωθείσης Χλόης,
θύσειν τῶν αἰγῶν τὴν ἀρίστην. Δραμὼν δὲ καὶ
ἐπὶ τὴν πίτυν, ἔνθα τὸ τοῦ Πανὸς ἄγαλμα
ἵδρυτο, τραγοσκελές, κερασφόρον, τῇ μὲν
σύριγγα, τῇ δὲ τράγον πηδῶντα κατέχον,
κἀκεῖνον προσεκύνει, καὶ ηὔχετο ὑπὲρ τῆς
Χλόης, καὶ τράγον θύσειν ἐπηγγέλλετο. Καὶ
μόλις ποτὲ περὶ ἡλίου καταφορὰς παυσάμενος
δακρύων καὶ εὐχῶν, ἀράμενος τὰς φυλλάδας
ἃς ἔκοψεν, ἐπανῆλθεν εἰς τὴν ἔπαυλιν, καὶ
τοὺς ἀμφὶ τὸν Λάμωνα πένθους ἀπαλλάξας,

Methymnaeans will find him no contemptible foe. Be not troubled: arise and show yourself to Lamon and Myrtale, who, like yourself, lie prostrate with sorrow, thinking that you also have been carried off. To-morrow Chloe will return with the sheep and goats; you shall tend them and play on the pipe together; leave the rest to the care of Love."

At this sight and at these words Daphnis started up from sleep. Weeping both for joy and grief, he did obeisance to the statues of the Nymphs and promised, if Chloe should be saved, that he would sacrifice to them the finest of his goats. He next ran to the pine tree, beneath which stood the statue of Pan, with the legs of a goat, his head surmounted by horns, in one hand holding his pipe, in the other a bounding goat. He did obeisance to him also, begged his assistance on behalf of Chloe, and promised to sacrifice a goat to him. The sun was almost set before he ceased from his tears and entreaties: then, taking up the green

εὐφροσύνης ἐμπλήσας, τροφῆς τε ἐγεύσατο,
καὶ ἐς ὕπνον ὥρμησεν, οὐδὲ τοῦτον ἄδακρυν·
ἀλλ᾿ εὐχόμενος μὲν αὖθις τὰς Νύμφας ὄναρ
ἰδεῖν, εὐχόμενος δὲ τὴν ἡμέραν γενέσθαι
ταχέως, ἐν ᾗ Χλόην ἐπηγγείλαντο αὐτῷ.
Νυκτῶν πασῶν ἐκείνη ἔδοξε μακροτάτη γεγονέναι. Ἐπράχθη δὲ ἐπ᾿ αὐτῆς τάδε.

Ὁ στρατηγὸς ὁ τῶν Μηθυμναίων, ὅσον
δέκα σταδίους ἀπελάσας, ἠθέλησε τῇ κατα-
δρομῇ τοὺς στρατιώτας κεκμηκότας ἀναλαβεῖν.
Ἄκρας οὖν ἐπεμβαινούσης τῷ πελάγει λαβόμενος, ἐπεκτεινομένης μηνοειδῶς, ἧς ἐντὸς
θάλαττα γαληνότερον τῶν λιμένων ὅρμον
εἰργάζετο, ἐνταῦθα τὰς ναῦς ἐπ᾿ ἀγκυρῶν
μετεώρους διορμίσας, ὡς μηδὲ μίαν ἐκ τῆς
γῆς τῶν ἀγροίκων τινὰ λυπῆσαι, ἀνῆκεν τοὺς
Μηθυμναίους εἰς τέρψιν εἰρηνικήν. Οἱ δὲ
ἔχοντες πάντων ἀφθονίαν ἐκ τῆς ἁρπαγῆς,
ἔπινον, ἔπαιζον, ἐπινίκιον ἑορτὴν ἐμιμοῦντο.

branches which he had cut, he returned
home, where his reappearance comforted
Lamon and Myrtale and filled them with
joy. Having taken a little food, he went
to bed: but even then his rest was disturbed by tears. He prayed that the
Nymphs might appear to him again in a
dream, and prayed for the speedy coming
of the day, on which they had promised
him that Chloe should return. Never had
a night seemed so long to him. Meanwhile, the following events had taken
place.

The Methymnaean captain, when he had
proceeded about ten stades, was desirous
of giving his men some rest, as they were
greatly fatigued with rowing. Accordingly,
having reached a promontory which jutted
out into the sea in the shape of a crescent,
the bay of which afforded a quieter port
than any harbour, he cast anchor, but at
some distance from the shore, for fear that
the inhabitants might annoy him; then
he allowed his crew to enjoy themselves
undisturbed. Since they were abundantly
supplied with everything, they drank and

Ἄρτι δὲ παυομένης ἡμέρας, καὶ τῆς τέρψεως
ἐς νύκτα ληγούσης, αἰφνίδιον μὲν πᾶσα ἡ γῆ
ἐδόκει λάμπεσθαι πυρὶ, κτύπος δὲ ἠκούετο
ῥόθιος κωπῶν, ὡς ἐπιπλέοντος μεγάλου
στόλου. Ἐβόα τις ὁπλίζεσθαι τὸν στρατη-
γόν· ἄλλος ἄλλον ἐκάλει, καὶ τετρῶσθαί τις
ἐδόκει, καὶ σχῆμά τι ἔκειτο νεκροῦ μιμούμενον.
Εἴκασεν ἄν τις ὁρᾶν νυκτομαχίαν οὐ παρόντων
πολεμίων.

Τῆς δὲ νυκτὸς αὐτοῖς τοιαύτης γενομένης,
ἐπῆλθεν ἡμέρα πολὺ τῆς νυκτὸς φοβερωτέρα.
Οἱ τράγοι μὲν οἱ τοῦ Δάφνιδος καὶ αἱ αἶγες
κιττὸν ἐν τοῖς κέρασι κορυμβοφόρον εἶχον·
οἱ δὲ κριοὶ καὶ αἱ ὄϊες τῆς Χλόης λύκων
ὠρυγμὸν ὠρύοντο. Ὤφθη δὲ καὶ αὐτὴ πίτυος
ἐστεφανωμένη. Ἐγίνετο καὶ περὶ τὴν θάλατταν αὐτὴν πολλὰ παράδοξα. Αἵ τε γὰρ
ἄγκυραι κατὰ βυθοῦ πειρωμένων ἀναφέρειν
ἔμενον, αἵ τε κῶπαι καθιέντων εἰς εἰρεσίαν

made merry, as if they had been cele-
brating a feast in honour of a victory.
But, when night began to fall and put an
end to their enjoyment, suddenly the whole
earth appeared in flames: the splash of
oars was heard upon the waters, as if a
numerous fleet were approaching. They
called upon the general to arm himself:
they shouted to each other: some thought
they were already wounded, others lay
as if they were dead. One would have
thought that they were engaged in a
battle by night, although there was no
enemy.

After a night thus spent, a day followed even more terrible to them than the
night. They saw Daphnis's goats with
ivy-branches, loaded with berries, on their
horns: while Chloe's rams and ewes were
heard howling like wolves: Chloe herself
appeared, crowned with a garland of pine.
Many marvellous things also happened on
the sea. When they attempted to raise
the anchors, they remained fast to the
bottom: when the oars were dipped into the
water to row, they snapped. Dolphins, leap-

ἐθραύοντο· καὶ δελφῖνες πηδῶντες, ταῖς οὐραῖς παίοντες τὰς ναῦς ἐξ ἀλὸς, ἕλυον τὰ γομφώματα. Ἠκούετό τις καὶ ὑπὲρ τῆς ὀρθίου πέτρας τῆς ὑπὸ τὴν ἄκραν σύριγγος ἦχος· ἀλλὰ οὐκ ἔτερπεν ὡς σύριγξ, ἐφόβει δὲ τοὺς ἀκούοντας ὡς σάλπιγξ. Ἐταράττοντο οὖν, καὶ ἐπὶ τὰ ὅπλα ἔθεον, καὶ πολεμίους ἐκάλουν τοὺς οὐ βλεπομένους· ὥστε πάλιν ηὔχοντο νύκτα ἐπελθεῖν, ὡς τευξόμενοι σπονδῶν ἐν αὐτῇ. Συνετὰ μὲν οὖν πᾶσιν ἦν τὰ γινόμενα τοῖς φρονοῦσιν ὀρθῶς, ὅτι ἐκ Πανὸς ἦν τὰ φαντάσματα καὶ ἀκούσματα μηνίοντός τι τοῖς ναύταις. Οὐκ εἶχον δὲ τὴν αἰτίαν συμβαλεῖν (οὐδὲν γὰρ ἱερὸν σεσύλητο Πανὸς,) ἔστε ἀμφὶ μέσην ἡμέραν εἰς ὕπνον οὐκ ἀθεεὶ τοῦ στρατηγοῦ καταπεσόντος, αὐτὸς ὁ Πὰν ὤφθη τοιάδε λέγων·

"Ὦ πάντων ἀνοσιώτατοι καὶ ἀσεβέστατοι, τί ταῦτα μαινομέναις φρεσὶν ἐτολμήσατε;

ing from the waves, lashed the ships with
their tails, and loosened the fastenings.
From the top of the steep rock over-
hanging the promontory was heard the
sound of a pipe: but the sound did not
soothe the hearers, but terrified them, like
the blast of a trumpet. Then, smitten
with affright they ran to arms, and called
upon their invisible enemies to appear:
after which, they prayed for the return
of night, hoping that it might afford them
some relief. All who possessed any in-
telligence clearly understood that all the
marvellous things that they had seen and
heard were the work of God Pan, who was
angry with them for some offence they had
committed against him: but they could
not guess the cause of it, for they had
not plundered any spot that was sacred
to him. At last, however, at mid-day,
when their general had fallen asleep, not
without the intervention of the Gods, Pan
himself appeared to him and spoke as
follows:

"O most impious and sacrilegious of
men! what has driven your frenzied minds

8—2

Πολέμου μὲν τὴν ἀγροικίαν ἐνεπλήσατε τὴν ἐμοὶ φίλην, ἀγέλας δὲ βοῶν καὶ αἰγῶν ἀπηλάσατε τὰς ἐμοὶ μελομένας· ἀπεσπάσατε δὲ βωμῶν παρθένον, ἐξ ἧς Ἔρως μῦθον ποιῆσαι θέλει· καὶ οὔτε τὰς Νύμφας ᾐδέσθητε βλεπούσας, οὔτε τὸν Πᾶνα ἐμέ. Οὔτε οὖν Μήθυμναν ὄψεσθε μετὰ τοιούτων λαφύρων πλέοντες, οὔτε τήνδε φεύξεσθε τὴν σύριγγα, τὴν ὑμᾶς ταράξασαν· ἀλλὰ ὑμᾶς βορὰν ἰχθύων θήσω καταδύσας, εἰ μὴ τὴν ταχίστην καὶ Χλόην ταῖς Νύμφαις ἀποδώσεις, καὶ τὰς ἀγέλας Χλόης, καὶ τὰς αἶγας, καὶ τὰ πρόβατα. Ἀνίστω δὴ, καὶ ἐκβίβαζε τὴν κόρην μεθ' ὧν εἶπον. Ἡγήσομαι δὲ ἐγὼ καί σοι τοῦ πλοῦ, κἀκείνῃ τῆς ὁδοῦ."

Πάνυ οὖν τεθορυβημένος ὁ Βρύαξις (τοῦτο γὰρ ἐκαλεῖτο ὁ στρατηγὸς) ἀναπηδᾷ, καὶ τῶν νεῶν καλέσας τοὺς ἡγεμόνας, ἐκέλευσε τὴν ταχίστην ἐν τοῖς αἰχμαλώτοις ἀναζητεῖσθαι

to such audacity? You have filled with war
the country that I love, and have carried
off the herds of cattle and flocks of sheep
and goats entrusted to my care : you have
dragged away from my altars a young girl
whom Love has reserved for himself, to
adorn a tale. Nay, you did not even
respect the presence of the Nymphs, nor
me, the great God Pan. Wherefore you
shall never again see Methymna with such
booty on board, nor shall you escape this
pipe, which has so smitten you with alarm:
I will swamp you in the waves and give
you as food to the fishes, unless you
speedily restore Chloe and her flocks,
sheep and goats, to the Nymphs. Arise
then, put ashore the young girl with all
that I have mentioned : and then I will
guide your course by sea, and Chloe's by
land."

Alarmed at this vision, Bryaxis—that
was the captain's name—started up, summoned the commanders of the ships, and
ordered them to search for Chloe with
all speed amongst the captives. They
soon found her and brought her before

Χλόην. Οἱ δὲ ταχέως καὶ ἀνεῦρον, καὶ εἰς ὀφθαλμοὺς ἐκόμισαν· ἐκαθέζετο γὰρ τῆς πίτυος ἐστεφανωμένη. Σύμβολον δὴ καὶ τοῦτο τῆς ἐν τοῖς ὀνείροις ὄψεως ποιούμενος, ἐπ᾽ αὐτῆς τῆς ναυαρχίδος εἰς τὴν γῆν αὐτὴν κομίζει. Κἀκείνη δὲ ἄρτι ἀποβεβήκει, καὶ σύριγγος ἦχος ἀκούεται πάλιν ἐκ τῆς πέτρας, οὐκέτι πολεμικὸς καὶ φοβερὸς, ἀλλὰ ποιμενικὸς, καὶ οἷος εἰς νομὴν ἡγεῖται ποιμνίων. Καὶ τά τε πρόβατα κατὰ τῆς ἀποβάθρας ἐξέτρεχεν, οὐκ ἐξολισθαίνοντα τοῖς κέρασι τῶν χηλῶν· καὶ αἱ αἶγες πολὺ θρασύτερον, οἷα καὶ κρημνοβατεῖν εἰθισμέναι.

Καὶ ταῦτα μὲν περιΐσταται κύκλῳ τὴν Χλόην ὥσπερ χορὸς, σκιρτῶντα, καὶ βληχώμενα, καὶ ὅμοια χαίρουσιν· αἱ δὲ τῶν ἄλλων αἰπόλων αἶγες, καὶ τὰ πρόβατα, καὶ τὰ βουκόλια κατὰ χώραν ἔμενεν ἐν κοίλῃ νηΐ, καθάπερ αὐτὰ τοῦ μέλους μὴ ἐκκαλοῦντος. Θαύματι πάντων ἐνεχομένων, καὶ τὸν Πᾶνα ἀνευφημούντων, ὤφθη τούτων ἐν τοῖς στοιχείοις ἀμφοτέροις θαυμα-

him : for she was sitting down, with a pine garland on her head. Recognising by this that it was she to whom his vision referred, he put her on board his own vessel, and conveyed her to land. As soon as she had gone ashore, the sound of the pipe again made itself heard from the summit of the rock, not martial and awe-inspiring, as before, but playing a pastoral air such as shepherds play when driving out their flocks to feed. Then immediately the sheep hurried down the gangway, without stumbling : while the goats descended with even greater confidence, being accustomed to climb steep places.

Then the sheep and the goats danced, skipped, and bleated around Chloe, as if they rejoiced with her : but the herds and flocks of the other shepherds remained where they were in the hollow ship, as if the sound of the pipe had not summoned them. While all were lost in admiration at this, and were singing the praises of Pan, stranger sights were seen on both elements. For the vessels of the

σιώτερα. ' Τῶν μὲν Μηθυμναίων, πρὶν ἀνα-
σπάσαι τὰς ἀγκύρας, ἔπλεον αἱ νῆες, καὶ τῆς
ναυαρχίδος ἡγεῖτο δελφὶν πηδῶν ἐξ ἁλός· τῶν
δὲ αἰγῶν καὶ τῶν προβάτων ἡγεῖτο σύριγγος
ἦχος ἥδιστος, καὶ τὸν συρίττοντα ἔβλεπεν
οὐδείς· ὥστε τὰ ποίμνια καὶ αἱ αἶγες προῄεσαν
ἅμα καὶ ἐνέμοντο τερπόμεναι τῷ μέλει.

Δευτέρας που νομῆς καιρὸς ἦν, καὶ ὁ Δάφνις
ἀπὸ σκοπῆς τινος μετεώρου θεασάμενος τὰς
ἀγελας καὶ τὴν Χλόην, μέγα βοήσας, ὦ Νύμφαι
καὶ Πὰν, κατέδραμεν εἰς τὸ πεδίον, καὶ περι-
πλακεὶς τῇ Χλόῃ καὶ λειποθυμήσας, κατέπεσε.
Μόλις δὲ ἔμβιος ὑπὸ τῆς Χλόης φιλούσης καὶ
ταῖς περιβολαῖς θαλπούσης γενόμενος, ἐπὶ τὴν
συνήθη φηγὸν ἔρχεται· καὶ ὑπὸ τῷ στελέχει
καθίσας, ἐπυνθάνετο πῶς ἀπέδρα τοσούτους
πολεμίους. Ἡ δὲ αὐτῷ κατέλεξε πάντα· τὸν
τῶν αἰγῶν κιττὸν, τὸν τῶν προβάτων ὠρυγμὸν,
τὴν ἐπανθήσασαν τῇ κεφαλῇ πίτυν, τὸ ἐν τῇ
γῇ πῦρ, τὸν ἐν τῇ θαλάττῃ κτύπον, τὰ συ-
ρίγματα ἀμφότερα, τὸ πολεμικὸν καὶ τὸ εἰρη-

Methymnaeans unmoored themselves of
their own accord, before the anchors were
pulled up, and a dolphin, leaping out of
the sea, piloted the commander's ship: on
land the sweet sounds of a pipe guided
the goats and sheep, although no one
could be seen playing upon it. Thus
the two flocks went on, feeding the while,
delighted to hear such strains.

It was about the time when the flocks
were being driven to the plains after mid-
day, when Daphnis, perceiving from a
lofty hill the approach of Chloe and the
herds, with a loud cry of " O Nymphs!
O Pan!" hastened down, ran towards
Chloe, and, after embracing her, fainted
from excess of joy. Even the hot kisses
of Chloe, as she clasped him in her arms,
scarcely revived him; but at last, having
regained consciousness, he made his way
to the well-known beech, and, sitting on
its trunk, inquired of her how she had
managed to escape her numerous foes.
Then she told him everything: the ivy
that grew on the horns of her goats, the
roaring of the sheep, the garland of pine

νικὸν, τὴν νύκτα τὴν φοβεράν, ὅπως αὐτῇ τὴν ὁδὸν ἀγνοούσῃ καθηγήσατο τῆς ὁδοῦ μουσική. Γνωρίσας οὖν ὁ Δάφνις τὰ τῶν Νυμφῶν ὀνείρατα, καὶ τὰ τοῦ Πανὸς ἔργα, διηγεῖται καὶ αὐτὸς ὅσα εἶδεν, ὅσα ἤκουσεν· ὅτι, μέλλων ἀποθνήσκειν, διὰ τὰς Νύμφας ἔζησε. Καὶ τὴν μὲν ἀποπέμπει κομίσουσαν τοὺς ἀμφὶ τὸν Δρύαντα καὶ Λάμωνα, καὶ ὅσα πρέποντα θυσίᾳ· αὐτὸς δὲ ἐν τούτῳ τῶν αἰγῶν τὴν ἀρίστην συλλαβὼν, καὶ κιττῷ στεφανώσας, ὥσπερ ὤφθησαν τοῖς πολεμίοις, καὶ γάλα τῶν κεράτων κατασπείσας, ἔθυσέ τε ταῖς Νύμφαις, καὶ κρεμάσας ἀπέδειρε, καὶ τὸ δέρμα ἀνέθηκεν.

Ἤδη δὲ παρόντων τῶν ἀμφὶ τὴν Χλόην, πῦρ ἀνακαύσας, καὶ τὰ μὲν ἑψήσας τῶν κρεῶν, τὰ δὲ ὀπτήσας, ἀπήρξατό τε ταῖς Νύμφαις, καὶ κρατῆρα ἀπέσπεισε μεστὸν γλεύκους· καὶ ἐκ φυλλάδος στιβάδας ὑποστορέσας, ἐντεῦθεν ἐν τροφῇ ἦν καὶ ποτῷ καὶ παιδιᾷ· καὶ ἅμα τὰς

leaves that sprouted upon her head, the
fire that blazed forth upon the land, the
noise of oars upon the sea, the two different sounds of the pipe, the martial and
the peaceful, the horrors of the night,
and how she had been guided on the road
which she did not know by the sound of
sweet music.

Then Daphnis, recognising the vision
of the Nymphs and the influence of Pan,
told her in turn all that he had seen and
heard, and how that, when he was on the
point of death, his life had been restored
by the Nymphs.   Then he sent her to
fetch Dryas and Lamon, and all that was
necessary for sacrifice : and, taking the
choicest of his goats, he crowned it with
ivy, just as the enemy had seen them, poured
a libation of milk between its horns, sacrificed it to the Nymphs, hung up and flayed
it, and consecrated its skin to them as a
votive offering.

When Chloe had returned, together with
Dryas and Lamon and their wives, he
roasted part of the flesh and boiled the
rest, after having offered the firstlings to

ἀγέλας ἐπεσκόπει, μὴ λύκος ἐμπεσὼν ἔργα ποιήσει πολεμίων. Ἦσάν τινας καὶ ᾠδὰς εἰς τὰς Νύμφας, παλαιῶν ποιμένων ποιήματα. Νυκτὸς δὲ ἐπελθούσης αὐτοῦ κοιμηθέντες ἐν τῷ ἀγρῷ, τῆς ἐπιούσης τοῦ Πανὸς ἐμνημόνευον· καὶ τῶν τράγων τὸν ἀγελάρχην στεφανώσαντες πίτυος, προσήγαγον τῇ πίτυϊ· καὶ ἐπισπεί- σαντες οἴνου, καὶ εὐφημοῦντες τὸν θεόν, ἔθυσαν, ἐκρέμασαν, ἀπέδειραν. Καὶ τὰ μὲν κρέα ὀπτή- σαντες καὶ ἑψήσαντες, πλησίον ἔθηκαν ἐν τῷ λειμῶνι, ἐν τοῖς φύλλοις· τὸ δὲ δέρμα κέρασιν αὐτοῖς ἐνέπηξαν τῇ πίτυϊ πρὸς τῷ ἀγάλματι, ποιμενικὸν ἀνάθημα ποιμενικῷ θεῷ. Ἀπήρ- ξαντο καὶ τῶν κρεῶν, ἀπέσπεισαν καὶ κρατῆρος μείζονος· ᾖσεν ἡ Χλόη, Δάφνις ἐσύρισεν.

Ἐπὶ τούτοις κατακλιθέντες, ἤσθιον· καὶ αὐτοῖς ἐφίσταται ὁ Φιλητᾶς βουκόλος κατὰ τύχην, στεφανίσκους τινὰς τῷ Πανὶ κομίζων, καὶ βότρυς ἔτι ἐν φύλλοις καὶ κλήμασι. Καὶ

the Nymphs, and poured a libation from a
full bowl of sweet wine.   Then, having
spread couches of leaves on the ground for
the use of the guests, he enjoyed himself
eating and drinking; but at the same time
he kept an eye upon his flocks, for fear
that a wolf might attack them.   After this
they sang some hymns in honour of the
Nymphs, composed by some ancient shepherds.   When night came on, they lay
down in the fields, and on the following
day bethought them of Pan.   They
crowned the goat that led the flock with
branches of pine, and led him to the tree
under which stood the image of the God:
then, having poured a libation of wine
over him, they sang praises to Pan, sacrificed, hung up, and flayed the goat.   They
roasted part of the flesh and boiled the
rest, and set it down close by in the
meadow on green leaves.   The skin with
the horns was hung up on the pine tree
near the statue, an offering of shepherds
to the shepherds' God.   They also gave
him of the firstlings, and poured libations
in his honour from a larger bowl, while

αὐτῷ τῶν παίδων ὁ νεώτατος εἵπετο Τίτυρος,
πυῤῥὸν παιδίον καὶ γλαυκὸν, λευκὸν παιδίον
καὶ ἀγέρωχον· καὶ ἥλλετο κοῦφα, βαδίζων
ὥσπερ ἔριφος. Ἀναπηδήσαντες οὖν, συνεστε-
φάνουν τὸν Πᾶνα, καὶ τὰ κλήματα τῆς κόμης
τῆς πίτυος ἐξήρτων· καὶ κατακλίναντες πλησίον αὐτῶν, συμπότην ἐποιοῦντο. Καὶ, οἷον
δὴ γέροντες ὑποβεβρεγμένοι, πρὸς ἀλλήλους
πολλὰ ἔλεγον· ὡς ἔνεμον ἡνίκα ἦσαν νέοι,
ὡς πολλὰς ληστῶν καταδρομὰς διέφυγον.
Ἐσεμνύνετό τις, ὡς λύκον ἀποκτείνας· ἄλλος,
ὡς μόνου τοῦ Πανὸς δεύτερα συρίσας· τοῦτο
τοῦ Φιλητᾶ τὸ σεμνολόγημα ἦν.

Ὁ δὲ Δάφνις καὶ ἡ Χλόη πάσας δεήσεις
προσέφερον μεταδοῦναι καὶ αὐτοῖς τῆς τέχνης,
συρίσαι τε ἐν ἑορτῇ θεοῦ σύριγγι χαίροντος.
Ἐπαγγέλλεται Φιλητᾶς, καίτοι τὸ γῆρας ὡς
ἄπνουν μεμψάμενος, καὶ ἔλαβε σύριγγα τὴν
τοῦ Δάφνιδος. Ἡ δὲ ἦν μικρὰ πρὸς μεγάλην

Chloe sang, and Daphnis played the flute.

After this they sat down and refreshed themselves. While they were thus engaged, by chance the herdsman Philetas came up, bringing some garlands of flowers to Pan, and some vine - branches full of bunches of grapes. He was accompanied by his youngest son Tityrus, a fair and impudent lad, with reddish hair and grey eyes, who ran and skipped along like a kid. When they saw Philetas and his son, the others, jumping up, went with them to place the garlands on the statue of Pan, and hung the vine-shoots on the branches of the pine: then, making Philetas sit down with them, they invited him to share their feast. After the manner of old men who are somewhat heated with wine, they began to tell all sorts of tales: how they tended their flocks when they were young, and how they had escaped many attacks of robbers. One boasted of having slain a wolf, and another (this was Philetas) of being inferior to Pan alone in his skill on the pipe.

Daphnis and Chloe begged him to give

τέχνην, οἷα ἐν στόματι παιδὸς ἐμπνεομένη.
Πέμπει οὖν Τίτυρον ἐπὶ τὴν ἑαυτοῦ σύριγγα,
τῆς ἐπαύλεως ἀπεχούσης σταδίους δέκα. Ὁ μὲν
ῥίψας τὸ ἐγκόμβωμα, γυμνὸς ὥρμησε τρέχειν
ὥσπερ νεβρός· ὁ δὲ Λάμων ἐπηγγείλατο αὐτοῖς
τὸν περὶ τῆς σύριγγος ἀφηγήσασθαι μῦθον, ὃν
αὐτῷ Σικελὸς αἰπόλος ᾖσεν ἐπὶ μισθῷ τράγῳ
καὶ σύριγγι.

"Αὕτη ἡ σύριγξ τὸ ἀρχαῖον οὐκ ἦν ὄργανον,
ἀλλὰ παρθένος καλή, καὶ τὴν φωνὴν μουσική.
Αἶγας ἔνεμεν, Νύμφαις συνέπαιζεν, ᾖδεν οἷον
νῦν. Πὰν, ταύτης νεμούσης, παιζούσης, ᾀδού-
σης, προσελθὼν, ἔπειθεν ἐς ὅ, τι ἔχρηζε· καὶ
ἐπηγγέλλετο τὰς αἶγας πάσας θήσειν διδυμο-
τόκους. Ἡ δὲ ἐγέλα τὸν ἔρωτα αὐτοῦ, οὐδὲ
ἐραστὴν ἔφη δέξασθαι, μήτε τράγον, μήτε ἄνθρωπον ὁλόκληρον. Ὁρμᾷ διώκειν ὁ Πὰν ἐς
βίαν· ἡ Σύριγξ ἔφευγε καὶ τὸν Πᾶνα, καὶ τὴν
βίαν· φεύγουσα, κάμνουσα, ἐς δόνακας κρύπ-

them a specimen of his skill, and to play
on his pipe at a feast in honour of the God
who delighted in such music.   Philetas
consented, although complaining that his
years had left him but little breath, and
took Daphnis's pipe.   But it was too small
for the display of great skill, being only fit
for a lad to play upon.   Philetas therefore
sent Tityrus to his cottage, which was
about ten stades distant, to fetch his own
pipe.   The lad, throwing off his smock,
ran off as swiftly as a fawn: meanwhile,
Lamon offered to tell them the story of
the pipe, which a Sicilian goatherd had
related to him in return for the present
of a goat and a pipe.

" This pipe in former times was not a
musical instrument, but a beautiful maiden,
who had a melodious voice.   She tended
goats, sported with the Nymphs, and sang
as now.   Pan, who saw her tending her
goats, sporting, and singing, tried to persuade her to yield to his advances, promising that her goats should always bring
forth twins.   But she scoffed at his love,
and declared that she would never have

9

τεται, εἰς ἕλος ἀφανίζεται. Πὰν, τοὺς δόνακας ὀργῇ ταμὼν, τὴν κόρην οὐχ εὑρὼν, τὸ πάθος μαθὼν, τὸ ὄργανον νοεῖ, καὶ τοὺς καλάμους κηρῷ συνδήσας ἀνίσους, καθ' ὅτι καὶ ὁ ἔρως ἄνισος αὐτοῖς· καὶ ἡ τότε παρθένος καλὴ νῦν ἐστι σύριγξ μουσική."

Ἄρτι πέπαυτο τοῦ μυθολογήματος ὁ Λάμων, καὶ ἐπῄνει Φιλητᾶς αὐτὸν, ὡς εἰπόντα μῦθον ᾠδῆς γλυκύτερον, καὶ ὁ Τίτυρος ἐφίσταται τὴν σύριγγα τῷ πατρὶ κομίζων, μέγα ὄργανον καὶ αὐλῶν μεγάλων· καὶ ἵνα κεκήρωτο, τῷ χαλκῷ πεποίκιλτο. Εἴκασεν ἄν τις εἶναι ταύτην ἐκείνην, ἣν ὁ Πὰν πρῶτον ἐπήξατο. Διεγερθεὶς οὖν ὁ Φιλητᾶς, καὶ καθίσας ἐν καθέδρᾳ ὄρθιον, πρῶτον μὲν ἀπεπειράθη τῶν καλάμων, εἰ εὔπνοοι· ἔπειτα μαθὼν ὡς ἀκώλυτον διατρέχει τὸ πνεῦμα, ἐνέπνει τὸ ἐντεῦθεν πολὺ καὶ νεανικόν. Αὐλῶν τις ἂν ᾠήθη συναυλούντων ἀκούειν· τοσοῦτον ἤχει τὸ σύριγμα. Κατ'

anything to do with a lover who was neither a goat nor a perfect man. Thereupon Pan was proceeding to violence, but Syrinx fled, until at last, weary of running, she flung herself into a swamp and disappeared amongst the reeds. Pan, enraged, cut down the reeds, and, not finding the maiden, understood what had happened. Then, cutting some reeds of unequal length, in token of an unequal love, he joined them together with wax and fashioned this instrument. Thus she who was once a beautiful maiden is now an instrument of music—the pipe."

Lamon had scarcely finished his story,—which was highly praised by Philetas, who declared that it was sweeter than any song, —when Tityrus returned with his father's pipe, which was very large and made of larger reeds than usual, while the waxen fastenings were overlaid with brass. One would have said that it was the very pipe which Pan had first made. Then Philetas sat upright, tried all the reeds to see if there was a free current of air, and, finding that his breath passed through unchecked,

ὀλίγον δὲ τῆς βίας ἀφαιρῶν, εἰς τὸ τερπνότεροι
μετέβαλλε τὸ μέλος. Καὶ πᾶσαν τέχνην ἐπι-
δεικνύμενος εὐνομίας μουσικῆς, ἐσύριττεν ὅσον
βοῶν ἀγέλῃ πρέπον, οἷον αἰπολίῳ πρόσφορον,
οἷον ποίμναις φίλον. Τερπνὸν ἦν τὸ ποιμνίων,
μέγα τὸ βοῶν, ὀξὺ τὸ αἰγῶν· ὅλως πάσας
σύριγγας μία σύριγξ ἐμιμήσατο.

Οἱ μὲν οὖν ἄλλοι σιωπῇ κατέκειντο τερπό-
μενοι· Δρύας δὲ ἀναστὰς, καὶ κελεύσας συρίζειν
διονυσιακὸν μέλος, ἐπιλήνιον αὐτοῖς ὄρχησιν
ὠρχήσατο. Καὶ ἐῴκει ποτὲ μὲν τρυγῶντι,
ποτὲ δὲ φέροντι ἀρρίχους, εἶτα πατοῦντι τοὺς
βότρυς, εἶτα πληροῦντι τοὺς πίθους, εἶτα
πίνοντι τοῦ γλεύκους. Ταῦτα πάντα οὕτως
εὐσχημόνως ὠρχήσατο Δρύας καὶ ἐναργῶς,
ὥστε ἐδόκουν βλέπειν καὶ τὰς ἀμπέλους,
καὶ τὴν ληνὸν, καὶ τοὺς πίθους, καὶ ἀληθῶς
Δρύαντα πίνοντα.

Τρίτος δὴ γέρων οὗτος εὐδοκιμήσας ἐπ᾽ ὀρ-

blew so loud and lustily, that it seemed
as if several pipes were being played at
once: then, gradually blowing more gently,
he changed his tune to a more pleasant
strain, and, displaying to them the most
perfect skill in pastoral music, he showed
them what strains were best for a herd
of oxen, or a flock of goats or sheep,—
sweet and gentle for sheep, loud and deep
for oxen, sharp and clear for goats: and
all these notes he imitated on a single
pipe.

While all, quietly reclining on the
ground, listened in silence, charmed by
the music, Dryas got up, begged Philetas
to strike up a Bacchanalian air and then
began the vintage dance. He seemed in
turns to be plucking the fruit, carrying
the baskets, treading the grapes, filling
the jars, and drinking the new wine: so
perfect was the imitation, and so naturally
did the dance represent the vines, the wine-
press, the jars, and Dryas drinking, to the
life.

The third old man, having thus danced
amid the applause of all, embraced Daphnis

χήσει, φιλεῖ Χλόην καὶ Δάφνιν. Οἱ δὲ μάλα
ταχέως ἀναστάντες, ὠρχήσαντο τὸν μῦθον τοῦ
Λάμωνος. Ὁ Δάφνις Πᾶνα ἐμιμεῖτο, τὴν
Σύριγγα Χλόη. Ὁ μὲν ἱκέτευε πείθων· ἡ
δὲ ἀμελοῦσα ἐμειδία. Ὁ μὲν ἐδίωκε, καὶ ἐπ'
ἄκρων τῶν ὀνύχων ἔτρεχε, τὰς χηλὰς μιμού-
μενος· ἡ δὲ ἐνέφαινε τὴν κάμνουσαν ἐν τῇ
φυγῇ. Ἔπειτα Χλόη μὲν εἰς τὴν ὕλην, ὡς
εἰς ἕλος, κρύπτεται· Δάφνις δὲ λαβὼν τὴν
Φιλητᾶ σύριγγα, τὴν μεγάλην, ἐσύρισε γοερὸν,
ὡς ἐρῶν, ἐρωτικὸν, ὡς πείθων, ἀνακλητικὸν, ὡς
ἐπιζητῶν· ὥστε Φιλητᾶς θαυμάσας, φιλεῖ τε
ἀναπηδήσας, καὶ τὴν σύριγγα χαρίζεται
φιλήσας, καὶ εὔχεται καὶ Δάφνιν καταλιπεῖν
αὐτὴν ὁμοίῳ διαδόχῳ. Ὁ δὲ τὴν ἰδίαν ἀναθεὶς
τῷ Πανὶ τὴν σμικρὰν, καὶ φιλήσας ὡς ἐκ φυγῆς
ἀληθινῆς εὑρεθεῖσαν τὴν Χλόην, ἀπήλαυνε τὴν
ἀγέλην συρίζων.

Νυκτὸς ἤδη γεγενημένης, ἀπήλαυνε καὶ ἡ

and Chloe, who quickly started up and
began to represent in the dance the
story told by Lamon.   Daphnis took
the part of Pan, and Chloe that of
Syrinx. He tried to persuade her with
his entreaties, while she rejected his
advances with a smile. He pursued her,
and ran on tiptoe, to represent the goat's
cloven feet : while Chloe pretended to
be weary in her flight and at last hid
herself in the forest which served as a
swamp.   Then Daphnis took Philetas's
large pipe, drew from it a mournful strain,
like the lamentations of a lover, then a
passionate air, to touch her heart, and,
lastly, a strain of recall, as if he had lost
and was seeking her.   So well did he play
that Philetas, overcome by admiration,
jumped up and embraced him, and made
him a present of his pipe, with a prayer
that Daphnis in his turn might leave it
to a successor like himself.   Daphnis
dedicated to the God Pan the small flute
which he had hitherto used, embraced
Chloe as if he had really lost and found
her again, and drove back his flock, playing on his pipe the while.

Χλόη τὴν ποίμνην, τῷ μέλει τῆς σύριγγος
συνάγουσα· καὶ αἵ τε αἶγες πλησίον τῶν
προβάτων ἦσαν, ὅτε Δάφνις ἐβάδιζεν ἐγγὺς
τῆς Χλόης· ὥστε ἐνέπλησαν ἕως νυκτὸς ἀλλήλους, καὶ συνέθεντο θᾶττον τὰς ἀγέλας τῆς
ἐπιούσης κατελάσαι· καὶ οὕτως ἐποίησαν.
Ἄρτι γοῦν ἀρχομένης ἡμέρας, ἦλθον εἰς τὴν
νομήν. Καὶ τὰς Νύμφας προτέρας, εἶτα τὸν
Πᾶνα προσαγορεύσαντες, τὸ ἐντεῦθεν ὑπὸ τῇ
δρυῖ καθεσθέντες, ἐσύριττον· εἶτα ἀλλήλους
ἐφίλουν, περιέβαλλον, κατεκλίνοντο· καὶ οὐδὲν
δράσαντες πλέον, ὑνίσταντο. Ἐμέλησεν αὐτοῖς καὶ τροφῆς· καὶ ἔπιον οἶνον, μίξαντες
γάλα.

Καὶ τούτοις ἅπασι θερμότεροι γενόμενοι
καὶ θρασύτεροι, πρὸς ἀλλήλους ἤριζον ἔριν
ἐρωτικήν, καὶ κατ' ὀλίγον εἰς ὅρκων πίστιν
προῆλθον. Ὁ μὲν δὴ Δάφνις τὸν Πᾶνα ὤμοσεν, ἐλθὼν ἐπὶ τὴν πίτυν, μὴ ζήσεσθαι μόνος
ἄνευ Χλόης, μηδὲ μιᾶς χρόνον ἡμέρας· ἡ δὲ
Χλόη Δάφνιδι τὰς Νύμφας, εἰσελθοῦσα εἰς τὸ

As night was close at hand, Chloe also drove back her sheep to the sound of the same pipe: the goats went side by side with the sheep, while Daphnis walked close to Chloe. Thus they enjoyed each other's society until nightfall, when they separated, after promising to drive their flocks to pasture earlier than usual on the following day, which they did. At day-break, they were in the fields. Having first saluted the Nymphs, and next, the God Pan, they sat down beneath the oak, where they played upon the pipe, kissed and embraced each other, and lay down side by side, but that was all. Then they got up and bethought themselves of food, and drank wine, mingled with milk. Warmed and further emboldened by what they had drunk, they commenced an amorous contest, and at last swore mutual fidelity. Daphnis swore by Pan beneath the pine tree that he could not live without Chloe, even for a single day: while Chloe, having entered the grotto, swore by the Nymphs to live and die with Daphnis. So simple and innocent was she that, when

ἄντρον, τὸν αὐτὸν ἕξειν θάνατον καὶ βίον. Τοσοῦτον δὲ ἄρα τῇ Χλόῃ τὸ ἀφελὲς ἦν ὡς κόρῃ, ὥστε ἐξιοῦσα τοῦ ἄντρου, καὶ δεύτερον ἠξίου λαβεῖν ὅρκον παρ' αὐτοῦ, "ὦ Δάφνι, λέγουσα, θεὸς ὁ Πὰν ἐρωτικός ἐστι καὶ ἄπιστος· ἠράσθη μὲν Πίτυος, ἠρασθη δὲ Σύριγγος· παύεται δὲ οὐδέποτε Δρυάσιν ἐνοχλῶν, καὶ Ἐπιμηλίσι Νύμφαις πράγματα παρέχων. Ὁ μὲν οὖν, ἀμεληθεὶς ἐν τοῖς ὅρκοις, ἀμελήσει σε κολάσαι, κᾂν ἐπὶ πλείονας ἔλθῃς γυναῖκας τῶν ἐν τῇ σύριγγι καλάμων· σὺ δέ μοι τὸ αἰπόλιον τοῦτο ὅμοσον, καὶ τὴν αἶγα ἐκείνην ἥ σε ἀνέθρεψε, μὴ καταλιπεῖν Χλόην, ἔστ' ἂν πιστή σοι μένῃ· ἄδικον δὲ εἰς σὲ καὶ τὰς Νύμφας γενομένην, καὶ φεῦγε, καὶ μίσει, καὶ ἀπόκτεινον ὥσπερ λύκον." Ἥδετο ὁ Δάφνις ἀπιστούμενος· καὶ στὰς εἰς μέσον τὸ αἰπόλιον, καὶ τῇ μὲν τῶν χειρῶν, αἰγός, τῇ δὲ, τράγου λαβόμενος, ὤμνυε Χλόην φιλῆσαι φιλοῦσαν· κᾂν ἕτερον προκρίνῃ Δάφνιδος, ἀντ' ἐκείνης αὐτὸν

she came out of the grotto, she demanded
that Daphnis should take a second oath.
" Daphnis," said she, " Pan is an amorous
and inconstant God : he was enamoured of
Pitys and Syrinx, he never ceases to annoy
the Dryads and the Epimelian Nymphs
with his solicitations. Wherefore, even if
you forget the oath that you have sworn by
him, he will forget to punish you, even
though you should have more mistresses
than there are reeds in your pipe. Do
you therefore swear by this herd of goats
and by the she-goat that reared you, that
you will never desert Chloe as long as
she remains true to you : but if she breaks
her vows to you and the Nymphs, flee
from her, loathe her, and kill her like a
wolf."

. Daphnis, pleased at being thus mis-
trusted, stood upright in the midst of his
flock, and, taking hold of a she-goat with
one hand, and of a he-goat with the other,
swore to love Chloe as long as she loved
him : and that, if she ever preferred
another, he would kill himself instead of
her. Then Chloe was delighted, and no

ἀποκτενεῖν. Ἡ δὲ ἔχαιρε, καὶ ἐπίστευεν ὡς κόρη, καὶ νέμουσα, καὶ νομίζουσα τὰς αἶγας καὶ τὰ πρόβατα ποιμένων καὶ αἰπόλων ἰδίους θεούς.

longer had any doubts : for she was young
and a simple shepherdess, and saw in the
sheep and goats the Gods of shepherds and
goatherds.

ΛΟΓΟΣ ΤΡΙΤΟΣ

Μιτυληναῖοι δὲ, ὡς ᾔσθοντο τὸν κατάπλουν τῶν δέκα νεῶν, καί τινες ἐμήνυσαν αὐτοῖς τὴν ἁρπαγὴν, ἐλθόντες ἐκ τῶν ἀγρῶν, οὐκ ἀνασχε- τὸν νομίσαντες ταῦτα ἐκ Μηθυμναίων παθεῖν, ἔγνωσαν καὶ αὐτοὶ τὴν ταχίστην ἐπ᾽ αὐτοὺς ὅπλα κινεῖν· καὶ καταλέξαντες ἀσπίδα τρισ- χιλίαν καὶ ἵππον πεντακοσίαν, ἐξέπεμψαν κατὰ γῆν τὸν στρατηγὸν Ἵππασον, ὀκνοῦντες ἐν ὥρᾳ χειμῶνος τὴν θάλατταν.

Ὁ δὲ ἐξορμηθεὶς, ἀγροὺς μὲν οὐκ ἐλεηλάτει τῶν Μηθυμναίων, οὐδὲ ἀγέλας καὶ κτήματα ἥρπαξε γεωργῶν καὶ ποιμένων, λῃστοῦ νομίζων ταῦτα ἔργα μᾶλλον ἢ στρατηγοῦ· ταχύνει δὲ ἐπὶ τὴν πόλιν αὐτὴν, ὡς ἐπιπεσούμενος ἀφρου- ρήτοις ταῖς πύλαις. Καὶ αὐτῷ σταδίους ὅσον ἑκατὸν ἀπέχοντι, κῆρυξ ἀπαντᾷ σπονδὰς κο- μίζων. Οἱ γὰρ Μηθυμναῖοι μαθόντες παρὰ

BOOK III

WHEN the Mitylenaeans heard of the
descent of the ten vessels, and were informed by certain persons who came from
the country of the plundering of their
territory, they considered such outrages
on the part of the Methymnaeans unbear-
able, and resolved to take up arms against
them without delay. Collecting a force of
three thousand heavy-armed infantry, and
five hundred cavalry, they despatched
them by land, under the command of
Hippasus, being afraid of journeying by
sea during the winter season.

Hippasus accordingly set out, but was
careful not to plunder the territory of
the Methymnaeans: he carried off neither
flocks nor any kind of booty from the
husbandmen and shepherds, considering
such conduct to be rather the act of a
brigand than of a general. He marched
with all speed against the city itself,

τῶν ἑαλωκότων, ὡς οὐδὲν ἴσασι Μιτυληναῖοι
τῶν γεγενημένων, ἀλλὰ γεωργοὶ καὶ ποιμένες
ὑβρίζοντας τοὺς νεανίσκους ἔδρασαν ταῦτα,
μετεγίνωσκον μὲν ὀξύτερα τολμήσαντες εἰς
γείτονα πόλιν ἢ σωφρονέστερα· σπουδὴν δὲ
εἶχον, ἀποδόντες πᾶσαν τὴν ἁρπαγὴν, ἀδεῶς
ἐπιμίγνυσθαι καὶ κατὰ γῆν καὶ κατὰ θάλατταν. Τὸν μὲν οὖν κήρυκα τοῖς Μιτυληναίοις ὁ
Ἵππασος ἀποστέλλει, καίτοι γε αὐτοκράτωρ
στρατηγὸς κεχειροτονημένος· αὐτὸς δὲ τῆς
Μηθύμνης ὅσον ἀπὸ δέκα σταδίων στρατό-
πεδον βαλόμενος, τὰς ἐκ τῆς πόλεως ἐντολὰς
ἀνέμενε. Καὶ δύο διαγενομένων ἡμερῶν, ἐλθὼν
ὁ ἄγγελος, τήν τε ἁρπαγὴν ἐκέλευσε κομί-
σασθαι, καὶ ἀδικήσαντα μηδὲν, ἀναχωρεῖν
οἴκαδε· πολέμου γὰρ καὶ εἰρήνης ἐν αἱρέσει
γενόμενοι, τὴν εἰρήνην εὕρισκον κερδαλεωτέραν.

Ὁ μὲν δὴ Μηθυμναίων καὶ Μιτυληναίων
πόλεμος ἀδόκητον λαβὼν ἀρχὴν καὶ τέλος,

hoping to be able to attack it while the
gates were left unguarded. When he was
about one hundred stades distant from
the city, a herald met them to propose a
truce. The Methymnaeans, having learnt
from the prisoners that the Mitylenaeans
knew nothing of what had taken place,
and that the whole affair was merely an
attack of a few shepherds and labourers
upon some insolent young men, regretted
that they had behaved with greater violence
than prudence towards a neighbouring city.
They were accordingly anxious to restore
all the plunder that they had taken, and
to re-establish friendly relations between
the two cities, both by sea and land. Hippasus sent the herald to the Mitylenaeans,
although he had been appointed commander with unlimited power: at the
same time he pitched his camp about ten
stades from Methymna, to await instructions from his government. At the end
of two days, the messenger returned with
orders to the commander to receive the
booty, and to return home without com-
mitting any act of hostility. Having the

οὕτω διελύθη. Γίνεται δὲ χειμὼν Δάφνιδι καὶ
Χλόῃ τοῦ πολέμου πικρότερος· ἐξαίφνης γὰρ
πεσοῦσα χιὼν πολλὴ, πάσας μὲν ἀπέκλεισε
τὰς ὁδοὺς, πάντας δὲ κατέκλεισε τοὺς γεωρ-
γούς. Λάβροι μὲν οἱ χείμαρροι κατέρρεον,
ἐπεπήγει δὲ κρύσταλλος· τὰ δένδρα ἐῴκει
κατεχωσμένοις· ἡ γῆ πᾶσα ἀφανὴς ἦν, ὅτι μὴ
περὶ πηγάς που καὶ ρεύματα. Οὔτ' οὖν
ἀγέλην τις εἰς νομὴν ἦγε, οὔτε αὐτὸς προῄει
τῶν θυρῶν· ἀλλὰ πῦρ καύσαντες μέγα περὶ
ᾠδὰς ἀλεκτρυόνων, οἱ μὲν λίνον ἔστρεφον, οἱ
δὲ αἰγῶν τρίχας ἔπλεκον, οἱ δὲ πάγας ὀρνίθων
ἐσοφίζοντο. Τότε βοῶν ἐπὶ φάτναις φροντὶς
ἦν ἄχυρον ἐσθιόντων, αἰγῶν καὶ προβάτων ἐν
τοῖς σηκοῖς, φυλλάδας, ὑῶν ἐν τοῖς συφεοῖς,
ἄκυλον καὶ βαλάνους.

'Αναγκαίας οὖν οἰκουρίας ἐπεχούσης ἄπαν-
τας, οἱ μὲν ἄλλοι γεωργοὶ καὶ νομεῖς ἔχαιρον,
πόνων τε ἀπηλλαγμένοι πρὸς ὀλίγον, καὶ

choice between peace and war, they were of opinion that peace would be more advantageous.

Thus ended the war between Methymna and Mitylene, as suddenly as it had commenced. Winter came on, a greater hardship than the war for Daphnis and Chloe: suddenly there was a heavy fall of snow, which blocked up all the roads and kept all the labourers indoors. Torrents rushed down with violence from the mountains, the water was frozen hard, the trees seemed buried beneath the hoar frost: the earth was completely hidden, except around the fountains and the banks of the streams. No herdsman led his flocks to pasture, or set foot outside his door: in the morning, at cockcrow, they lighted a large fire, round which they gathered, some twisting hemp, others weaving goats' hairs or making snares for birds. The only thing they had to think about was to give the oxen in the stalls straw to eat, the sheep and goats in the cotes plenty of leaves, and the pigs in the sties acorns and beech-nuts.

τροφὰς ἑωθινὰς ἐσθίοντες, καὶ καθεύδοντες
μακρὸν ὕπνον· ὥστε αὐτοῖς τὸν χειμῶνα δοκεῖι
καὶ θέρους καὶ μετοπώρου καὶ ἦρος αὐτοῦ γλυ-
κύτερον· Χλόη δὲ καὶ Δάφνις ἐν μνήμῃ γενόμενοι τῶν καταλειφθέντων τερπνῶν, ὡς ἐφίλουν
ὡς περιέβαλλον, ὡς ἅμα τὴν τροφὴν προσ-
εφέροντο, νύκτας τε ἀγρύπνους διῆγον καὶ
λυπηρὰς, καὶ τὴν εἰαρινὴν ὥραν ἀνέμενον, ἐκ
θανάτου παλιγγενεσίαν. Ἐλύπει δὲ αὐτοὺς,
ἢ πήρα τις ἐλθοῦσα εἰς χεῖρας, ἐξ ἧς ἤσθιον,
ἢ γαυλὸς ὀφθεὶς, ἐξ οὗ συνέπιον, ἢ σύριγξ
ἀμελῶς ἐρριμμένη, δῶρον ἐρωτικὸν γεγενημένη.
Εὔχοντο δὴ ταῖς Νύμφαις καὶ τῷ Πανὶ, καὶ
τούτων αὐτοὺς ἐκλύσασθαι τῶν κακῶν, καὶ
δεῖξαί ποτε αὐτοῖς καὶ ταῖς ἀγέλαις ἥλιον·
ἅμα τε εὐχόμενοι τέχνην ἐξήτουν δι' ἧς ἀλλήλους θεάσονται. Ἡ μὲν δὴ Χλόη δεινῶς ἄπορος
ἦν καὶ ἀμήχανος· ἀεὶ γὰρ αὐτῇ συνῆν ἡ δοκοῦσα
μήτηρ, ἔριά τε ξαίνειν διδάσκουσα, καὶ ἀτράκ-

The necessity of remaining at home glad-
dened the hearts of the other labourers and
shepherds, who thus enjoyed some relaxa-
tion from their daily task, and, after they
had breakfasted, had a long sleep. In this
respect the winter seemed to them more
enjoyable than spring, summer, or winter.
But Daphnis and Chloe had always in
mind the pleasant pastimes which they
were now forced to abandon—their kisses,
embraces, and meals shared together: they
passed sad and sleepless nights, and waited
for the return of spring as a resurrection.
It grieved them sorely when they touched
a wallet from which they had eaten, or
saw a pail from which they had drunk
together, or a pipe, carelessly thrown
aside, that had been a gift of affection.
They prayed to Pan and the Nymphs to
put an end to their sorrows, and to show
the sun again to them and their flocks ; at
the same time, they endeavoured to find
some means of seeing each other. Chloe
was terribly embarrassed, and did not
know what to do : for her supposed mother
never left her for a moment: she taught

τους στρέφειν, καὶ γάμου μνημονεύουσα· ὁ δὲ
Δάφνις, οἷα σχολὴν ἄγων, καὶ συνετώτερος κόρης, τοιόνδε σόφισμα εὗρεν ἐς θέαν τῆς Χλόης.

Πρὸ τῆς αὐλῆς τοῦ Δρύαντος, ὑπ᾿ αὐτῇ τῇ
πύλῃ, μυῤῥίναι μεγάλαι δύο καὶ κιττὸς ἐπε-
φύκει. Αἱ μυῤῥίναι πλησίον ἀλλήλων, ὁ κιττὸς
δὲ ἀμφοτέρων μέσος· ὥστε ἐφ᾿ ἑκατέραν δια-
θεὶς τοὺς ἀκρέμονας ὡς ἄμπελος, ἄντρου σχῆμα
διὰ τῶν φύλλων ἐπαλλαττόντων ἐποίει· καὶ ὁ
κόρυμβος πολὺς καὶ μέγας ὅσος βότρυς κλημάτων ἐξεκρέματο. Ἦν οὖν πολὺ πλῆθος περὶ
αὐτὸν τῶν χειμερινῶν ὀρνίθων, ἀπορίᾳ τῆς ἔξω
τροφῆς· πολὺς μὲν κόψιχος, πολλὴ δὲ κίχλη,
καὶ φᾶτται, καὶ ψᾶρες, καὶ ὅσον ἄλλο κιττο-
φάγον πτερόν. Τούτων τῶν ὀρνίθων ἐπὶ προ-
φάσει θήρας ἐξώρμησεν ὁ Δάφνις, ἐμπλήσας
μὲν τὴν πήραν ὀψημάτων μεμελιτωμένων, κομίζων δὲ ἐς πίστιν ἰξὸν καὶ βρόχους. Τὸ μὲν
οὖν μεταξὺ, σταδίων ἦν οὐ πλέον δέκα· οὔπω δὲ
ἡ χιὼν λελυμένη πολὺν κάματον αὐτῷ παρέ-

her to card wool, and turn the spindle, and
talked to her of marriage. Daphnis, however, since he had more time to himself,
and was cleverer than the young girl, de-
vised the following scheme for seeing her.

In front of Dryas's cottage, close to the
courtyard gate, grew two large myrtles and
an ivy plant. The myrtles almost touched,
and the ivy had worked its way between
them in such a manner that, spreading
its branches on either side like a vine, it
formed a kind of arbour shaded by its inter-
twining foliage : berries, large as grapes,
hung down from the branches, upon which
settled swarms of birds, which were unable to procure food outside—blackbirds,
thrushes, doves, starlings, and all the birds
that are fond of feeding on ivy. Daphnis
went out under pretence of catching some
of these birds, taking with him a wallet
full of honey-cakes, and some birdlime
and snares, so as to allay all suspicion.
Although the distance was ten stades at
the most, the snow, which was not yet
melted, caused him great inconvenience :
but Love can make its way through every-

σχεν· ἔρωτι δὲ ἄρα πάντα βάσιμα, καὶ πῦρ, καὶ ὕδωρ, καὶ Σκυθικὴ χιών.

Δρόμῳ οὖν πρὸς τὴν αὐλὴν ἔρχεται· καὶ ἀποσεισάμενος τῶν σκελῶν τὴν χιόνα, τούς τε βρόχους ἔστησε, καὶ τὸν ἰξὸν ῥάβδοις μακραῖς ἐπήλειψε· καὶ ἐκαθέζετο τὸ ἐντεῦθεν ὄρνιθας καὶ τὴν Χλόην μεριμνῶν. Ἀλλ' ὄρνιθες μὲν καὶ ἧκον πολλοὶ καὶ ἐλήφθησαν ἱκανοί· ὥστε πράγματα μυρία ἔσχε συλλέγων αὐτούς, καὶ ἀποκτιννὺς, καὶ ἀποδύων τὰ πτερά· τῆς δὲ αὐλῆς προῆλθεν οὐδεὶς, οὐκ ἀνήρ, οὐ γυναίκιον, οὐ κατοικίδιος ὄρνις, ἀλλὰ πάντες τῷ πυρὶ παραμένοντες ἔνδον κατεκέκλειντο· ὥστε πάνυ ἠπορεῖτο ὁ Δάφνις, ὡς οὐκ αἰσίοις ὄρνισιν ἐλθών· καὶ ἐτόλμα, πρόφασιν σκηψάμενος, ὤσασθαι διὰ θυρῶν, καὶ ἐξήτει πρὸς αὐτὸν ὅ,τι λεχθῆναι πιθανώτερον· "Πῦρ ἐναυσόμενος ἦλθον—Μὴ γὰρ οὐκ ἦσαν ἀπὸ σταδίου γείτονες; Ἄρτους αἰτησόμενος ἧκον—Ἀλλ' ἡ πήρα μεστὴ τροφῆς. Οἴνου δέομαι—Καὶ μὴν

thing, through fire, water, and the snows of Scythia.

He made all haste to the cottage, and, having shaken the snow from his feet, he set up his snares, and smeared some long sticks with birdlime: then he sat down waiting for the birds and thinking of Chloe. The birds came in great numbers, and he caught so many that he had plenty to do to pick them up, kill, and pluck them. But no one left the house, neither man, nor woman, nor fowl: for all had shut themselves up and were seated round the fire. Daphnis was utterly at a loss what to do, and cursed his unlucky star: then he thought of venturing to knock at the door, but did not know what plausible excuse to make. He discussed the matter with himself as follows: " If I say that I have come to fetch something to light a fire with, they will ask me. if I have no nearer neighbours. If I ask for some bread, they will tell me that my wallet is full of food. If I say I want wine, they will answer that we have only just got in the vintage. If I say I have been chased by a wolf, they will ask

χθὲς καὶ πρώην ἐτρύγησας. Λύκος με ἐδίωκε—
Καὶ ποῦ τὰ ἴχνη τοῦ λύκου; Θηράσων ἀφικό-
μην τοὺς ὄρνιθας—Τί οὖν θηράσας οὐκ ἄπει;
Χλόην θεάσασθαι βούλομαι . . . πατρὶ δὲ τίς
καὶ μητρὶ παρθένου ὁμολογεῖ; Παίδων δὴ
πανταχοῦ σιωπή·[1] ἀλλ' οὐδὲν τούτων ἁπάντων
ἀνύποπτον. Ἄμεινον ἄρα σιγᾶν· Χλόην δὲ
ἦρος ὄψομαι, ἐπεὶ μὴ εἵμαρτο, ὡς ἔοικε, χει-
μῶνός με ταύτην ἰδεῖν." Τοιαῦτα δή τινα
διανοηθεὶς, καὶ τὰ θηραθέντα συλλαβὼν, ὥρ-
μητο ἀπιέναι· καὶ, ὥσπερ αὐτὸν οἰκτείραντος
τοῦ Ἔρωτος, τάδε γίνεται.

Τράπεζαν εἶχον οἱ ἀμφὶ τὸν Δρύαντα· κρέα
διῃρεῖτο, ἄρτοι παρετίθεντο, κρατὴρ ἐκιρνᾶτο.
Εἷς δὴ κύων τῶν προβατευτικῶν, ἀμέλειαν φυλάξας, κρέας ἁρπάσας, ἔφυγε διὰ τῶν θυρῶν.
Ἀλγήσας ὁ Δρύας, (καὶ γὰρ ἦν ἐκείνου μοῖρα)
ξύλον ἁρπασάμενος, ἐδίωκε κατ' ἴχνος ὥσπερ
κύων. Διώκων δὲ, καὶ κατὰ τὸν κιττὸν γενόμενος, ὁρᾷ τὸν Δάφνιν ἀνατεθειμένον ἐπὶ τοὺς

---

[1] This passage is corrupt.

where his footprints are. If I say that I
came to catch birds, they will ask me why I
do not return home, now that I have caught
enough. And, as for declaring openly that
I want to see Chloe, who would make such
a confession to a girl's mother and father?
All such excuses are open to suspicion:
the best thing will be to hold my tongue.
I shall see Chloe again in the spring, since
I am not destined to see her this winter."
After this soliloquy he picked up his birds
and was preparing to go, when, as if Love
had taken compassion upon him, the following incident occurred.

Dryas was at table with his family: the
meat had been cut up and distributed, the
bread served, and the goblet mixed, when
one of the sheep dogs, taking advantage of
the moment when no one was watching
him, seized a piece of meat, and ran out
of doors. Dryas, greatly enraged (for the
piece of meat was his own portion),
snatched up a cudgel, and ran after him
like another dog. In his pursuit, he
passed close to the ivy, and saw Daphnis
who had just flung his spoil over his

ὤμους τὴν ἄγραν, καὶ ἀποσοβεῖν ἐγνωκότα.
Κρέως μὲν καὶ κυνὸς αὐτίκα ἐπελάθετο· μέγα
δὲ βοήσας, χαῖρε, ὦ παῖ, περιεπλέκετο καὶ
κατεφίλει, καὶ περιῆγεν ἔσω λαβόμενος.
Μικροῦ μὲν οὖν ἰδόντες ἀλλήλους, εἰς τὴν
γῆν κατερρύησαν· μεῖναι δὲ καρτερήσαντες
ὀρθοὶ, προσηγόρευσάν τε καὶ κατεφίλησαν·
καὶ τοῦτο οἰονεὶ ἔρεισμα αὐτοῖς τοῦ μὴ πεσεῖν
ἐγένετο.

Τυχὼν δὲ ὁ Δάφνις παρ' ἐλπίδας καὶ φιλήματος καὶ Χλόης, τοῦ τε πυρὸς ἐκαθέσθη
πλησίον, καὶ ἐπὶ τὴν τράπεζαν ἀπὸ τῶν ὤμων
τὰς φάττας ἀπεφορτίσατο καὶ τοὺς κοψίχους·
καὶ διηγεῖτο πῶς ἀσχάλλων πρὸς τὴν οἰκουρίαν,
ὥρμησε πρὸς τὴν ἄγραν· καὶ ὅπως τὰ μὲν
βρόχοις αὐτῶν, τὰ δὲ ἰξῷ λάβοι, τῶν μύρτων
καὶ τοῦ κιττοῦ γλιχόμενα. Οἱ δὲ ἐπήνουν τὸ
ἐνεργὸν, καὶ ἐκέλευον ἐσθίειν ὧν ὁ κύων κατέλιπεν. Ἐκέλευον δὲ τῇ Χλόῃ πιεῖν ἐγχέαι·
καὶ ἥδε χαίρουσα τοῖς τε ἄλλοις ὤρεξε, καὶ

shoulders, and had made up his mind to depart. Then, immediately forgetting all about the meat and the dog, he shouted, "Good-day, my lad," embraced him, and led him into the house. When Daphnis and Chloe saw each other, they nearly fainted for joy: however, they managed to keep on their feet, and greeted and saluted each other : and this helped to prevent them from falling.

Thus Daphnis, having, beyond all expectation, both seen and kissed Chloe, took a seat near the fire, and laid upon the table the doves and blackbirds with which his shoulders were burdened. He told them how, weary of being obliged to stay at home, he had set out to catch birds, and how he had trapped them with snares and birdlime, owing to their greediness for myrtle and ivy - berries. They praised his activity, and pressed him to eat some of what the dog had left. Chloe was bidden to pour out wine for them to drink, which she gladly did. She served all the rest first, reserving Daphnis for the last: for she pretended to be angry

Δάφνιδι μετὰ τοὺς ἄλλους· ἐσκήπτετο γὰρ ὀργίζεσθαι διότι ἐλθὼν, ἔμελλεν ἀποτρέχειν οὐκ ἰδών. Ὅμως μέντοι πρὶν προσενεγκεῖν, ἀπέπιεν, εἶθ' οὕτως ἔδωκεν. Ὁ δὲ, καίτοι διψῶν, βραδέως ἔπινε, παρέχων ἑαυτῷ διὰ τῆς βραδυτῆτος μακροτέραν ἡδονήν.

Ἡ μὲν δὴ τράπεζα ταχέως ἐγένετο κενὴ ἄρτων καὶ κρεῶν· καθήμενοι δὲ περὶ τῆς Μυρτάλης καὶ τοῦ Λάμωνος ἐπυνθάνοντο, καὶ εὐδαιμόνιζον αὐτοὺς τοιούτου γηροτρόφου εὐτυχήσαντας. Καὶ τοῖς ἐπαίνοις μὲν ἥδετο, Χλόης ἀκρωμένης· ὅτε δὲ κατεῖχον αὐτὸν, ὡς θύσοντες Διονύσῳ τῆς ἐπιούσης ἡμέρας, μικροῦ δεῖν ὑφ' ἡδονῆς ἐκείνους ἀντὶ τοῦ Διονύσου προσεκύνησεν. Αὐτίκα οὖν ἐκ τῆς πήρας προεκόμιζε μελιττώματα πολλὰ, καὶ τοὺς θηραθέντας δὲ τῶν ὀρνίθων· καὶ τούτους ἐς τράπεζαν νυκτερινὴν ηὐτρέπιζον. Δεύτερος κρατὴρ ἵστατο, καὶ δεύτερον πῦρ ἀνεκάετο. Καὶ ταχὺ μάλα νυκτὸς γενομένης, δευτέρας

with him because, having come so far, he was on the point of going home without seeing her. However, before she offered him the cup, she dipped her lips into it, and then gave it to him: and he, although very thirsty, drank the contents slowly, in order to make the pleasure last longer.

The bread and meat soon disappeared from the table: then, remaining seated, his hosts began to ask him about Myrtale and Lamon, at the same time congratulating them upon having such a support in their old age. Daphnis was delighted at their commendation, since Chloe heard them: but when they invited him to stay until the following day, when they intended to offer sacrifice to Dionysus, he was ready to fall down and worship them in place of the God. He immediately pulled out the honey-cakes from his wallet and all the birds which he had caught: and they got them ready for the evening meal. A second goblet was prepared, and the fire relighted: and, when it was night, they sat down to another hearty meal. After this they sang

τραπέζης ἐνεφοροῦντο· μεθ' ἢν τὰ μὲν μυθο-
λογήσαντες, τὰ δὲ ᾄσαντες, εἰς ὕπνον ἐχώρουν,
Χλόη μετὰ τῆς μητρὸς, Δρύας ἅμα Δάφνιδι.
Χλόῃ μὲν οὖν οὐδὲν χρηστὸν ἦν, ὅτι μὴ τῆς
ἐπιούσης ἡμέρας ὀφθησόμενος ὁ Δάφνις· Δάφνις
δὲ κενὴν τέρψιν ἐτέρπετο· τερπνὸν γὰρ ἐνόμιζε καὶ πατρὶ συγκοιμηθῆναι Χλόης· ὥστε καὶ
περιέβαλλεν αὐτὸν, καὶ κατεφίλει πολλάκις
ταῦτα πάντα ποιεῖν Χλόην ὀνειροπολούμενος.

Ὡς ἐγένετο ἡμέρα, κρύος μὲν ἦν ἐξαίσιον
καὶ αὖρα βόρειος ὑπέκᾳε πάντα. Οἱ δὲ ἀναστάντες, θύουσι τῷ Διονύσῳ κριὸν ἐνιαύσιον·
καὶ πῦρ ἀνακαύσαντες μέγα, παρεσκευάζοντο
τροφήν. Τῆς οὖν Νάπης ἀρτοποιούσης, καὶ
τοῦ Δρύαντος τὸν κριὸν ἕψοντος, σχολῆς ὁ
Δάφνις καὶ ἡ Χλόη λαβόμενοι, προῆλθον τῆς
αὐλῆς ἵνα ὁ κιττός· καὶ πάλιν βρόχους στήσαντες, καὶ ἰξὸν ἐπαλείψαντες, ἐθήρων πλῆθος
οὐκ ὀλίγον ὀρνίθων. Ἦν δὲ αὐτοῖς καὶ φιλη-
μάτων ἀπόλαυσις συνεχὴς, καὶ λόγων ὁμιλία
τερπνή· "Διὰ σὲ ἦλθον, Χλόη.—Οἶδα, Δάφνι.

and told stories, and then went to bed, Chloe with her mother, and Daphnis with Dryas. Chloe thought of nothing but the happiness of seeing Daphnis on the following day; while Daphnis satisfied himself with an idle enjoyment : he thought it happiness even to sleep with Chloe's father, clasped him in his arms, and kissed him again and again, dreaming that he was kissing and embracing Chloe.

At daybreak, it was bitterly cold, and a north wind was nipping everything. The family got up, and having sacrificed a year-old ram to Dionysus, lighted a large fire, and made preparations for a meal. While Nape was making the bread, and Dryas cooking the meat, Daphnis and Chloe, being left to themselves, retired to the ivy-bower in front of the yard, where they again set up the nets and smeared the twigs with birdlime, and caught a large number of birds. In the meantime, they continually kissed each other and held delightful converse.

"It was for your sake that I came, dear Chloe." "I know it, Daphnis." "It is

11

Διὰ σὲ ἀπολλύω τοὺς ἀθλίους κοψίχους· τίς
οὖν σοι γίνομαι; Μέμνησό μου.—Μνημονεύω,
νὴ τὰς Νύμφας, ἃς ὤμοσά ποτε εἰς ἐκεῖνο τὸ
ἄντρον, εἰς ὃ ἤξομεν εὐθὺς ἂν ἡ χιὼν τακῇ.
᾽Αλλὰ πολλή ἐστι, Χλόη, καὶ δέδοικα μὴ ἐγὼ
πρὸ ταύτης τακῶ.—Θάρρει, Δάφνι· θερμός
ἐστιν ὁ ἥλιος. Εἰ γὰρ οὕτως γένοιτο, Χλόη,
θερμὸς, ὡς τὸ κᾶον πῦρ τὴν καρδίαν τὴν ἐμήν.
Παίζεις ἀπατῶν με.—Οὐ μὰ τὰς αἶγας ἃς σύ
με ἐκέλευες ὀμνύειν."

Ταῦτα ἀντιφωνήσασα πρὸς τὸν Δάφνιν ἡ
Χλόη καθάπερ ἠχὼ, καλούντων αὐτοὺς τῶν
περὶ τὴν Νάπην, εἰσέδραμον, πολὺ περιττο-
τέραν τῆς χθιζῆς θήραν κομίζοντες· καὶ ἀπαρ-
ξάμενοι τῷ Διονύσῳ κρατῆρος, ἤσθιον, κιττῷ
τὰς κεφαλὰς ἐστεφανωμένοι. Καὶ ἐπεὶ καιρὸς
ἦν, ἰακχάσαντες καὶ εὐάσαντες, προέπεμπον τὸν
Δάφνιν, πλήσαντες αὐτοῦ τὴν πήραν κρεῶν καὶ
ἄρτων. ῎Εδωκαν δὲ καὶ τὰς φάττας καὶ τὰς
κίχλας Λάμωνι καὶ Μυρτάλῃ κομίζειν, ὡς αὐτοὶ

for your sake that I am destroying these poor birds. What then am I to you? Do not forget me." "I do not forget you, I swear by the Nymphs whom I formerly invoked as the witnesses of my oath in the grotto, whither we will soon return, as soon as the snow melts." "It lies very deep, Chloe: I am afraid that I myself shall melt first." "Courage, Daphnis: the sun is hot." "Would that it were as hot as the fire which consumes my heart.' "You are laughing at me and trying to deceive me." "No, I swear it by the goats, by which you bade me swear."

While Chloe was thus answering Daphnis, like an echo, Nape called them. They ran into the house with their catch, which was much larger than that of the previous day. After they had poured libations to Dionysus, they ate, crowned with garlands of ivy. Then, when the time came, after they had celebrated the praises of Bacchus and chanted Evoe, Dryas and Nape sent Daphnis on his way, having first filled his wallet with bread and meat. They also gave him

θηράσοντες ἄλλοτε ἄλλας, ἔστ' ἂν ὁ χειμὼν
μένῃ, καὶ ὁ κιττὸς μὴ λείπῃ. Ὁ δὲ ἀπῄει,
φιλήσας αὐτοὺς προτέρους Χλόης, ἵνα τὸ
ἐκείνης φίλημα καθαρὸν μείνῃ. Καὶ ἄλλας δὲ
πολλὰς ἦλθεν ὁδοὺς ἐπ' ἄλλαις τέχναις· ὥστε
μὴ παντάπασιν αὐτοῖς γενέσθαι τὸν χειμῶνα
ἀνέραστον.

Ἤδη δὲ ἦρος ἀρχομένου, καὶ τῆς μὲν χιόνος
λυομένης, τῆς δὲ γῆς γυμνουμένης, καὶ τῆς πόας
ὑπανθούσης, οἵ τε ἄλλοι νομεῖς ἦγον τὰς
ἀγέλας εἰς νομὴν, καὶ πρὸ τῶν ἄλλων Χλόη
καὶ Δάφνις, οἷα μείζονι δουλεύοντες ποιμένι.
Εὐθὺς οὖν δρόμος ἦν ἐπὶ τὰς Νύμφας καὶ τὸ
ἄντρον· ἐντεῦθεν ἐπὶ τὸν Πᾶνα καὶ τὴν πίτυν·
εἶτα ἐπὶ τὴν δρῦν, ὑφ' ἣν καθίζοντες καὶ τὰς
ἀγέλας ἔνεμον καὶ ἀλλήλους κατεφίλουν.
Ἀνεζήτησάν τε καὶ ἄνθη, στεφανῶσαι θέλοντες
τοὺς θεούς· τὰ δὲ ἄρτι ὁ Ζέφυρος τρέφων καὶ
ὁ ἥλιος θερμαίνων ἐξῆγεν· ὅμως δὲ εὑρέθη καὶ
ἴα καὶ νάρκισσος, καὶ ἀναγαλλὶς, καὶ ὅσα

the wood-pigeons and thrushes to take to
Lamon and Myrtale, since they knew that
they would be able to catch as many as
they wanted, as long as the winter and
the ivy-berries lasted. Then Daphnis departed, after kissing them all—Chloe last,
that her kiss might remain pure and without alloy. He afterwards found several
fresh excuses for returning, so that they
did not pass the winter entirely deprived
of the joys of love.

With the commencement of spring the
snow began to melt, the earth again became visible, and the green grass sprouted.
The shepherds again drove their flocks
into the fields, Daphnis and Chloe first of
all, since they served a mightier shepherd.
They ran first to the grotto of the
Nymphs, then to the pine tree and the
image of Pan, and after that to the oak,
under which they sat down, watching their
flocks and kissing each other. Then, to
weave chaplets for the Gods, they went in
search of some flowers, which were only just
beginning to blossom under the fostering
influence of Zephyr and the warmth of the

ἦρος πρωτοφορήματα. Ἡ μὲν Χλόη καὶ ὁ
Δάφνις ἀπὸ αἰγῶν καὶ ἀπὸ οἴων τινῶν γάλα
νέον, καὶ τοῦτο, στεφανοῦντες τὰ ἀγάλματα,
κατέσπεισαν. Ἀπήρξαντο καὶ σύριγγος, καθάπερ τὰς ἀηδόνας ἐς τὴν μουσικὴν ἐρεθίζοντες·
αἱ δὲ ὑπεφθέγγοντο ἐν ταῖς λόχμαις, καὶ τὸν
Ἴτυν κατ' ὀλίγον ἠκρίβουν, ὥσπερ ἀναμιμνη-
σκόμεναι τῆς ᾠδῆς ἐκ μακρᾶς σιωπῆς.

Ἐβληχήσατό που καὶ ποίμνιον· ἐσκίρτησάν
που καὶ ἄρνες, καὶ ταῖς μητράσιν ὑποκλάσαντες
αὑτούς, τὴν θηλὴν ἔσπασαν· τὰς δὲ μήπω
τετοκυίας οἱ κριοὶ καταδιώκοντες, καὶ κάτω
στήσαντες, ἔβαινον ἄλλος ἄλλην. Ἐγίνοντο
καὶ τράγων διώγματα, καὶ ἐς τὰς αἶγας ἐρωτι-
κώτερα πηδήματα, καὶ ἐμάχοντο περὶ τῶν
αἰγῶν· καὶ ἕκαστος εἶχεν ἰδίας, καὶ ἐφύλαττε
μή τις αὐτὰς μοιχεύσῃ λαθών. Καὶ γέροντας
ὁρῶντας ἐξώρμησεν εἰς ἀφροδίτην τὰ τοιαῦτα
θεάματα· οἱ δέ, καὶ νέοι, καὶ σφριγῶντες, καὶ
πολὺν ἤδη χρόνον ἔρωτα ζητοῦντες, ἐξεκάοντο
πρὸς τὰ ἀκούσματα, καὶ ἐτήκοντο πρὸς τὰ

sun : however, they found some violets, hyacinths, pimpernel, and other flowers of early spring. After they had drunk some new milk drawn from the sheep and goats, they crowned the images, and poured libations. Then they began to play upon their pipes, as if challenging to song the nightingales, which were warbling in the thickets and gradually perfecting their lamentation for Itys, as if anxious, after long silence, to recall their strains.

The sheep began to bleat, the lambs gamboled, or stooped under their mothers' bellies to suck their teats. The rams chased the sheep which had not yet borne young, and mounted them. The he-goats also chased the she-goats with even greater heat, leaped amorously upon them, and fought for them. Each had his own mate, and jealously guarded her against the attacks of a wanton rival. At this sight even old men would have felt the fire of love rekindled within them : the more so Daphnis and Chloe, who were young and tortured by desire, and had long been in quest of the delights of love. All that they

θεάματα, καὶ ἐζήτουν καὶ αὐτοὶ περιττότερόν
τι φιλήματος καὶ περιβολῆς, καὶ μάλιστα δὲ
ὁ Δάφνις. Οἷα γοῦν ἐνηβήσας τῇ κατὰ τὸν
χειμῶνα οἰκουρίᾳ καὶ ἀσχολίᾳ, πρός τε τὰ
φιλήματα ὥργα, καὶ πρὸς τὰς περιβολὰς
ἐσκιτάλιζε, καὶ ἦν ἐς πᾶν ἔργον περιεργότερος
καὶ θρασύτερος.

Ἦτει δὴ τὴν Χλόην χαρίσασθαί οἱ πᾶν
ὅσον βούλεται, καὶ γυμνὴν γυμνῷ συγκατακλιθῆναι μακρότερον ἢ πρόσθεν εἰώθεσαν·
τοῦτο γὰρ δὴ λείπειν τοῖς Φιλητᾶ παιδεύ-
μασιν, ἵνα δὴ γένηται τὸ μόνον ἔρωτα παῦον
φάρμακον. Τῆς δὲ πυνθανομένης τί πλέον
ἐστὶ φιλήματος καὶ περιβολῆς, καὶ αὐτῆς
κατακλίσεως, καὶ τί ἔγνω δρᾶσαι γυμνὸς γυμνῇ
ἐγκατακλινείς· "Τοῦτο, εἶπεν, ὃ οἱ κριοὶ
ποιοῦσι τὰς οἶς, καὶ οἱ τράγοι τὰς αἶγας.
Ὁρᾷς ὡς μετὰ τοῦτο τὸ ἔργον, οὔτε ἐκεῖναι
ἔτι φεύγουσιν αὐτούς, οὔτε ἐκεῖνοι κάμνουσι
διώκοντες, ἀλλ' ὥσπερ κοινῆς λοιπὸν ἀπο-

heard inflamed them, all that they saw
melted them, and they longed for something more than mere embraces and kisses,
but especially Daphnis, who, having spent
the winter in the house doing nothing,
kissed Chloe fiercely, pressed her wantonly
in his arms, and showed himself in every
respect more curious and audacious.

He begged her to grant him all he desired, and to lie with him naked longer
than they had been accustomed to do:
" This," said he, " is the only one of
Philetas's instructions that we have not
yet followed, the only remedy that can
appease Love." When Chloe asked him
what else there could be besides kisses,
embraces, and lying together, and what
he meant to do, if they both lay naked
together, he replied: " The same as the
rams and the he-goats do to their mates.
You see how, after this has been accomplished, the former no longer pursue the
latter, nor the latter flee from the former:
but, from that moment, they feed quietly
together, as if they had enjoyed the same
pleasure in common. This pastime, me-

λαύοντες ἡδονῆς συννέμονται. Γλυκύ τι, ὡς
ἔοικεν, ἔστι τὸ ἔργον, καὶ νικᾷ τὸ ἔρωτος
πικρόν.—Εἶτ' οὐχ ὁρᾷς, ὦ Δάφνι, τὰς αἶγας,
καὶ τοὺς κριοὺς, καὶ τοὺς τράγοις, καὶ τὰς οἶς,
ὡς ὀρθοὶ μὲν ἐκεῖνοι δρῶσιν, ὀρθαὶ δὲ ἐκεῖναι
πάσχουσιν· οἱ μὲν, πηδήσαντες, αἱ δὲ, κατα-
νωτισάμεναι; Σὺ δέ με ἀξιοῖς συγκατακλιθῆναι,
καὶ ταῦτα γυμνήν; Καίτοι γε ἐκεῖναι πόσον
ἐνδεδυμένης ἐμοῦ λασιώτεραι; " Πείθεται
Δάφνις, καὶ συγκατακλινεὶς αὐτῇ, πολὺν
χρόνον ἔκειτο, καὶ οὐδὲν ὧν ἕνεκα ὤργα, ποιεῖν
ἐπιστάμενος, ἀνίστησιν αὐτὴν, καὶ κατόπιν
περιεφύετο μιμούμενος τοὺς τράγοις. Πολὺ
δὲ μᾶλλον ἀπορηθεὶς, καθίσας ἔκλαυσεν, εἰ καὶ
κριῶν ἀμαθέστερος εἰς τὰ ἔρωτος ἔργα.

Ἦν δὲ τις αὐτῷ γείτων, γεωργὸς γῆς ἰδίας,
Χρῶμις τὸ ὄνομα, παρηβῶν ἤδη τὸ σῶμα.
Τούτῳ γυναίκιον ἦν ἐπακτὸν ἐξ ἄστεος, νέον
καὶ ὡραῖον, καὶ ἀγροικίας ἁβρότερον· τούτῳ
Λυκαίνιον ὄνομα ἦν. Αὕτη ὁρῶσα τὸν Δάφνιν

thinks, is something sweet, which can overcome the bitterness of love." "But," answered Chloe, "do you not see that he-goats and she-goats, rams and sheep, all satisfy their desire standing upright: the males leap upon the females, who receive them on their backs? You ask me to lie down with you naked: but see how much thicker their fleece is than my garments." Daphnis obeyed, lay down by her side, and held her for a long time clasped in his arms: but, not knowing how to do what he was burning to do, he made her get up, and embraced her behind, in imitation of the he-goats, but with even less success: then, utterly at a loss what to do, he sat down on the ground and began to weep at the idea of being more ignorant of the mysteries of love than the rams.

In the neighbourhood there dwelt a labourer named Chromis, already advanced in years, who farmed his own estate. He had a wife whom he had brought from the city, young, beautiful, and more refined than the countrywomen: her name was

καθ' ἑκάστην ἡμέραν παρελαύνοντα τὰς αἶγας
ἔωθεν εἰς νομὴν, νύκτωρ ἐκ νομῆς, ἐπεθύμησεν
ἐραστὴν κτήσασθαι δώροις δελεάσασα. Καὶ
δή ποτε λοχήσασα μόνον, καὶ σύριγγα δῶρον
ἔδωκε, καὶ μέλι ἐν κηρίῳ, καὶ πήραν ἐλάφου.
Εἰπεῖν δὲ τι ὤκνει, τὸν Χλόης ἔρωτα κατα-
μαντευομένη· πάνυ γὰρ ἑώρα προσκείμενον
αὐτὸν τῇ κόρῃ. Πρότερον μὲν οὖν ἐκ νευμάτων
καὶ γέλωτος συνεβάλετο τοῦτο· τότε δὲ ἐξ
ἑωθινοῦ σκηψαμένη πρὸς Χρῶμιν ὡς παρὰ
τίκτουσαν ἄπεισι γείτονα, κατόπιν αὐτοῖς
κατηκολούθησε, καὶ εἴς τινα λόχμην ἐγκρύ-
ψασα ἑαυτὴν, ὡς μὴ βλέποιτο, πάντα ἤκουσεν ὅσα εἶπον, πάντα εἶδεν ὅσα ἔπραξαν· οὐκ
ἔλαθεν αὐτὴν οὐδὲ κλαύσας ὁ Δάφνις. Συν-
αλγήσασα δὴ τοῖς ἀθλίοις, καὶ καιρὸν ἥκειν
νομίσασα διττὸν, τὸν μὲν εἰς ἐκείνων σωτηρίαν,
τὸν δὲ εἰς τὴν ἑαυτῆς ἐπιθυμίαν, ἐπιτεχνᾶταί
τι τοιόνδε.

Τῆς ἐπιούσης ὡς παρὰ τὴν γυναῖκα Λάβα[1] τὴν

---

[1] The reading is uncertain here.

Lycaenium. Every morning she saw
Daphnis driving his goats to pasture, and
back again at night. She was seized with
a desire of winning him for her lover by
presents. Having watched until he was
alone, she gave him a pipe, a honeycomb,
and a deer-skin wallet, but she was afraid
to say anything, suspecting his love for
Chloe. For she had observed that he was
devoted to the girl, although hitherto she
had only guessed his affection from having
seen them interchange nods and smiles.
One day, in the morning, making the
excuse to Chromis that she was going to
visit a neighbour who had been brought
to bed, she followed them, concealed herself in a thicket to avoid being seen, and
heard all they said, and saw all they did.
Even Daphnis's tears did not escape her.
Pitying the poor young couple, and thinking that she had a two-fold opportunity—
of getting them out of their trouble and,
at the same time, satisfying her own
desires, she had recourse to the following
stratagem.

The next day, having gone out again on

τίκτουσαν ἀπιοῦσα, φανερῶς ἐπὶ τὴν δρῦν ὑφ' ᾗ
ἐκαθέζετο. Δάφνις καὶ Χλόη, παραγίνεται, καὶ
ἀκριβῶς μιμησαμένη τὴν τεταραγμένην, "σῶσόν
με, εἶπε, Δάφνι, τὴν ἀθλίαν· ἐκ γάρ μοι τῶν
χηνῶν τῶν εἴκοσιν ἕνα τὸν κάλλιστον ἀετὸς
ἥρπασε· καὶ, οἷα μέγα φορτίον ἀράμενος, οὐκ
ἐδυνήθη μετέωρος ἐπὶ τὴν συνήθη τὴν ὑψηλὴν
κομίσαι ἐκείνην πέτραν· ἀλλὰ εἰς τήνδε τὴν
ὕλην τὴν ταπεινὴν ἔχων κατέπεσε. Σὺ τοίνυν,
πρὸς τῶν Νυμφῶν καὶ τοῦ Πανὸς ἐκείνου,
εἰσελθὼν εἰς τὴν ὕλην, σῶσόν μου τὸν χῆνα
(μόνη γὰρ δέδοικα εἰσελθεῖν), μηδὲ περιΐδῃς
ἀτελῆ μου τὸν ἀριθμὸν γενόμενον. Τάχα δὲ
καὶ αὐτὸν τὸν ἀετὸν ἀποκτενεῖς, καὶ οὐκ ἔτι
πολλοὺς ὑμῶν ἄρνας καὶ ἐρίφους ἁρπάσει. Τὴν
δὲ ἀγέλην τέως φρουρήσει Χλόη· πάντως αὐτὴν
ἴσασιν αἱ αἶγες ἀεί σοι συννέμουσαν."

Οὐδὲν τῶν μελλόντων ὑποπτεύσας ὁ Δάφνις,
εὐθὺς ἀνίσταται, καὶ ἀράμενος τὴν καλαύροπα,
κατόπιν ἠκολούθει τῇ Λυκαινίῳ. Ἡ δὲ ἡγεῖτο
ὡς μακροτάτω τῆς Χλόης· καὶ ἐπειδὴ κατὰ τὸ

pretence of visiting her sick neighbour, she proceeded straight to the oak under which Daphnis and Chloe were sitting, and, pretending to be in great distress, cried : " Help me, Daphnis : I am most unhappy. An eagle has just carried off the finest of my twenty geese : but, as the burden was a heavy one, he could not carry it up to the top of the rock, his usual refuge, but has alighted with his prey at the end of the wood. In the name of the Nymphs and Pan yonder, I beseech you, go with me into the forest, for I am afraid to go alone : save my goose, and do not leave the number of my flock imperfect. Perhaps you will also be able to slay the eagle, and he will no longer carry off your kids and lambs. Meanwhile, Chloe can look after your goats : they know her as well as you : for you always tend your flocks together."

Daphnis, suspecting nothing of what was to come, immediately got up, took his crook and followed Lycaenium. She took as far from Chloe as possible, and, when they came to the thickest part of the

πυκνότατον ἐγένοντο, πηγῆς πλησίον καθίσαι
κελεύσασα αὐτὸν, " ἐρᾷς, εἶπε, Δάφνι, Χλόης,
καὶ τοῦτο ἔμαθον ἐγὼ νύκτωρ παρὰ τῶν
Νυμφῶν. Δι' ὀνείρατος ἐμοὶ τὰ χθιζά σου
αἱ Νύμφαι διηγήσαντο δάκρυα, καὶ ἐκέλευσάν
σε σῶσαι διδαξαμένην τὰ ἔρωτος ἔργα. Τὰ
δέ ἐστιν οὐ φιλήματα καὶ περιβολὴ, καὶ οἷα
δρῶσι κριοὶ καὶ τράγοι, ἀλλὰ ταῦτα πηδήματα
καὶ τῶν ἐκεῖ γλυκύτερα· πρόσεστι γὰρ αὐτοῖς
χρόνος μακροτέρας ἡδονῆς. Εἰ δή σοι φίλον
ἀπηλλάχθαι κακῶν, καὶ ἐν πείρᾳ γενέσθαι
ζητουμένων τερπνῶν, ἴθι, παραδίδου μοι
τερπνὸν σαυτὸν μαθητήν· ἐγὼ δὲ, χαριζομένη
ταῖς Νύμφαις ἐκείναις, διδάξω."

Οὐκ ἐκαρτέρησεν ὁ Δάφνις ὑφ' ἡδονῆς, ἀλλ'
ἅτε ἄγροικος καὶ αἰπόλος, καὶ ἐρῶν καὶ νέος,
πρὸ τῶν ποδῶν καταπεσὼν, τὴν Λυκαίνιον
ἱκέτευεν ὅτι τάχιστα διδάξαι τὴν τέχνην, δι'
ἧς ὃ βούλεται δράσει Χλόην· καὶ, ὥσπερ τι
μέγα καὶ θεόπεμπτον ἀληθῶς μέλλων διδά-
σκεσθαι, καὶ ἔριφον αὐτῇ δώσειν ἐπηγγείλατο

forest, she bade him sit down near a fountain, and said: "Daphnis, you are in love with Chloe: the Nymphs revealed this to me last night. They told me in a dream of the tears you shed yesterday, and bade me relieve you of your trouble by teaching you the mysteries of love. These consist not in kisses and embraces alone, or the practices of sheep and goats, but in connexion far more delightful than these: for the pleasure lasts longer. If then you wish to be freed from your troubles and to try the delights of which you are in search, come, put yourself in my hands, a delightful pupil: out of gratitude to the Nymphs, I will be your instructress."

Daphnis, at these words, could no longer contain himself for joy: but, being a simple countryman and goatherd, young and amorous, he threw himself at her feet and begged her to teach him without delay the art which would enable him to do to Chloe what he desired: and, as if it had been some profound and heaven-sent secret, he promised to give her a kid

καὶ τυροὺς ἁπαλοὺς πρωτορρύτου γάλακτος,
καὶ τὴν αἶγα αὐτήν. Εὑροῦσα δὴ ἡ Λυκαίνιον
αἰπολικὴν ἀφθονίαν οἵαν οὐ προσεδόκησεν,
ἤρχετο παιδεύειν τὸν Δάφνιν, τοῦτον τὸν
τρόπον. Ἐκέλευσεν αὐτὸν καθίσαι πλησίον
αὐτῆς ὡς ἔχει, καὶ φιλήματα φιλεῖν οἷα εἰώθει
καὶ ὅσα, φιλοῦντα ἅμα καὶ περιβάλλειν καὶ
κατακλίνεσθαι χαμαί. Ὡς δὲ ἐκαθέσθη, καὶ
ἐφίλησε, καὶ κατεκλίθη, μαθοῦσα ἐνεργεῖν
δυνάμενον καὶ σφριγῶντα, ἀπὸ μὲν τῆς ἐπὶ
πλευρὰν κατακλίσεως ἀνίστησιν· αὐτὴν δὲ
ὑποστορέσασα ἐντέχνως, ἐς τὴν τέως ζητου-
μένην ὁδὸν ἦγε· τὸ δὲ ἐντεῦθεν οὐδὲν περι-
ηγάγετο ξένον· αὐτὴ γὰρ ἡ φύσις λοιπὸν
ἐπαίδευε τὸ πρακτέον.

Τελεσθείσης δὲ τῆς ἐρωτικῆς παιδαγωγίας,
ὁ μὲν Δάφνις ἔτι ποιμενικὴν ἔχων γνώμην,
ὥρμησε τρέχειν ἐπὶ τὴν Χλόην, καὶ ὅσα ἐπε-
παίδευτο, δρᾶν αὐτίκα, καθάπερ δεδοικὼς μὴ
βραδύνας ἐπιλάθοιτο· ἡ δὲ Λυκαίνιον κατα-
σχοῦσα αὐτὸν, ἔλεξεν ὧδε· "Ἔτι καὶ ταῦτα

lately weaned, fresh cheeses made of new milk, and even the mother herself. Lycaenium seeing, from his generous offer, that Daphnis was more simple than she had imagined, began to instruct him in the following manner. She ordered him to sit down by her side just as he was, and to kiss her as he had been accustomed to kiss Chloe, and, while kissing, to embrace her and lie down by her side. When he had done so, Lycaenium, finding that he was ready for action and inflamed with desire, lifted him up a little, and, cleverly slipping under him, set him on the road he had sought so long in vain: and, without more ado, Nature herself taught him the rest.

When this lesson in the mysteries of Love was finished, Daphnis, still as simple as before, would have hastened at once to Chloe, to teach her all that he had learnt, for fear of forgetting it, if he delayed. But Lycaenium stopped him, and said: "There is something else you must know, Daphnis: I am a woman, and you have not hurt me: for, long ago, another man taught me

δεῖ σε μαθεῖν, ὦ Δάφνι· ἐγὼ γυνὴ τυγχάνουσα
πέπονθα νῦν οὐδέν· πάλαι γάρ με ταῦτα ἀνὴρ
ἄλλος ἐπαίδευσε, μισθὸν τὴν παρθενίαν λαβών·
Χλόη δὲ συμπαλαίουσά σοι ταύτην τὴν πάλην,
καὶ οἰμώξει, καὶ κλαύσεται, καὶ αἵματι κείσεται
πολλῷ, καθάπερ πεφονευμένη. Ἀλλὰ σὺ τὸ
αἷμα μὴ φοβηθῇς· ἀλλ' ἡνίκα ἂν πείσῃς αὐτήν
σοι παρασχεῖν, ἄγαγε αὐτὴν εἰς τοῦτο τὸ
χωρίον, ἵνα κἂν βοήσῃ, μηδεὶς ἀκούσῃ, κἂν
δακρύσῃ, μηδεὶς ἴδῃ, κἂν αἱμαχθῇ, λούσηται
τῇ πηγῇ· καὶ μέμνησο ὅτι σε ἄνδρα ἐγὼ πρὸ
Χλόης πεποίηκα."

Ἡ μὲν οὖν Λυκαίνιον τοσαῦτα ὑποθεμένη,
κατ' ἄλλο μέρος τῆς ὕλης ἀπῆλθεν, ὡς ἔτι
ζητοῦσα τὸν χῆνα· ὁ δὲ Δάφνις εἰς λογισμὸν
ἄγων τὰ εἰρημένα, τῆς μὲν προτέρας ὁρμῆς
ἀπήλλακτο, διοχλεῖν δὲ τῇ Χλόῃ περιττότερον
ὤκνει φιλήματος καὶ περιβολῆς, μήτε βοῆσαι
θέλων αὐτὴν, ὡς πρὸς πολέμιον, μήτε δακρύσαι,
ὡς ἀλγοῦσαν, μήτε αἱμαχθῆναι, καθάπερ πεφο-

what I have just taught you, and took my maidenhead as his reward. But Chloe, when she enters upon this struggle with you for the first time, will weep and cry out, and will bleed as if she had been wounded. But you need not be afraid at the sight of the blood : when you have persuaded her to yield to your desire, bring her here, where, if she cries, no one can hear her; if she weeps, no one can see her; if she bleeds, she can wash herself in the spring. And never forget that I made you a man before Chloe."

After she had given him this advice, Lycaenium went off to another part of the wood, as if she was still looking for her goose. Daphnis, thinking over what she had said, felt his passion somewhat cooled, and hesitated to press Chloe to grant him anything more than kisses and embraces. He did not wish to make her cry out, as if she was being attacked by an enemy, or to make her weep, as if she were in pain, or to make her bleed, as if she had been wounded : for, being a novice

νευμένην· ἀρτιμαθὴς γὰρ ὢν ἐδεδοίκει τὸ αἷμα,
καὶ ἐνόμιζεν ὅτι ἄρα ἐκ μόνου τραύματος αἷμα
γίνεται. Γνοὺς δὲ τὰ συνήθη τέρπεσθαι μετ᾽
αὐτῆς, ἐξέβη τῆς ὕλης· καὶ ἐλθὼν ἵνα ἐκάθητο
στεφανίσκον ἴων πλέκουσα, τόν τε χῆνα τῶν
τοῦ ἀετοῦ ὀνύχων ἐψεύσατο ἐξαρπάσαι, καὶ
περιθεὶς ἐφίλησεν, οἷον ἐν τῇ τέρψει Λυκαίνιον·
τοῦτο γὰρ ἐξῆν ὡς ἀκίνδυνον. Ἡ δὲ τὸν στέφανον ἐφήομοσεν αὐτοῦ τῇ κεφαλῇ, καὶ τὴν
κόμην ἐφίλησεν, ὡς τῶν ἴων κρείττονα. Καὶ
πήρας προκομίσασα παλάθης μοῖραν, καὶ ἄρτους τινὰς, ἔδωκε φαγεῖν· καὶ ἐσθίοντος ἀπὸ
τοῦ στόματος ἥρπαζε, καὶ οὕτως ἤσθιεν ὥσπερ
νεοττὸς ὄρνιθος.

Ἐσθιόντων αὐτῶν καὶ περιττότερον φιλούν-
των ὧν ἤσθιον, ναῦς ἁλιέων ὤφθη παραπλέουσα.
Ἄνεμος μὲν οὐκ ἦν, γαλήνη δὲ ἦν, καὶ ἐρέττειν
ἐδόκει. Καὶ ἤρεττον ἐῤῥωμένως· ἠπείγοντο
γὰρ νεαλεῖς ἰχθῦς εἰς τὴν πόλιν διασώσασθαι
τῶν τινὶ πλουσίων. Οἷον οὖν εἰώθασι ναῦται

in the art of love, he was afraid of this blood, thinking it impossible that it could proceed from anything but a wound. He accordingly left the wood, resolved to enjoy himself with her in the usual way, and, when he reached the place where she was sitting weaving a chaplet of violets, he pretended that he had rescued the goose from the eagle's claws : then he embraced and kissed her, as he had kissed Lycaenium while they toyed together : for this at least he thought was free from danger. Chloe crowned his head with the chaplet, and kissed his hair, which smelt sweeter to her than the violets : then she took out of her wallet a piece of fruit-cake and some bread and gave him to eat : and, while he was eating, she would snatch a morsel from his mouth, and eat it, just like a young bird pecking from its mother's beak.

While they were eating, and were even more busily engaged in kissing each other, a fishing-boat came in sight proceeding along the coast. There was no wind, and the sea was calm : wherefore the crew decided to use their oars, and rowed on

ὁρᾶν εἰς καμάτων ἀμέλειαν, τοῦτο κἀκεῖνοι
ὁρῶντες, τὰς κώπας ἀνέφερον. Εἷς μὲν αὐτοῖς
κελευστὴς ναυτικὰς ᾖδεν ᾠδάς· οἱ δὲ λοιποί,
καθάπερ χορὸς, ὁμοφώνως κατὰ καιρὸν τῆς
ἐκείνου φωνῆς ἐβόων. Ἡνίκα μὲν οὖν ἀνα-
πεπταμένῃ τῇ θαλάττῃ ταῦτα ἔπραττον, ἠφα-
νίζετο ἡ βοὴ, χεομένης τῆς φωνῆς εἰς πολὺν
ἀέρα· ἐπεὶ δὲ ἄκρᾳ τινὶ ὑποδραμόντες, εἰς
κόλπον μηνοειδῆ καὶ κοῖλον εἰσήλασαν, μείζων
μὲν ἠκούετο βοὴ, σαφῆ δὲ ἐξέπιπτεν εἰς τὴν γῆν
τὰ τῶν κελευσμάτων ᾄσματα. Κοῖλος γὰρ τῷ
πεδίῳ αὐλὼν ὑποκείμενος, καὶ τὸν ἦχον εἰς αὑτὸν
ὡς ὄργανον δεχόμενος, πάντων τῶν λεγομένων
μιμητὴν φωνὴν ἀπεδίδου, ἰδίᾳ μὲν τῶν κωπῶν
τὸν ἦχον, ἰδίᾳ δὲ τὴν φωνὴν τῶν ναυτῶν· καὶ
ἐγίνετο ἄκουσμα τερπνόν. Φθανούσης τῆς
ἀπὸ τῆς θαλάττης φωνῆς, ἡ ἐκ τῆς γῆς φωνὴ
τοσοῦτον ἐπαύετο βράδιον, ὅσον ἤρξατο.

Ὁ μὲν οὖν Δάφνις εἰδὼς τὸ πραττόμενον,
μόνῃ τῇ θαλάττῃ προσεῖχε. Καὶ ἐτέρπετο

vigorously, for they were taking some fish that they had just caught to one of the wealthy citizens. After the custom of sailors, in order to lighten their toil, one of them sang a song of the sea, which regulated the movement of the oars, while the rest, like a chorus, joined in with the singer at intervals. As long as they were in the open sea, their song was but faintly heard, since their voices were lost in the expanse of air : but when they ran under a promontory, or entered a deep crescent-shaped bay, their voices sounded louder, and the refrain of their song was heard more distinctly on the land : for the bottom of the bay terminated in a hollow valley, which received the sound like a musical instrument, and gave back an echo which represented separately the plash of the oars and the voice of the singers, delightful to hear : for, when one sound came from the sea, the answering echo from the land took it up, and lasted longer, since it had commenced later.

Daphnis, knowing what it was, had eyes for nothing but the sea. He was delighted

τῇ νηῒ παρατρεχούσῃ τὸ πεδίον θᾶττον πτε-
ροῦ, καὶ ἐπειρᾶτό τινα διασώσασθαι τῶν ᾀσμά-
των, ὡς γένοιτο τῆς σύριγγος μέλη. Ἡ δὲ
Χλόη τότε πρῶτον πειρωμένη τῆς καλουμένης
ἠχοῦς, ποτὲ μὲν εἰς τὴν θάλατταν ἀπέβλεπε,
τῶν ναυτῶν κελευόντων, ποτὲ δὲ εἰς τὴν ὕλην
ὑπέστρεφε, ζητοῦσα τοὺς ἀντιφωνοῦντας. Καὶ
ἐπεὶ παραπλευσάντων ἦν κἂν τῷ αὐλῶνι σιγὴ,
ἐπυνθάνετο τοῦ Δάφνιδος, εἰ καὶ ὀπίσω τῆς
ἄκρας ἐστὶ θάλαττα, καὶ ναῦς ἄλλη παραπλεῖ,
καὶ ἄλλοι ναῦται τὰ αὐτὰ ᾖδον, καὶ ἅμα
πάντες σιωπῶσι. Γελάσας οὖν ὁ Δάφνις ἡδὺ,
καὶ φιλήσας ἥδιον φίλημα, καὶ τὸν τῶν ἴων
στέφανον ἐκείνῃ περιθεὶς, ἤρξατο αὐτῇ μυθο-
λογεῖν τὸν μῦθον τῆς Ἠχοῦς, αἰτήσας, εἰ
διδάξειε, μισθὸν παρ' αὐτῆς ἄλλα φιλήματα
δέκα.

"Νυμφῶν, ὦ κόρη, πολὺ γένος, Μέλιαι,
Δρυάδες καὶ Ἕλειοι· πᾶσαι καλαὶ, πᾶσαι
μουσικαί. Καὶ μιᾶς τούτων θυγάτηρ Ἠχὼ
γίνεται· θνητὴ μὲν, ὡς ἐκ πατρὸς θνητοῦ· καλὴ

at the sight of the boat gliding along the
coast swifter than a bird on the wing, and
endeavoured to catch some of the airs that
he might play them on his pipe. Chloe,
who had never heard an echo before, looked
first towards the sea, while the fishermen
were singing, and then towards the wood,
to see whose voices answered. When the
boat had passed, all was silent in the valley.
Then Chloe asked Daphnis whether there
was another sea behind the promontory, or
another boat with another crew singing
the same strains, and whether they all
ceased singing at once. Then Daphnis
smiled pleasantly, and kissed her more
tenderly : and, placing upon her head the
chaplet of violets, began to tell her the
story of Echo, demanding as his reward
ten kisses more.

"There are several kinds of Nymphs,
my dear Chloe, Nymphs of the forest, of
the woods, and of the meadows : they are
all beautiful, and all skilled in singing.
Echo was the daughter of one of these :
she was mortal, since her father was a
mortal, and beautiful, being born of a

δὲ, ὡς ἐκ μητρὸς καλῆς. Τρέφεται μὲν ὑπὸ
Νυμφῶν, παιδεύεται δὲ ὑπὸ Μουσῶν συρίζειν,
αὐλεῖν, τὰ πρὸς λύραν, τὰ πρὸς κιθάραν,
πᾶσαν ᾠδήν· ὥστε καὶ παρθενίας εἰς ἄνθος
ἀκμάσασα, ταῖς Νύμφαις συνεχόρευε, ταῖς
Μούσαις συνῇδεν· ἄρρενας δὲ ἔφευγε πάντας,
καὶ ἀνθρώπους καὶ θεοὺς, φιλοῦσα τὴν παρθενίαν. Ὁ Πὰν ὀργίζεται τῇ κόρῃ, τῆς
μουσικῆς φθονῶν, τοῦ κάλλους μὴ τυχών·
καὶ μανίαν ἐμβάλλει τοῖς ποιμέσι καὶ τοῖς
αἰπόλοις. Οἱ δὲ, ὥσπερ κύνες, ἢ λύκοι,
διασπῶσιν αὐτὴν, καὶ ῥίπτουσιν εἰς πᾶσαν
γῆν ἔτι ᾄδοντα τὰ μέλη. Καὶ τὰ μέλη Γῆ,
χαριζομένη Νύμφαις, ἔκρυψε πάντα. Καὶ
ἐτήρησε τὴν μουσικὴν, καὶ γνώμῃ Μουσῶν
ἀφίησι φωνὴν, καὶ μιμεῖται πάντα, καθάπερ
τότε ἡ κόρη, θεοὺς, ἀνθρώπους, ὄργανα, θηρία·
μιμεῖται καὶ αὐτὸν συρίττοντα τὸν Πᾶνα. Ὁ
δὲ ἀκούσας, ἀναπηδᾷ καὶ διώκει κατὰ τῶν ὀρῶν,
οὐκ ἐρῶν τυχεῖν ἀλλ' ἢ τοῦ μαθεῖν τίς ἐστιν
ὁ λανθάνων μαθητής." Ταῦτα μυθολογήσαντα

beautiful mother. She was brought up by
the Nymphs, and taught by the Muses to
play on the flute and pipe, the lyre and
the lute, and to sing all kinds of songs:
when she grew up, she danced with the
Nymphs and sang with the Muses: but,
jealous of her virginity, she avoided all
males, both Gods and men. Pan was
incensed against the maiden, being jealous
of her singing, and vexed that he could
not enjoy her beauty. He inspired with
frenzy the shepherds and goatherds, who,
like dogs or wolves, tore the maiden to
pieces, and flung her limbs here and there,
still quivering with song. Earth, out of
respect for the Nymphs, received and hid
them in her bosom, where they still
preserve their gift of song, and, by the
will of the Muses, speak and imitate all
sounds, as the maiden did when alive—
the voices of men and Gods, musical instruments, and the cries of wild beasts: they
even imitate the notes of Pan when playing on his pipe. And he, when he hears
it, springs up and rushes down the mountains, with the sole desire of finding out

τὸν Δάφνιν, οὐ δέκα μόνον φιλήματα, ἀλλὰ
πάνυ πολλὰ κατεφίλησεν ἡ Χλόη· μικροῦ
γὰρ καὶ τὰ αὐτὰ εἶπεν Ἠχώ, καθάπερ μαρτυ-
ροῦσα ὅτι μηδὲν ἐψεύσατο.

Θερμοτέρου δὲ καθ' ἑκάστην ἡμέραν γιγνο-
μένου τοῦ ἡλίου, οἷα τοῦ μὲν ἦρος παυομένου,
τοῦ δὲ θέρους ἀρχομένου, πάλιν αὐτοῖς ἐγίνοντο
καιναὶ τέρψεις καὶ θέρειοι. Ὁ μὲν γὰρ ἐνήχετο
ἐν τοῖς ποταμοῖς, ἡ δὲ ἐν ταῖς πηγαῖς ἐλούετο·
ὁ μὲν ἐσύριξεν, ἁμιλλώμενος πρὸς τὰς πίτυς,
ἡ δὲ ᾖδε, ταῖς ἀηδόσιν ἐρίζουσα. Ἐθήρων
ἀκρίδας λάλους, ἐλάμβανον τέττιγας ἠχοῦντας,
ἄνθη συνέλεγον, δένδρα ἔσειον, ὀπώρας ἤσθιον.
Ἤδη ποτὲ καὶ γυμνοὶ συγκατεκλίθησαν, καὶ
ἓν δέρμα αἰγὸς ἐπεσύραντο. Καὶ ἐγένετο ἂν
γυνὴ Χλόη ῥᾳδίως, εἰ μὴ Δάφνιν ἐτάραξε τὸ
αἷμα. Ἀμέλει καὶ δεδοικὼς μὴ νικηθῇ τὸν
λογισμόν ποτε, πολλὰ γυμνοῦσθαι τὴν Χλόην
οὐκ ἐπέτρεπεν· ὥστε ἐθαύμαζε μὲν ἡ Χλόη,
τὴν δὲ αἰτίαν ᾐδεῖτο πυθέσθαι.

who is the pupil who thus conceals himself." When Daphnis had finished his story, Chloe gave him, not ten, but ten times ten kisses: for Echo had repeated nearly all her words, as if to testify that he had spoken nothing but the truth.

The sun grew daily hotter—for spring was at its close and summer was beginning, and the delights of summer returned to them once more. Daphnis swam in the rivers, Chloe bathed in the springs: he played on the pipe, in rivalry with the rustling of the pines, she emulated the nightingales in her song : they chased the noisy locusts, caught the chirping grasshoppers, plucked the flowers, shook the fruit from the trees and ate it: they even sometimes lay naked together side by side under the same goat-skin. Then Chloe would have soon become a woman, had not Daphnis been deterred by his horror of blood. Often, being afraid that he might not be able to contain himself, he would not allow Chloe to strip: whereat she was astonished, but was too bashful to inquire the reason.

Ἐν τῷ θέρει τῷδε καὶ μνηστήρων πλῆθος ἦν
περὶ τὴν Χλόην, καὶ πολλοὶ πολλαχόθεν ἐφοί-
των παρὰ Δρύαντα, πρὸς γάμον αἰτοῦντες
αὐτήν· καὶ οἱ μέν τι δῶρον ἔφερον, οἱ δὲ ἐπηγ-
γέλλοντο μεγάλα. Ἡ μὲν οὖν Νάπη ταῖς
ἐλπίσιν ἐπαιρομένη, συνεβούλευσεν ἐκδιδόναι
τὴν Χλόην, μηδὲ κατέχειν οἴκοι πρὸς πλέον
τηλικαύτην κόρην, ἣ τάχα μικρὸν ὕστερον
νέμουσα τὴν παρθενίαν ἀπολέσει, καὶ ἄνδρα
ποιήσεταί τινα τῶν ποιμένων ἐπὶ μήλοις ἢ
ῥόδοις· ἀλλ' ἐκείνην τε ποιῆσαι δέσποιναν
οἰκίας, καὶ αὐτοὺς πολλὰ λαβόντας, ἰδίῳ φυλάττειν αὐτὰ καὶ γνησίῳ παιδίῳ· (ἐγεγόνει δὲ
αὐτοῖς ἄρρεν παιδίον οὐ πρὸ πολλοῦ τινος).
Ὁ δὲ Δρύας ποτὲ μὲν ἐθέλγετο τοῖς λεγο-
μένοις· (μείζονα γὰρ ἢ κατὰ ποιμαίνουσαν
κόρην δῶρα ὠνομάζετο παρ' ἑκάστου·) ποτὲ
δὲ ὡς κρείττων ἐστὶν ἡ παρθένος μνηστήρων
γεωργῶν, καὶ ὡς, εἴ ποτε τοὺς ἀληθινοὺς γονέας
εὕροι, μεγάλως αὐτοὺς εὐδαίμονας θήσει, ἀνε-
βάλλετο τὴν ἀπόκρισιν, καὶ εἷλκε χρόνον ἐκ

During this summer, a number of suitors for the hand of Chloe presented themselves, coming from all parts to ask her of Dryas in marriage. Some brought presents, others made lavish promises. Nape, her hopes being thus excited, advised him to let Chloe marry, and not keep a girl of her age at home, who might, at any moment, while tending her flocks, lose her virginity, and bestow herself upon some shepherd for a present of roses or apples : it would be better, said she, to make her mistress of a home and to keep the presents they had received for their own son lately born. Sometimes Dryas felt tempted by these arguments : for each of the suitors made far handsomer offers than might have been expected in the case of a simple shepherdess ; but at other times he came to the conclusion that the girl was too good for a rustic husband, and that, if she ever found her parents again, they might make him and Nape rich. He accordingly put off answering from day to day, receiving in the meantime a considerable number of presents. Chloe, seeing all this, was over-

13

χρόνου, καὶ ἐν τῷ τέως ἀπεκέρδαινεν οὐκ ὀλίγα
δῶρα. Ἡ μὲν δὴ μαθοῦσα, λυπηρῶς πάνυ διῆγε,
καὶ τὸν Δάφνιν ἐλάνθανεν ἐπιπολύ, λυπεῖν οὐ
θέλουσα· ὡς δὲ ἐλιπάρει καὶ ἐνέκειτο πυνθανό-
μενος, καὶ ἐλυπεῖτο μᾶλλον μὴ μανθάνων ἢ
ἔμελλε μαθών, πάντα αὐτῷ διηγεῖται· τοὺς
μνηστευομένους, ὡς πολλοὶ καὶ πλούσιοι, τοὺς
λόγους οὓς ἡ Νάπη σπεύδουσα πρὸς τὸν γάμον
ἔλεγεν, ὡς οὐκ ἀπείπατο Δρύας, ἀλλ' ὡς εἰς τὸν
τρυγητὸν ἀναβέβληται.

Ἔκφρων ἐπὶ τούτοις ὁ Δάφνις γίνεται, καὶ
ἐδάκρυσε καθήμενος, ἀποθανεῖσθαι, μηκέτι νεμούσης Χλόης, λέγων· καὶ οὐκ αὐτὸς μόνος,
ἀλλὰ καὶ τὰ πρόβατα μετὰ τοιοῦτον ποιμένα. Εἶτα ἀνενεγκὼν ἀνεθάρρει, καὶ πείσειν
ἐνενόει τὸν πατέρα, καὶ ἕνα τῶν μνωμένων
αὐτὸν ἠρίθμει, καὶ πολὺ κρατήσειν ἤλπιζε τῶν
ἄλλων. Ἕν αὐτὸν ἐτάραττεν· οὐκ ἦν Λάμων
πλούσιος· τοῦτο αὐτοῦ τὴν ἐλπίδα μόνον

come with grief, which she for a long time
concealed from Daphnis to avoid giving
him pain : but at last, as he importuned
her with questions, and was even more
unhappy than if he knew all, she told him
everything—her numerous and wealthy
suitors, Nape's reasons for hastening on
her marriage, and how Dryas, without
absolutely refusing his consent, had de-
ferred his answer to the next vintage.

When Daphnis heard this, he nearly
went out of his mind : he sat down and
began to weep, declaring that he should
die if Chloe no longer came to tend her
flocks in the fields; and not he alone, but
her sheep also, if they lost such a shepherdess. Then, having recovered himself
a little, he took courage and thought of
asking her father for her hand himself.
He already reckoned himself one of her
suitors, and hoped to be easily preferred
before the rest. One thing alone disturbed
him : Lamon was not rich [and even
though he had been rich, he was not
free]: this alone made his chances slighter.
Nevertheless, he decided to prefer his suit,

λεπτὴν εἰργάζετο. Ὅμως δὲ ἐδόκει μνᾶσθαι,
καὶ τῇ Χλόῃ συνεδόκει. Τῷ Λάμωνι μὲν οὖν
οὐδὲν ἐτόλμησεν εἰπεῖν, τῇ Μυρτάλῃ δὲ
θαρρήσας καὶ τὸν ἔρωτα ἐμήνυσε, καὶ περὶ
τοῦ γάμου λόγους προσήνεγκεν· ἡ δὲ τῷ
Λάμωνι νύκτωρ ἐκοινωνήσατο. Σκληρῶς δὲ
ἐκείνου τὴν ἔντευξιν ἐνεγκόντος, καὶ λοιδορή-
σαντος εἰ παιδὶ θυγάτριον ποιμένων προξενεῖ
μεγάλην ἐν τοῖς γνωρίσμασιν ἐπαγγελλομένῳ
τύχην, ὃς αὐτοὺς, εὑρὼν τοὺς οἰκείους, καὶ
ἐλευθέρους θήσει, καὶ δεσπότας ἀγρῶν μειζόνων,
ἡ Μυρτάλη διὰ ἔρωτα φοβουμένη μὴ τελέως
ἀπελπίσας ὁ Δάφνις τὸν γάμον, τολμήσει τι
θανατῶδες, ἄλλας αὐτῷ τῆς ἀντιρρήσεως αἰτίας
ἐπήγγελλε. "Πένητές ἐσμεν, ὦ παῖ, καὶ δεό-
μεθα νύμφης φερούσης τι μᾶλλον· οἱ δὲ πλούσιοι, καὶ πλουσίων νυμφίων δεόμενοι. Ἴθι δὴ,
πεῖσον Χλόην, ἡ δὲ τὸν πατέρα, μηδὲν αἰτεῖν
μέγα, καὶ γαμεῖν. Πάντως δέ που κἀκείνη

and Chloe approved his resolution. He
did not, however, venture to speak directly
to Lamon, but, feeling bolder with Myrtale,
he told her of his love and spoke to her
of his wish to marry Chloe. At night, she
told Lamon, who was greatly annoyed at
the proposal : he sharply rebuked her for
wanting to marry, to the daughter of a
simple shepherd, a youth who, to judge
from the tokens found with him when he
lay exposed, might look forward to a
higher destiny, and who, if he found his
parents again, might not only grant them
their freedom, but might bestow upon
them a larger estate even than the one on
which they worked. Myrtale, fearing that
Daphnis might do something desperate, or
even take his own life, if he lost all hope
of winning Chloe, gave him other reasons
for Lamon's refusal. " We are poor, my
son," she said to him, " we rather want
a bride who will bring a dowry with her :
while they[1] are wealthy, and seek wealthy
suitors. But, come, persuade Chloe, and let
her try and persuade her father, not to ask
for a large settlement, but to allow you to

[1] Dryas and Nape.

φιλεῖ σε, καὶ βούλεται συγκαθεύδειν πένητι
καλῷ μᾶλλον ἢ πιθήκῳ πλουσίῳ."

Μυρτάλη μὲν οὔποτε ἐλπίσασα Δρύαντα
τούτοις συντεθήσεσθαι, μνηστῆρας ἔχοντα
πλουσιωτέρους, εὐπρεπῶς ᾤετο παρῃτῆσθαι
τὸν γάμον· Δάφνις δὲ οὐκ εἶχε μέμφεσθαι τὰ
λελεγμένα· λειπόμενος δὲ πολὺ τῶν αἰτου-
μένων, τὸ σύνηθες ἐρασταῖς πενομένοις ἔπρατ-
τεν· ἐδάκρυε, καὶ τὰς Νύμφας αὖθις ἐκάλει
βοηθούς. Αἱ δὲ αὐτῷ καθεύδοντι νύκτωρ ἐν
τοῖς αὐτοῖς ἐφίστανται σχήμασιν, ἐν οἷς δὲ
πρότερον. Ἔλεγε δὲ ἡ πρεσβυτάτη πάλιν·
"Γάμου μὲν μέλει τῆς Χλόης ἄλλῳ θεῷ· δῶρα
δέ σοι δώσομεν ἡμεῖς, ἃ θέλξει Δρύαντα. Ἡ
ναῦς, ἡ τῶν Μηθυμναίων νεανίσκων, ἧς τὴν
λύγον αἱ σαί ποτε αἶγες κατέφαγον, ἡμέρᾳ
μὲν ἐκείνῃ μακρὰν τῆς γῆς ὑπηνέχθη πνεύματι·
νυκτὸς δὲ, πελαγίου ταράξαντος ἀνέμου τὴν
θάλατταν, εἰς τὴν γῆν, εἰς τὰς ἄκρας πέτρας
ἐξεβράσθη. Αὐτὴ μὲν οὖν διεφθάρη, καὶ πολλὰ

marry. No doubt she loves you and would
prefer for her bed-fellow a handsome youth,
though poor, to an ape, however wealthy."

Myrtale, who never expected that Dryas
would give his consent, since there were
far wealthier suitors for the hand of Chloe,
thought that she had very cleverly avoided
the question of the marriage. Daphnis, on
his part, could find nothing to say against
this : but, finding how little chance he had
of getting what he wanted, he did what
poor lovers usually do—he began to weep,
and again implored the assistance of the
Nymphs, who appeared to him at night,
while he was asleep, in the same dress and
form as on the first occasion. The eldest
of them again addressed him : "Chloe's
marriage is the business of another God :
but we will give you some presents which
will soften the heart of Dryas. The vessel
which belonged to the young Methymnaeans, the osier cable of which your goats
formerly ate, was carried far out to sea all
that day by the winds. But, during the
night, when a violent breeze blew from
the sea, it was driven ashore on the rocky

τῶν ἐν αὐτῇ· βαλάντιον δὲ τρισχιλίων δραχμῶν
ὑπὸ τοῦ κύματος ἀπεπτύσθη, καὶ κεῖται φυκίοις
κεκαλυμμένον πλησίον δελφῖνος νεκροῦ, δι᾽ ὃν
οὐδεὶς οὐδὲ προσῆλθεν ὁδοιπόρος, τὸ δυσῶδες
τῆς σηπεδόνος παρατρέχων. Ἀλλὰ σὺ πρόσ-
ελθε, καὶ προσελθὼν ἀνελοῦ, καὶ ἀνελόμενος,
δός. Ἱκανόν σοι δόξαι νῦν μὴ πένητι· χρόνῳ
δὲ ὕστερον ἔσῃ καὶ πλούσιος."

Αἱ μὲν ταῦτα εἰποῦσαι, τῇ νυκτὶ συναπῆλ-
θον. Γενομένης δὲ ἡμέρας ἀναπηδήσας ὁ Δάφνις
περιχαρὴς, ἤλαυνε ῥοίζῳ πολλῷ τὰς αἶγας εἰς
τὴν νομήν· καὶ τὴν Χλόην φιλήσας, καὶ τὰς
Νύμφας προσκυνήσας, κατῆλθεν ἐπὶ θάλατταν
ὡς περιρράνασθαι θέλων· καὶ ἐπὶ τῆς ψάμμου,
πλησίον τῆς κυματωγῆς, ἐβάδιζε ζητῶν τὰς
τρισχιλίας. Ἔμελλε δὲ ἄρα οὐ πολὺν κάματον
ἕξειν· ὁ γὰρ δελφὶς οὐκ ἀγαθὸν ὀδωδὼς, αὐτῷ
προσέπιπτεν ἐρριμμένος καὶ μυδῶν· οὗ τῇ
σηπεδόνι καθάπερ ἡγεμόνι χρώμενος ὁδοῦ,
προσῆλθέ τε εὐθὺς, καὶ τὰ φυκία ἀφελὼν,
εὑρίσκει τὸ βαλάντιον ἀργυρίου μεστόν.

promontory. The vessel was shattered
to pieces, and nearly all that was in it was
lost : but a purse of 3,000 drachmas was
cast up by the waves, and it now lies upon
the shore, hidden under some seaweed,
close to a dead dolphin, the stench from
which is so noisome that no passer-by will
go near it. Go, take the purse, and give
it to Dryas. It is enough for you now
to show that you are not poor : but a day
will come when you will be even wealthy."

With these words, they disappeared, and
night with them. At daybreak, Daphnis
jumped up full of joy, and eagerly drove
his goats to pasture. Having kissed Chloe
and paid his respects to the Nymphs, he
went down to the shore, saying he was
going to bathe, and walked along the
sand on the beach, looking for the 3,000
drachmas. He had not to trouble himself
long : for the evil smell of the dolphin,
which lay rotting on the shore, soon
reached his nostrils. Following the smell
as a guide, he soon reached the spot, removed the seaweed, and found the purse
full of money. He took it, stowed it away

τῶν ἐν αὐτῇ· βαλάντιον δὲ τρισχιλίων δραχμῶν
ὑπὸ τοῦ κύματος ἀπεπτύσθη, καὶ κεῖται φυκίοις
κεκαλυμμένον πλησίον δελφῖνος νεκροῦ, δι' ὃν
οὐδεὶς οὐδὲ προσῆλθεν ὁδοιπόρος, τὸ δυσῶδες
τῆς σηπεδόνος παρατρέχων. Ἀλλὰ σὺ πρόσ-
ελθε, καὶ προσελθὼν ἀνελοῦ, καὶ ἀνελόμενος,
δός. Ἱκανόν σοι δόξαι νῦν μὴ πένητι· χρόνῳ
δὲ ὕστερον ἔσῃ καὶ πλούσιος."

Αἱ μὲν ταῦτα εἰποῦσαι, τῇ νυκτὶ συναπῆλ-
θον. Γενομένης δὲ ἡμέρας ἀναπηδήσας ὁ Δάφνις
περιχαρὴς, ἤλαυνε ῥοίζῳ πολλῷ τὰς αἶγας εἰς
τὴν νομήν· καὶ τὴν Χλόην φιλήσας, καὶ τὰς
Νύμφας προσκυνήσας, κατῆλθεν ἐπὶ θάλατταν
ὡς περιρράνασθαι θέλων· καὶ ἐπὶ τῆς ψάμμου,
πλησίον τῆς κυματωγῆς, ἐβάδιζε ζητῶν τὰς
τρισχιλίας. Ἔμελλε δὲ ἄρα οὐ πολὺν κάματον
ἕξειν· ὁ γὰρ δελφὶς οὐκ ἀγαθὸν ὀδωδὼς, αὐτῷ
προσέπιπτεν ἐρριμμένος καὶ μυδῶν· οὗ τῇ
σηπεδόνι καθάπερ ἡγεμόνι χρώμενος ὁδοῦ,
προσῆλθέ τε εὐθὺς, καὶ τὰ φυκία ἀφελὼν,
εὑρίσκει τὸ βαλάντιον ἀργυρίου μεστόν.

promontory. The vessel was shattered
to pieces, and nearly all that was in it was
lost : but a purse of 3,000 drachmas was
cast up by the waves, and it now lies upon
the shore, hidden under some seaweed,
close to a dead dolphin, the stench from
which is so noisome that no passer-by will
go near it. Go, take the purse, and give
it to Dryas. It is enough for you now
to show that you are not poor : but a day
will come when you will be even wealthy."

With these words, they disappeared, and
night with them. At daybreak, Daphnis
jumped up full of joy, and eagerly drove
his goats to pasture. Having kissed Chloe
and paid his respects to the Nymphs, he
went down to the shore, saying he was
going to bathe, and walked along the
sand on the beach, looking for the 3,000
drachmas. He had not to trouble himself
long : for the evil smell of the dolphin,
which lay rotting on the shore, soon
reached his nostrils. Following the smell
as a guide, he soon reached the spot, removed the seaweed, and found the purse
full of money. He took it, stowed it away

Τοῦτο ἀνελόμενος, καὶ εἰς τὴν πήραν ἐνθέμενος, οὐ πρόσθεν ἀπῆλθε, πρὶν τὰς Νύμφας εὐφημῆσαι καὶ αὐτὴν τὴν θάλατταν· καίπερ γὰρ αἰπόλος ὤν, ἤδη καὶ τὴν θάλατταν ἐνόμιζε τῆς γῆς γλυκυτέραν, ὡς εἰς τὸν γάμον αὐτῷ τὸν Χλόης συλλαμβάνουσαν.

Εἰλημμένος δὲ τῶν τρισχιλίων, οὐκέτ᾽ ἔμελλεν· ἀλλ᾽, ὡς πάντων ἀνθρώπων πλουσιώτατος, οὐ μόνον τῶν ἐκεῖ γεωργῶν, αὐτίκα ἐλθὼν παρὰ τὴν Χλόην, διηγεῖται τὸ ὄναρ, δείκνυσι τὸ βαλάντιον, κελεύει τὰς ἀγέλας φυλάττειν ἔστ᾽ ἂν ἐπανέλθῃ, καὶ συντείνας, σοβεῖ παρὰ τὸν Δρύαντα· καὶ εὑρὼν πυροὺς τινας ἀλωνοτριβοῦντα μετὰ τῆς Νάπης, πάνυ θρασὺν ἐμβάλλει λόγον περὶ γάμου· "Ἐμοὶ δὸς Χλόην γυναῖκα· ἐγὼ καὶ συρίζειν οἶδα καλῶς, καὶ κλᾶν ἄμπελον, καὶ φυτὰ κατορύττειν. Οἶδα καὶ γῆν ἀροῦν, καὶ λικμῆσαι πρὸς ἄνεμον. Ἀγέλην δὲ ὅπως νέμω, μάρτυς Χλόη· πεντήκοντα αἶγας παραλαβών, διπλασίονας πεποίηκα· ἔθρεψα

in his wallet, and, before departing, gave
thanks to the Nymphs and the sea itself:
for, although he was a goatherd, he began
to think that the sea was pleasanter than
the earth, since it had assisted his marriage
with Chloe.

Having gained possession of the 3,000
drachmas, he delayed no longer. He
thought himself the richest man, not only
amongst the husbandmen in the neighbourhood, but of all men living, hastened
to Chloe, told her of the dream, showed
her the purse, told her to mind the flocks
till he returned, and then ran with all
speed to Dryas, whom he found with Nape,
beating some wheat on a threshing-floor.
Then, quite confidently, he approached the
subject of marriage: "Give Chloe to me
to wife: I know how to play on the pipe,
to prune vines, and to plant trees: I also
know how to plough, and to winnow the
corn in the breeze: how I can tend flocks,
Chloe herself can testify. I had fifty goats
at first, I have doubled their number. I
have reared some fine large he-goats,
whereas before I was obliged to borrow

καινότατον, μνᾶσθαι νυμφίον. Εὑρὼν δὲ κἀκείνους κριθία μετροῦντας οὐ πρὸ πολλοῦ
λελικμημένα, ἀθύμως τε ἔχοντας ὅτι, μικροῦ
δεῖν, ὀλιγώτερα ἦν τῶν καταβληθέντων σπερ-
μάτων, ἐπ' ἐκείνοις μὲν παρεμυθήσατο, κοινὴν
ὁμολογήσας αἰτίαν πανταχοῦ γεγονέναι· τὸν
δὲ Δάφνιν ᾐτεῖτο Χλόη, καὶ ἔλεγεν ὅτι,
"πολλὰ ἄλλων διδόντων, οὐδὲν παρ' αὐτῶν
λήψεται, μᾶλλον δέ τοι οἴκοθεν αὐτοῖς ἐπι-
δώσει· συντετράφθαι γὰρ ἀλλήλοις, κἂν τῷ
νέμειν συνῆφθαι φιλίᾳ ῥᾳδίως λυθῆναι μὴ δυνα-
μένῃ· ἤδη δὲ καὶ ἡλικίαν ἔχειν ὡς καθεύδειν καὶ
μετ' ἀλλήλων." Ὁ μὲν ταῦτα, καὶ ἔτι πλείω
ἔλεγεν, οἷα τοῦ πεῖσαι ἆθλον ἔχων τὰς τρισχι-
λίας· ὁ δὲ Λάμων ἔτι μήτε πενίαν προβάλ-
λεσθαι δυνάμενος, (αὐτοὶ γὰρ οὐχ ὑπερηφάνουν)
μήτε ἡλικίαν Δάφνιδος, (ἤδη γὰρ μειράκιον ἦν)
τὸ μὲν ἀληθὲς οὐδ' ὡς ἐξηγόρευσεν ὅτι κρείττων ἐστὶ τοιούτου γάμου· χρόνον δὲ σιωπή-
σας ὀλίγον, οὕτως ἀπεκρίνατο·

nowed, and greatly disheartened, because
the crop was disproportionate to the seed
that had been sown. He tried to console
them, saying that the same complaint was
to be heard everywhere : and then asked
the hand of Daphnis for Chloe, saying :
"Although others offer much for the
honour, I will take nothing from you, but
will rather give you something out of my
own purse. They have been brought up
together, and, while tending their flocks,
have become so attached to each other,
that it would be hard to separate them :
and they are now both of marriageable
age." This and more said Dryas, as a
man who was to have 3,000 drachmas for
a reward, if he persuaded Lamon and
Myrtale. Lamon, being no longer able to
allege his poverty as an excuse (since the
parents of the girl did not reject the
alliance), nor the age of Daphnis (for he
was now a well-grown youth), nevertheless
shrunk from stating the real reason for
his hesitation, namely, that Daphnis was
above such a connection. He remained
silent for a while, and then said :

" Δίκαια ποιεῖτε τοὺς γείτονας προτιμῶντες
τῶν ξένων, καὶ πενίας ἀγαθῆς πλοῦτον μὴ
νομίζοντες κρείττονα. Ὁ Πὰν ὑμᾶς ἀντὶ
τῶνδε καὶ αἱ Νύμφαι φιλήσειαν. Ἐγὼ δὲ
σπεύδω μὲν καὶ αὐτὸς τὸν γάμον· καὶ γὰρ
ἂν μαινοίμην, ἡμιγέρων τε ὢν ἤδη, καὶ χειρὸς
εἰς τὰ ἔργα δεόμενος περιττοτέρας, ὡς μὴ
καὶ τὸν ὑμέτερον οἶκον φίλον προσλαβεῖν.
Ἀγαθόν τι μέγα· περισπούδαστος δὲ καὶ
Χλόη, καλὴ καὶ ὡραία κόρη, καὶ πάντα ἀγαθή·
δοῦλος δὲ ὢν, οὐδενός εἰμι τῶν ἐμῶν κύριος·
ἀλλὰ δεῖ τὸν δεσπότην μανθάνοντα ταῦτα
συγχωρεῖν. Φέρε οὖν, ἀναβαλλώμεθα τὸν
γάμον εἰς τὸ μετόπωρον. Ἀφίξεσθαι τότε
λέγουσιν αὐτὸν οἱ παραγινόμενοι πρὸς ἡμᾶς
ἐξ ἄστεος. Τότε ἔσονται ἀνὴρ καὶ γυνή· νῦν
δὲ φιλείτωσαν ἀλλήλους ἀδελφοί. Ἴσθι
μόνον, ὦ Δρύα, τοσοῦτον· σπεύδεις περὶ
μειράκιον κρεῖττον ἡμῶν." Ὁ μὲν ταῦτα
εἰπὼν, ἐφίλησέ τε αὐτὸν, καὶ ὤρεξε ποτὸν, ἤδη

" You do right in preferring neighbours
to strangers, and in esteeming riches above
honourable poverty. May Pan and the
Nymphs reward you for it. I myself am
anxious for this marriage : for I should
be mad, seeing that I am now an old man,
and have need of more hands to help
me, if I did not consider it a great honour
to enter into an alliance with your family.
Chloe herself is much sought after, being
a good and beautiful girl. But, as I am
a serf, I have nothing of which I can
dispose : I must first inform my master
and gain his consent. Come then, let us
put off the marriage until autumn, when,
according to those who have visited us
from the city, he will be here. Then
they shall become man and wife : in the
meantime, let them love each other like
brother and sister. But let me tell you
this, Dryas : you are asking for the hand
of a youth whose station is superior to
our own." When he had thus spoken,
Lamon kissed Dryas, and offered him
wine to drink, for the sun was at its
height : then he accompanied him part

14

μεσημβρίας ἀκμαζούσης, καὶ προὔπεμψε μέχρι
τινὸς, φιλοφρονούμενος πάντα.

Ὁ δὲ Δρύας οὐ παρέργως ἀκούσας τὸν
ὕστερον λόγον τοῦ Λάμωνος, ἐφρόντιζε βαδίζων καθ' αὐτὸν ὅστις ὁ Δάφνις. " Ἐτράφη
μὲν ὑπὸ αἰγὸς, ὡς κηδομένων θεῶν· ἔστι δὲ
καλὸς καὶ οὐδὲν ἐοικὼς σιμῷ γέροντι καὶ
μαδώσῃ γυναικί. Εὐπόρησε δὲ καὶ τρισχιλίων,
ὅσον οὐδὲ ἀχράδων εἰκὸς ἔχειν αἰπόλον. Ἆρα
καὶ τοῦτον ἐξέθηκέ τις ὡς Χλόην; Ἆρα καὶ
τοῦτον εὗρε Λάμων, ὡς ἐκείνην ἐγώ; Ἆρα καὶ
γνωρίσματα ὅμοια παρέκειτο τοῖς εὑρεθεῖσιν
ὑπ' ἐμοῦ; Ἐὰν ταῦτα οὕτως, ὦ δέσποτα Πὰν
καὶ Νύμφαι φίλαι, τάχα οὗτος, τοὺς ἰδίους
εὑρὼν, εὑρήσει τι καὶ τῶν Χλόης ἀπορρήτων."
Τοιαῦτα μὲν πρὸς αὐτὸν ἐφρόντιζε καὶ ὠνειρο-
πόλει μέχρι τῆς ἅλω· ἐλθὼν δὲ ἐκεῖ, καὶ τὸν
Δάφνιν μετέωρον πρὸς τὴν ἀκοὴν καταλαβὼν,
ἀνέρρωσέ τε γαμβρὸν προσαγορεύσας, καὶ τῷ
μετοπώρῳ τοὺς γάμους θήσειν ἐπαγγέλλεται,

of the way home, with every mark of affection.

Dryas, who had listened attentively to Lamon's last words, began to think, as he was walking along, who this Daphnis might be: " He was reared by a goat, as if the Gods watched over him: he is fair to look upon, and in no way resembles this snub - nosed old man or his bald-headed wife. He has been able to lay his hands upon 3,000 drachmas, a larger sum than a man in his position could make out of pears. Was he exposed by some one, like Chloe? did Lamon find him, as I found her? were any tokens found with him, like those I found with Chloe? If this be so, O Pan and you, dear Nymphs, perhaps Daphnis will one day find his parents and find out the mystery attached to Chloe."

Thus reflecting and dreaming, Dryas went on until he reached the threshing-floor, where he found Daphnis eagerly waiting to hear what news he had brought. He cheered him, called him his son-in-law, promised that the marriage should

δεξιάν τε ἔδωκεν, ὡς οὐδενὸς ἐσομένης, ὅτι μὴ
Δάφνιδος, Χλόης.

Θᾶττον οὖν νοήματος, μηδὲν πιὼν, μηδὲ
φαγὼν, παρὰ τὴν Χλόην κατέδραμε· καὶ
εὑρὼν αὐτὴν ἀμέλγουσαν καὶ τυροποιοῦσαν,
τόν τε γάμον εὐηγγελίζετο, καὶ ὡς γυναῖκα
λοιπὸν μὴ λανθάνων κατεφίλει, καὶ ἐκοινώνει
τοῦ πόνου. Ἤμελγε μὲν εἰς γαυλοὺς τὸ
γάλα, ἐνεπήγνυ δὲ ταρσοῖς τοὺς τυρούς·
προσέβαλλε ταῖς μητράσιν ἄρνας καὶ τοὺς
ἐρίφους. Καλῶς δὲ ἐχόντων τούτων, ἀπελού-
σαντο, ἐνέφαγον, ἔπιον, περιῄεσαν ζητοῦντες
ὀπώραν ἀκμάζουσαν. Ἦν δὲ ἀφθονία πολλὴ
διὰ τὸ τῆς ὥρας πάμφορον· πολλαὶ μὲν
ἀχράδες, πολλαὶ δὲ ὄχναι, πολλὰ δὲ μῆλα·
τὰ μὲν ἤδη πεπτωκότα κάτω, τὰ δὲ ἔτι ἐπὶ
τῶν φυτῶν· τὰ ἐπὶ τῆς γῆς, εὐωδέστερα· τὰ
ἐπὶ τῶν κλάδων, εὐανθέστερα· τὰ μὲν, οἷον
οἶνος ἀπῶζε· τὰ δὲ, οἷον χρυσὸς ἀπέλαμπε.
Μία μηλέα τετρύγητο, καὶ οὔτε καρπὸν εἶχεν,

take place in the autumn, and pledged him his word that Chloe should never marry anyone but Daphnis.

Then, quicker than thought, without tasting food or drink, Daphnis ran straight to Chloe, whom he found milking the cows and making cheese. He told her the good news of their approaching marriage, and kissed her, openly and without concealment, as his betrothed, and assisted her in all her tasks. He drew the milk into the pails, curdled the cheeses in the crates, and put the lambs and kids under their mothers. When all this was done, they washed themselves, ate and drank, and went in search of ripe fruit, of which they found abundance, since it was the fruitful season of the year—wild and garden pears and apples, some fallen on the ground, and others still on the trees. Those on the ground were more fragrant, and smelt like wine: those on the trees were fresher, and glittered like gold. There was one apple-tree, the fruit of which had already been plucked, and which was stripped of its fruit and leaves. All its branches were bare,

οὔτε φύλλον. Γυμνοὶ πάντες ἦσαν οἱ κλάδοι,
καὶ ἓν μῆλον ἐλείπετο ἐν αὐτοῖς ἄκροις ἀκρο-
τατον, μέγα καὶ καλὸν, καὶ τῶν πολλῶν
τὴν εὐωδίαν ἐνίκα μόνον. Ἔδεισεν ὁ τρυγῶν
ἀνελθεῖν, ἠμέλησε καθελεῖν· τάχα δὲ καὶ
ἐφυλάττετο τὸ καλὸν μῆλον ἐρωτικῷ ποιμένι.

Τοῦτο τὸ μῆλον ὡς εἶδεν ὁ Δάφνις, ὥρμα
τρυγᾶν ἀνελθὼν, καὶ, Χλόης κωλυούσης, ἠμέλη-
σεν. Ἡ μὲν ἀμεληθεῖσα, ὁρμηθεῖσα πρὸς τὰς
ἀγέλας ἀπῆλθε· Δάφνις δὲ ἀναδραμὼν, ἐξί-
κετο τρυγῆσαι, καὶ κομίσαι δῶρον Χλόῃ, καὶ
λόγον τοιόνδε εἶπεν ὠργισμένῃ· "Ὦ παρθένε,
τοῦτο τὸ μῆλον ἔφυσαν Ὧραι καλαὶ, καὶ φυτὸν
καλὸν ἔθρεψε, πεπαίνοντος ἡλίου, καὶ ἐτήρη-
σεν ἡ Τύχη· καὶ οὐκ ἔμελλον αὐτὸ καταλιπεῖν
ὀφθαλμοὺς ἔχων, ἵνα πέσῃ χαμαὶ, καὶ ἢ ποίμνιον αὐτὸ πατήσῃ νεμόμενον, ἢ ἑρπετὸν φαρ-
μάξῃ συρόμενον, ἢ χρόνος δαπανήσῃ κείμενον,
βλεπόμενον, ἐπαινούμενον. Τοῦτο Ἀφροδίτη
κάλλους ἔλαβεν ἆθλον· τοῦτο ἐγὼ σοὶ δίδωμι

and only a single apple remained on the topmost bough, fine and large, more fragrant than all the rest. He who had plucked the others had not ventured to climb so high, or had forgotten to take it : or it may be that so fine an apple was reserved for a love-sick shepherd. When Daphnis saw this apple, he was eager to climb and pluck it, and, when Chloe tried to prevent him, he paid no heed to her, and she went off to her flocks. Then Daphnis climbed the tree, reached and plucked the apple, and took it to Chloe. Seeing that she was annoyed, he said : " Dear Chloe, the beautiful seasons have made this apple to grow, a beautiful tree has nourished it, the sun has ripened it, and chance has preserved it. I should have been blind not to see it, and foolish to leave it there, to fall to the ground and be trodden under foot by a grazing herd or poisoned by some creeping serpent, or to be consumed by time, though admired by all who saw it. Aphrodite was presented with an apple as the prize of beauty : I present this to you as the meed of victory. You are

νικητήριον. Ὁμοίως ἔχομεν τοὺς σοὺς μάρ-
τυρας·[1] ἐκεῖνος ἦν ποιμήν, αἰπόλος ἐγώ."
Ταῦτα εἰπών, ἐντίθησι τοῖς κόλποις· ἡ δε
ἐγγὺς γενόμενον κατεφίλησεν· ὥστε ὁ Δάφνις
οὐ μετέγνω τολμήσας ἀνελθεῖν εἰς τοσοῦτον
ὕψος· ἔλαβε γὰρ κρεῖττον καὶ χρυσοῦ μήλου
φίλημα.

---

[1] The text is corrupt here.

as beautiful as Aphrodite : your judges are
alike : Paris was a shepherd, I am a goatherd." With these words, he placed the
apple in Chloe's bosom, and, when he
drew near, she kissed him, so that he did
not regret that he had been bold enough to
climb so high, for he was rewarded with
a kiss that he valued above the golden
apples of the Hesperides.

ΛΟΓΟΣ ΤΕΤΑΡΤΟΣ.

῍Ηκων δέ τις ἐκ τῆς Μιτυλήνης ὁμόδουλος τοῦ Λάμωνος, ἤγγειλεν ὅτι ὀλίγον πρὸ τοῦ τρυγητοῦ ὁ δεσπότης ἀφίξεται, μαθησόμενος μή τι τοὺς ἀγροὺς ὁ τῶν Μηθυμναίων εἴσπλους ἐλυμήνατο. ῍Ηδη οὖν τοῦ θέρους ἀπιόντος, καὶ τοῦ μετοπώρου προσιόντος, παρεσκεύαζεν αὐτῷ τὴν καταγωγὴν ὁ Λάμων εἰς πᾶσαν θέας ἡδονήν. Πηγὰς ἐξεκάθαιρεν, ὡς ὕδωρ καθαρὸν ἔχοιεν· τὴν κόπρον ἐξεφόρει τῆς αὐλῆς, ὡς ἀπόζουσα μὴ διοχλοίη· τὸν παράδεισον ἐθεράπευεν, ὡς ὀφθείη καλός.

῍Ην δὲ ὁ παράδεισος πάγκαλόν τι χρῆμα, καὶ κατὰ τοὺς βασιλικούς. Ἐκτέτατο μὲν εἰς σταδίου μῆκος, ἐπέκειτο δὲ ἐν χώρῳ μετεώρῳ τὸ εὖρος ἔχων πλέθρων τεττάρων. Εἴκασεν ἄν

BOOK IV

MEANWHILE, one of Lamon's fellow-servants arrived from Mitylene and informed him that their master would visit his estate a little before the vintage, to see whether the inroad of the Methymnaeans had done any damage. As the summer was nearly over, and autumn was close at hand, Lamon made preparations to receive his master, and put his house and garden in order, that he might find everything pleasant to look upon. He cleaned the fountains, that the water might be bright and pure, removed the dung from the yard, that he might not be annoyed by the smell, and put the grounds in order, that they might look as pleasant as possible.

These grounds were very beautiful, like royal parks. They were about a stade in length, situated on high ground, about

τις αὐτὸν πεδίῳ μακρῷ. Εἶχε δὲ πάντα δένδρα,
μηλέας, μυρρίνας, ὄχνας, καὶ ῥοιὰς, καὶ συκῆν,
καὶ ἐλαίας· ἑτέρωθι ἄμπελον ὑψηλήν· καὶ
ἐπέκειτο ταῖς μηλέαις καὶ ταῖς ὄχναις, περ-
κάθουσα, καθάπερ περὶ τοῦ καρποῦ αὐταῖς
προσερίζουσα· τοσαῦτα ἤμερα. Ἦσαν δὲ καὶ
κυπάριττοι, καὶ δάφναι, καὶ πλάτανοι, καὶ
πίτυες. Ταύταις πάσαις ἀντὶ τῆς ἀμπέλου
κιττὸς ἐπέκειτο· καὶ ὁ κόρυμβος αὐτοῦ μέγας
ὢν καὶ μελαινόμενος, βότρυν ἐμιμεῖτο. Ἔνδον
ἦν τὰ καρποφόρα φυτὰ, καθάπερ φρουρού-
μενα· ἔξωθεν περιειστήκει τὰ ἄκαρπα, καθάπερ
θριγκὸς χειροποίητος· καὶ ταῦτα μέντοι λεπ-
τῆς αἱμασιᾶς περιέθει περίβολος. Τέτμητο
καὶ διεκέκριτο πάντα, καὶ στέλεχος στελέχους
ἀφειστήκει. Ἐν μετεώρῳ δὲ οἱ κλάδοι συνέ-
πιπτον ἀλλήλοις, καὶ ἐπήλλαττον τὰς κόμας·
ἐδόκει μέντοι καὶ ἡ τούτων φύσις εἶναι τέχνης.
Ἦσαν καὶ ἀνθῶν πρασιαί, ὧν τὰ μὲν ἔφερεν ἡ
γῆ, τὰ δὲ ἐποίει τέχνη· ῥοδωνιὰ, καὶ ὑάκινθοι,

four plethra in breadth, so that they
were rectangular in shape. All kinds of
trees were to be found there, apple-trees,
myrtles, pear - trees, pomegranates, fig-
trees, and olives : on one side was a lofty
vine, which with its black grapes over-
spread the apple and pear-trees, as if to
contend with them in fruitfulness. These
were the cultivated trees : but there were
also cypresses, laurels, planes, and pines,
over which, instead of the vine, spread
branches of ivy, whose large berries turn-
ing black looked like ripe grapes. The fruit
trees were in the centre of the garden, as
if for better protection : those that did
not bear fruit stood round them like
an artificial fence, and the whole was
shut in by a little wall. Everything was
admirably arranged and distributed : the
trunks of the trees were kept apart, but,
overhead, the branches were so inter-
twined that what was due to Nature
seemed to be the work of art. There
were also beds of flowers, some growing
wild, others cultivated — roses, hyacinths,
and lilies that had been planted : violets,

καὶ κρίνα, χειρὸς ἔργα· ἰωνιὰς, καὶ ναρκίσσους,
καὶ ἀναγαλλίδας ἔφερεν ἡ γῆ. Σκιά τε ἦν
θέρους, καὶ ἦρος ἄνθη, καὶ μετοπώρου τρύγη,
καὶ κατὰ πᾶσαν ὥραν ὀπώρα.

Ἐντεῦθεν εὔοπτον μὲν ἦν τὸ πεδίον, καὶ ἦν
ὁρᾶν τοὺς νέμοντας· εὔοπτος δὲ ἡ θάλαττα,
καὶ ἑωρῶντο οἱ παραπλέοντες· ὥστε καὶ ταῦτα
μέρος ἐγίνετο τῆς ἐν παραδείσῳ τρυφῆς. Ἵνα
τοῦ παραδείσου τὸ μεσαίτατον ἐπὶ μῆκος
καὶ εὖρος ἦν, νεὼς Διονύσου καὶ βωμὸς ἦν·
περιεῖχε τὸν μὲν βωμον κιττὸς, τὸν νεὼν
δὲ κλήματα. Εἶχε δὲ καὶ ἔνδοθεν ὁ νεὼς
Διονυσιακὰς γραφὰς, Σεμέλην τίκτουσαν,
Ἀριάδνην καθεύδουσαν, Λυκοῦργον δεδεμένον,
Πενθέα διαιρούμενον. Ἦσαν καὶ Ἰνδοὶ νικώ-
μενοι, καὶ Τυρρηνοὶ μεταμορφούμενοι· πανταχοῦ Σάτυροι, πανταχοῦ Βάκχαι χορεύουσαι·
οὐδὲ ὁ Πὰν ἠμέλητο. Ἐκαθέζετο δὲ καὶ αὐτὸς
συρίζων ἐπὶ πέτρας, ὅμοιος ἐνδιδόντι κοινὸν
μέλος καὶ τοῖς πατοῦσι καὶ ταῖς χορευούσαις.

Τοιοῦτον ὄντα τὸν παράδεισον ὁ Λάμων

narcissuses, and pimpernel, which grew wild. There was shade in summer, flowers in spring, grapes in autumn, and fruit in every season of the year.

From this spot the plain could be seen, with the shepherds feeding their flocks ; also the sea, and the vessels passing along, which added enjoyment to this delightful spot. In the very centre of the garden, there was a temple and altar of Dionysus, the latter covered with ivy, the former with vine-branches. Within the temple were pictures representing incidents in the life of the God : Semele brought to bed, Ariadne asleep, Lycurgus bound in chains, Pentheus being torn to pieces, conquered Indians, Tyrrhenians changed into dolphins, and everywhere Satyrs and Bacchantes leading the dance. Nor was Pan forgotten : he was seated on a rock, playing upon his pipe, so that he seemed to be playing the same air both for those who were treading the wine-press and for the Bacchantes who were dancing.

Such were the grounds to which Lamon devoted all his attention, lopping off the

ἐθεράπευε, τὰ ξηρὰ ἀποτέμνων, τὰ κλήματα
ἀναλαμβάνων. Τὸν Διόνυσον ἐστεφάνωσε τοῖς
ἄνθεσιν· ὕδωρ ἐπωχέτευσε πηγή τις, ἣν εὗρεν
ἐς τὰ ἄνθη Δάφνις· Ἐσχόλαζε μὲν τοῖς ἄνθεσιν ἡ πηγὴ, Δάφνιδος δὲ ὅμως ἐκαλεῖτο
πηγή. Παρεκελεύετο δὲ καὶ τῷ Δάφνιδι ὁ
Λάμων πιαίνειν τὰς αἶγας ὡς δυνατὸν μάλιστά
που, πάντως κἀκείνας λέγων ὄψεσθαι τὸν δεσπότην ἀφικόμενον διὰ μακροῦ· ὁ δὲ ἐθάρρει
μὲν, ὡς ἐπαινηθησόμενος ἐπ᾽ αὐταῖς· διπλα-
σίονάς τε γὰρ ὧν ἔλαβεν, ἐποίησε, καὶ λύκος
οὐδὲ μίαν ἥρπαζε, καὶ ἦσαν πιότεραι τῶν οἰῶν.
Βουλόμενος δὲ προθυμότερον αὐτὸν γενέσθαι
πρὸς τὸν γάμον, πᾶσαν θεραπείαν καὶ προθυ-
μίαν προσέφερεν, ἄγων τε αὐτὰς πάνυ ἔωθεν,
καὶ ἀπάγων τὸ δειλινόν. Δὶς ἡγεῖτο ἐπὶ ποτὸν,
ἀνεζήτει δὲ εὐνομώτατα τῶν χωρίων. Ἐμέλησεν αὐτῷ καὶ σκαφίδων καινῶν, καὶ γαυλῶν
πολλῶν, καὶ ταρσῶν μειζόνων. Τοσαύτη δὲ ἦν
κηδεμονία, ὥστε καὶ τὰ κέρατα ἤλειφε, καὶ τὰς

dry leaves and tying up the vine-branches. He placed a garland of flowers upon the head of Dionysus, and conveyed water to the flower-beds from a spring which had been discovered by Daphnis, and was hence called " Daphnis's spring." Lamon also advised Daphnis to get his goats into as good condition as possible, as his master would want to inspect them, since he had not visited his estate for so long a time. Daphnis had no fear of not being praised for the condition of his flock: he had doubled their number, not one of them had been carried off by wolves, and they were fatter than the sheep. But, as he was eager to do everything to obtain his master's approval of his marriage, he spared no pains to make them sleek and fat, driving them out to pasture in the early morning, and not driving them home until late in the evening. He took them twice to drink, and carefully sought for the places where there was the best pasturage. He also took care that there were new drinking-vessels, plenty of milk-pails, and larger cheese-vats. He was so

15

τρίχας ἐθεράπευε. Πανὸς ἄν τις ἱερὰν ἀγέλην
ἔδοξεν ὁρᾶν. Ἐκοινώνει δὲ παντὸς εἰς αὐτὰς
καμάτου καὶ ἡ Χλόη· καὶ τῆς ποίμνης παρα-
μελοῦσα, τὸ πλέον ἐκείναις ἐσχόλαζε· ὥστε
ἐνόμιζεν ὁ Δάφνις δι' ἐκείνην αὐτὰς φαίνεσθαι
καλάς.

Ἐν τούτοις οὖσιν αὐτοῖς, δεύτερος ἄγγελος
ἐλθὼν ἐξ ἄστεος ἐκέλευεν ἀποτρυγᾶν τὰς ἀμπέλους ὡς τάχιστα· καὶ αὐτὸς ἔφη παραμένειν
ἔστ' ἂν τοὺς βότρυς ποιήσωσι γλεῦκος, εἶτα
οὕτως κατελθὼν εἰς τὴν πόλιν, ἄξειν τὸν δεσπότην, ἤδη τῆς μετοπωρινῆς τρύγης. Τοῦτόν
τε οὖν Εὔδρομον (οὕτω γὰρ ἐκαλεῖτο, ὅτι ἦν
αὐτῷ ἔργον τρέχειν) ἐδεξιοῦντο πᾶσαν δεξίω-
σιν, καὶ ἅμα τὰς ἀμπέλους ἀπετρύγων, τοὺς
βότρυς ἐς τὰς ληνοὺς κομίζοντες, τὸ γλεῦκος
εἰς τοὺς πίθους φέροντες, τῶν βοτρύων τοὺς
ἡβῶντας ἐπὶ κλημάτων ἀφαιροῦντες, ὡς εἴη
καὶ τοῖς ἐκ τῆς πόλεως ἐλθοῦσιν ἐν εἰκόνι καὶ
ἡδονῇ γενέσθαι τρυγητοῦ.

particular that he even anointed their horns, and combed their hair : you would have thought you were looking upon Pan's sacred flock. Chloe also assisted him in his labours, and, neglecting her sheep, devoted the greater part of her time to the goats : so that Daphnis declared it was owing to her that they looked in such good condition.

While they were thus engaged, a second messenger arrived from the city, bidding them gather the grapes as speedily as possible; since he had been ordered to stay until the new wine was made, when he was to return to the city to fetch his master in time for the autumn vintage. They gave Eudromus (so was the slave called, because he acted as his master's courier) a hearty reception, stripped the vines, pressed the grapes, put the new wine into casks, and cut off a number of branches with the grapes still unpicked, so that those who came from the city might have an idea of the delights of the vintage and might think that they had taken part in them.

Μέλλοντος δὲ ἤδη σοβεῖν ἐς ἄστυ τοῦ
Εὐδρόμου, καὶ ἄλλα μὲν οὐκ ὀλίγα αὐτῷ
Δάφνις ἔδωκεν· (ἔδωκε δὲ καὶ ὅσα ἀπὸ αἰπόλου
δῶρα) τυροὺς εὐπαγεῖς, ἔριφον ὀψίγονον,
δέρμα αἰγὸς λευκὸν καὶ λάσιον, ὡς ἔχοι χειμῶνος ἐπιβάλλεσθαι τρέχων· ὁ δὲ ἤδετο καὶ
ἐφίλει τὸν Δάφνιν, καὶ ἀγαθόν τι ἐρεῖν περὶ
αὐτοῦ πρὸς τὸν δεσπότην ἐπηγγέλλετο. Καὶ
ὁ μὲν ἀπῄει φίλα φρονῶν· ὁ δὲ Δάφνις
ἀγωνιῶν τῇ Χλόῃ συνέμενεν. Εἶχε δὲ κἀκείνη
πολὺ δέος· μειράκιον γὰρ εἰωθὸς αἶγας βλέπειν, καὶ ὄρος, καὶ γεωργοὺς, καὶ Χλόην,
πρῶτον ἔμελλεν ὄψεσθαι δεσπότην, οὗ πρῶτον
μόνον ἤκουε τὸ ὄνομα. Ὑπέρ τε οὖν τοῦ
Δάφνιδος ἐφρόντιζεν, ὅπως ἐντεύξεται τῷ
δεσπότῃ, καὶ περὶ τοῦ γάμου τὴν ψυχὴν
ἐταράττετο, μὴ μάτην ὀνειροπολοῦσιν αὐτόν.
Συνεχῆ μὲν οὖν τὰ φιλήματα, καὶ ὥσπερ
συμπεφυκότων αἱ περιβολαί· καὶ τὰ φιλή-

When Eudromus was ready to hurry
back to the city, Daphnis gave him several
presents, such as a goatherd might have
been expected to give, some well-made
cheeses, a young kid, and the shaggy skin
of a white goat, to wear during the winter
when he was running messages. Eudromus was highly pleased, kissed Daphnis,
and promised to say everything in his
favour to his master. Then he departed,
full of kindly feelings: but Daphnis, full of
anxiety, remained with Chloe in the fields.
She felt equally timid, when she remembered that Daphnis, a youth who had
never seen anything but goats, mountains,
husbandmen, and herself, was now for the
first time to see his master, whom he
had hitherto only known by name. She
was very anxious to know how Daphnis
would address his master, and was greatly
disturbed in mind regarding their marriage,
for fear it might prove an idle dream.
They kissed each other over and over
again, and embraced tenderly: but their
kisses were mingled with apprehension
and their embraces were tinged with sad-

ματα δειλὰ ἦν, καὶ αἱ περιβολαὶ σκυθρωπαί,
καθάπερ ἤδη παρόντα τὸν δεσπότην φοβου-
μένων, ἢ λανθανόντων. Προσγίνεται δέ τις
αὐτοῖς καὶ τοιόσδε τάραχος.

Λάμπις τις ἦν ἀγέρωχος βουκόλος. Οὗτος
καὶ αὐτὸς ἐμνᾶτο τὴν Χλόην παρὰ τοῦ Δρύαντος, καὶ δῶρα ἤδη πολλὰ ἐδεδώκει σπεύδων
τὸν γάμον. Αἰσθόμενος οὖν ὡς, εἰ συγχωρη-
θείη παρὰ τοῦ δεσπότου, Δάφνις αὐτὴν ἄξεται,
τέχνην ἐζήτει δι᾽ ἧς τὸν δεσπότην αὐτοῖς
ποιήσειε πικρόν· καὶ εἰδὼς πάνυ αὐτὸν τῷ
παραδείσῳ τερπόμενον, ἔγνω τοῦτον, ὅσον
οἷός τέ ἐστι, διαφθεῖραι καὶ ἀποκοσμῆσαι.
Δένδρα μὲν οὖν τέμνων, ἔμελλεν ἁλώσεσθαι
διὰ τὸν κτύπον· ἐπεῖχε δὲ τοῖς ἄνθεσιν, ὥστε
διαφθεῖραι αὐτά. Νύκτα δὴ φυλάξας, καὶ
ὑπερβὰς τὴν αἱμασιάν, τὰ μὲν ἀνώρυξε, τὰ δὲ
κατέκλασε, τὰ δὲ κατεπάτησεν ὥσπερ σῦς.
Καὶ ὁ μὲν λαθὼν ἀπεληλύθει· Λάμων δὲ τῆς

ness, as if their master were already present, and they were afraid of him or were obliged to keep their love a secret. While they were in this distress, the following trouble came upon them.

In the neighbourhood there lived a cow-herd named Lampis, a man of insolent and overweening disposition. He also sought Chloe's hand from Dryas, and had already given him several presents to further his suit. Seeing that, if his master's consent were obtained, Daphnis would marry her, he cast about for the means of embittering the master against the young couple. Knowing that he took great pride in his garden, he determined to spoil and rob it of its beauty. Since, if he cut down the trees, he might be betrayed by the noise, he determined to devote his energies to destroying the flowers. He waited until it was night, climbed over the low wall, pulled up, broke off, and trod down the flowers like a wild boar, and then withdrew without having been seen by anybody. The next morning, Lamon went into the garden to water the flowers from his spring; and,

ἐπιούσης παρελθὼν εἰς τὸν κῆπον, ἔμελλεν ὕδωρ
αὐτοῖς ἐκ τῆς πηγῆς ἐπάξειν. Ἰδὼν δὲ πᾶν τὸ
χωρίον δεδῃωμένον, καὶ ἔργον οἷον ἂν ἐχθρὸς,
οὐ λῃστὴς ἐργάσαιτο, κατερρήξατο μὲν εὐθὺς
τὸν χιτωνίσκον, βοῇ δὲ μεγάλῃ θεοὺς ἀνεκάλει·
ὥστε καὶ ἡ Μυρτάλη τὰ ἐν χερσὶ καταλιποῦσα,
ἐξέδραμε, καὶ ὁ Δάφνις ἐλάσας τὰς αἶγας,
ἀνέδραμε· καὶ ἰδόντες ἐβόων, καὶ βοῶντες
ἐδάκρυον.

Καὶ ἦν μὲν κενὸν πένθος ἀνθῶν, ἀλλ' οἱ μὲν
φοβούμενοι δεσπότην, ἔκλαιον· ἔκλαυσε δ' ἂν
τις καὶ ξένος ἐπιστάς· ἀποκεκόσμητο γὰρ ὁ
τόπος, καὶ ἦν λοιπὸν πᾶσα ἡ γῆ πηλώδης.
Τῶν δὲ εἴ τι διέφυγε τὴν ὕβριν, ὑπήνθει καὶ
ἔλαμπε, καὶ ἦν ἔτι καλὸν καὶ κείμενον. Ἐπέ-
κειντο δὲ αὐτοῖς καὶ μέλιτται συνεχεῖς, καὶ
ἄπαυστον βομβοῦσαι, καὶ θρηνούσαις ὅμοιον.
Ὁ μὲν γὰρ Λάμων ὑπ' ἐκπλήξεως κἀκεῖνα
ἔλεγε· "Φεῦ τῆς ῥοδωνιᾶς, ὡς κατακέκλασται.
Φεῦ τῆς ἰωνιᾶς, ὡς πεπάτηται. Φεῦ τῶν

when he saw the whole place thus ravaged, at the sight of this desolation, which was clearly the work of an enemy rather than of a robber, he immediately rent his cloak, and invoked the Gods with loud cries. Myrtale at once threw down what she had in her hands and ran out: Daphnis, who was driving out his goats, turned back: and when they saw what had happened they cried aloud and burst into tears.

It was idle to lament the loss of the flowers, but the fear of their master made them weep. Even a stranger would have wept at the sight: the whole place was in disorder, and nothing could be seen but upturned earth and mud. If by chance some flower had escaped the general destruction, it still looked gay and bright, and retained its former beauty, although lying on the ground. Swarms of bees hovered round, humming incessantly, as if they too lamented what had happened. Lamon cried out in his consternation: "Alas! my rose trees, how they are broken! Alas! my violets, how they are trodden under foot! Alas! my hyacinths

ὑακίνθων καὶ τῶν ναρκίσσων, οὓς ἀνώρυξέ τις πονηρὸς ἄνθρωπος. Ἀφίξεται τὸ ἦρ· τὰ δὲ οὐκ ἀνθήσει. Ἔσται τὸ θέρος· τὰ δὲ οὐκ ἀκμάσει. Μετόπωρον· ἀλλὰ τάδε οὐδένα στεφανώσει. Οὐδὲ σὺ, δέσποτα Διόνυσε, τὰ ἄθλια ταῦτα ἠλέησας ἄνθη, οἷς παρῴκεις, καὶ ἔβλεπες, ἀφ’ ὧν ἐστεφάνωσά σε πολλάκις; Πῶς δείξω νῦν τὸν παράδεισον τῷ δεσπότῃ; Τίς ἐκεῖνος, θεασάμενος, ἔσται; Κρεμᾷ γέροντα ἄνθρωπον ἐκ μιᾶς πίτυος ὡς Μαρσύαν· τάχα δὲ καὶ Δάφνιν, ὡς τῶν αἰγῶν ταῦτα εἰργασμένων.”

Δάκρυα ἦν ἐπὶ τούτοις θερμότερα· καὶ ἐθρήνουν οὐ τὰ ἄνθη λοιπόν, ἀλλὰ τὰ αὑτῶν σώματα. Ἐθρήνει καὶ Χλόη Δάφνιν εἰ κρεμήσεται, καὶ ηὔχετο μηκέτι ἐλθεῖν τὸν δεσπότην αὐτῶν, καὶ ἡμέρας διήντλει μοχθηρὰς, ὡς ἤδη Δάφνιν βλέπουσα μαστιγούμενον. Καὶ ἤδη νυκτὸς ἀρχομένης, ὁ Εὔδρομος αὐτοῖς

and narcissuses, which the hand of some
wretch has uprooted ! The spring will
return, but they will blossom no more :
the summer will come, but they will not
bloom : autumn will come again, but they
will not deck anyone's head. And you,
my lord Dionysus, had you no pity for
these unhappy flowers, near which you
dwelt, with which I have often crowned
your brows ? How can I show the garden
to my master ? What will he think when
he sees it ? he will hang the old man on
a pine tree, like Marsyas : and perhaps
Daphnis as well, thinking that his goats
have done this damage."

At these words, they wept even more
bitterly, not so much on account of the
flowers as themselves. Chloe was bitterly
distressed, at the thought that Daphnis
would be hung : she prayed that their
master might not come, and passed her
days in bitterness, thinking that she
already saw Daphnis under the lash.
One evening, Eudromus came to inform
them that the master himself would not
arrive for three days, but that his son

ἀπήγγελλεν, ὅτι ὁ μὲν πρεσβύτερος δεσπότης μεθ' ἡμέρας ἀφίξεται τρεῖς, ὁ δὲ παῖς αὐτοῦ τῆς ἐπιούσης πρόεισι. Σκέψις οὖν ὑπὲρ τῶν συμβεβηκότων, καὶ κοινωνὸν εἰς τὴν γνώμην τὸν Εὔδρομον παρελάμβανον· ὁ δὲ, εὔνους ὢν τῷ Δάφνιδι, παρήνει τὸ συμβὰν ὁμολογῆσαι πρότερον τῷ νέῳ δεσπότῃ, καὶ αὐτὸς συμπράττειν ἐπηγγέλλετο, τιμώμενος ὡς ὁμογάλακτος· καὶ ἡμέρας γενομένης, οὕτως ἐποίησαν.

῟Ηκε μὲν ὁ ῎Αστυλος ἐφ' ἵππου, καὶ παράσιτος αὐτοῦ, καὶ οὗτος ἐφ' ἵππου· ὁ μὲν, ἀρτιγένειος· ὁ δὲ Γνάθων (τουτὶ γὰρ ἐκαλεῖτο), τὸν πώγωνα ξυρώμενος πάλαι· ῾Ο δὲ Λάμων ἅμα τῇ Μυρτάλῃ καὶ τῷ Δάφνιδι, πρὸ τῶν ποδῶν αὐτοῦ καταπεσὼν, ἱκέτευεν οἰκτεῖραι γέροντα ἀτυχῆ, καὶ πατρῴας ὀργῆς ἐξαρπάσαι τὸν οὐδὲν ἀδικήσαντα· ἅμα τε αὐτῷ καταλέγει πάντα. Οἰκτείρει τὴν ἱκεσίαν ὁ ῎Αστυλος, καὶ ἐπὶ τὸν παράδεισον ἐλθὼν, καὶ τὴν ἀπώ-

would be there on the morrow.   They accordingly thought over what had happened,
and took Eudromus into their confidence.
He, being well disposed towards Daphnis,
advised him to tell everything to their
young master beforehand, promising to
do his best for them, since he possessed
some influence with him, being his foster-
brother.   When the day came, they did
as he had advised them.

Astylus arrived on horseback, accompanied by his parasite, also on horseback.
Astylus's beard was only just beginning
to grow, but Gnathon's (so was the parasite named) had long been familiar with
the razor.   Lamon, together with Daphnis
and Myrtale, fell at his feet and besought
him to have compassion upon an unfortu-
nate old man, and to save from his father's
wrath one who had committed no offence:
and at the same time he told him all
that had occurred.   Astylus was moved to
pity by his supplication : he went to the
garden, inspected the damage done to the
flowers, promised to make his father relent,
and undertook to lay the blame upon his

λειαν τῶν ἀνθῶν ἰδὼν, αὐτὸς ἔφη παραιτή-
σεσθαι τὸν πατέρα, καὶ κατηγορήσειν τῶν
ἵππων, ὡς ἐκεῖ δεθέντες ἐξύβρισαν, καὶ τὰ
μὲν κατέκλασαν, τὰ δὲ κατεπάτησαν, τὰ δὲ
ἀνώρυξαν λυθέντες. Ἐπὶ τούτοις ηὔχοντο
μὲν αὐτῷ πάντα τὰ ἀγαθὰ Λάμων καὶ Μυρ-
τάλη· Δάφνις δὲ δῶρα προσεκόμισεν ἐρίφους,
τυροὺς, ὄρνιθας, καὶ τὰ ἔκγονα αὐτῶν, βότρυς
ἐπὶ κλημάτων, μῆλα δὲ ἐπὶ κλάδων. Ἦν ἐν
τοῖς δώροις καὶ ἀνθοσμίας οἶνος Λέσβιος,
ποθῆναι κάλλιστος οἶνος.

Ὁ μὲν δὴ Ἄστυλος ἐπῄνει ταῦτα, καὶ περὶ
θήραν εἶχε λαγῶν, οἷα πλούσιος νεανίσκος,
καὶ τρυφῶν ἀεὶ, καὶ ἀφιγμένος εἰς τὸν ἀγρὸν
εἰς ἀπόλαυσιν ξένης ἡδονῆς. Ὁ δὲ Γνάθων,
οἷα μαθὼν ἐσθίειν ἄνθρωπος καὶ πίνειν εἰς
μέθην, καὶ οὐδὲν ἄλλο ὢν ἢ γνάθος, καὶ γαστὴρ,
καὶ τὰ ὑπὸ γαστέρα, οὐ παρέργως εἶδε τὸι
Δάφνιν τὰ δῶρα κομίσαντα· ἀλλὰ καὶ φύσει

own horses, and to say that they had
been fastened up in the garden, but,
having become frisky, had broken loose,
and trampled down, trodden under foot,
and uprooted the flowers. Lamon and
Myrtale wished him all prosperity in return for his kindness: and Daphnis presented him with some kids, cheeses, birds
with their young, grapes still on the
vine-branches, and apples on the boughs:
to these he added some fragrant Lesbian
wine, most delightful to drink.

Astylus, having expressed his satisfac-
tion, went to hunt the hares, like a wealthy
young man who had nothing to do but
amuse himself, and was visiting the
country in search of some fresh diversion.
Gnathon, who knew nothing except how to
eat till he could eat no more, and to drink
till he was drunk, and was all throat and
belly and lust, had carefully observed
Daphnis when he brought the presents to
Astylus. Being naturally fond of boys,
and finding Daphnis handsomer than any
of the youths in the city, he resolved to
make advances to him, thinking that he

παιδεραστὴς ὤν, κάλλος, οἷον οὐδὲ ἐπὶ τῆς
πόλεως, εὑρὼν, ἐπιθέσθαι διέγνω τῷ Δάφνιδι,
καὶ πείσειν ᾤετο ῥᾳδίως, ὡς αἰπόλον. Γνοὺς
δὲ ταῦτα, θήρας μὲν οὐκ ἐκοινώνει τῷ ᾿Αστύλῳ,
κατιὼν δὲ ἵνα ἔνεμεν ὁ Δάφνις, λόγῳ μὲν, τῶν
αἰγῶν, τὸ δὲ ἀληθὲς, Δάφνιδος ἐγίνετο θεατής.
Μαλθάσσων δὲ αὐτὸν, τάς τε αἶγας ἐπήνει,
καὶ συρίσαι τὸ αἰπολικὸν ἠξίωσε· καὶ ἔφη
ταχέως ἐλεύθερον θήσειν, τὸ πᾶν δυνάμενος.

῾Ως δὲ εἶχε χειροήθη, νύκτωρ λοχήσας ἐκ
τῆς νομῆς ἐλαύνοντα τὰς αἶγας, πρῶτον μὲν
ἐφίλησε προδραμών· εἶτα ὄπισθεν παρασχεῖν
τοιοῦτον οἷον αἱ αἶγες τοῖς τράγοις. Τοῦ δὲ
βραδέως νοήσαντος, καὶ λέγοντος, "ὡς αἶγας
μὲν βαίνειν τράγους, καλόν· τράγον δὲ οὔπω
ποτέ τις εἶδε βαίνοντα τράγον, οὐδὲ κριὸν
ἀντὶ τῶν οἴων κριὸν, οὐδὲ ἀλεκτρυόνας ἀντὶ
τῶν ἀλεκτορίδων ἀλεκτρυόνας," οἷός τε ἦν ὁ
Γνάθων βιάζεσθαι, τὰς χεῖρας προσφέρων· ὁ

would find no difficulty in seducing a simple goatherd. Having made up his mind to this, instead of accompanying Astylus to the chase, he went down to the place where Daphnis was tending his flock, under pretence of looking at the goats, but in reality he had eyes for nothing but Daphnis. In order to coax him, he praised his goats, and begged him to play a pastoral air upon his pipe : then he promised to obtain his freedom for him shortly, saying that he was all-powerful with his master.

When Gnathon thought he had won Daphnis's affection, he lay in wait for him one evening as he was driving back his goats from pasture, ran up to him and kissed him. Then he asked him to turn his back to him and let him do to him what the he-goats did to the she-goats. Daphnis was slow to understand, but at last he said to himself that, while it was quite natural for he-goats to mount she-goats, no one had ever seen a he-goat mounting a he-goat, or a ram another ram instead of a sheep, or a cock treading

16

δὲ μεθύοντα ἄνθρωπον καὶ ἑστῶτα μόλις
παρωσάμενος, ἔσφηλεν εἰς τὴν γῆν, καὶ, ὥσπερ
σκύλαξ ἀποδραμὼν, κείμενον κατέλιπεν, ἀνδρὸς,
οὐ παιδὸς, πρὸς χειραγωγίαν δεόμενον. Οὐκέτι
προσίετο ὅλως, ἀλλὰ ἄλλοτε ἄλλῃ τὰς αἶγας
ἔνεμεν, ἐκεῖνον μὲν φεύγων, Χλόην δὲ τηρῶν.
Οὐδὲ ὁ Γνάθων ἔτι περιειργάζετο, καταμαθὼν
ὡς οὐ μόνον καλὸς, ἀλλὰ καὶ ἰσχυρός ἐστιν.
Ἐπετήρει δὲ καιρὸν διαλεχθῆναι περὶ αὐτοῦ
τῷ Ἀστύλῳ, καὶ ἤλπιζε δῶρον αὐτὸν ἕξειν
παρὰ τοῦ νεανίσκου πολλὰ καὶ μεγάλα χαρίζε-
σθαι θέλοντος.

Τότε μὲν οὖν οὐκ ἠδυνήθη· προσῄει γὰρ ὁ
Διονυσοφάνης ἅμα τῇ Κλεαρίστῃ· καὶ ἦν
θόρυβος πολὺς κτηνῶν, οἰκετῶν, ἀνδρῶν,
γυναικῶν· μετὰ δὲ τοῦτο συνέταττε λόγον
καὶ ἐρωτικὸν καὶ μακρόν. Ἦν δὲ ὁ Διονυσοφάνης μεσαιπόλιος μὲν ἤδη, μέγας δὲ καὶ καλὸς,
καὶ μειρακίοις ἁμιλλᾶσθαι δυνάμενος· ἀλλὰ

a cock in place of a hen. Meanwhile, Gnathon attempted to lay violent hands upon
Daphnis, who dealt him a vigorous blow,
which felled him to the ground, since he
was already drunk and could hardly stand.
After this, Daphnis ran away as swiftly as
a fawn, leaving Gnathon on the ground,
more in need of the assistance of a man,
than of a boy, to help him along. From
that time Daphnis shunned him altogether,
changing the pasturage of his goats from
one place to another, avoiding Gnathon as
carefully as he sought Chloe. Nor did
Gnathon trouble him any more, when he
found that he was not only handsome, but
also strong and vigorous. But he watched
for an opportunity to speak to Astylus
about him, hoping that his young master
would make him a present of Daphnis,
since he knew that he was ready to grant
almost every favour he asked.

For the moment he could do nothing:
for Dionysophanes had just arrived with
Clearista, and nothing was heard but the
noise of animals, slaves, men, and women.
In the meantime, Gnathon set about com-

16—2

καὶ πλούσιος ἐν ὀλίγοις, καὶ χρηστὸς ὡς οὐδεὶς
ἕτερος. Οὗτος ἐλθών, τῇ πρώτῃ μὲν ἡμέρα
θεοῖς ἔθυσεν ὅσοι προεστᾶσιν ἀγροικίας,
Δήμητρι, καὶ Διονύσῳ, καὶ Πανὶ, καὶ Νύμφαις,
καὶ κοινὸν πᾶσι τοῖς παροῦσιν ἔστησε κρατῆρα·
ταῖς δὲ ἄλλαις ἡμέραις ἐπεσκόπει τὰ τοῦ
Λάμωνος ἔργα· καὶ ὁρῶν τὰ μὲν πεδία ἐν
αὔλακι, τὰς δὲ ἀμπέλους ἐν κλήματι, τὸν δὲ
παράδεισον ἐν κάλλει (περὶ γὰρ τῶν ἀνθῶν
Ἄστυλος τὴν αἰτίαν ἀνελάμβανεν) ἥδετο πε-
ριττῶς, καὶ τὸν Λάμωνα ἐπῄνει, καὶ ἐλεύθερον
ἀφήσειν ἐπηγγέλλετο. Κατῆλθε μετὰ ταῦτα
καὶ εἰς τὸ αἰπόλιον, τάς τε αἶγας ὀψόμενος
καὶ τὸν νέμοντα.

Χλόη μὲν οὖν εἰς τὴν ὕλην ἔφυγεν, ὄχλον
τοσοῦτον αἰδεσθεῖσα καὶ φοβηθεῖσα· ὁ δὲ
Δάφνις εἱστήκει δέρμα λάσιον αἰγὸς ἐζωσμένος,
πήραν νεορραφῆ κατὰ τῶν ὤμων ἐξηρτημένος,
κοατῶν ταῖς χερσὶν ἀμφοτέραις, τῇ μὲν, ἀρτι-

posing a long and amorous discourse upon
Daphnis. Dionysophanes, whose hairs
were already beginning to turn grey, was
a tall, handsome man, who need not have
shrunk from rivalry with many a young
man : in addition to this, he was richer
than most men, and none were more
virtuous. On the first day of his arrival,
he offered sacrifice to all the Gods who
preside over husbandry, to Demeter,
Dionysus, Pan, and the Nymphs, and
gave a feast to all the household. On the
following days, he went to see how Lamon
had done his work: and, at the sight of
the ploughed fields, the well-kept vines,
and the beautiful garden—for Astylus had
taken the blame for the damage done to
the flowers—he was delighted, congratulated Lamon, and promised him his
freedom. After this he went to see the
goats and the goatherd.

Chloe immediately ran away into the
forest, feeling bashful and afraid of so
many visitors : but Daphnis remained
where he was, with a shaggy goat-skin
fastened round him, and a new wallet

παγεῖς τυροὺς, τῇ δὲ, ἐρίφους γαλαθηνούς. Εἴ
ποτε Ἀπόλλων Λαομέδοντι θητεύων ἐβουκό-
λησε, τοιόσδε ἦν, οἷος τότε ὤφθη Δάφνις.
Αὐτὸς μὲν οὖν εἶπεν οὐδὲν, ἀλλὰ ἐρυθήματος
πλησθεὶς, ἔνευσε κάτω, προτείνας τὰ δῶρα·
ὁ δὲ Λάμων, "οὗτος," εἶπε, "σοὶ, δέσποτα,
τῶν αἰγῶν αἰπόλος. Σὺ μὲν ἐμοὶ πεντήκοντα
νέμειν ἔδωκας, καὶ δύο τράγους· οὗτος δέ σοι
πεποίηκεν ἑκατὸν, καὶ δέκα τράγους. Ὁρᾷς
ὡς λιπαραὶ καὶ τὰς τρίχας λάσιαι, καὶ τὰ
κέρατα ἄθραυστοι. Πεποίηκεν αὐτὰς καὶ
μουσικάς· σύριγγος γοῦν ἀκούουσαι ποιοῦσι
πάντα."

Παροῦσα τοῖς λεγομένοις ἡ Κλεαρίστη,
πεῖραν ἐπεθύμησε τοῦ λεχθέντος λαβεῖν, καὶ
κελεύει τὸν Δάφνιν ταῖς αἰξὶν οἷον εἴωθε
συρίσαι, καὶ ἐπαγγέλλεται συρίσαντι χαρί-
σασθαι χιτῶνα καὶ χλαῖναν καὶ ὑποδήματα.
Ὁ δὲ καθίσας αὐτοὺς ὥσπερ θέατρον, στὰς
ὑπὸ τῇ φηγῷ, καὶ ἐκ τῆς πήρας τὴν σύριγγα

hanging from his shoulder, holding in one hand some fresh cheeses, and in the other some sucking kids. If ever Apollo tended the flocks of Laomedon as a hired servant, he must have looked like Daphnis, who, without saying a word, his face covered with blushes, bowed and presented his gifts. Then Lamon said: "O master, this is the goatherd: you gave me fifty goats and two he-goats to look after: he has doubled the number of the goats, and increased the he-goats to ten. You see how fat and sleek they are, what long hair they have, and how sound their horns are. He has also taught them to understand music: when they hear the sound of his pipe, they are ready to do anything."

Clearista, who was present and heard what was said, was anxious to put it to the proof: she ordered Daphnis to play on his pipe to his goats as he was accustomed to do, and promised to give him a cloak, a tunic, and a pair of shoes for his trouble. Daphnis made them sit down as if they were at the theatre, stood up under the beech tree, took his pipe out

κομίσας, πρῶτα μὲν ὀλίγον ἐνέπνευσε· καὶ αἱ
αἶγες ἔστησαν, τὰς κεφαλὰς ἀράμεναι. Εἶτα
ἐνέπνευσε τὸ νόμιον· καὶ αἱ αἶγες ἐνέμοντο,
νεύσασαι κάτω. Αὖθις λιγυρὸν ἔδωκε· καὶ
ἀθρόαι κατεκλίθησαν. Ἐσύρισέ τε καὶ ὀξὺ
μέλος· αἱ δὲ, ὥσπερ λύκου προσιόντος, εἰς τὴν
ὕλην κατέφυγον. Μετ᾽ ὀλίγον ἀνακλητικὸν
ἐφθέγξατο· καὶ ἐξελθοῦσαι τῆς ὕλης, πλησίον
αὐτοῦ τῶν ποδῶν συνέδραμον. Οὐδὲ ἀνθρώπους
οἰκέτας εἶδεν ἄν τις οὕτω πειθομένους προσ-
τάγματι δεσπότου. Οἵ τε οὖν ἄλλοι πάντες
ἐθαύμαζον, καὶ πρὸ πάντων ἡ Κλεαρίστη, καὶ
δῶρα ἀποδώσειν ὤμοσε καλῷ τε ὄντι αἰπόλῳ
καὶ μουσικῷ· καὶ ἀνελθόντες εἰς τὴν ἔπαυλιν,
ἀμφὶ ἄριστον εἶχον, καὶ τῷ Δάφνιδι ἀφ᾽ ὧν
ἤσθιον ἔπεμψαν.

Ὁ δὲ μετὰ τῆς Χλόης ἤσθιε, καὶ ἤδετο γενόμενος ἀστυκῆς ὀψαρτυσίας, καὶ εὔελπις ἦν
τεύξεσθαι τοῦ γάμου, πείσας τοὺς δεσπότας.
Ὁ δὲ Γνάθων προσεκκανθεὶς τοῖς κατὰ τὸ

of his wallet, and, to commence with, drew from it merely a feeble strain. The goats immediately stood up, and lifted their heads. Then he piped to pasture and the goats began to browse, with their heads towards the ground. He played a clear sweet strain, and they all lay down. He played a shrill air, and they fled towards the forest, as if a wolf was approaching. After a brief interval, he piped a recall, and they came out of the forest, and ran to his feet. They obeyed the notes of the pipe more readily than servants obey their masters' orders. The visitors were astonished, especially Clearista, who swore to give what she had promised to the gentle goatherd who played so well. Then they returned to the homestead for dinner, and sent Daphnis something from their own table.

Daphnis shared the food with Chloe, highly pleased at tasting city cookery, and feeling sanguine of obtaining his master's consent to his marriage. Gnathon, inflamed still more by what he had seen of the goatherd, and considering that life

αἰπόλιον γεγενημένοις, καὶ ἀβίωτον νομίζων
τὸν βίον, εἰ μὴ τεύξεται Δάφνιδος, περιπα-
τοῦντα τὸν Ἄστυλον ἐν τῷ παραδείσῳ φυλάξας, καὶ ἀναγαγὼν εἰς τὸν τοῦ Διονύσου
νεὼν, πόδας καὶ χεῖρας κατεφίλει. Τοῦ δὲ πυν-
θανομένου, τίνος ἕνεκα ταῦτα δρᾷ, καὶ λέγειν κε-
λεύοντος, καὶ ὑπουργήσειν ὀμνύοντος, " Οἴχεταί
σοι Γνάθων," ἔφη, " δέσποτα. Ὁ μέχρι νῦν μόνης
τραπέζης ἐρῶν, ὁ πρότερον ὀμνὺς ὅτι μηδέν
ἐστιν ὡραιότερον οἴνου γέροντος, ὁ κρείττους
τῶν ἐφήβων τῶν ἐν Μιτυλήνῃ τοὺς σοὺς ὀψαρ-
τυτὰς λέγων, μόνον λοιπὸν καλὸν εἶναι Δάφνιν
νομίζω. Καὶ τροφῆς μὲν τῆς πολυτελοῦς οὐ
γεύομαι, καίτοι τοσούτων παρασκευαζομένων
ἑκάστης ἡμέρας, κρεῶν, ἰχθύων, μελιττωμάτων,
ἡδέως δ' ἂν αἲξ γενόμενος πόαν ἐσθίοιμι καὶ
φύλλα, τῆς Δάφνιδος ἀκούων σύριγγος, καὶ
ὑπ' ἐκείνῳ νεμόμενος. Σὺ δὲ σῶσον Γνάθωνα
τὸν σὸν, καὶ τὸν ἀήττητον ἔρωτα νίκησον. Εἰ
δὲ μὴ, σοὶ ἐπόμνυμι τὸν ἐμὸν θεὸν, ξιφίδιον

would not be endurable if he did not get possession of Daphnis, waited his opportunity until Astylus was walking in the garden : then, leading him up to the temple of Dionysus, he kissed his hands and feet. When Astylus asked what was the meaning of his behaviour, and bade him speak, swearing that he would grant whatever favour he asked, Gnathon replied : " Your poor Gnathon is lost, O master. I who hitherto cared for nothing but the pleasures of the table, who used to swear that there was nothing more delightful than old wine, who considered your cooks far superior to all the youths of Mitylene—I now think that there is nothing beautiful in the world but Daphnis. I do not so much as taste the most dainty dishes, although so many are prepared each day— meat, fish, and honey-cakes. I should like to be a goat, I should like to eat grass and leaves, listening to his pipe and tended by him. Save Gnathon, I beseech you, and remedy a love that is irremediable. If you do not, I swear to you by my God that I will take a hearty meal, and then

λαβὼν, καὶ ἐμπλήσας τὴν γαστέρα τροφῆς,
ἐμαυτὸν ἀποκτενῶ πρὸ τῶν Δάφνιδος θυρῶν·
σὺ δὲ οὐκέτι καλέσεις Γναθωνάριον, ὥσπερ
εἰώθεις παίζων ἀεί."

Οὐκ ἀντέσχε κλαίοντι, καὶ αὖθις τοὺς πόδας
καταφιλοῦντι, νεανίσκος μεγαλόφρων, οὐκ ἄπει-
ρος ἐρωτικῆς λύπης, ἀλλ᾽ αἰτήσειν αὐτὸν παρὰ
τοῦ πατρὸς ἐπηγγέλλετο, καὶ κομίσειν εἰς τὴν
πόλιν, αὐτῷ μὲν δοῦλον, ἐκείνῳ δὲ ἐρώμενον.
Εἰς εὐθυμίαν δὲ καὶ αὐτὸν ἐκεῖνον θέλων προ-
αγαγεῖν, ἐπυνθάνετο μειδιῶν, εἰ οὐκ αἰσχύνεται
Λάμωνος υἱὸν φιλῶν, ἀλλὰ καὶ σπουδάζει συγκατακλιθῆναι νέμοντι αἶγας μειρακίῳ; Καὶ
ἅμα ὑπεκρίνετο τὴν τραγικὴν δυσωδίαν μυσάτ-
τεσθαι. Ὁ δὲ, οἷα πᾶσαν ἐρωτικὴν μυθο-
λογίαν ἐν τοῖς τῶν ἀσώτων συμποσίοις πε-
παιδευμένος, οὐκ ἀπὸ σκοποῦ καὶ ὑπὲρ αὐτοῦ
καὶ ὑπὲρ τοῦ Δάφνιδος, ἔλεγεν· "Οὐδεὶς
ταῦτα, δέσποτα, ἐραστὴς πολυπραγμονεῖ·
ἀλλ᾽ ἐν οἵῳ ποτὲ ἂν σώματι εὕρῃ τὸ κάλλος,

stab myself in front of Daphnis's door :
and you will never again call me your
dear little Gnathon, as you used to do
in jest."

When Gnathon began to kiss his feet
again, Astylus could no longer resist his
entreaties, for he was a generous youth,
who had himself felt the pains of love.
He promised to ask his father for Daphnis
and to take him to the city, nominally as
his slave, but really as Gnathon's minion.
Then, wishing to cheer him up, he asked
him with a smile if he were not ashamed
of being in love with Lamon's son, and
why he was so anxious to sleep with this
young goatherd, at the same time pretending that the smell of goats disgusted
him. But Gnathon, like one who had
gone through the whole course of erotic
lore at the tables of debauchees, replied
shrewdly enough in regard to himself and
Daphnis : " No lover troubles himself
about such things : in whatever form he
finds beauty, he is smitten with it. Men
have been known to become enamoured of
a plant, a river, or a wild beast : and yet

ἑάλωκε. Διὰ τοῦτο καὶ φυτοῦ τις ἠράσθη, καὶ ποταμοῦ, καὶ θηρίου. Καίτοι τίς οὐκ ἂν ἐραστὴν ἠλέησεν ὃν ἔδει φοβεῖσθαι τὸν ἐρώμενον; Ἐγὼ δὲ σώματος μὲν ἐρῶ δούλου, κάλλους δὲ ἐλευθέρου. Ὁρᾷς, ὡς ὑακίνθῳ μὲν τὴν κόμην ὁμοίαν ἔχει, λάμπουσι δὲ ὑπὸ ταῖς ὀφρύσιν οἱ ὀφθαλμοί, καθάπερ ἐν χρυσῇ σφενδόνῃ ψηφίς; Καὶ τὸ μὲν πρόσωπον ἐρυθήματος μεστόν, τὸ δὲ στόμα λευκῶν ὀδόντων ὥσπερ ἐλέφαντος; Τίς ἐκεῖθεν οὐκ ἂν εὔξαιτο λαβεῖν ἐραστὴς λευκὰ φιλήματα; Εἰ δὲ νέμοντος ἠράσθην, θεοὺς ἐμιμησάμην. Βουκόλος ἦν Ἀγχίσης, καὶ ἔσχεν αὐτὸν Ἀφροδίτη· αἶγας ἔνεμε Βράγχιος, καὶ Ἀπόλλων αὐτὸν ἐφίλησε· ποιμὴν ἦν Γανυμήδης, καὶ αὐτὸν ὁ Ζεὺς ἥρπασε. Μὴ καταφρονῶμεν παιδός, ᾧ καὶ αἶγας, ὡς ἐρώσας, πειθομένας εἴδομεν· ἀλλ᾽ εἰ ἔτι μένειν ἐπὶ γῆς ἐπιτρέπουσι τοιοῦτο κάλλος, χάριν ἔχωμεν τοῖς Διὸς ἀετοῖς."

Ἡδὺ δὲ γελάσας ὁ Ἄστυλος ἐπὶ τούτῳ μά-

who would not pity a lover who has to
fear what he loves? No doubt the form
that I love is that of a slave, but its
beauty is free. Do you see how like his
hair is to the hyacinth, how his eyes
glitter beneath his brows, like a jewel
in a setting of gold? His face is
ruddy, his teeth are white as ivory.
Who would not long for a tender kiss
from his lips? In loving a goatherd, I
am but following the example of the
Gods. Anchises was a cowherd, and
Aphrodite possessed him : Branchius tended goats, and Apollo loved him : Gany-
mede was a shepherd, and Zeus carried
him up to heaven. Let us not despise
a lad, whose goats we see obey him, as if
even they were enamoured of him : let
us rather thank the eagles of Zeus for
allowing such beauty to remain upon the
earth."

Astylus, who was highly amused by
this speech, laughed and told Gnathon
that love produced very plausible orators :
at the same time, he promised to watch

λιστα τῷ λεχθέντι, καὶ ὡς μεγάλους ὁ Ἔρως
ποιεῖ σοφιστὰς, εἰπὼν, ἐπετήρει καιρὸν ἐν ᾧ
τῷ πατρὶ περὶ Δάφνιδος διαλέξεται. Ἀκούσας
δὲ τὰ λεχθέντα κρύφα πάντα ὁ Εὔδρομος, καὶ
τὰ μὲν τὸν Δάφνιν φιλῶν, ὡς ἀγαθὸν νεανίσκον,
τὰ δὲ ἀχθόμενος εἰ Γνάθωνος ἐμπαροίνημα
γενήσεται τοιοῦτο κάλλος, αὐτίκα καταλέγει
πάντα κἀκείνῳ καὶ Λάμωνι. Ὁ μὲν οὖν Δάφνις
ἐκπλαγεὶς, ἐγίνωσκεν ἅμα τῇ Χλόῃ τολμῆσαι
φυγεῖν, ἢ ἀποθανεῖν, κοινωνὸν κἀκείνην λαβών.
Ὁ δὲ Λάμων προσκαλεσάμενος ἔξω τῆς αὐλῆς
τὴν Μυρτάλην· "Οἰχόμεθα, εἶπεν, ὦ γύναι.
Ἥκει καιρὸς ἐκκαλύπτειν τὰ κρυπτά. Ἔρημοι
δὲ αἱ αἶγες καὶ τὰ λοιπὰ πάντα· ἀλλὰ, μὰ
τὸν Πᾶνα, καὶ τὰς Νύμφας, οὐδ' εἰ μέλλω
βοῦς, φασὶν, ἐν αὐλείῳ καταλείπεσθαι, τὴν
Δάφνιδος τύχην ἥτις ἐστὶν οὐ σιωπήσω μὲν,
ἀλλὰ καὶ ὅ, τι εὗρον ἐκκείμενον, ἐρῶ, καὶ ὅπως
τρεφόμενον, μηνύσω, καὶ ὅσα εὗρον συνεκκεί-
μενα, δείξω. Μαθέτω Γνάθων ὁ μιαρὸς οἷος

for an opportunity to speak to his father about Daphnis. But Eudromus had heard all that was said without being seen. His friendship for Daphnis, whom he considered a worthy young man, and his indignation at the idea of such beauty being handed over to the insults of a drunken wretch like Gnathon, made him go and tell Daphnis and Lamon at once. Daphnis, in great consternation, at first thought of flight in company with Chloe, or of dying together with her. Then Lamon called Myrtale out, and said to her : " We are lost, my dear wife : the moment is come to reveal what has long been hidden. Although the goats and everything else be abandoned, I swear, by Pan and the Nymphs, even though I should be left like a worn-out ox in the stall, that I will no longer hold my tongue in regard to the history of Daphnis. I will tell how I found him exposed : I will declare how he has been brought up : and I will show all the tokens that I found exposed with him. That infamous wretch Gnathon shall know what manner of man

17

ὧν οἴων ἐρᾷ. Παρασκεύαζέ μοι μόνον εὐτρεπῆ
τὰ γνωρίσματα."

Οἱ μὲν ταῦτα συνθέμενοι, ἀπῆλθον εἴσω πά-
λιν· ὁ δὲ Ἄστυλος σχολὴν ἄγοντι τῷ πατρὶ
προσρυεὶς, αἰτεῖ τὸν Δάφνιν εἰς τὴν πόλιν
καταγαγεῖν, ὡς καλόν τε ὄντα καὶ ἀγροικίας
κρείττονα, καὶ ταχέως ὑπὸ Γνάθωνος καὶ τὰ
ἀστυκὰ διδαχθῆναι δυνάμενον. Χαίρων ὁ πατὴρ
δίδωσι· καὶ μεταπεμψάμενος τὸν Λάμωνα καὶ
τὴν Μυρτάλην, εὐηγγελλίζετο αὐτοῖς, ὅτι
Ἄστυλον θεραπεύσει λοιπὸν ἀντὶ αἰγῶν καὶ
τράγων Δάφνις· ἐπηγγέλλετο δὲ δύο ἀντ'
ἐκείνου δώσειν αὐτοῖς αἰπόλους. Ἐνταῦθα ὁ
Λάμων, πάντων ἤδη συνερρυηκότων, καὶ ὅτι
καλὸν ὁμόδουλον ἕξουσιν ἡδομένων, αἰτήσας
λόγον, ἤρξατο λέγειν· "Ἄκουσον, ὦ δέσποτα,
παρὰ ἀνδρὸς γέροντος ἀληθῆ λόγον· ἐπόμνυμι
δὲ τὸν Πᾶνα καὶ τὰς Νύμφας, ὡς οὐδὲν ψεύ-
σομαι. Οὐκ εἰμὶ Δάφνιδος πατὴρ, οὐδ' εὐ-

he is, and who it is that he has the audacity to love. Do you look after the tokens, and see that I have them ready to hand."

Having settled this, they went indoors. Meanwhile, Astylus, finding his father disengaged, hastened to him and asked permission to take Daphnis home with him to the city, declaring that he was a handsome lad and too superior to be left in the country, and that Gnathon would soon teach him city manners. His father willingly gave his consent, and, having sent for Lamon and Myrtale, told them the good news that Daphnis would in future serve his son Astylus instead of tending goats, and promised to give them two goatherds to take his place. Then, when all the other slaves had gathered together, delighted at the prospect of having so handsome a fellow - servant, Lamon asked leave to speak, and, on its being granted, began as follows: "O master, hear a true story from an old man: I swear by Pan and the Nymphs that I will not utter a word that is false.

τύχησε Μυρτάλη μήτηρ γενέσθαι. Ἄλλοι
πατέρες ἐξέθηκαν τοῦτο τὸ παιδίον, ἴσως παι-
δίων πρεσβυτέρων ἅλις ἔχοντες· ἐγὼ δὲ εὗρον
ἐκκείμενον, καὶ ὑπὸ αἰγὸς ἐμῆς τρεφόμενον, ἣν
καὶ ἀποθανοῦσαν ἔθαψα ἐν τῷ περικήπῳ, φιλῶν
ὅτι ἐποίησε μητρὸς ἔργα. Εὗρον αὐτῷ καὶ
γνωρίσματα συνεκκείμενα· ὁμολογῶ, δέσποτα,
καὶ φυλάττω· τύχης γάρ ἐστι μείζονος ἢ καθ'
ἡμᾶς σύμβολα. Ἀστύλου μὲν οὖν εἶναι δοῦλον
αὐτὸν οὐχ ὑπερηφανῶ, καλὸν οἰκέτην καλοῦ καὶ
ἀγαθοῦ δεσπότου· παροίνημα δὲ Γνάθωνος οὐ
δύναμαι περιϊδεῖν γενόμενον, ὃς ἐς Μιτυλήνην
αὐτὸν ἄγειν ἐπὶ γυναικῶν ἔργα σπουδάζει."

Ὁ μὲν Λάμων ταῦτα εἰπὼν ἐσιώπησε, καὶ
πολλὰ ἀφῆκε δάκρυα. Τοῦ δὲ Γνάθωνος θρασυνο-
μένου, καὶ πληγὰς ἀπειλοῦντος, ὁ Διονυσοφάνης
τοῖς εἰρημένοις ἐκπλαγεὶς, τὸν μὲν Γνάθωνα
σιωπᾶν ἐκέλευσε, σφόδρα τὴν ὀφρῦν εἰς αὐτὸν

I am not the father of Daphnis, nor has Myrtale the good fortune to be his mother. He was exposed when a child by other parents, who perhaps had enough children already. I found him abandoned, and being suckled by one of my goats, which I buried in the garden when it died: for I loved it because it had performed the part of a mother towards the infant. I also found some tokens lying by its side: this I confess, master, and also that I kept them: for they show that he belongs to a higher rank of life than our own. I have no objection to his serving Astylus, for he will be a good servant to a good and honourable master: but I cannot endure that he should become the laughing-stock of the drunken Gnathon, who wants to take him to Mitylene and make him play the part of a woman."

After this Lamon was silent and burst into tears. But when Gnathon waxed bolder and threatened to chastise him, Dionysophanes, astounded at what Lamon had said, knitted his brows and ordered Gnathon to hold his tongue: then he again

τοξοποιήσας· τὸν δὲ Λάμωνα πάλιν ἀνέκρινε, καὶ
παρεκελεύετο τὰ ληθῆ λέγειν, μηδὲ ὅμοια πλάτ-
τειν μύθοις, ἐπὶ τῷ κατέχειν τὸν υἱόν. Ὡς δὲ
ἀτενὴς ἦν, καὶ κατὰ πάντων ὤμνυε θεῶν, καὶ
ἐδίδου βασανίζειν αὐτὸν, εἴ τι ψεύδεται, καθη-
μένης τῆς Κλεαρίστης ἐβασάνιζε τὰ λελεγμένα.
" Τί δ' ἂν ἐψεύδετο Λάμων, μέλλων ἀνθ' ἑνὸς
δύο λαμβάνειν αἰπόλους ; Πῶς δ' ἂν καὶ ταῦτα
ἔπλασεν ἄγροικος ; Οὐ γὰρ εὐθὺς ἦν ἄπιστον,
ἐκ τοιούτου γέροντος καὶ μήτρας εὐτελοῦς
υἱὸν καλὸν οὕτω γενέσθαι ; "

Ἐδόκει μὴ μαντεύεσθαι ἐπιπλέον, ἀλλὰ ἤδη
τὰ γνωρίσματα σκοπεῖν, εἰ λαμπρᾶς καὶ ἐνδοξ-
οτέρας τύχης. Ἀπῄει μὲν Μυρτάλη κομί-
σουσα πάντα φυλαττόμενα ἐν πήρᾳ παλαιᾳ.
Κομισθέντα δὲ πρῶτος Διονυσοφάνης ἔβλεπε,
καὶ ἰδὼν χλαμύδιον ἁλουργὲς, πόρπην χρυσή-
λατον, ξιφίδιον ἐλεφαντόκωπον, μέγα βοήσας,

questioned the old man, exhorting him to speak the truth, and not to invent some story, in order that he might keep his son. When Lamon persisted in his tale, swore by all the Gods that it was true, and offered to submit to the torture if he had lied, Dionysophanes, with Clearista sitting by his side, carefully considered what he had said. " What object could Lamon have in speaking falsely, seeing that he was to have two goatherds in place of one? how could a rude peasant have invented such a story? again, was it not at the outset incredible that so handsome a youth should be the offspring of an old man like Lamon and a shabby old woman like Myrtale ? "

They determined not to trust any further to conjecture, but to examine the tokens at once, to see if they indicated that Daphnis belonged to a higher rank of life. Myrtale immediately went to fetch them out of an old sack in which they had been stored away. When they were brought, Dionysophanes looked at them first, and when he saw the little purple tunic with

ὦ Ζεῦ δέσποτα, καλεῖ τὴν γυναῖκα θεασομένην.
Ἡ δὲ ἰδοῦσα, μέγα καὶ αὐτὴ βοᾷ· "Φίλαι
Μοῖραι· οὐ ταῦτα ἡμεῖς συνεξεθήκαμεν ἰδίῳ
παιδὶ, καὶ εἰς τούτους τοὺς ἀγροὺς κομίζουσαν
Σωφροσύνην ἀπεστείλαμεν; Οὐκ ἄλλα μὲν οὖν,
ἀλλὰ ταὐτά· φίλε ἄνερ, ἡμέτερόν ἐστι τὸ
παιδίον· σὸς υἱός ἐστι Δάφνις, καὶ πατρῴας
ἔνεμεν αἶγας."

Ἔτι λεγούσης αὐτῆς, καὶ τοῦ Διονυσοφάνους
τὰ γνωρίσματα φιλοῦντος, καὶ ὑπὸ περιττῆς
ἡδονῆς δακρύοντος, ὁ Ἄστυλος συνεὶς ὡς ἀδελφός ἐστι, ῥίψας θοἰμάτιον, ἔθει κατὰ τοῦ
παραδείσου, πρῶτος τὸν Δάφνιν φιλῆσαι
θέλων. Ἰδὼν δὲ αὐτὸν μετὰ πολλῶν, καὶ
βοῶντα, Δάφνι, νομίσας ὅτι συλλαβεῖν αὐτὸν
βουλόμενος τρέχει, ῥίψας τὴν πήραν καὶ τὴν
σύριγγα, πρὸς τὴν θάλατταν ἐφέρετο, ῥίψων
ἑαυτὸν ἀπὸ τῆς μεγάλης πέτρας. Καὶ ἴσως

its golden clasp, and the dagger with the ivory handle, he cried aloud, "O Lord and master *Zeus*," and called his wife to look: and she, as soon as she saw them, in like manner cried aloud, "O kindly Fates: are not these the jewels which we gave to Sophrosyne to put by the side of our own son when she exposed him? There is no doubt about it: they are the same. Dear husband, the child is ours. Daphnis is your son, and has fed his father's goats."

While she was still speaking, Dionysophanes kissed the token, and wept from excess of joy. Then Astylus, understanding that Daphnis was his brother, immediately threw off his cloak, and hastened to the garden, wishing to be the first to embrace him. But when Daphnis saw him coming towards him, accompanied by a number of people, and shouting "Daphnis," thinking that he wanted to seize him, he threw away his wallet and his pipe, and fled towards the sea, intending to throw himself from the top of the rock: and perhaps, by a strange caprice of Fortune, Daphnis,

ἂν τὸ καινότατον εὑρεθεὶς ἀπολώλει Δάφνις,
εἰ μὴ συνεὶς ὁ Ἄστυλος ἐβόα πάλιν· " Στῆθι,
Δάφνι, μηδὲν φοβηθῇς· ἀδελφός εἰμί σου; καὶ
γονεῖς, οἱ μέχρι νῦν δέσποται. Νῦν ἡμῖν
Λάμων τὴν αἶγα εἶπε, καὶ τὰ γνωρίσματα
ἔδειξεν· ὅρα δὲ ἐπιστραφεὶς πῶς ἴασι φαιδροὶ
καὶ γελῶντες. Ἀλλ' ἐμὲ πρῶτον φίλησον·
ὄμνυμι δὲ τὰς Νύμφας, ὡς οὐ ψεύδομαι."

Μόλις καὶ μετὰ τὸν ὅρκον ἔστη, καὶ τὸν
Ἄστυλον τρέχοντα περιέμεινε, καὶ προσελ-
θόντα κατεφίλησεν. Ἐν ᾧ δὲ ἐκεῖνον ἐφίλει,
πλῆθος τὸ λοιπὸν ἐπιρρεῖ θεραπόντων, θερα-
παινῶν, αὐτὸς ὁ πατὴρ, ἡ μήτηρ μετ' αὐτοῦ.
Οὗτοι πάντες περιέβαλλον, κατεφίλουν χαίροντες, κλάοντες. Ὁ δὲ τὸν πατέρα καὶ τὴν
μητέρα πρὸ τῶν ἄλλων ἐφιλοφρονεῖτο· καὶ
ὡς πάλαι εἰδὼς προσεστερνίζετο, καὶ ἐξελθεῖν
τῶν περιβολῶν οὐκ ἤθελεν· οὕτω φύσις ταχέως
πιστεύεται. Ἐξελάθετο καὶ Χλόης πρὸς
ὀλίγον· καὶ ἐλθὼν εἰς τὴν ἔπαυλιν, ἐσθῆτά τε
ἔλαβε πολυτελῆ, καὶ παρὰ τὸν πατέρα τὸν
ἴδιον καθεσθείς, ἤκουεν αὐτοῦ λέγοντος οὕτως.

who had just been found, would have been lost, had not Astylus, perceiving his intention, shouted to him: "Stop, Daphnis: fear nothing: I am your brother: your former master and mistress are your parents. Lamon has told us all about the goat, and shown us the tokens: look, turn round and see how glad and cheerful they seem. But kiss me first: I swear by the Nymphs that I am speaking the truth."

Even when he heard this oath, Daphnis was loth to stop: however, he waited for Astylus, and kissed him when he came running up to him. In the meantime, all the household, men and women servants, and his mother and father came and embraced and kissed him, with tears of joy. Daphnis welcomed them all affectionately, but especially his father and mother, whom he clasped to his bosom as if he had already known them for a long time: so quickly does Nature make her claim felt. For a while he even forgot Chloe: and when he reached the homestead, they gave him a handsome dress, and he sat down by the side of his father, who addressed him and Astylus as follows:

"Ἔγημα, ὦ παῖδες, κομιδῇ νέος, καὶ χρόνου διελθόντος ὀλίγου, πατὴρ, ὡς ᾤμην, εὐτυχὴς ἐγεγόνειν. Ἐγένετο γάρ μοι πρῶτος υἱὸς, καὶ δευτέρα θυγάτηρ, καὶ τρίτος Ἄστυλος. Ὤμην ἱκανὸν εἶναι τὸ γένος, καὶ γενόμενον ἐπὶ πᾶσι τοῦτο τὸ παιδίον ἐξέθηκα, οὐ γνωρίσματα ταῦτα συνεκθεὶς, ἀλλὰ ἐντάφια. Τὰ δὲ τῆς Τύχης ἄλλα βουλεύματα. Ὁ μὲν γὰρ πρεσβύτερος παῖς καὶ ἡ θυγάτηρ ὁμοίᾳ νόσῳ μιᾶς ἡμέρας ἀπώλοντο· σὺ δέ μοι προνοίᾳ θεῶν ἐσώθης, ἵνα πλείους ἔχωμεν χειραγωγούς. Μήτε οὖν σύ μοι μνησικακήσῃς ποτὲ τῆς ἐκθέσεως· (ἑκὼν γὰρ οὐκ ἐβουλευσάμην), μήτε σὺ λυπηθῇς, Ἄστυλε, μέρος ληψόμενος ἀντὶ πάσης τῆς οὐσίας· (κρεῖττον γὰρ τοῖς εὐφρονοῦσιν ἀδελφοῦ κτῆμα οὐδέν·) ἀλλὰ φιλεῖτε ἀλλήλους, καὶ χρημάτων γ᾽ ἕνεκα καὶ βασιλεῦσιν ἐρίζετε. Πολλὴν μὲν γὰρ ὑμῖν καταλείψω

" My sons, I married when I was a very young man, and, after a short time, I became a happy father, as I then imagined. My first child was a son, the second a daughter, and the third, Astylus. I thought that three children were enough, and, when another son was born, I exposed him together with these jewels and tokens, which I considered rather as funeral ornaments than as tokens by which he might be afterwards recognised. But Fortune willed otherwise. My eldest son and daughter died of the same complaint on the same day : but you, Daphnis, have been preserved to us by the providence of the Gods that we may have greater support in our old age. Do not bear a grudge against me, my son, for having exposed you : for, though I did so, it was sorely against my will. Nor do you, Astylus, be annoyed that you will have to share your inheritance, for to a wise man a brother is better than all possessions. Love one another : as far as wealth is concerned, you need not envy even a king. For I will leave to both large estates,

γῆν, πολλοὺς δὲ οἰκέτας δεξιοὺς, χρυσὸν, ἄρ-
γυρον, ὅσα ἄλλα εὐδαιμόνων κτήματα. Μόνον
ἐξαίρετον τοῦτο Δάφνιδι τὸ χωρίον δίδωμι, καὶ
Λάμωνα καὶ Μυρτάλην, καὶ τὰς αἶγας ἃς αὐτὸς
ἔνεμεν."

Ἔτι αὐτοῦ λέγοντος, Δάφνις ἀναπηδήσας,
"καλῶς με, εἶπε, ταῦτα, πάτερ, ἀνέμνησας.
Ἄπειμι τὰς αἶγας ἀπάξων ἐπὶ τὸν ποτὸν, αἳ
που νῦν διψῶσαι παραμένουσι τὴν σύριγγα
τὴν ἐμὴν, ἐγὼ δὲ ἐνταυθοῖ καθέξομαι." Ἡδὺ
πάντες ἐγέλασαν, ὅτι δεσπότης γεγενημένος,
ἔτι θέλει εἶναι αἰπόλος. Κἀκείνας μὲν θερα-
πεύσων ἐπέμφθη τις ἄλλος· οἱ δὲ θύσαντες Διὶ
Σωτῆρι, συμπόσιον συνεκρότουν. Εἰς τοῦτο
τὸ συμπόσιον μόνος οὐχ ἧκε Γνάθων· ἀλλὰ
φοβούμενος ἐν τῷ νεῷ τοῦ Διονύσου καὶ τὴν
ἡμέραν ἔμεινε καὶ τὴν νύκτα, ὥσπερ ἱκέτης.
Ταχείας δὲ φήμης εἰς πάντας ἐλθούσης, ὅτι
Διονυσοφάνης εὗρεν υἱὸν, καὶ ὅτι Δάφνις ὁ
αἰπόλος δεσπότης τῶν ἀγρῶν εὑρέθη, ἅμα ἔῳ

a number of clever and industrious servants, gold, silver, and all other blessings
that rich men enjoy. But I specially wish
that Daphnis should have this estate, and
I make him a present of Lamon and
Myrtale, and the goats which he has
tended."

While he was still speaking, Daphnis
suddenly started up and said: " You have
just reminded me, father: I will go and
take my goats to drink: they are thirsty
about this time, and are waiting for the
sound of my pipe, while I am sitting
here." Hereupon all laughed, at the idea
that Daphnis, who had just become a
master, should still wish to perform the
duties of a goatherd. They sent some
one else to look after his goats, offered
sacrifice to *Z*eus Soter, and held high
festival. Gnathon alone was not present,
but, seized with alarm, he remained day
and night in the temple of Dionysus, as
a suppliant. The report soon spread that
Dionysophanes had found his son, and
that the goatherd Daphnis had become
master of the estate : and, the next morn-

συνέτρεχον ἄλλος ἀλλαχόθεν, τῷ μὲν μειρακίῳ συνηδόμενοι, τῷ δὲ πατρὶ αὐτοῦ δῶρα κομίζοντες, ἐν οἷς καὶ ὁ Δρύας πρῶτος, ὁ τρέφων τὴν Χλόην.

Ὁ δὲ Διονυσοφάνης κατεῖχε πάντας, κοινωνοὺς μετὰ τὴν εὐφροσύνην καὶ τῆς ἑορτῆς ἐσομένους. Παρεσκεύαστο δὲ πολὺς μὲν οἶνος, πολλὰ δὲ ἄλευρα, ὄρνιθες ἕλειοι, χοῖροι γαλαθηνοὶ, μελιτώματα ποικίλα· καὶ ἱερεῖα δὲ πολλὰ τοῖς ἐπιχωρίοις θεοῖς ἐθύετο. Ἐνταῦθα ὁ Δάφνις συναθροίσας πάντα τὰ ποιμενικὰ κτήματα, διένειμεν ἀναθήματα τοῖς θεοῖς. Τῷ Διονύσῳ μὲν ἀνέθηκε τὴν πήραν καὶ τὸ δέρμα· τῷ Πανὶ τὴν σύριγγα καὶ τὸν πλάγιον αὐλόν· τὴν καλαύροπα ταῖς Νύμφαις, καὶ τοὺς γαυλοὺς οὓς αὐτὸς ἐτεκτήνατο. Οὕτω δὲ ἄρα τὸ σύνηθες ξενιζούσης εὐδαιμονίας τερπνότερόν ἐστιν, ὥστε ἐδάκρυσεν ἐφ' ἑκάστῳ τούτων ἀπαλλαττόμενος· καὶ οὔτε τοὺς γαυλοὺς ἀνέθηκε, πρὶν ἀμέλξαι, οὔτε τὸ δέρμα, πρὶν ἐνδύσασθαι, οὔτε τὴν σύριγγα, πρὶν συρίσαι· ἀλλὰ καὶ ἐφίλησεν

ing, the peasants gathered together from
all parts to congratulate the young man,
and offer presents to his father, the first
to arrive being Dryas, who had brought
up Chloe.

Dionysophanes made them all stay for
the festivities : for he had prepared abundance of bread and wine, water-fowl,
sucking-pigs, honey-cakes of all kinds,
and victims to be offered as a sacrifice to
the Gods of the country. Then Daphnis,
having collected all his pastoral equip-
ments, distributed them as offerings to the
Gods. To Dionysus he consecrated his
wallet and goat-skin, to Pan his pipe and
flute, to the Nymphs his crook and the
milk-pails which he had made himself.
But—so much sweeter is that to which we
are accustomed than strange and unexpected
good fortune—Daphnis wept as he parted
with each of these things. He did not
offer up his milk-pails before he had
milked his goats once again, nor his goat-
skin before he had put it on again, nor
his pipe before he had played upon it:
he kissed them all, spoke to his goats,

αυτὰ πάντα, καὶ τὰς αἶγας προσεῖπε, καὶ τοὺς
τράγους ἐκάλεσεν ὀνομαστί· τῆς μὲν γὰρ
πηγῆς καὶ ἔπιεν, ὅτι πολλάκις καὶ μετὰ
Χλόης. Οὔπω δὲ ὡμολόγει τὸν ἔρωτα, καιρὸν
παραφυλάττων.

Ἐν ᾧ δὲ Δάφνις ἐν θυσίαις ἦν, τάδε γίνεται
περὶ τὴν Χλόην. Ἐκάθητο κλάουσα, τὰ
πρόβατα νέμουσα, λέγουσα οἷα εἰκὸς ἦν·
"ἐξελάθετό μου Δάφνις· ὀνειροπολεῖ γάμους
πλουσίους. Τί γὰρ αὐτὸν ὀμνύειν ἀντὶ τῶν
Νυμφῶν τὰς αἶγας ἐκέλευον; Κατέλιπε καὶ
ταύτας ὡς καὶ Χλόην. Οὐδὲ θύων ταῖς Νύμφαις καὶ τῷ Πανὶ ἐπεθύμησεν ἰδεῖν Χλόην.
Εὗρεν ἴσως παρὰ τῇ μητρὶ θεραπαίνας ἐμοῦ
κρείττονας. Χαιρέτω· ἐγὼ δὲ οὐ ζήσομαι."

Τοιαῦτα λέγουσαν, τοιαῦτα ἐννοοῦσαν, ὁ
Λάμπις ὁ βουκόλος μετὰ χειρὸς γεωργικῆς
ἐπιστάς, ἥρπασεν αὐτήν· ὡς οὔτε Δάφνιδος ἔτι
γαμήσοντος, καὶ Δρύαντος ἐκεῖνον ἀγαπήσον-

and called his he-goats by name: he also
went and drank at the fountain, because
he had often done so before with Chloe.
But he did not yet venture to declare
his love, since he was waiting for a better
opportunity.

While Daphnis was engaged in these
ceremonies, this was what happened to
Chloe. She was sitting down, weeping,
while she tended her flock, and lamenting,
as indeed was only natural: " Daphnis
has forgotten me: he is dreaming of a
wealthy match. Why did I make him
swear by his goats instead of the Nymphs?
he has abandoned them as he has abandoned Chloe: even when he was sacrificing
to the Nymphs and Pan, he felt no desire
to come and see me. Perhaps he has
found some handmaids at his mother's
house whom he prefers. May he be
happy: but I can live no longer."

While she thus gave utterance to her
thoughts, the herdsman Lampis came up
with a band of peasants and carried her
off, being persuaded that Daphnis would
no longer care to marry her and that

τος. Ἡ μὲν οὖν ἐκομίζετο βοῶσα ἐλεεινόν·
τῶν δέ τις ἰδόντων ἐμήνυσε τῇ Νάπῃ, κἀκείνη
τῷ Δρύαντι, καὶ ὁ Δρύας τῷ Δάφνιδι. Ὁ δὲ
ἔξω τῶν φρενῶν γενόμενος, οὔτε εἰπεῖν πρὸς
τὸν πατέρα ἐτόλμα, καὶ καρτερεῖν μὴ δυνάμενος, εἰς τὸν περίκηπον εἰσελθὼν ὠδύρετο,
"ὦ πικρᾶς ἀνευρέσεως," λέγων. "Πόσον ἦν μοι
κρεῖττον νέμειν; Πόσον ἤμην μακαριώτερος,
δοῦλος ὤν; Τότε ἔβλεπον Χλόην· νῦν δὲ τὴν
μὲν Λάμπις ἁρπάσας οἴχεται, νυκτὸς δὲ γενομένης, κοιμήσεται. Εγὼ δέ πίνω, καὶ τρυφῶ,
καὶ μάτην τὸν Πᾶνα, καὶ τὰς αἶγας, καὶ τὰς
Νύμφας ὤμοσα."

Ταῦτα τοῦ Δάφνιδος λέγοντος ἤκουσεν ὁ
Γνάθων ἐν τῷ παραδείσῳ λανθάνων· καὶ καιρὸν
ἥκειν διαλλαγῶν πρὸς αὐτὸν νομίζων, τινὰς τῶν
τοῦ Ἀστύλου νεανίσκων προσλαβὼν, μετα-
διώκει τὸν Δρύαντα. Καὶ ἡγεῖσθαι κελεύσας
ἐπὶ τὴν τοῦ Λάμπιδος ἔπαυλιν, συνέτεινε

Dryas would accept him [1] as her husband.
As she was being carried off, uttering
piercing cries, some one who had seen
what had taken place went and told Nape,
who informed Dryas, who in his turn told
Daphnis. The latter, almost beside himself, had neither the courage to confess
everything to his father, nor the strength
of mind to resign himself to this misfor-
tune; he entered the garden-walk, and
thus lamented: "What a painful discovery!
how much better would it have been for
me to remain a shepherd ! how much
happier I was when I was a slave ! Then
I used to see Chloe: but now Lampis has
carried her off, and at night he will sleep
with her. But I am drinking and enjoying
myself, and in vain have I taken an oath
by Pan, my goats, and the Nymphs."

Daphnis's lamentations were heard by
Gnathon, who was concealed in the
garden. Thinking this a good opportunity for making peace with him, he
went in search of Dryas, accompanied by
some young men of Astylus's retinue,
ordered him to conduct him to Lampis's

[1] Lampis.

δρόμον· καὶ καταλαβὼν ἄρτι εἰσάγοντα τὴν
Χλόην, ἐκείνην τε ἀφαιρεῖται, καὶ ἀνθρώπους
γεωργοὺς συνηλόησε πληγαῖς. Ἐσπούδαξε δὲ
καὶ τὸν Λάμπιν δήσας ἄγειν ὡς αἰχμάλωτον
ἐκ πολέμου τινὸς, εἰ μὴ φθάσας ἀπέδρα. Κατ-
ορθώσας δὲ τηλικοῦτον ἔργον, νυκτὸς ἀρχομένης ἐπανέρχεται. Καὶ τὸν μὲν Διονυσοφάνην
εὑρίσκει καθεύδοντα, τὸν δὲ Δάφνιν ἀγρυπ-
νοῦντα, καὶ ἔτι ἐν τῷ περικήπῳ δακρύοντα.
Προσάγει δὴ τὴν Χλόην αὐτῷ, καὶ διδοὺς
διηγεῖται πάντα, καὶ δεῖται μηδὲν ἔτι μνησι-
κακοῦντα, δοῦλον ἔχειν οὐκ ἄχρηστον, μηδὲ
ἀφελέσθαι τραπέζης, μεθ' ἣν τεθνήξεται λιμῷ.
Ὁ δὲ ἰδὼν Χλόην, καὶ ἔχων ἐν χερσὶ, τῷ μὲν ὡς
εὐεργέτῃ διηλλάττετο, τῇ δὲ ὑπὲρ τῆς ἀμελείας
ἀπελογεῖτο.

Βουλευομένοις δὲ αὐτοῖς ἐδόκει τὸν γάμον
κρύπτειν, ἔχειν δὲ κρύφα τὴν Χλόην, πρὸς
μόνην ὁμολογήσαντα τὸν ἔρωτα τὴν μητέρα·

house, and hastened thither with him. He came upon the herdsman just as he was taking Chloe inside, snatched her away from him, and severely beat the peasants who were with him. He was anxious to bind Lampis, and to take him away like a prisoner of war, but he got the start and ran away. Having accomplished this exploit, Gnathon returned at nightfall. He found Dionysophanes in bed, but Daphnis was still up, weeping in the garden. Gnathon conducted Chloe to him, told him what had taken place, begged him not to bear him ill-will any longer, but to keep him—for he would be a useful servant—and not to drive him away from his table, otherwise he would die of hunger. When Daphnis saw Chloe, and clasped her in his arms, he pardoned Gnathon in consideration of the service he had rendered him, and excused himself to Chloe for his own neglect.

After taking counsel together, they re-solved not to mention their marriage as yet : meanwhile, Daphnis would see Chloe secretly, and only tell her mother of his

ἀλλ' οὐ συνεχώρει Δρύας, ἠξίου δὲ τῷ πατρὶ
λέγειν, καὶ πείσειν αὐτὸς ἐπηγγέλλετο. Καὶ
γενομένης ἡμέρας, ἔχων ἐν τῇ πήρᾳ τὰ γνωρίσματα, πρόσεισι τῷ Διονυσοφάνει καὶ τῇ Κλεα-
ρίστῃ, καθημένοις ἐν τῷ παραδείσῳ· (παρῆν δὲ
καὶ ὁ Ἄστυλος, καὶ αὐτὸς ὁ Δάφνις·) καὶ
σιωπῆς γενομένης, ἤρξατο λέγειν· " Ὁμοία με
ἀνάγκη Λάμωνι τὰ μέχρι νῦν ἄρρητα ἐκέλευσε
λέγειν. Χλόην ταύτην οὔτε ἐγέννησα, οὔτε
ἀνέθρεψα· ἀλλὰ ἐγέννησαν μὲν ἄλλοι, κειμένην
δὲ ἐν ἄντρῳ Νυμφῶν ἀνέτρεφεν οἷς. Εἶδον
τοῦτο αὐτὸς καὶ ἰδὼν ἐθαύμασα καὶ θαυμάσας,
ἔθρεψα. Μαρτυρεῖ μὲν καὶ τὸ κάλλος, ἔοικε
γὰρ οὐδὲν ἡμῖν· μαρτυρεῖ δὲ καὶ τὰ γνωρίσματα, πλουσιώτερα γὰρ ἢ κατὰ ποιμένα.
Ἴδετε ταῦτα, καὶ τοὺς προσήκοντας τῃ
κόρῃ ζητήσατε, ἂν ἀξία ποτὲ Δάφνιδος
φανῇ."

love. Dryas, however, did not agree with this: he thought it best to tell Daphnis's father, and himself promised to obtain his consent. At daybreak, he put the tokens which had been found with Chloe into his wallet, and presented himself before Diony-sophanes and Clearista, whom he found seated in the garden, together with Astylus and Daphnis. When all were silent, he addressed them as follows : " A necessity, similar to that which forced Lamon to speak, compels me to reveal what has hitherto been kept a secret. Chloe is not my daughter, neither did I rear her. She is the daughter of other parents who exposed her in the grotto of the Nymphs, where she was suckled by an ewe. I saw this with my own eyes, and when I saw it, I wondered, and brought up the child as my own. Her beauty is sufficient proof of this: she in no way resembles us. The tokens also bear witness; for they are too valuable to belong to shepherds. Look at them, try and discover the girl's parents, and see whether you consider her worthy of marriage with Daphnis."

Τοῦτο οὔτε Δρύας ἀσκόπως ἔρριψεν, οὔτε
Διονυσοφάνης ἀμελῶς ἤκουσεν, ἀλλὰ ἰδὼν εἰς
τὸν Δάφνιν, καὶ ὁρῶν αὐτὸν χλωριῶντα, καὶ
κρύφα δακρύοντα, ταχέως ἐφώρασε τὸν ἔρωτα·
καὶ ὡς ὑπὲρ παιδὸς ἰδίου μᾶλλον ἢ κόρης ἀλλο-
τρίας δεδοικὼς, διὰ πάσης ἀκριβείας ἤλεγχε
τοὺς λόγους τοῦ Δρύαντος. Ἐπεὶ δὲ καὶ τὰ
γνωρίσματα εἶδε κομισθέντα, τὰ ὑποδήματα κα-
τάχρυσα, τὰς περισκελίδας, τὴν μίτραν, προσκαλεσάμενος τὴν Χλόην, παρεκελεύετο θαρρεῖν,
ὡς ἄνδρα μὲν ἔχουσαν ἤδη, ταχέως δὲ εὑρήσουσαν
καὶ τὸν πατέρα καὶ τὴν μητέρα. Καὶ τὴν μὲν
ἡ Κλεαρίστη παραλαβοῦσα, ἐκόσμει λοιπὸν
ὡς υἱοῦ γυναῖκα· τὸν δὲ Δάφνιν ὁ Διονυσοφάνης
ἀναστήσας μόνον, ἀνέκρινεν εἰ παρθένος ἐστί·
τοῦ δὲ ὁμόσαντος μηδὲν γεγονέναι φιλήματος
καὶ ὅρκων πλέον, ἡσθεὶς ἐπὶ τῷ συνωμοσίῳ,
κατέκλινεν αὐτούς.

Ἦν οὖν μαθεῖν οἷόν ἐστι τὸ κάλλος, ὅταν

Dryas did not say this without a purpose, and it was not lost upon Dionysophanes, who, casting his eyes upon Daphnis, and seeing that he turned pale and was weeping silently, easily discovered the secret of his love. He accordingly took the greatest pains to verify what Dryas had said, being more anxious about his own son than about a young girl who was a stranger to him. When he saw the tokens — the gilt shoes, the anklets, and the head-dress, he called Chloe to him, and bade her be of good cheer, since she already had a husband, and would soon find her father and mother. Then Clearista took her and dressed her as became her son's intended wife : while Dionysophanes took Daphnis aside, and inquired of him whether Chloe was a virgin : and when he swore that nothing more had taken place between them than kisses and vows of fidelity, he expressed himself pleased at the oath they had taken, and made them sit down to table.

Then could be seen the power of beauty, when it is adorned : for Chloe, richly

κόσμον προσλάβῃ· ἐνδυθεῖσα γὰρ ἡ Χλόη,
καὶ ἀναπλεξαμένη τὴν κόμην, καὶ ἀπολούσασα
τὸ πρόσωπον, εὐμορφοτέρα τοσοῦτον ἐφάνη
πᾶσιν, ὥστε καὶ Δάφνις αὐτὴν μόλις ἐγνώρισεν.
Ὤμοσεν ἄν τις καὶ ἄνευ τῶν γνωρισμάτων, ὅτι
τοιαύτης κόρης οὐκ ἦν Δρύας πατήρ. Ὅμως
μέντοι παρῆν καὶ αὐτὸς, καὶ συνειστιᾶτο μετὰ
τῆς Νάπης, συμπότας ἔχων ἐπὶ κλίνης ἰδίᾳ
τὸν Λάμωνα καὶ τὴν Μυρτάλην. Πάλιν οὖν
ταῖς ἐξῆς ἡμέραις ἐθύετο ἱερεῖα, καὶ κρατῆρες
ἵσταντο, καὶ ἀνετίθει καὶ Χλόη τὰ ἑαυτῆς, τὴν
σύριγγα, τὴν πήραν, τὸ δέρμα, τοὺς γαυλούς.
Ἐκέρασε δὲ καὶ τὴν πηγὴν οἴνῳ, τὴν ἐν τῷ
ἄντρῳ, ὅτι καὶ ἐτράφη παρ᾽ αὐτῇ, καὶ ἐλούσατο πολλάκις ἐν αὐτῇ. Ἐστεφάνωσε καὶ τὸν
τάφον τῆς ὄϊος, δείξαντος Δρύαντος. Καὶ
ἐσύριξέ τι καὶ αὐτὴ τῇ ποίμνῃ· καὶ ταῖς θεαῖς
συρίσασα, ηὔξατο τοὺς ἐκθέντας εὑρεῖν ἀξίους
τῶν Δάφνιδος γάμων.

dressed, with her hair plaited and her face washed, appeared far handsomer to all who saw her, so that even Daphnis scarcely recognised her. Leaving the tokens out of consideration, anyone would have been ready to swear that Dryas could not be the father of such a daughter. However he was present, and sat on the same couch with Nape, Lamon, and Myrtale. On the next and following days, victims were sacrificed, goblets of wine were prepared, and Chloe also consecrated to the Gods everything that belonged to her — her pipe, wallet, goat-skin, and milk-pails. She poured some wine into the water of the fountain at the bottom of the grotto, because she had been suckled on its brink, and had often bathed in it: she also crowned with a garland of flowers the tomb of the sheep, which was pointed out to her by Dryas. She also piped to her flocks, and, having sung a hymn to the Nymphs, she prayed to them that the parents who had exposed her might be found worthy to be allied by marriage with Daphnis.

Ἐπεὶ δὲ ἅλις ἦν τῶν κατ' ἀγρὸν ἑορτῶν,
ἔδοξε βαδίζειν εἰς τὴν πόλιν, καὶ τούς τε τῆς
Χλόης πατέρας ἀναζητεῖν, καὶ περὶ τὸν γάμον
αὐτῶν μηκέτι βραδύνειν. Ἕωθεν οὖν ἐνσκευασά-
μενοι, τῷ Δρύαντι μὲν ἔδωκαν ἄλλας τρισχιλίας, τῷ Λάμωνι δὲ τὴν ἡμίσειαν μοῖραν τῶν
ἀγρῶν θερίζειν καὶ τρυγᾶν, καὶ τὰς αἶγας ἅμα
τοῖς αἰπόλοις, καὶ ζεύγη βοῶν τέτταρα, καὶ
ἐσθῆτας χειμερινὰς, καὶ ἐλευθέραν τὴν γυναῖκα.[1]
Καὶ μετὰ τοῦτο ἤλαυνον ἐπὶ Μιτυλήνην ἵπποις,
καὶ ζεύγεσι, καὶ τρυφῇ πολλῇ. Τότε μὲν οὖν
ἔλαθον τοὺς πολίτας, νυκτὸς κατελθόντες· τῆς
δὲ ἐπιούσης, ὄχλος ἠθροίσθη περὶ τὰς θύρας,
ἀνδρῶν, γυναικῶν. Οἱ μὲν τῷ Διονυσοφάνει
συνήδοντο παῖδα εὑρόντι, καὶ μᾶλλον, ὁρῶντες
τὸ κάλλος τοῦ Δάφνιδος· αἱ δὲ τῇ Κλεα-
ρίστῃ συνέχαιρον ἅμα κομιζούσῃ καὶ παῖδα
καὶ νύμφην. Ἐξέπληξε γὰρ κἀκείνας ἡ Χλόη,
κάλλος ἐκφαίνουσα παρευδοκιμηθῆναι μὴ δυνά-

---

[1] Read: καὶ ἐλεύθερον εἶναι αὐτοῦ τε καὶ τὴν
γυναῖκα.

When they became tired of the rustic festivities, they resolved to return to the city, to try and find out who Chloe's parents were, and to hasten on the marriage. Accordingly, in the morning, they packed up their things, and made ready for their journey: but, before they started, they gave Dryas another 3,000 drachmas, and to Lamon the privilege of gathering the corn and grapes of half the estate, together with the goats and goatherds, four yoke of oxen, some winter garments, and freedom for himself and his wife. After this, they set out for Mitylene, with a splendid equipage of horses and chariots. As they reached the city at night, the inhabitants were not aware of their arrival: but, on the following day, a crowd of men and women assembled round the house. The former congratulated Dionysophanes on having found a son, and all the more, when they saw how handsome Daphnis was: the latter shared Clearista's joy at having found, not only a son, but a wife for him. They also were struck with astonishment at Chloe's incomparable

μενον. Ὅλη γὰρ ἐκινεῖτο ἡ πόλις ἐπὶ τῷ
μειρακίῳ καὶ τῇ παρθένῳ, καὶ εὐδαιμόνιζον μὲν
ἤδη τὸν γάμον· ηὔχοντο δὲ καὶ τὸ γένος ἄξιον
τῆς μορφῆς εὑρεθῆναι τῆς κόρης· καὶ γυναῖκες
πολλαὶ τῶν μέγα πλουσίων ἠράσαντο θεοῖς
αὐταὶ πιστευθῆναι μητέρες θυγατρὸς οὕτω
καλῆς.

Ὄναρ δὲ Διονυσοφάνει μετὰ φροντίδα πολλὴν
εἰς βαθὺν ὕπνον κατενεχθέντι, τοιόνδε γίνεται·
ἐδόκει τὰς Νύμφας δεῖσθαι τοῦ Ἔρωτος, ἤδη
ποτ' αὐτοῖς κατανεῦσαι τὸν γάμον· τὸν δὲ
ἐκλύσαντα τὸ τοξάριον, καὶ ἀποθέμενον παρὰ
τὴν φαρέτρην, κελεῦσαι τῷ Διονυσοφάνει, πάντας τοὺς ἀρίστους τῶν Μιτυληναίων θέμενον
συμπότας, ἡνίκα ἂν τὸν ὕστατον πλήσῃ κρατῆρα, τότε δεικνύειν ἑκάστῳ τὰ γνωρίσματα·
τὸ δὲ ἐντεῦθεν ᾄδειν τὸν ὑμέναιον. Ταῦτα ἰδὼν
καὶ ἀκούσας, ἕωθεν ἀνίσταται, καὶ κελεύσας
λαμπρὰν ἑστίασιν παρασκευασθῆναι τῶν ἀπὸ
γῆς, τῶν ἀπὸ θαλάττης, καὶ εἴ τι ἐν λίμναις,

beauty. The whole city was in a state of excitement over the young man and the maiden : their union was already looked upon as a happy one, and hopes were expressed that Chloe's birth might be found to be worthy of her beauty. More than one wealthy woman prayed to the Gods that she might be credited with being the mother of so beautiful a daughter.

Dionysophanes, weary with constant thought, fell into a deep sleep, and dreamed a dream. It seemed to him that the Nymphs were begging Love to give his consent to the marriage. Then the God unbent his bow, placed it on the ground by the side of his quiver, and ordered Dionysophanes to invite all the nobles of Mitylene to a banquet, and, when the last cup was filled, to show the tokens to each guest, and to sing the song of Hymen. Struck with this vision and the directions given by the God, when he rose in the morning, he ordered a sumptuous banquet to be prepared, furnished with every dainty that the land, the sea, the lakes, and rivers could produce, and invited all the nobles

καὶ εἴ τι ἐν ποταμοῖς, πάντας τοὺς ἀρίστους Μιτυληναίων ποιεῖται συμπότας. Ὡς δὲ ἤδη νὺξ ἦν, καὶ ἐπέπληστο κρατὴρ ἐξ οὗ σπένδουσιν Ἑρμῇ, εἰσκομίζει τις ἐπὶ σκεῦος ἀργυροῦν θεράπων τὰ γνωρίσματα, καὶ περιφέρων ἐνδέξια πᾶσιν ἐδείκνυε.

Τῶν μὲν οὖν ἄλλων ἐγνώρισεν οὐδείς· Μεγακλῆς δέ τις διὰ γῆρας ὕστατος κατακείμενος, ὡς εἶδε, γνωρίσας, πάνυ μέγα καὶ νεανικὸν ἐβόα· "Τίνα ὁρῶ ταῦτα; Τί γέγονάς μοι θυγάτριον; Ἆρα καὶ σὺ ζῇς; Ἢ ταῦτά τις ἐβάστασε μόνα ποιμὴν ἐντυχών; Δέομαι, Διονυσόφανες, εἰπέ μοι· πόθεν ἔχεις ἐμοῦ παιδίου γνωρίσματα; Μὴ φθονήσῃς μετὰ Δάφνιν εὑρεῖν τι κἀμέ." Κελεύσαντος δὲ τοῦ Διονυσοφάνους πρότερον ἐκεῖνον λέγειν τὴν ἔκθεσιν, ὁ Μεγακλῆς οὐδὲν ὑφελὼν τοῦ τόνου τῆς φωνῆς, ἔφη· "Ἦν ὀλίγος μοι βίος τὸν πρότερον χρόνον· ὃν γὰρ εἶχον, εἰς χορηγίας καὶ τριηραρχίας ἐξεδαπάνησα. Ὅτε ταῦτα ἦν, γίνεταί μοι θυγάτριον. Τοῦτο τρέφειν ὀκνήσας ἐν πενίᾳ,

of Mitylene. At evening, after the cup
with which libations are offered to Hermes
had been filled, one of the attendants
brought in the tokens upon a silver vessel,
and carried them round and showed them
to each of the guests.

All declared that they did not recognise
them, with the exception of one Megacles,
who, on account of his great age, had been
placed at the end of the table. As soon
as he beheld them, he shouted out loudly :
" What is this I see ? my daughter, what
has become of you ? are you still alive ?
or did some shepherd find these tokens
and pick them up ? Dionysophanes, I
beseech you, tell me, where did you get
these tokens of my child ? Now that you
have found Daphnis, do not grudge me
the happiness of finding something." Dionysophanes at first desired him to state
how she had been exposed : and Megacles,
in as firm a tone and voice as before, replied : " Formerly I was badly off, for I
had spent what I possessed upon the public games and triremes. While I was thus
situated, a daughter was born to me.

τούτοις τοῖς γνωρίσμασι κοσμήσας ἐξέθηκα,
εἰδὼς ὅτι πολλοί καὶ οὕτω σπουδάζουσι πατέρες γενέσθαι. Καὶ τὸ μὲν ἐξέκειτο ἐν ἄντρῳ
Νυμφῶν, πιστευθὲν ταῖς θεαῖς· ἐμοὶ δὲ πλοῦ-
τος ἐπέρρει καθ᾽ ἑκάστην ἡμέραν, κληρονόμον
οὐκ ἔχοντι. Οὐκέτι γοῦν οὔτε θυγατρίου γενέσθαι πατὴρ ηὐτύχησα· ἀλλ᾽ οἱ θεοὶ ὥσπερ
γέλωτά με ποιούμενοι, νύκτωρ ὀνείρους μοι
ἐπιπέμπουσι, δηλοῦντες ὅτι με πατέρα ποιήσει
ποίμνιον.''

Ἀνεβόησεν ὁ Διονυσοφάνης μεῖζον τοῦ Με-
γακλέους, καὶ ἀναπηδήσας, εἰσάγει Χλόην πάνυ
καλῶς κεκοσμημένην, καὶ λέγει· ''Τοῦτο τὸ
παιδίον ἐξέθηκας. Ταύτην σοι τὴν παρθένον οἷς
προνοίᾳ Νυμφῶν ἐξέθρεψεν, ὡς αἲξ Δάφνιν ἐμοί.
Λάβε τὰ γνωρίσματα καὶ τὴν θυγατέρα·
λαβὼν δὲ, ἀπόδος Δάφνιδι νύμφην. Ἀμφοτέρους ἐξεθήκαμεν, ἀμφοτέρους εὑρήκαμεν· ἀμφοτέρων ἐμέλησε Πανί, καὶ Νύμφαις, καὶ
Ἔρωτι.'' Ἐπήνει τὰ λεγόμενα ὁ Μεγακλῆς,
καὶ τὴν γυναῖκα Ῥόδην μετεπέμπετο, καὶ τὴν

Being afraid to bring her up in poverty,
I decked her out with these tokens and
exposed her, for I knew that there were
many people who are ready to adopt the
children of others. She was exposed in
the grotto of the Nymphs, and intrusted
to the protection of the Goddesses. In
the meantime, Fortune favoured me : my
wealth increased daily, but I had no heir,
for I have not been fortunate to have
even another daughter. The Gods also,
as if to mock me, send me visions at
night, announcing that a ewe shall make
me a father."

Then Dionysophanes shouted even louder
than Megacles : he started up, brought in
Chloe richly attired, and said : "Here is
the child you exposed : thanks to the providence of the Nymphs, a ewe nourished this
maiden, as a goat suckled Daphnis for me.
Take the tokens and your daughter, and
give her to Daphnis as his bride. We
exposed them both : we have found them
both : both have been under the care of
Pan, the Nymphs, and the God of Love."
Megacles approved, clasped Chloe in his

Χλόην ἐν τοῖς κόλποις εἶχε. Καὶ ὕπνον αὐτοῦ μένοντες εἵλοντο· Δάφνις γὰρ οὐδενὶ διώμνυτο προήσεσθαι τὴν Χλόην, οὐδὲ αὐτῷ τῷ πατρί.

Ἡμέρας δὲ γενομένης, συνθέμενοι, πάλιν εἰς τὸν ἀγρὸν ἤλαυνον· ἐδεήθησαν γὰρ τοῦτο Δαφνις καὶ Χλόη, μὴ φέροντες τὴν ἐν ἄστει διατριβήν. Ἐδόκει δὲ κἀκείνοις ποιμενικούς τινας αὐτοῖς ποιῆσαι τοὺς γάμους. Ἐλθόντες οὖν παρὰ τὸν Λάμωνα, τόν τε Δρύαντα τῷ Μεγακλεῖ προσήγαγον, καὶ τῇ Ῥόδῃ τὴν Νάπην συνέστησαν, καὶ τὰ πρὸς τὴν ἑορτὴν παρεσκευάζοντο λαμπρῶς. Παρέδωκε μὲν οὖν ἔπι ταῖς Νύμφαις τὴν Χλόην ὁ πατήρ, καὶ μετ' ἄλλων πολλῶν ἐποίησεν ἀναθήματα τὰ γνωρίσματα, καὶ Δρύαντι τὰς λειπούσας εἰς τὰς μυρίας ἐπλήρωσεν.

Ὁ δὲ Διονυσοφάνης, εὐημερίας οὔσης, αὐτοῦ πρὸ τοῦ ἄντρου στιβάδας ὑπεστόρεσεν ἐκ χλωρᾶς φυλλάδος, καὶ πάντας τοὺς κωμήτας κατακλίνας, εἱστία πολυτελῶς. Παρῆσαν δὲ Λάμων καὶ Μυρτάλη, Δρύας καὶ Νάπη, οἱ Δόρ-

arms, and sent for his wife Rhode. They
slept that night at the house of Dionysophanes: for Daphnis had sworn that he
would not intrust Chloe to anyone, not
even to her own father.

At daybreak they agreed to return to
the country, at the earnest request of
Daphnis and Chloe, who could not get
used to city life: besides, they had decided
that the wedding should be a rustic one.
They returned to Lamon's house, where
Dryas was presented to Megacles, and
Nape to Rhode, and all preparations were
made for a brilliant festival. Megacles
consecrated Chloe in presence of the
Nymphs, and, amongst other offerings,
dedicated the tokens to them, and made
up to Dryas the sum of 10,000 drachmas.

As it was a very fine day, Dionysophanes
ordered couches of green leaves to be
spread in front of the grotto, invited all
the villagers to the festivities, and entertained them handsomely. Lamon and
Myrtale were there, together with Dryas
and Nape, Dorcon's relations; Philetas and
his sons, Chromis and Lycaenium: even

κωνι προσήκοντες, Φιλητᾶς, οἱ Φιλητᾶ παῖδες,
Χρῶμις καὶ Λυκαίνιον· οὐκ ἀπῆν οὐδὲ Λάμπις
συγγνώμης ἀξιωθείς. Ἦν οὖν, ὡς ἐν τοιοῖσδε
συμπόταις, πάντα γεωργικὰ καὶ ἄγροικα· ὁ
μὲν ᾖδεν οἷα ᾄδουσι θερίζοντες· ὁ δὲ ἔσκωπτε
τὰ ἐπὶ ληνοῖς σκώμματα· Φιλητᾶς ἐσύρισε·
Λάμπις ηὔλησε· Δρύας καὶ Λάμων ὠρχήσαντο·
Χλόη καὶ Δάφνις ἀλλήλους κατεφίλουν. Ἐνέμοντο δὲ καὶ αἱ αἶγες πλησίον, ὥσπερ καὶ
αὐταὶ κοινωνοῦσαι τῆς ἑορτῆς. Τοῦτο τοῖς
μὲν ἀστυκοῖς οὐ πάνυ τερπνὸν ἦν· ὁ δὲ Δάφνις
καὶ ἐκάλεσέ τινας αὐτῶν ὀνομαστί, καὶ φυλλάδα χλωρὰν ἔδωκε, καὶ κρατήσας ἐκ τῶν
κεράτων κατεφίλησε.

Καὶ ταῦτα οὐ τότε μόνον, ἀλλ' ἔστε ἔζων,
τὸν πλεῖστον χρόνον ποιμενικὸν εἶχον, θεοὺς
σέβοντες, Νύμφας, καὶ Πᾶνα, καὶ Ἔρωτα,
ἀγέλας δὲ προβάτων καὶ αἰγῶν πλείστας
κτησάμενοι, ἡδίστην δὲ τροφὴν νομίζοντες
ὀπώραν καὶ γάλα. Αἰγὶ καὶ ἄρρεν μὲν παιδίον
ὑπέθηκαν, καὶ θυγάτριον γενόμενον δεύτερον,

Lampis was forgiven, and allowed to be present. All the amusements were of a rustic and pastoral character, as was natural, considering the guests. One sang a reaper's song, another repeated the jests of the vintage season: Philetas played the pipe, Lampis the flute, Dryas and Lamon danced: Daphnis and Chloe embraced each other. The goats also were feeding close at hand, as if they desired to take part in the banquet. This was not altogether to the taste of the city people: but Daphnis called some of them by name, gave them some green leaves to eat, took them by the horns and kissed them.

And not only then, but as long as they lived, they devoted most of their time to a pastoral life. They paid especial reverence to the Nymphs, Pan, and Love, acquired large flocks of goats and sheep, and considered fruit and milk superior to every other kind of food. When a son was born to them, they put him to suck a goat: their daughter was suckled by a ewe: and they called the former Philo-

οἱὸς ἑλκύσαι θηλὴν ἐποίησαν· καὶ ἐκάλεσαν
τὸν μὲν, Φιλοποίμενα, τὴν δὲ, Ἀγέλην· οὕτως
αὐτοὶ κἀνταῦθα συνεγήρασαν. Οὗτοι καὶ τὸ
ἄντρον ἐκόσμησαν, καὶ εἰκόνας ἀνέθεσαν, καὶ
βωμὸν ἐποιήσαντο Ποιμένος Ἔρωτος, καὶ τῷ
Πανὶ δὲ ἔδοσαν ἀντὶ τῆς πίτυος οἰκεῖν νεών,
Πᾶνα Στρατιώτην ὀνομάσαντες.

Ἀλλὰ ταῦτα μὲν ὕστερον ὠνόμασαν καὶ
ἔπραξαν· τότε δὲ νυκτὸς γενομένης, πάντες
αὐτοὺς παρέπεμπον εἰς τὸν θάλαμον, οἱ μὲν
συρίττοντες, οἱ δὲ αὐλοῦντες, οἱ δὲ δᾷδας
μεγάλας ἀνίσχοντες. Καὶ ἐπεὶ πλησίον ἦσαν
τῶν θυρῶν, ᾖδον σκληρᾷ καὶ ἀπηνεῖ τῇ φωνῇ,
καθάπερ τριαίναις γῆν ἀναρρηγνύντες, οὐχ
ὑμέναιον ᾄδοντες· Δάφνις δὲ καὶ Χλόη γυμνοὶ
συγκατακλιθέντες, περιέβαλλον ἀλλήλους καὶ
κατεφίλουν, ἀγρυπνήσαντες τῆς νυκτὸς ὅσον
οὐδὲ γλαῦκες· καὶ ἔδρασέ τι Δάφνις ὧν αὐτὸν
ἐπαίδευσε Λυκαίνιον· καὶ τότε Χλόη πρῶτον
ἔμαθεν, ὅτι τὰ ἐπὶ τῆς ὕλης γινόμενα ἦν
ποιμένων παίγνια.

poemen, and the latter Agele.   Thus they lived to a good old age in the fields, decorated the grotto, set up statues, and erected an altar to Shepherd Love, and, in place of the pine, built a temple for Pan to dwell in, and dedicated it to Pan the Soldier.

But this did not take place until later. After the banquet, when night came, all the guests accompanied them to the nuptial chamber, playing on the pipe and flute, and carrying large blazing torches. When they were near the door, they began to sing in a harsh and rough voice, as if they were breaking up the earth with forks, instead of singing the marriage hymn.   Daphnis and Chloe, lying naked side by side, embraced and kissed each other, more wakeful than the owl, the whole night long. Daphnis put into practice the lessons of Lycaenium, and then for the first time Chloe learned that all that had taken place between them in the woods was nothing more than the childish amusement of shepherds.

APPENDIX.

APPENDIX.

APPENDIX.

The following fragment, which fills up the hiatus in the narrative indicated by the asterisks on page 14, was discovered by P. L. Courier, in 1809, in the Laurentian Library at Florence.[1]

* * * And Daphnis, standing by the spring, began to wash his hair and his whole person. His hair was dark and thick, and his body tanned by the sun; one would have thought that it was darkened by the reflection of his hair. Chloe looked at him, and he seemed to her to be very handsome: and, because she had never thought him handsome before, she imagined that he owed his beauty to his bath. She washed his back and shoulders, and, finding his skin soft and yielding beneath her hand,

[1] See Introduction.

she more than once secretly touched herself, to see whether her own skin was more delicate. Then, as it was near sunset, they drove back their flocks to the homestead: and, from that moment, Chloe had but one thought, one desire—to see Daphnis in the bath again.

The following day, when they returned to the pasture, Daphnis sat down under his favourite oak-tree and played on his pipe, looking awhile at his goats, which, lying at his feet, seemed to be listening to his strains. Chloe, seated near him, was also looking after her sheep, but her eyes were more frequently fixed upon Daphnis. She again thought him handsome as he was playing on his pipe, and this time, imagining that he owed his beauty to the music, she took the pipe herself, to see whether she could make herself beautiful. She persuaded him to take a bath again, saw him in the bath and touched him : then, on her way home, she again began to praise his beauty, and this praise was the beginning of love. She did not know what was the matter with her, being a young girl brought

up in the country, who had never even
heard anyone mention the name of Love.
But her heart was a prey to languor, she
no longer had control over her eyes, and
she often uttered the name of Daphnis.
She ate little, could not sleep at night, and
neglected her flock: by turns she laughed
and cried, slept and started up: her face
was pale one moment, and covered with
blushes the next: a cow, stung by the
gadfly, was not more uneasy than Chloe.
Sometimes, when she was quite alone, she
talked to herself in the following strain:

"I am ill, but I do not know the nature
of my illness: I feel pain, but I am not
wounded: I am sad, but I have lost none
of my sheep. I am burning, although seated
in the shade. The brambles have often torn
my flesh, but I did not weep: the bees have
often stung me, but I ate my food. The
evil which now gnaws my heart must be
sharper than all those. Daphnis is beautiful, but so are the flowers: his pipe gives
forth sweet notes, but so do the nightingales: but yet I care not for them. Would
that I were his pipe, that I might receive

20

his breath! Would that I were one of his goats, that I might be tended by him! O cruel water, that hast made Daphnis so beautiful, while I have washed in thee in vain! I perish, O beloved Nymphs, and you, too, refuse to save the girl who has been brought up in your midst. When I am dead, who will crown you with garlands? Who will feed my poor sheep? Who will look after the noisy grasshopper, which I took so much trouble to catch, that it might send me to sleep, chirping in front of the grotto? But now Daphnis has robbed me of sleep, and the grasshopper chirps in vain."

Such were the words she spoke in her suffering, seeking in vain for the name of Love. But Dorcon, the herdsman who had extricated Daphnis and the goat from the pit, a youth whose beard was just beginning to grow, who knew the name of Love and what it meant, had felt an affection for Chloe ever since that day, and, as time went on, his passion increased. Thinking little of Daphnis, whom he looked upon as a mere child, he resolved

to gain his object, either by bribery or violence. He first made them presents: to
Daphnis he gave a rustic pipe, the nine
reeds of which were fastened together
with brass instead of wax, and to Chloe
a spotted fawn's skin, such as Bacchus was
wont to wear. Then, thinking that he was
on sufficiently friendly terms with them,
he gradually began to neglect Daphnis,
while every day he brought Chloe a fresh
cheese, a garland of flowers, or some ripe
fruit; and once he presented her with a
young calf, a gilt cup, and some young
birds, which he had caught on the mountains. She, knowing nothing of the arts
of lovers, was delighted to receive the presents, because she could pass them on to
Daphnis. One day—since Daphnis also
was destined to learn what Love meant—
a discussion arose between him and Dorcon
as to which of them was the handsomer.
Chloe was appointed judge: and the victor's
reward was to be a kiss. Dorcon spoke
first:

" I am taller than Daphnis: I am a cow-
herd, while he is only a goatherd, as much

superior to him as cows are superior to goats. I am white as milk, ruddy as corn fit for the sickle: my mother reared me, not a wild beast. He is short, beardless as a woman, black as a wolf. He tends goats, and stinks like them. He is so poor that he cannot even keep a dog: and if, as is reported, a goat has suckled him, he differs little from a kid."

After Dorcon had spoken thus, Daphnis replied:

" Yes, like Zeus, I was suckled by a goat: I tend goats that are larger than his cows, and I do not smell of them, any more than Pan, who is more like a goat than anything else. I am content with cheese, hard bread, and sweet wine: if he have these, a man is rich in the country. I am beardless, so was Dionysus: I am dark, so is the hyacinth: and yet Dionysus is superior to the Satyrs, the hyacinth to the lily. He is as red as a fox, bearded like a goat, white as a woman from the city. If you kiss me, you will kiss my mouth: but, if you kiss him, you will only kiss the hairs on his chin. Lastly, O

maiden, remember that you were suckled
by a sheep: and yet how beautiful you
are!"

Chloe could wait no longer: delighted
at such praise, and having long been eager
to kiss Daphnis, she jumped up and kissed
him, simply and artlessly, but yet her kiss
had power to inflame his heart. Dorcon,
deeply annoyed, hastened away, to think
of some other way of satisfying his desires.
Daphnis, on the other hand, seemed to
have received a sting, rather than a kiss.
He immediately became sad and pensive:
he was seized with a chill, and was unable
to restrain his palpitating heart: he wanted
to look at Chloe, and, when he did so, his
face was covered with blushes. Then, for
the first time, he admired her fair hair,
her eyes as large as those of a heifer, her
face whiter than goats' milk: it seemed as
if he then began for the first time to see,
and had hitherto been blind. He merely
tasted his food, and hardly moistened his
lips with drink. He who was once more
noisy than the locusts, remained silent: he
who was formerly more active than his

goats, sat idle: his flock was neglected, his pipe lay on the ground, his face was paler than the grass in summer. He could only speak of Chloe: and, whenever he was away from her * * *.

EXPLANATORY NOTE.

EXPLANATORY NOTE

PAUL LOUIS COURIER, the writer of the letter which follows, had discovered at Florence, at the monastery of Monte Cassino, a complete MS. of the Pastorals of Longus, which had hitherto been printed only in a mutilated form, and was preparing to publish the Greek text, together with a translation, when he received permission to dedicate the whole to the Princess, as Élise, the sister of Bonaparte, was called in Tuscany. This permission, announced to Courier by the Prefect of Florence in the presence of a number of people, caused him surprise. It was the last thing he expected, and he refused to take advantage of it, alleging as his excuse that the public always ridiculed such dedications : but the excuse was considered frivolous ; the public, at that time, counted for nothing, and Courier was looked upon as a man not sufficiently devoted to the dynasty which was considered worthy to occupy every throne. He was accordingly branded as a philosopher, inde-

pendent or even worse, and deprived of the protection of the Government.   He was immediately
attacked : the newspapers denounced him at first
as a philosopher, then as a thief.   One Signor
Puccini, the Italian chamberlain of the august
Élisa, wrote about the matter in France and
Germany : the virtuous princess herself sent a
message to Paris that a certain person who had
by accident discovered a fragment of valuable
Greek, had seized it in order to sell it to the
English.   This meant that the man was to be
shot and his Greek confiscated, if the opportunity
occurred ; for the *savants* were already in possession of the unearthed fragment which completed
Longus—the fragment that was really very valuable, printed and distributed gratis with Courier's
version.

Another Florentine, a professor of Greek named
Furia, very ignorant of Greek and every other language, annoyed at the stir this discovery produced
amongst the Italian men of letters, took his pen in
hand and composed a pamphlet. Pamphlets were
rare in the time of the great Napoleon : this was
read beyond the mountains, and even reached
Paris.   M. Renouard, the publisher, who was
accused in the pamphlet of having an understanding with Courier to steal the monks' Greek,

alone replied : Courier was thinking of something else.

Prints also appeared, one of which represented him in a library, upsetting all the ink from his inkhorn upon an open book, which book was the MS. of Longus. For, as will be explained, he had made a blot in it while copying it, which was the sole pretext for the persecution and clamour that was raised against him. It was declared that he intended to destroy the original text, in order to be the sole possessor of a complete Longus. A high official considered this reasoning admirable, and, without making further inquiries, ordered the confiscation of the Greek and French published by Courier at Florence : this was truly amusing, for, for fear that he might be the sole possessor of what he was giving to the whole world, the librarian, who knew nothing about Greek or MSS., and as little about Longus as about his translator, had at first written to stop the sale of the work, whatever it was: then, learning that it was not on sale, but that the Greek and French were being presented to a small number of learned men, he caused all the copies to be confiscated, to prevent Courier from appropriating them. The latter, without betraying any emotion, left his Chloe in the hands of

the police, having resolved to take no steps to get out of the difficulty ; but at length he was informed that it was intended to arrest him himself. This made him consider the matter with attention, and he began to think how he might get out of the difficulty, when he was summoned by the Prefect of Rome (where he was at the time) to give information concerning his conduct, connections, position, property, birth, and the blot of ink, all in accordance with orders from his superiors. He wrote to the Prefect as follows :

"Monsieur, I have not thought it worth while to reply to the slanders that have been published against me during the past year, believing that such follies would make little impression upon sensible minds ; but, since the minister attaches importance to them, and I must at length explain myself in regard to this miserable affair, I intend to offer the public, before whom I am accused, as clear and precise a justification of myself as lies within my power. You shall receive the first copy of this brief pamphlet, in which his Excellency will find the information he requires."

The Prefect replied : " Monsieur, beware of publishing anything in regard to the matter in question : you will expose yourself to great risk,

and the printer who lends you his services will be equally compromised."

It was a question of a blot of ink, and observe (for there is a moral in all history, and everything supplies material for instruction to him who will reflect) and wonder at the doctrine of power: slanders are printed, the reply to them is not. Anyone who pleases can tell the public in pamphlets and in the newspapers that Courier is a thief, while he must not address the same public and prove that he is an honest man. The minister carries the matter before his cabinet, where he alone will decide, and will declare Paul Louis an honest man or a scoundrel according as he thinks it will please her Majesty, according to the pleasure of her Imperial Highness Madame Bacciocchi.[1]

Courier, although forbidden, wrote to the Prefect again as follows : "Monsieur, I did not know that your permission to print my little justificatory pamphlet was necessary ; but, since it is, I beg you will let me have it."

As he had fully expected, he received no answer. Fortunately, he remembered a poor devil of a printer named Lino Contadini, who lived near the Sapience, who printed nothing but almanacks, and was little in harmony with

[1] Élisa, the sister of Napoleon I., was married to a Corsican named Felice Pasquale Bacciocchi.

the new censorship. He went to him and said:
"Quick, get this printed for his Excellency the
Prefect of Police;" to which the worthy man
replied, "My dear sir, how can I do it? I do
not understand a word of French; how, then, can
I make out this scrawl, full of erasures?" "Well,
then," rejoined Courier, "we will work at it
together; but let us be quick, the Prefect is
waiting." So then they set to work, and Courier
was compositor, corrector, printer, and everything
else. The copy was a wonderful work: there
were ten mistakes in every line, but with great
effort it was capable of being deciphered. When
it was finished, the worthy printer felt certain
qualms of conscience. "Do we not want a
permit," he asked, "to do what we are doing?"
"No." "Yes," said Lino. "What, for the Prefect?" "Wait," said Lino, "I will be back
directly." He went off to the Prefect, and, in
the meantime, Courier made up a parcel of 100
copies or so, which he carried away with him. A
quarter of an hour later the printing-office was full
of *sbirri* (gendarmes).

Having now obtained almost all he wanted,
Courier wrote a final letter to the Prefect: "Monsieur, I have deceived Lino the printer. I made
him believe that he was working for you: I spoke

to him in your name and as if I had been com-
missioned by you. I hurried him on by declaring
that you were waiting impatiently for the result of
his work ; in fact, I have employed all the means
I could think of to deceive this man, who, thinking that he was serving you, was ignorant of what
he was doing. After this declaration on my part,
Monsieur, I feel sure that you are too sensible to
lay upon him, instead of upon me alone, the blame
for the publication of my literary polemic. I will
only ask you to be kind enough to send it,
together with this letter, to the Minister, who is
curious to know what I am working at and who
I am."

Poor Lino was arrested, questioned, repri-
manded, and then dismissed. The Prefect did
not forward either the letter or pamphlet to the
Minister, but soon afterwards he received a sharp
reproof from his master. What a blunder on the
part of a Prefect—to allow the complaint of an
ill-treated man to be printed and published !
The trickery of which he had been the dupe
did not excuse him in the eyes of a strong
Government. He was responsible; the complaint had appeared ; it was his fault,—the man
who was paid for the very purpose of preventing
such things. He nearly lost his post, and it would

have been really a pity; he would not be what he is at the present day (a State councillor) if he had ceased at that time to serve the dynasties.

After this, Courier lived quietly at Rome, and heard no more of the Prefect or the Minister. His letter made a stir, especially in Italy. The Lombards were delighted to see Florence laughed at and treated as ignorant. Some pamphlets appeared supporting Courier; those who wanted to answer them were forbidden to do so by the Government, which enjoined silence on all. At that time, the least discussion, in which the public would have been the judge, was dreaded. The present dispute, which at first was merely silly and ridiculous, led to serious, even tragic results. It made Furia ill and killed Puccini: the latter, when dining one day with the Comtesse d'Albani, the widow of the English Pretender, began to quarrel with one of the guests, who was defending Courier, and became so enraged that, when he returned home in the evening, he wrote a letter of excuses to Madame d'Albani, took to his bed and died, regretted by all, for he was a worthy man, except for his violent temper. Courier was not responsible for this, as he has been reproached with being; but, if he had been able to foresee such a catastrophe, the fear of causing

the death of a Chamberlain would not have hindered him from writing in his own defence, when he thought it his duty to do so.

What gave offence in this pamphlet was a freedom of style, an air of discontent which was considered very extraordinary at that time, and the disrespectful manner in which he spoke of the Government employees ; but, above all, the fact that it revealed the hatred of Italy for this Government and the French name. Bonaparte believed he was worshipped everywhere ; his police assured him of the fact every morning ; a voice which gave utterance to a contrary opinion was highly embarrassing to the police, and might possibly have attracted Bonaparte's attention, as in fact happened : for he spoke of it one day, and wanted to know who was the retired officer who lived at Rome and was having Greek printed. What he heard about him induced him to leave him in peace.

A LETTER

FROM

P. L. COURIER

TO

MONSIEUR RENOUARD

MONSIEUR,—I have seen your notice of a fragment of Longus recently discovered, that is to
say, your apology in reference to this discovery,
in which you were accused of having had some
ulterior object. It seems to me that you have
completely justified yourself, and I should rejoice
with you, if I could rejoice ; but this affair, which
you have come out of with such flying colours, has
taken a different turn as far as I am concerned ;
and, while you have escaped our common enemies, I really do not know what is going to
become of me.

I have heard from Florence that this poor
translation, of the existence of which you have
informed the public, has just been seized at the
bookseller's ; that a search is being made for the
translator, and that, while he is still undiscovered,

he is still the subject of legal proceedings. There is a talk of prosecution, inquiries, evidence, and nothing is said about the rest.[1] Such, Monsieur, is the pretty mess in which you have involved me; for, if you remember, it was you who first thought of giving this unhappy fragment to the public; I, who had been acquainted with it since I spoke of it to you at Bologna, two years before, had not even thought of reading it. "Were it not for this fragment fatal to the tranquillity of my life, my days would pass away quietly and leisurely, free rom the attacks of jealousy;"[2] I should not have had anything to do with the *savants* of Florence; no one would ever have suspected that they knew their trade so ill, and the ignorance of these gentlemen, which is only made manifest in their works, would have remained unknown.

For you know well that in that lies all the mischief, and that no one cares about this blot, as to which so much fuss has been made; you did not like to say so, because you are wise. You confine yourself within the strict limits of your justification; and, in a spirit of unexampled moderation,

[1] *Et l'on se tait du reste*, a quotation from Corneille, an allusion to the intervention of the Princess Élisa, the sister of Bonaparte.

[2] Sans ce fragment fatal au repos de ma vie,
Mes jours dans le loisir couleront sans envie.

when replying to the lies which are published against you, you maintain silence about the truths which might have caused annoyance to your calumniators. In fact, of what use would it have been to you, who felt sure of being able to clear yourself of blame, to irritate persons who, utterly contemptible as they are, have a licence, a salary, and a livery—who, without being of much importance, are of some consideration, and whose hatred is capable of injuring? And then, you well knew that I should be obliged to state what you said nothing about, that you would thus be avenged without striking a blow, and that the devil would lose nothing by it.[1]

As for myself, as long as the attacks upon me were confined to certain articles inserted in the Italian newspapers, and to certain obscure libels signed by pedants, I laughed at them together with my friends, for I knew that, as you well put it, few persons take an interest in such matters, and these would not fail to understand the reasons of such frenzy and gross calumnies. During the eight months that these gentlemen have honoured me with their insults, you know in what terms I have written to you ; I told you that they were a

---

[1] *Le diable n'y perdroit rien :* A phrase used in reference to a violent emotion, which, though held in check for a time, is bound to show itself later.

rabble whom I was obliged to allow to bark. I had reason to despise them; but I was wrong not to fear them, and now that I should like to put myself upon my guard against them, there is no longer time.

Sometimes, however, it somewhat consoles me to reflect that Columbus discovered America, and was clapped into a dungeon; that Galileo discovered the true system of the universe, and his reward was a prison. I have discovered five or six pages in which it is a question of knowing who is to kiss Chloe : shall I be treated worse than them ? I ought at most to be censured by the Court ; but the punishment is not always proportionate to the offence, and it is that which makes me uneasy.

You say that the facts are notorious ; nevertheless, your story and M. Furia's do not agree. His contains many falsehoods ; yours, many omissions. You do not state all you know ; perhaps even you do not know all ; I, who am less cautious, better informed, and equally trustworthy, will fill up the gap caused by your silence.

When staying at Florence about three years ago, I went with one of my friends, M. Akerblad,[1] a member of the Institute, to see the library of the Abbey in that city. There, amongst other MSS. of great antiquity, I was shown one of Longus. I examined it for some time, and the

[1] A Swedish Orientalist.

first book, which everybody knows is incomplete
in all the editions, appeared to me complete in
this MS.; I gave it back and thought no more
about it.   At that time I was occupied with very
different matters.   Afterwards, having travelled
through France, Germany, and Switzerland, I returned to Italy, and with you to Florence, where,
finding myself at leisure, I copied from this MS.
what was missing in the printed edition.   In this
task I secured the assistance of MM. Furia and
Bencini, who were both employed at the library
of Saint Laurence, where the MS. was at the
time.   While working with them, I was so careless
as to make a blot of ink which spread over about
twenty words in the inedited passage already
transcribed by me.   To repair in some degree
this trifling disaster, I offered, without being
asked, to give up my copy, that is to say,
that which had been made by myself, M. Furia,
and his assistant, and which, being the work of
three hands and taken from the original, and
revised by three persons before the accident
occurred, possessed an exactness and authenticity which was wanting in every other copy.
At first my offer was treated with contempt, on
the ground that the copy could not take the place
of the original ; afterwards it was demanded from

me, but at that time I had reasons for refusing it.
I paid these gentlemen, and went from Florence
to Rome, where, having found, as I had hoped,
other MSS. of Longus, I had the text of this
author printed at my own expense, with the
variants of Rome and Florence. This edition
is not on sale, I make a present of it to anyone
I please ; but the Florentine fragment, printed
separately, is given gratis to anyone who desires
to have it.

In regard to all this, I need not call for your
evidence, which happily I can dispense with. I
understand your caution ; I can appreciate your
carefulness, and I have no wish to bring you into
collision with the authorities, by obliging you to
explain yourself in matters of such importance.
If anyone speaks to you about them, shrug your
shoulders, lift your eyes to Heaven, heave a sigh,
or smile, and say that it is a fine day.

But, before I go further, allow me to complain
of the manner in which you have introduced me
to the public. You announce me as the author
of a translation of Longus, entirely unknown, an
anonymous *brochure*, of which there are only a
very few copies in the hands of a few friends ;
and, as I am no better known than my translation, you inform your readers that I am a very

"clever Hellenist," to use your words. You could
not have found a worse expression ; if I am clever,
I have not shown it on this occasion. After I have
discovered this trifle, which completes a beautiful
work which has been mutilated for so many gene-
rations, you see what advantage I have been able
to derive from it. I have made a present of it to
the public, and I am considered to have not only
stolen, but utterly destroyed it ; you yourself
deplore the loss of it. The Italian journals
denounce me as the destroyer of one of the
most beautiful monuments of antiquity. M.
Furia is in mourning for it, his clique cries ven-
geance, and, while this supplement is in the hands
of those who can read it, thanks to my efforts and
my purse, a libel is being scattered broadcast
against me, entitled, *The history of the discovery
and sudden loss of a fragment of Longus.* So
much for my cleverness. Anyone else would at
least have gained some honour ; I have lost my
money and my reputation, and I shall think
myself lucky if nothing worse happens to me.
Believe me, Monsieur, the clever literary men are
those who, like Pascal's Jesuits, "do not read at
all, write little, and intrigue much."

Neither am I a "Hellenist," or else I do not know
myself. If I understand this word properly (and

I confess it is new to me), you use the word
"Hellenist" like "chemist" and "druggist":
following this analogy, a "Hellenist" would be
a man who displays Greek to the public, who
lives by it, and sells it to the public, to the book-
sellers, to the Government. That is very different
from what I do. You are well aware, Monsieur,
that I devote myself to these studies simply from
inclination, or rather, from caprice, and when I
have no other fancies ; that I attach no importance to them, and derive no profit from them ;
that my name has never been seen at the head of
any book ; that I desire none of the positions
which are attained by these means, and that, had
it not been for the chance which has induced me to
give this text of a few pages to the public, the latter
would never have had this proof of my cleverness;
and that, lastly, even after that, unless you had
revealed, unnecessarily and contrary to all the
rules of politeness, this cleverness, which you are
pleased to assume in me, it would never have
been attributed to me, or would still be a secret
confined to persons capable of judging of it.

Pray tell me, Monsieur, what is the use of a
notice of a book which is not for sale, which is
given to a few people, and cannot even be given
again ? And what does it matter to anyone who

reads your works whether this book be good or
bad, if people cannot have it? It is quite natural
that you should defend yourself against the crime
imputed to you by naming the person who has
executed the translation ; but no one accused you
of having executed it. I do not wish to press you
too hard upon this point, or to appear more
angry than I really am. You thought it a matter
of trifling importance, and rightly judged that
such a work could do me neither great honour
nor great harm ; but you might have dispensed with
mentioning my name, at least as translator, and if
you had thought better of it, you would not have
said that I was either "clever" or a "Hellenist."

Nor are you more accurate in speaking of M.
Furia. Without any further explanation, you describe him simply as librarian, guardian of a
literary trust which is celebrated throughout
Europe. Consider, Monsieur. You are writing
at Paris, you are addressing Frenchmen, who,
seeing these posts occupied by persons of recognised merit, some of whom are even Italians, will
most certainly believe that M. Furia is a person of
importance from his position and learning. I can
understand that this mistake is a matter of indif-
ference to you, and that, having apparently more
reasons to spare him than to complain of him, you

are glad to leave him the importance attached to his title in the country in which you are ; but it is important for me, whom he attacks with the support of a clique of pedants, that he should be appreciated at his just value ; nor can I endure that he should be confounded with persons whose learning and good taste are an honour to Italy.

If you had desired to give a just idea of the little known persons of whom you had to speak, after having stated that I was an old soldier, a Hellenist, and since you will have it so, "very clever," you ought to have added ; M. Furia is a pedant, a retired shoemaker like his father, the keeper of a library which he ought still to be sweeping, who at the present time makes bad books, never having been able to make good shoes, a Hellenist the reverse of clever, with a salary of 800 francs, copying Greek for those who pay him to do it, the pupil and successor of Signor Bandini, whose ignorance is famous. You ought not only to have said that this man discovers offences in the merest accidents, but that he is interested in discovering them, because he is an angry pedant whose rage and cruelly wounded vanity serve as instruments of a hatred which does not venture to display itself in any other manner.

These are the things upon which you maintain a prudent silence. Voltaire says somewhere: Fontenelle was full of this circumspection; he would not, for anything in the world, have consented even to whisper that F * * * * * was a rascal. Voltaire concealed his thoughts less; but it is safer to imitate Fontenelle. Unfortunately, the choice does not rest with me, and I am obliged to tell all.

To begin with Signor Furia's possible reasons for not being as disinterested in this matter as one might imagine, you must know that the discovery of the precious fragment of Longus was made in a MS. on which Furia had worked for several years, and which he regarded as, in a manner, his own property; that the discovery was made exactly at the moment when Signor Furia had just presented the public with a very full and, according to him, "very accurate" account of this MS., in which is set forth, page by page, and in great detail, all that he found worthy of observation; that his work upon this little volume, announced a long time before, has lasted six years, during which he has never ceased to examine and describe it with extraordinary patience; that he has even, according to his own account, extracted from it several variants of the

pretended fables of Aesop, which are reprinted by him at the end of his account; for these silly productions of some monk, with which we begin the study of Greek at school, are to be found at the end of the romance by Longus, and M. Furia has not failed to profit by them; that, lastly, hardly had he finished his work, which he sold himself, and in which he thought that he had exhausted all there was to be said about the divine MS., than by chance there comes someone who, at the first glance, finds and points out to the public the only really interesting thing in it, and the only thing also that Signor Furia had not observed.

At the present day it is common enough for persons to write about what they understand the least. Every petty scholar sets himself up for a doctor: to judge by what is printed every day, one would say that every one thinks himself obliged to show his ignorance. But proofs of such strength of mind are not common, and Signor Bandini himself, famous for similar blunders, never did anything to approach that.

We possess narratives of travel, the authors of which are suspected of never having been out of their study; and, in another field, "How many have given accounts of battles which they

have never been near";[1] but an account of a book by one who has not read it is quite a new kind of buffoonery, for which the public ought to be obliged to Signor Furia. I do not mean to imply by that that he has not examined it with considerable attention. On the contrary, I am astonished that he has been able to enter into all these details and to have made two volumes of them. His work (which I have not read) will some day be useful to the binder to prevent any mistake in the arrangement of the sheets. In a word, in the account which he has given of this book, and which, according to him, was so interesting that it has occupied him six years, he has thought of everything, except reading it.

It is to be regretted for your sake, Monsieur, that you did not witness the effect produced upon him by the first sight of this lacuna in the printed work, and the inedited fragment in the MS. which filled it up. His surprise was very great, and when he found that the fragment consisted, not merely of a few lines, but of several pages, I assure you I could not help pitying him. At first he seemed dazed : you would perhaps have laughed at him at first, but soon you would have been afraid of him, for in a moment he became

---

[1] Combien de gens ont fait des récits de batailles
    Dont ils s'étoient tenus loin !
                                        MOLIÈRE

furious. I had never before seen a pedant in a rage : you cannot think what one is like. " The quadruped foams and his eye flashes fire."[1] If looks could have bitten me, I should have had a bad time of it.

From that time Signor Furia believed himself a disgraced man. You know that Vatel[2] killed himself because his master had no roast meat for supper. In his way, as the King said when he heard of his death, he was a man of honour. M. Furia did not kill himself, because soon afterwards he conceived the hope of regaining to some extent his reputation at the expense of mine : for I think it was two days later that I made the blot in the MS., for which he is in his heart so grateful to me, although he so loudly complains of it. After having copied all the inedited fragment, I finished the collation of the rest with these gentlemen. In order to mark in the volume the place where the supplement was to be found, I put in it a sheet of paper, without noticing that it was smeared with ink underneath. This paper stuck to the sheet, and made a blot which spread over a few words in a few lines.

[1] Le quadrupède écume et son œil étincelle.—LA FON-TAINE.

[2] The *maître d'hôtel* of the Prince de Condé. The occasion referred to was a dinner given by the latter to Louis XIV.

M. Furia has described, in historic prose, the
history of this event. It is said to be his best
work : it is at any rate the only one that has been
read. He has inserted in it a great deal of his
own, both in matter and style ; but the chief part
of it is taken from the Pharsalia and Seneca's
tragedies.

I confess that the accident seemed to me a very
trifling one. I did not know that this book was
the Palladium of Florence, that the destiny of
this city depended upon the words which I had
just effaced ; however, I ought to have suspected
that these were sacred objects to the Florentines,
since they never touch them. But I was not
conscious of my blood freezing in my veins, or
of my hair standing up on end ; I did not lose
my voice for a moment, my breath did not stop,
my pulse did not cease to beat. M. Furia declares that this was what happened to him ; but
I looked carefully, and I swear that I did not
see in him any of these alarming symptoms of
approaching faintness, except when I put his nose
to the fragment of Greek which he had been
unable to see without my assistance.

M. Furia's expressions, in which he describes
the shock he felt at the sight of this blot, which
covered, as I have told you, about twenty words,
are written in very high style, and in a tone of

pathos rare even in Italy. You have been struck
by them, Monsieur, and you have quoted them, but
without venturing to translate them. Perhaps
you imagined that the weakness of our language
could not attain such elevation of style; I
am more venturesome, and I think that, whatever Horace may say, one may attempt to translate
Pindar and M. Furia; it is all the same. Here
is my literal version:

At this horrible sight (he means the blot I
made on his old book) my blood froze in my
veins, and, for several instants, when I attempted
to cry or speak, my voice stopped in my throat
a cold shiver seized upon my numbed limbs . . .
Do you see, Monsieur? this blot of ink is for him
the head of Medusa. He is stupified; he asserts it positively, and it is the only assertion that
is proved by his book.

But there is as much malice as frankness in
this confession; for he wants to make people
believe that it is I who have produced this effect
upon him, to the great detriment of literature.
For my part, I maintain that, long before he saw
this frightful blot, "the mere recollection of which
fills him with horror and indignation," he was
dazed, or certainly very nearly so, since he has
held, turned over, examined, described, and

marked in detail each page of this little volume,
without even suspecting what it contained.

When his director, or his preserver as he sometimes calls him, Signor Thomas Puzzini,[1] "heard
of this strange accident through the loud-sounding
trumpet of Fame, which ever unwearied re-echoed
it in his ear;" in short, when he was told of the
incident of the blot, "he was seized with horror;
he shuddered at the recital of so atrocious an
action." In fact, there may be greater crimes,
but none blacker. Besides, M. Furia represents
"Florence in deep distress, a whole city in tears,
the citizens in a state of consternation;" as for
him, in the midst of this public mourning, when
everyone was weeping, you may guess that he did
not spare himself. From the time when "his
voice stuck in his throat," he never said a word,
and doubtless he thought no more about it, for
he "became dazed." But, "during the night, in
his dreams, this cruel (he did not venture to say
bloody) image presented itself to his eyes." And
he declares, at the outset, that the obligation of
relating this fact "weighs heavily upon him, is a
very heavy burden for him, because it recalls to

[1] His real name was Puccini: the writer, by way of a
joke, has changed this into Puzzini, meaning "stinking";
as Regnier says, "he smelt much more strongly, but not
sweeter, than roses."

him the liveliest recollections of the bitterness of
an event which, while no length of time could
ever veil it in oblivion for him, he can never think
of again without feeling himself overwhelmed with
horror." Here I translate word for word. Here
it is Virgil amplified in proportion to the subject;
for, what the poet said of the whole massacre of a
whole people did not seem strong enough to M.
Furia for a blot of ink. Do you not wonder,
Monsieur, that a man writing in this style attaches
such importance to the text of Longus, which is
simplicity itself? It is zeal for old books which
inflames M. Furia and causes him to speak like a
prophet. For the rest, hyperbole is familiar to
him, and it is in that that he is most successful.
Do you want a good instance of it? One of his
patrons (for he has several, all fired with the
same zeal and desperately enraged against me)
undertook to print one of his books, when the
publishers refused it: immediately M. Furia pro-
claimed him, in his dedication, to be the foremost
man of the age, and assured him that "no age to
come would ever cease to praise him." Cicero
formerly said as much to the conquerors of the
world.[1] Now, if a man who spends fifty crowns
on printing Signor Furia's foolish effusions de-

[1] Nulla aetas de tuis laudibus conticescet.
Oratio pro Marcello.

serves to have altars erected to him, it is clear
that he who, although involuntarily, makes everyone see and feel the ignorance of the said Signor
is worthy of every punishment: that is the
substance of the libel which he has published
against me.

We are agreed upon the facts and circumstances which he relates: most of them, of his
own invention, are really unimportant. What does
it really matter whether he was the first to notice
this blot, as he declares, or whether I showed it to
him, as soon as I saw it myself, which is the truth?
whether it was he who showed me this MS. of
Longus, or whether I had been acquainted with
it a long time before, as you, Monsieur, know to
be the case, and all the other persons to whom I
had written or spoken about it? whether, as he
says, I copied the whole supplement at his dictation, or whether I deciphered and explained to
him the passages which he was unable to read,
because he did not understand the meaning,—
all this has nothing to do with the matter.

I have made the blot, "the horrible blot," and
I have given a declaration to that effect to
M. Furia, without his having thought of asking
me for it, whatever he may say. After having
offered him my copy, which he did not ask me

for either, I afterwards refused it to him. I
am far from regretting it, and you shall hear
why.

I at first offered this copy to M. Furia, as I
have stated, on my own initiative, and he accepted
my offer without appearing to attach much importance to it, very judiciously observing that
no copy could repair the injury done to the MS.
I continued my work : you arrived two days later,
and you saw the "disaster," as M. Furia called
it. On that day, as far as I remember, he laid
but little stress upon the promised copy ; however,
I see, from your account, that it was talked about,
and no doubt I promised it again. It was not
until the next day, when you were no longer at
Florence, that M. Furia pressed me for this copy.
I told him that I had not time to make a dupli-
cate of it for myself, but that, as soon as I had
finished collating the MS., I would think about
satisfying him. The same day, when I looked
at the blot, it seemed to me larger, and I began
to have my suspicions. In the evening, when I
went out of the library, M. Furia pressed me
strongly to call at my rooms with him, to give
him the copy. He wanted it immediately, he
said, because it might get lost with me. His
eagerness added to the mistrust I already felt,

and I replied that, having carefully considered
the matter, I should be glad to keep this copy
for myself; since, as it had been written by three
hands, it was the only and the only authentic
proof which I could give of the text I intended
to publish, as far as the passage that was obliterated was concerned. "For this very reason,"
said he to me, "it is the only one that properly
belongs to the library, and in my hands it will
run no risk of being lost." I did not tell him
what I thought, but I refused point-blank. He
got angry, I got angrier, and I sent him about his
business in language which cannot be described.

Did I not warn you, Monsieur, when you
wanted to take away the paper that was gummed
to the MS.? Did I not exclaim: "Take care;
touch nothing; you do not know the people
with whom you are dealing." I perhaps made use
of other words dictated by the occasion and the
contempt which I felt for them, but that was in
the main the meaning, and you recollect it. Fear
nothing, Monsieur; this cannot compromise you.
You did not heed what I said; you put your
hand upon the fatal blot; you have suffered for
it; but your conduct showed that you always
think well of people "who occupy a position,"
whatever their position may be. You may there-

fore admit, without fear of becoming embroiled
with anyone, that I warned you of what would
happen to you, and you will do so, for we like
to tell the truth when it cannot hurt us.

You see, Monsieur, that from that time I had
divined their spiteful intention ; I did not as yet
know what they were meditating ; but I knew,
when I refused my copy to M. Furia.

In order to understand the importance which
we both attached to it, you must know how this copy
was made. The character of the MS. was strange
to me : MM. Furia and Bencini, having had it
long enough to be tolerably familiar with it, at
first dictated to me while I wrote, and, while
writing, I left blank spaces in the passages which
they had not been able to read in the original,
because the characters were effaced or blurred.
When I had in this manner finished writing all
that was missing in the printed copy, I in my
turn took the MS., and, guided by the sense,
which I understood better than they did, made
out or conjectured the words which these gentlemen had been unable to decipher, while they,
holding the pen, wrote what I dictated to them,
and filled up the blanks which I had left in my
copy. In addition, there were certain mistakes
in what I had written from their dictation, which

I made them correct in accordance with the MS., which caused a number of erasures. Thus, on every page, almost in every line, amongst the words written by me, are to be found words written by one of them, and it is this which establishes the authenticity of the whole ; you also see that M. Furia, in his diatribe against me, attests the accuracy of this copy, which he could not deny without injuring himself.

Several persons at Florence, when speaking to me at the time of the blot made in the MS., appeared to me to be convinced that it was an idea of my own, so that I might be able to alter the text in an obscure passage, and in this manner avoid its difficulties. These reports were spread by M. Furia, who, by any means in his power, wished to discredit the edition which you had announced, and of which he believed that you and I hoped to make a most profitable speculation ; for he could neither believe nor understand that I should do all that gratuitously, and, now that he is obliged to believe it, he does not understand it any the more.

Even at that time you were able to read in the *Milan Gazette* an article written by one of M. Furia's clique, in which the public was warned "not to attach any credit to a supplement of

Longus which was about to be published at Paris,
considering the destruction of the original MS.,"
and so forth.   You may imagine, Monsieur, that,
in this state of things, M. Furia was the last
person to whom I could have intrusted the deposit which he required.   How could I repair the
injury done to the MS., except by giving to the
public the text, printed from an authentic copy?
and could I put the only proof of the text, which
I was going to publish, into the hands of a man
who accused me of wishing to falsify this text?

You will observe that this document, so necessary to me, is perfectly useless to the library; it
cannot possess, in the eyes of learned men, the
authority of the MS., and, consequently, cannot
take its place.   If there is any error in my edition, it is because I have wrongly read the
original, and my copy cannot be of any use in
correcting it.   It is useless to those who might
doubt the accuracy of the printed text, of which
it is not the source; but it is useful to me against
the disloyalty and bad faith of Signor Furia, who,
if he had it in his hands, could bring suspicion
upon the whole by altering a single word, whereas
his own writing now obliges him to confess the
authenticity of this text, which he would assuredly
deny, if he were able to do so.

If M. Furia had had this copy in his hands, he would first have published lengthy discussions upon the erasures, of which it is full. It is easy to guess the conclusion at which he would have arrived, and the foolishness of his arguments would only have been seen by really clever men, who are few in number, and can never decide about anything; therefore, far from intrusting it to him, I refused even to show it to him : for, if he could only have known what were the words written by his own hand, it would have been enough to enable him to fill the newspapers with fresh impertinences. In a word, every request on his part was bound to be suspected by me, and his eagerness was the first reason for my refusal.

Assuredly the rage of these gentlemen was manifested too openly for me to be mistaken as to their intentions. A few days after your departure, the directors, inspectors, and preservers of Signor Furia met, together with him, at the house of Signor Puzzini, Chamberlain and Keeper of the Museum ; the sacred MS., "attended by the four faculties," was conveyed thither with all ceremony. There, the chemists, who had been summoned to give their opinion upon the blot, unanimously declared that they could not understand it at all; that this blot was made with an

extraordinary ink, the composition of which, invented on purpose by myself for this great scheme, was beyond their capacity, resisted all analysis, and could not be removed by any known means. An official report was issued and published in the newspapers. M. Furia described at length all that took place at this memorable sitting ; it is the finest episode of his history of the blot of ink, and finished in the style of *Diafoirus*[1] or *Chiampol la perruque*. As for myself, I cannot help saying, even if it makes me fresh enemies, that it only proves that the Professors of Florence are not more skilled in chemistry than in literature, for any binder in Paris could have proved to them that it was ink *de la petite vertu*, and could have removed it before their eyes by a method which, as you know, is practised every day.

But what do you think, Monsieur, of this devotion to old books ? To judge from the importance that these gentlemen attach to their MSS. would you not say that they read them ? You will naturally imagine that, being paid to direct, inspect, and preserve the letters and arts at Florence, they carefully look after the deposit that is intrusted to their charge, without exactly knowing what it is, and regard their careful

[1] The name of two characters in Molière's *Malade imaginaire.*

attention as a merit, the only one which they
can claim. But this zeal of the house of the
Lord is, I assure, quite a new thing with them :
it has never been aroused on quite a recent occasion, of far greater importance, as you shall see.

The Abbey of Florence, whence this text of
Longus originally comes, was known throughout
Europe as containing the most valuable MSS. in
existence. Few persons had seen them; for,
during several centuries, this library remained
inaccessible, only monks could enter it, that is to
say, no one entered it. The collection which it
contained, the more interesting as it was so little
known, was an entirely new mine for the learned
to work : it was there that could have been found
not only a Longus, but a Plutarch, a Diodorus, a
Polybius, more complete than we at present
possess them. I at last managed to get in, as I
have told you, with M. Akerblad, when the
French Government took possession of Tuscany,
and in an hour we saw a sight that would have
roused the ecstasy of all the " Hellenists " (to use
your term) in the world—eighty MSS. of the 9th
and 10th centuries. We especially noticed the
Plutarch of which I have so often spoken to you.
What we were able to read of it appeared to me
to belong to the life of Epaminondas, which is

wanting in the printed editions. Some months later, this volume disappeared, and with it the most valuable treasure of the library, with the exception of the Longus, which was too well known by the recent account given of it by M. Furia, for anyone to venture to sell it. In consequence of complaints made by M. Akerblad and myself, the Junta gave orders for the recovery of the MSS. It was known where they were, who had bought them, who had sold them ; nothing would have been easier than to find them again ; it was a matter to exercise the zeal of the conservators, and we pressed these gentlemen strongly to act, but they replied that " they did not wish to cause pain to anyone." The matter went no further. I have kept a copy of the letter which I wrote on the subject to M. Chaban, a member of the Junta.

Livourne, Sept. 30th, 1808.

MONSIEUR,—The orders which I have received have compelled me to depart in such haste, that I hardly had the time to leave my card with you at an hour when I had little hope of being able to speak to you—a way of taking leave of you which was quite at variance with my plans ; for, after the marks of kindness which you had shown me, I had intended to pay my respects to you and to take advantage of your favourable disposition

towards me to collect and preserve anything else of value that might be found in your monastic libraries. But, since my duties prevent me from taking part in this good work, I desire at least to assist it by my prayers. I beseech you, then, to be good enough to give instructions that all the MSS. of the Abbey should be removed to the library of Saint-Laurent, and that those which are missing, according to the existing catalogue, should be searched for. I have recently noticed that some of the most important of them have already disappeared ; but it will be easy to trace them, and to prevent these monuments of antiquity passing into foreign hands, which are only too eager to secure them, or even being lost in the hands of those who conceal them, as has frequently happened, &c., &c."

Fresh orders were given for the search for the MSS. I was even nominated by the Junta, a commissioner for this object, together with M. Akerblad, but we refused the honour, he as a foreigner, I, as being engaged elsewhere. The task was accordingly intrusted to MM. Puzzini and Furia, whom nothing could induce to give the slightest attention to it—"they did not at the time wish to cause pain to anybody." Those who had the MSS. kept them, and still have them in their possession.

Now, will it be believed that these persons, who were so indifferent to the loss of a collection of all the classic authors, are the very same as those who, at the present moment—for the sake of a few words of a single page of a romance, a few words which, had it not been for me, they would never have known, a few words which are printed, and which they could read, if they knew how to read —are now working with such zeal to stir up the Government and the public against me, are filling the newspapers with insults and ridiculous slanders, and, by means of circulars, promise the literary *canaille* of Italy the pleasure of soon seeing me treated as a State criminal? M. Puzzini answers for it; he no doubt knows what he is saying, and, "upon my honour, I myself begin to believe a little," as Sosia says.

It will surprise you to learn, Monsieur, that not one of them knows me. Not one of them, with the exception of Signor Furia, has ever had the least quarrel, or connection of any kind with me. I have spoken for a quarter of an hour with M. Puccini, and I do not even recall his features; therefore their hatred against me cannot be personal. The reason of their waging such cruel war against me, and for such a trifle, considering that they are "naturally disinclined to cause pain to anyone," is something quite different from per-

sonal animosity.   The offence which I have involuntarily given to Signor Furia concerns him
particularly; the rage of his clique has a more
general cause.

~ You remember the Spanish expression : Not as
French, but as heretics.[1]   These gentlemen certainly say something like it; but I assure you
that they but ill-disguise the true reasons of their
hatred; everybody knows it.   My first crime was
that I discovered their ignorance, but that alone
would have been nothing ; for, if they persecuted
all those who knew more than themselves, whom
would they be able to pardon?   The second,
which renders me utterly unworthy of pardon,
is that I do not pronounce the word *ciceri*[2] as
they do.   That is a kind of original sin which
nothing can obliterate.

If I had the least influence, or could promise
them any post, however unimportant, or offer
them any reward or bribe, they would all be at
my feet, and would think of as many petty mean-
nesses, to pay their court to me, as they now invent
calumnies, in order to injure me.   You may rest
assured, Monsieur, that, before making up their

[1] The Spaniards in Florida hung and burned the French,
"not as French, but as heretics," according to the placards,
to which the filibusters subsequently replied by massacreing
the Spaniards, "not as Spaniards, but as assassins."
[2] The Shibboleth of the Sicilian Vespers.

minds to attack me, they have taken good care
to find out whether I had anyone to support me,
and, when they found out that I had nothing
to depend upon, that I lived alone with a few
friends as unknown as myself, that I kept away
from the great, and that no highly-placed per-
sonage took any interest in me, they declared
war against me.   You must confess that they are
clever people : it was certainly something for the
worthy Spaniards to make an *auto-da-fé* of the
French in Florida, it was something to praise
God for ; but what a triumph, what fun to cause
a Frenchman to be burned by the French themselves !   I see here people reading this gloomy
rhapsody of Furia against myself: his style is bad,
they say, but his intention is good.   According
to what these gentlemen say, the discovery I have
made in the MS. is nothing, it is the most trifling
thing that could ever have been discovered, but
the harm that I have done is " immense."
Understand this well, Monsieur, the whole fragment is nothing, but a few words of it, unfortunately obliterated, are an immense loss, even
when the whole is printed.   M. Furia has extended this loss as far as he possibly could, since
the blot is now twice as large as when I made it,
if the sketch of it as published by him is correct.

He has increased it to this extent in order to be able to say that it was immense ; for he accommodates, not the epithet to the thing, but the thing to the epithet which he desires to employ. With all that, the damage is far from being immense, and even if I had drowned all his old books as well as himself, in ink, the evil would still be small.

However, M. Furia understands, or rather agrees, that this discovery is common to us, for it is clear that the whole credit of it belongs to him, since it is he, as he asserts, who made me acquainted with the MS., showed and deciphered it to me, whereas without his assistance I should have been unable to discover it, or to read it when discovered. This, in truth, is the chief aim of his pamphlet, and all the details invented by him tend in this direction. Without employing much skill, he has found his readers disposed to believe him and to adjudge him half the credit, for it would be too much for one man to enjoy the whole.

What hatred accompanies fame! how difficult it is to escape neglect and jealousy! Of all the roads which lead to the temple of Memory, I have followed the most obscure: my reputation rests upon eight pages of Greek, and these are

disputed with me! M. Furia wants his share of
them; he cries in the newspapers, he arranges
and prints a tissue of lies in order to arrive at the
expression, "our common discovery." You see
the trick, Monsieur, and far from revealing it, you
endeavour to profit by it by slipping between us
two. You seem to say to each of us: At least
allow me to be your shadow; Furia would consent;
but I am intractable; I desire to go down to pos-
terity alone.

Reputation is very rare at the present day; one
would never believe it: in this enlightened and
triumphant age there are not two men certain of
leaving a name behind them. As for me, if I
have completed the text of Longus, as long as
people read Greek, there will always be four or
five "Hellenists" who will know that I once
existed. A thousand years hence, some learned
man will prove, in a dissertation, that my name
was Paul Courier, that I was born at such and
such a place, in such and such a year, that I died
on such and such a day in the year of grace * * *,
without anyone having ever known anything about
it, and, for this famous discovery, he will be made
a member of the Academy. Let me try, then, to
prove that I am the real, the only restorer of the
mutilated work of Longus; it is worth the trouble;
it is a question of nothing less than immortality.

You know the truth, Monsieur, although you do not state it, and M. Clavier, to whom I wrote as follows from Milan, knows it as well :

Milan, October 13th, 1809.

Please send me your Greek commissions without delay ; I shall be at Florence for a month, at Rome during the whole winter, and I will give you a good account of the MSS. of Pausanias. There is not an old book in Italy over which I shall not be willing to lose my eyesight for love of you and of Greek. I shall also examine on my own account the MSS. in the Abbey of Florence. There was something of value for you and me in about one hundred volumes belonging to the ninth and tenth centuries; what has not been sold by the monks still remains ; perhaps I shall find what you want there. With Dorville's[1] Chariton there is a Longus which I believe to be complete; at least, I did not discover any lacunas when I examined it ; but, really, one needs to be a magician in order to read it. I hope, however, to manage to do so, " by having frequent recourse to spectacles," as Maître François[2] says. It is really a pity that this pretty little romance, which has

---

[1] Jacques Philippe d'Orville, a well known *littérateur* and archæologist.

[2] Rabelais.

been translated into every language and meets with universal approval, should be in its present condition. If I could offer it you in a perfect state, I should think my time profitably spent and my name amply commended to the Greeks, present and future. I want little glory; it is enough for me that it should one day be known that I have shared your studies and your friendship."

M. Lamberti read this letter, in which he was mentioned, and promised me that he would translate the supplement, as he could do it better than anyone. He well remembers all the circumstances, and the following is his letter:

"The hope which you entertained of finding in the Florentine MSS. a complete text of Longus was communicated to me by you as soon as you arrived at Milan, and I spoke about it to several friends, who cannot fail to remember it. Mention was also made of a translation of the supplement into Italian, if your hopes of the discovery did not turn out ill-founded; and I bound myself to undertake it by a solemn promise, founded upon the friendship which unites us. It was therefore with great astonishment that I afterwards saw the silly nonsense written by Signor Furia, who, in his *brochure*, claimed to have had a share in the discovery."

Lastly, here is a letter from M. Akerblad, which sufficiently shows when it was that I saw this MS. for the first time :

" I certainly remember that, three years ago, we went together to the library of the Abbey at Florence, where, amongst other MSS., we were shown that which contains the romances of Longus, and several other of the Greek " erotic " writers. I also remember quite well that, while I was occupied in going through the catalogue of these MSS., the finest of which have since disappeared, you stopped long enough to examine that of Longus, the same one which supplied you with the interesting fragment which you have just published." Thus, certainly before this MS. passed into the library of Saint-Laurent at Florence, I had seen it at the Abbey of Florence : I knew that it was perfect ; I had spoken or written to that effect to all those whom it might interest. Since then, M. Furia " showed " me in the library the book which I asked him for, and which I knew better than he did, although I had not had it in my possession so long, and it was I who " showed " him what he had not seen in the MS. during the six years he had spent in describing it and extracting its rubbish. This clearly shows that all M. Furia's story, and the trivialities

with which he has embellished it, in order to
show that chance caused us both to make this
discovery together, which he calls "common,"
are so many falsehoods.   Now if, in dealing with
a fact so well known, M. Furia lies with such
effrontery, it is easy to judge of his good faith in
things which he asserts on his testimony alone;
for to this lie, of little importance in itself, he has
added other impostures, the most innocent of
which would certainly deserve a hundred lashes.
It was this upon which he counted "so as to be
a little at his ease," like the *huissier* in the
Plaideurs.[1]   I might have fallen into the snare
twenty years ago; but now I know these tricks,
and I advise him to turn his attention somewhere
else.   I might certainly, in my absent-mindedness,
have let the ink-bottle fall upon the old book;
but, in falling upon the pedant, I should not
have the same excuse, and I know what it would
cost me.

Since the insertion in the *Gazette* of Florence
of the article in which you announced an edition
of the supplement and of the entire work, I was
in full possession of my discovery, and more interested than anyone else in its preservation.
Everyone knew that I had discovered this fragment of Longus, that I intended to work upon it

[1] By Racine.

and print it : thus my " privilege " and my right of discovery were assured ; it cannot therefore be imagined that I purposely made the blot on the MS. in order to appropriate the inedited fragment, which belonged to me.   Nevertheless, this is what M. Furia alleges ; he says that this blot of ink was made in order to deprive him of his share in the little find (you have seen, by what precedes, to what this share reduces itself), and in order to prevent him or any other equally capable person from bringing out an edition of it.   This, according to him, is proved by my refusal to let him have the copy.

Such language can only find credit with those who have no idea of such a work ; for who would have been able to undertake it at Florence, even if your announcement had not informed the public both of the discovery and of the person to whom it belonged ?   Do not take my word for it, Monsieur ; consult the learned men of your acquaintance, and they will all tell you that there was no one at Florence capable of producing a tolerable edition of this text according to a single MS.   This requires a knowledge of the Greek language, not indeed very extraordinary, but far superior to that possessed by the Florentine Professors.

Imagine to yourself, Monsieur, eight pages without stops or commas, in every place words mutilated, transposed, omitted and added, glosses confused with the text, entire phrases altered by the ignorance, and, more frequently, the impertinent corrections of the copyists. Schrevelius[1] affords little assistance in clearing up this confusion to one who only knows the *Fables of Aesop*. I can flatter myself that I have been completely successful, although I was without all the necessary aids ; but, with the exception of one or two places, which those who have books will be easily able to correct, I have restored the whole to such a condition that even M. Furia, with my translation and his Schrevelius, would easily be able to follow the author's meaning from one end to the other. All this can be done by others, and better than by myself, at Venice or Milan, but not at Florence.

The Florentines are witty, but they know very little Greek, and I believe that they care very little about it ; there are amongst them several talented persons, well informed and agreeable; they speak the most beautiful of living languages admirably, which enables them to dispense readily with Greek.

What preface, I ask you, could M. Furia have written for this book, if he had edited it ? He

[1] A Dutch scholar, who compiled a Greek Lexicon.

would have been obliged to say : In my lengthy
work upon this MS., from which I have extracted
what is of very little interest, I forgot to say that
it contained the complete work of Longus : this
fact has just been brought to my notice.   On
that point he would have quoted your article in
the *Gazette*.   You see, Monsieur, how many
reasons there were why I should have little fear
that he or any other person would think of dis-
turbing me in the possession of the blessed
fragment.   I refused to give M. Furia, not *any*
copy, which would have been useless to him as
librarian, but a *particular* copy, which he wanted to
misuse as my declared enemy ; and this misuse
did not consist in his wish to publish it, for he
could not do that, but to alter it, so as to throw
doubt upon what I was going to publish.   All
this is, I think, sufficiently clear.

But if it is positively declared that, against my
own, obvious interest, I mutilated this fragment,
which I had then just unearthed and which
belonged to me, apparently for the purpose of
consoling M. Furia for the trifling annoyance
which this discovery caused him, it will have to
be confessed that the worshippers of Longus owe
me far more thanks than reproaches.   If this
text is so sacred, I deserve a statue for having

completed it. The blot which has destroyed a few words in the MS. cannot be a State crime unless the restoration of the whole in the printed copies be not a public benefit: but if all the work, as some very sensible persons think, is in itself only a piece of silliness, what is this blot, about which such a fuss is made? In all sincerity, the affair of Figaro, which also turned upon a blot of ink, and the case of the Intimé, are, compared with this, serious matters: "and, even if it should be true that, out of pure mischief, I purposely spoiled the whole or part of the said fragment, let what I have done since then be regarded as a set-off,"[1] and the edition of the supplement which is distributed gratis, and that of the whole work which is "presented" to the learned, and lastly, this translation of which you give an account, which certainly clears up the text more than the blot obscures it. You will not be suspected of partiality for me, Monsieur. You are of opinion that I have completed Amyot's version so "skilfully" that there appears very little incongruity between his work and my additions, and you confess that "the task was diffi-

---

[1] Et quand il seroit vrai que, par pure folie,
   J'aurois exprès gâté le tout ou bien partie
   Du dit fragment, qu'on mette en compensation
   Ce que nous avons fait depuis cette action.

cult." I am not here in a position to play the modest man : an accused man in the dock, who sees that things are going badly for him, recommends himself whenever he can and takes advantage of everything. This translation of Amyot is generally admired, and is considered one of the most beautiful works in our language. A whole volume could be made of the commendation which has been passed upon it even during the last four or five years, in the journals and in various books. One considers it a masterpiece of *naïveté* ; another calls Amyot the creator of a style which no one has been able to imitate ; a third declares the translation inimitable, and even goes so far as to attribute to him the great reputation of Longus's work. Now, this inimitable masterpiece, this model which no one has been able to reach, has not only been imitated by me very "skilfully," to use your expression, but I have corrected it throughout, and you cannot say that any of the beauties of the original have been lost. The undertaking was of such a nature that, before it was carried out, everybody would have laughed at the idea, because, in fact, there were very few persons capable of carrying it out. There are five or six people in Europe who know Greek ; those who know French are fewer. But it is not

only Greek and French that have helped me to
finish this beautiful copy, after having been so
fortunate as to restore the original ; it is rather
the excellent Italian writers, from whom I have
derived more benefit than from our own, and
who are the real origin of the beauties of Amyot ;
for, in order to touch up and finish Amyot's work,
it was necessary to possess his knowledge of the
three languages (a sufficiently rare combination)
which have formed his style.   Thus this trifle,
trifle though it is, and certainly a very small one,
could have been produced by few.

I can understand, Monsieur, that your judg-
ment is not that of everyone else, and that what
has met with your approval may seem ridiculous
to others ; but, as the work is only known by your
notice of it, the public ought, for the moment, to
be favourably disposed towards me ; and, if this
prejudice in favour of my translation is able to
procure my acquittal from the charge of *lèse-
manuscrit*, it does not matter to me whether it is
afterwards considered good or bad.

I would ask, then, that it should be considered
whether the merit of having completed, corrected,
and perfected this version, which everybody reads
with such delight, and of having given to the
learned a text which will soon be translated into

every language, can atone for the crime of having
involuntarily obliterated a few words in an old
book which no one before me has ever read, and
which no one will read after me? If I possessed
M. Furia's eloquence, I would here summon the
shade of Longus, and, if I related the incident to
him, I would wager that he would laugh at it, and
would embrace me for having at last "restored
his amorous work to the light of day." You may
imagine what a face he would make at M. Furia,
who left him to be eaten with worms in the vener-
able old book.

I have the honour to be, Monsieur, &c.

Tivoli, Sept. 28th, 1810.

P.S.—Is it worth while to tell you the reason
why I have not sent you either the text or the
translation which I promised? Being accused
of entering into a speculation with you in regard
to this fragment, of which I made you a present,
as you admit, was not my only course to "give
it" to the public myself? I will also confess that
your ambition alarmed me. If, after having accompanied me into a library, you had said and
printed at Milan, "We have discovered, we are
going to bring out a complete Longus," would
it not have been clear that, once master and

publisher of this text, you would have said, like Archimedes, Εὕρηκα. You and M. Furia would have decked yourself in my finest feathers, and I should have been left with my spot of ink, of which no one disputed possession with me. I had meant to make a division: the profit for you, the honour for me; you wanted to have both, and to leave me nothing but the blot. Such a claim upset all our arrangements.

BIBLIOGRAPHY[1]

PASTORALIUM de Daphnide et Chloe libri quatuor, græce, ex bibliotheca Aloisii Alamani, cum notis Columbanii, Florentiæ, apud Ph. Junctam, 1598, superiorum permissu.

> (The MS. from which this edition was printed was compared by one of Columbanus's friends, Fulvius Ursinus, with a MS. at Rome.)

Achillis Tatii de Clitophontis et Leucippes amoribus libri viii. Longi Sophistæ de Daphnide et Chloes amoribus libri iv., etc., græce et latine. Ex officina Commeliniana, Heidelbergæ, 1601.

Pastoralium de Daphnide et Chloe libri quatuor, gr. lat. Hanoviae, typis Wechelianis, 1605, cum notis Jungermanni.

Longi Pastoralium de Daphnide et Chloe libri quatuor. Editio nova, gr. lat., una cum emenda· tionibus, uncis inclusis, cura J. S. Bernard, Lutetiæ Parisiorum, in gratiam curiosorum et Amstelo· dami, 1754.

Iidem libri, græce. Recensuit Lud. Dutens. Parisiis : ex typographia F. A. Didot, 1776. (Only 200 copies printed.)

[1] Mainly from N. Pons, in the Paris edition of 1878.

Iidem libri. Curavit varietatem lectionis ac notas Jungermanni, Mollii et suas cum Gambaræ expositis addidit B. G. L. Boden, Lipsiae, 1777.

Iidem libri, gr. lat., ex recensione et cum anim-adversionibus J. B. Casparis d'Ansse de Villoison. Excudebat F. A. Didot, Parisiis, 1778.

Iidem libri, græce, cum proloquio de libris ero-ticis antiquorum (P. M. Paciaudi): Parmæ, ex reg. typogr., 1786.

Scriptores erotici græci, ed. Mitscherlich, Deux-Ponts, 1794.

Longi Pastoralia, græce, curante A. Coray, Paris, P. Didot, 1802.

Longi Pastoralia, gr. lat. cum proloquio Paciaudi de libris eroticis antiquorum, græca recensuit, no-tasque adjecit G. H. Schaefer, Lipsiæ, 1803.

Longi sophistæ pastoralia Lesbiaca, poema a textu græco in latinum numeris heroicis deductum erotico poimenikon, Paris, 1809.

Longi Pastoralia e duobus codicibus manu-scriptis italicis primum integra græce, edidit P. L. Courier, Romæ, 1810.

(This is the first edition containing the passage dis-covered by Courier at Florence, of which an account is given in the Introduction.

Longi Pastoralia edidit P. L. Courier, exemplar
romanum, emendatius et auctius typis reedendum
curavit Lud. de Simner, Paris, Didot, 1829.

Longi Pastoralia . . . adnotationes suas adjecit
Eduardus Seiler, Lipsiæ, 1835 and 1843.

Erotici Græci Scriptores, ex nova recensione
Guillelmi Adriani Hirschig, græce et latine, cum
indice historico, 1856. (Part of the Didot Collection des auteurs grecs.)

Les Amours Pastorales de Daphnis et Chloe,
Paris, Vinçent Sertenaz, 1559. The first edition
of Amyot's original work: no indication is given
as to the manuscript used by him, or how the
Greek text came into his hands. It is noteworthy
that this French translation precedes the publication of the *editio princeps* of the Greek text by
forty years. This edition was reprinted a large
number of times in Paris and Amsterdam. We
may mention :

Les Amours Pastorales de Daphnis et Chloé
(traduites du grec en français), 1718. Frontispice
d'après Coypel et figures d'après les tableaux du
Régent, gravés par Benoît Audran.

Amours de Daphnis et de Chloé, traduit du grec
par Amyot, avec les notes d'Ant. Lancelot, publié
par Falconnet, Paris, 1731.

Les Amours Pastorales de Daphnis et Chloé par Longus, double traduction du grec en français du M. Amyot et d'un anonyme (L. Cannes), mis en parallèle et ornées des estampes originales du fameux B. Audran, gravées au dépens du feu Duc d'Orléans, régent de France.

Traduction complète d'après le manuscrit de Florence. Florence, Piatti, 1810. Here commences the series of the revised (by Courier) editions of Amyot's translations.

Romans grecs, traduits en français par Ch. Zevort. Charpentier, 1856.

Daphnis and Chloe, d'après la traduction de J. Amyot, revue et completée par P. L. Courier. Compositions de R. Collin, gravées à l'eau forte par Champollion. Préface de Jules Claretie. Paris, 1890. (An *édition de luxe*.)

Daphnis und Chloe, aus dem griechischen des Longus, von F. Grillo. Berlin, 1765.
There are also German translations by Krabinger (1809), F. Passow (Leipzig, 1811), and F. Jacobs (1832).

Gli Amori Pastorali di Dafni e Cloè volgarizzati da G. Gozzi. Parigi, 1781.

Gli Amori Pastorali di Dafni e di Cloè tradotti della lingua greca nella nostra toscana dal commendatore Annibal Caro. Parma, 1786.

Another edition of Gozzi's translation, col sup-
plimento tradotto da S. Ciampi e da A. Verri;
Collezione de' Classici Italiani, vol. 80.

Dáfnis y Cloe : traduccion con introduccion y
notas por un Aprendiz de Hellenista : Madrid,
1880.

Daphnis and Chloe, a most sweet and pleasant
pastoral romance for young ladies, translated by
G. Thornley, London, 1657.

The Pastoral Amours of Daphnis and Chloe, a
novel written originally in Greek by Longus, and
translated into English by James Craggs, London,
1712.   Several times reprinted : in 1764, with six
drawings, by J. B. Scotin.

Daphnis and Chloe, a pastoral novel, now first
selectly translated into English, by C. V. le Grice :
Penzance, 1803.

The Amours of Daphnis and Chloe, translated
by R. Smith (forming part of Bohn's Classical
Library) : London, 1848.

Daphnis and Chloe, a pastoral romance (the
translation based upon that of C. V. le Grice),
illustrated with engravings after designs by
Prudhon, etc.   London, 1890.

Paul Louis Courier et la tache d'encre du
manuscrit de Longus de Florence, par H. Omont.

Notice sur une nouvelle édition de la traduction française de Longus par Amyot et sur la découverte d'un fragment grec de cet ouvrage, par A. T. Renouard (Répertoire des bibliographies speciales).

Histoire et Amours Pastorales de Daphnis et Chloé, écrite premièrement en grec par Longus et maintenant mise en français: ensemble un débat judicial de Folie et d'Amour, fait par Dame L. L. L. (Louise Labé Lyonnoise), plus quelques vers français, lesquels ne sont pas moins plaisants que récréatifs, par M. D. R. (Madame des Roches), poicterine, Paris, Jean Parens, 1578: in-16 de 4 feuillets préliminaires et 132 chiffres. (Very rare.)

Histoire des Pastorales et Bocagères Amours de Daphnis et Chloé, traduite du grec en français (par J. Amyot). Dernière édition, revue, corrigée, et augmentée d'additions en marge, outre les précédentes, et de quelques gaytés champestres tirées du plaisir des champs du Seigneur Gauchet. Paris, Anth. du Breuil, 1594 et 1596. A third edition was published in 1609.

Daphnis et Chloé, traduit de l'original grec en notre langue par le Sieur de Marcassus. Paris, Toussaint du Bray, rue Saint-Jacques, aux Épis mûrs, 1626.

Les Amours Pastorales de Daphnis et Chloé, écrites en grec par Longus et traduites en français

par Amyot. Paris, chez les héritiers de Cramoisy, 1712 et 1716.

Les Amours Pastorales de Daphnis et Chloe. Paris, Coutelier, 1747.

Les Amours de Daphnis et Chloé, traduction nouvelle par Fr. Valentin Mulot, chanoine régulier de Saint-Victor à Mitylène, Reims, Cazin, 1783 : réimprimé chez Patris, à Paris, en 1795.

Les mêmes, traduction nouvelle par de Bure de Saint-Fauxbin, Paris, Lamy, imprimeur de Monsieur, 1787, 29 planches en bistre, gravées par Martini d'après le Régent.

Les mêmes, traduction nouvelle (de P. Blanchard ?), Paris, Maradan et Deseune, avec 5 coquettes figures dessinées par Monsiau et gravées par Dupréel.

Les mêmes, traduction d'Amyot, Paris, Didot aîné, 1800, 9 figures d'après Gérard et Prudhon. Fait partie de la collection des auteurs classiques imprimés pour l'éducation du Dauphin.

Les mêmes, Paris, Renouard, 1803.[1]

Les Pastorales de Longus, ou Daphnis et Chloé, traduction complète d'après le texte grec des meilleurs manuscrits, Paris, F. Didot, 1813 (500 copies).

[1] The copy of this edition in the British Museum has added to it the series of illustrations engraved for the edition of 1718 by B. Andrau, from the designs of Philip, Duke of Orleans, as well as some other plates, which are proofs before letters, and printed on India paper or satin.

Les mêmes, traduction de Messire Jacques Amyot, en son vivant evêque d'Auxerre, et grand aumônier de France : revue, corrigée, complétée, de nouveau refaite en grande partie par P. L. Courier, vigneron, membre de la légion d'honneur, ci-devant canonnier à cheval, aujourd'hui en prison à Saint·Pélagie, Paris, Alex. Cowéard, 1821.

Les mêmes, traduction complète par P. L. Courier, nouvelle édition, revue et corrigée, Paris, J. S. Merlin, 1825, avec un dessin représentant la leçon de flûte. (This is the last edition that had the benefit of Courier's personal revision, as he was assassinated, April 12th, 1825.)

Romans grecs, Daphnis et Chloé de Longus, traduction d'Amyot, Lefèvre, et Charpentier, 1851.

Les Romans illustrés, anciens et modernes. Daphnis et Chloé, traduction d'Amyot, revue par P. L. Courier, 1849.

Les Pastorales de Longus, Daphnis et Chloé, traduction d'Amyot et de Courier, avec une préface d'Amaury Duval, Paris, Hetzel, 1862. (Remark·able for some drawings by Léopold Burtle.)

Les mêmes, chez Marpon et Dubuisson, 1862 (Reproduced several times.)

Les mêmes, Paris, Leclère, 1862, avec 9 photo·gravures des figures de Prudhon.

Les mêmes, Leclère, 1863, avec de charmantes vignettes et gravures d'après Wille et Eisen.

Les mêmes, Paris, Picard, 1866.

Les mêmes, Paris, Jouaust, 1872.

Les mêmes, édition revue et complétée, avec une glossaire des mots difficiles, par Jannet, Paris, Lemerre, 1873.

Les mêmes, chez J. Maury et Cie.

Les mêmes, traduction d'Amyot, complétée par Courier, suivie de la lettre de celui-ci à M. Renouard, Paris, De la Rue, 1876.

Les mêmes, traduction de Courier, suivies des Poésies d'Anacreon et de Sapho.

Les IV. Livres de l'Histoire de Daphnis et Chloé, par le docteur Nicolaus Piccolos, chez Lainé et Savard, 1866. (A learned critical edition by a modern Greek.)

Della Scoperta e Subitanea Perdita di una parte inedita del primo libro dei Pastorali di Longo, par Furia, Florence, 1810. (See Courier's Letter.)

Dunlop's History of Fiction, vol. i.

Villemain, Essai sur les Romans Grecs.

Blackwood's Magazine, vol. liv., p. 109; lv., p. 33.

Foreign Quarterly Review, vol. v.

Westminster Review, cxxxvii.